VASILY MAHANENKO

CLANS WAR

Books are the lives
we don't have
time to live,

Vasily Mahanenko

THE WAY OF THE SHAMAN
BOOK 7

MAGIC DOME BOOKS

Clans War
The Way of the Shaman, Book # 7
Copyright © V. Mahanenko 2018
Cover Art © V. Manyukhin 2018
Translator © Boris Smirnov 2018
Published by Magic Dome Books, 2018
All Rights Reserved
ISBN: 978-80-88231-59-2

TABLE OF CONTENTS:

Chapter One. Return to Barliona...............................1

Chapter Two. Unforeseen Difficulties......................41

Chapter Three. Erebus..78

Chapter Four. The Harbinger..............................110

Chapter Five. The Hermit....................................150

Chapter Six. A Friendly Visit..............................186

Chapter Seven. Betrayal......................................221

Chapter Eight. Lait the Reborn...........................248

Chapter Nine. The Bard of Shadow.....................283

Chapter Ten. The Chess Set of Karmadont...........316

Chapter Eleven. The Burden of the Creator..........345

Chapter Twelve. The Arena..................................381

Chapter Thirteen. The Pryke Copper Mine.............431

Chapter Fourteen. The Tomb of the Creator..........474

Chapter Fifteen. The Greater Evil........................529

Epilogue..537

CHAPTER ONE
RETURN TO BARLIONA

"*W*ELCOME TO BARLIONA. *While the capsule configuration is in progress, please review the latest update notes...*"

A soothing female voice began to list off the updated game mechanics and their particularities; however, I'd already examined these back in reality. Stacey had summarized the major changes to me: The level of the Emperor NPCs had been raised from 500 to 1000, which meant that even a dozen scrolls of Armageddon wouldn't pose any danger to these characters. The levels of Advisers and Heralds had also been raised to 900 and 800 respectively. Meanwhile, the developers had played a mean trick on the players and removed the max stat cap entirely. Now, the most stubborn among us could increase their stats infinitely. At the same time, the stat points gained from every new level had been decreased. The gaming forums immediately burst into flames with the outrage of high-level players who had long ago reached their maximum stat points and therefore lost the bonuses from all the levels they had gained since. Still, the Corporation stayed firm and no one would be receiving any extra bonuses. The greatest concession here was that players were still permitted to allocate the unused stat points they had saved up, and at least now everyone knew what the deal was. We'd have to be happy with that at least.

There weren't any other global changes to the mechanics, aside from several new classes and races as well as locations for them. Likewise, the continent's area grew due to some kind of earthquake caused by an island ramming the land mass. I believe it was this island where the new races appeared, though I was only half listening to the update notes. Instead, my eyes were fixed on the 3D image of my character, decked out in sumptuous Shamanic armor. I hadn't looked like that before blowing up Geranika. It didn't occur to me to complain, however. The violet glow of Legendary items radiating from my new gear let me know that I would be happy when I got around to checking their properties.

After all, my former Thricinian gear lost its efficacy after Level 300.

The Corporation had decided to resurrect Geranika and his army. It turned out that my five Armageddon scrolls destroyed not only the Lord of Shadow and his attendants, but also the new Shadow Dragon that the devs had placed so much of their hopes in. This time James and his team didn't bother reinventing the wheel and simply asked Mr. Johnson to restore Barliona to its state an hour before the global disconnection. They wrote mountains of explanatory letters and assessed the compensation they would pay the players for their loss of an hour's worth of grinding, after which Mr. Johnson personally pushed the big 'Reset' button. Geranika and his Dragon of Shadow sprang back to life, the players received their due compensation, but the Corporation didn't bother touching my character. Mahan retained all the XP he had earned. Moreover, the Corp outfitted my Shaman with such loot that every time I ran into their representatives all they did was smile mysteriously and remind me to return to the game as soon as possible in order to personally see their generosity.

In the meantime, after leaving the capsule, my life had become one big fairy tale. Three days in the rehab center was all it took to get me back on my feet. This was followed by a week of court where I testified as a witness instead of a suspect. Then there were unique agreements with the Corporation regarding my character; Anastaria's appearance and her speech; our half-hour-long silence as we sat and simply looked into each other's eyes, unwilling to say a single word; the tempestuous and passionate lovemaking that followed; the mad and foolish words of apology and confessions of love...My disconnection from reality. Tears. Happiness. Love.

If it weren't for Stacey's father insisting that we return to Barliona, perhaps our fairy tale would have gone on forever. But all good things have to end at some point, so...

Enter!

Quest list updated. Please review it.

The first thing that appeared before my eyes when Barliona replaced reality was a notification that my quest list had been updated. This enormous notification refused to be swiped aside, telling me one thing — until I open the quest list and review it, this notification won't be going anywhere. Making sure just in case that I had spawned in a safe location — the main hall of Altameda by the looks of it — I took a seat in my beloved rocking throne and began to peruse my to do list. Something tells me that until I familiarize myself with all the changes that have been made to my Shaman, I won't even be allowed to leave Altameda.

'The Creator of the World.'
Description: Speak with the hermit living in the foothills of the Elma Mountains. He shall help guide your craft in the proper direction.
'The Pirate Brethren. Step 3: Armward Ho!'
Description: Assault the capital of the Shadow

Empire with the pirates. Destroy the Heart of Chaos (15 days until expiration) or plunder the city. This quest must be done on your own ship.

'Training: Level 2.'

Description: Complete the training grounds of the Vampire Patriarch. Training duration: six weeks. Reward: +60 to all stats, +5 Levels.

'Audience with the Emperor.'

Description: You have earned Exalted status with the Emperor and the Empire of Malabar. The Emperor wishes to see you in order to grant you your reward.

'Audience with the Dark Lord.'

Description: You have earned Exalted status with the Dark Lord and the Empire of Kartoss. The Dark Lord wishes to see you in order to grant you your reward.

'The Emperor's Reward.'

Description: You have earned a First Kill and received two tickets to an audience with the Emperor. The Imperial audience will be held in five months.

'The Tomb of the Creator.'

Description: You have received the Original Key to the Tomb of the Creator. Any items acquired in this Dungeon will be Unique or rarer. The minimal level of monsters in the Dungeon is equal to that of the highest-level player on your continent. All clans of Barliona have received this information.

'Tight-knit family. Step 1.'

Description: Meet up 30 times over the course of 3 calendar months, spending at least 1 hour together in questing or speaking to one another. Quest type: Unique, family. Reward: +2000 Reputation with the Priests of Eluna, +1000 with Goddess Eluna and the next quest in the chain.

Ok...Look at all these new things I've learned, reading a simple old list. First of all, the quest descriptions have been adjusted, since there was never a reward of five levels in the Patriarch's training quest. Second, my Reputation with Malabar and Kartoss had reached its ultimate peak. Feeling a twinge of curiosity, I opened my list of unlocked Achievements, but didn't see anything new about being the first to reach Exalted status with two Empires at once. Someone had earned it before me. It's too bad. Third, the list now omitted several social quests, which I had received in times immemorial, and which I hadn't gotten around to or didn't feel like doing. It seemed that the Corporation's people had deemed these quests unnecessary and deleted them.

Character updated. Please familiarize yourself with the changes.

The next step of familiarizing myself with the changes to my character involved the statistics and equipment. I had actually wanted to check them out in the very beginning, but the quests thing popped up first. Opening the properties I instantly encountered the first item and pulled up its properties before me. Let's see what Legendary items the devs had gifted me.

Edka's LXXII Breastplate.

Description: One of the founders of Shamanism, the ancient troll Edka was renowned for his taste in armor. Hard to please, Edka either didn't like the description or the item didn't offer sufficient bonuses or the item didn't look convincing enough. Then one day, the troll came across the LXXII Breastplate and had a nervous breakdown because of how perfect it was.

Bonuses: +2500 to Stamina, +3200 to Intellect, +600 to Strength, +900 to Agility, +40 to Energy. +3400 Resistance to all damage types.

Stacking bonus with 2 set items: +5000 Intellect.

Stacking bonus with 6 set items: +5000 Stamina and +10000 to Intellect.

Bonus for equipping the entire set: +30% to all base stats.

Item class: Legendary Set. Restriction: Shaman, Level 300+.

I swallowed hard and glanced over at my Hoarding Hamster and Greed Toad, who had collapsed in a fit on their backs. I hadn't expected a present like this — nine Legendary items. Edka's full set. The devs had kindly stored my old Thricinian items in my bag — and that's where they stayed after I compared their stats with my new gear. At Level 300, the gap between the Thricinian items and the new set was monstrous. It was almost twofold. The only item that even stood up to the new gear were the boots the Emperor had given me and if it weren't for the set bonus, I'd probably wear them.

All my other equipment remained unchanged. For example, I still had some Minor Copper chain on my neck, granting me a mere +12 to Intellect and serving as a bold reminder that it was time to do some crafting. I closed the window with the equipment and stats, wishing to move on to my mail, when a new notification popped up before me:

Please allocate your free stat points.

There was no other choice. As hard as I tried to close the window that had popped open behind the notification, the system insisted I do its bidding. Even popping out to reality didn't help the situation. As soon as I returned to the game, the stats screen reappeared covering everything in sight and insisting I distribute my 1500 free stat points. There was no way out...

Statistics for player Mahan, companion of Anastaria					
Experience	0	of	18,000,000	Additional Stats	
Race	Dragon			Dragon Rank	16
Class	Harbinger			Minutes in Dragon Form	160
Main Profession	Jeweler			Physical damage	3,782
Character level	300			Magical damage	160,416
Hit Points	240,830			Physical defense	20,100
Mana	517,470			Magic resistance	20,100
Energy	430			Fire resistance	20,100
Stats	Scale	Base	+ Items	Cold resistance	20,100
Stamina	64%.	592	24,083	Poison resistance	100%.
Agility	11%.	84	7,276		
Strength	84%.	98	2,282	Dodge chance	41.20%
Intellect	35%.	1,214	51,747	Critical hit chance	25.60%
Charisma	41%.	80	88	Shamanic Blessing	10%
Crafting	0%.	16	18	Eluna's Blessing	15%
Endurance.	43%	154	178	Water Spirit Rank:	12
Spirituality	0%	89	98	Totem Level	112
Unused Stat Points:			0	Item bonus	5%
Professions				**Specialization**	
Jewelcrafting	23%	165	165	Gem Cutter	3
Mining	77%	86	86	Hardiness 2	10%
Trade	25%	19	19	-	
Cooking	20%	32	32	-	
Cartography	50%	99	99	Scroll Scribe	10%
Smithing	20%	129	129	Smelter 2	10%
Repair	0%	6	6	Leather Repair	

"Master!" No sooner had the stats screen closed, than my majordomo, Viltrius, popped in to visit me. The system had decided that it had completed its mission of informing me about Barliona's new update and finally allowed me to swipe away all the other annoying windows and deal with the game itself. "Do you have any orders?"

"Fill me in on what's been going on with the castle lately."

Viltrius adjusted his jacket's lapel in a serious

manner, as if gathering his thoughts, and then proudly raised his green mug and began to speak with feeling, sense and composure. I could hardly contain my smile, since all the goblin was missing was a small podium. That would complete the image of a small boy who was being forced to recite verses at Christmas dinner to get his present from Santa Claus.

There hadn't been many changes to or happenings in the castle. Considering the relative remoteness of Altameda from the places that NPCs lived in and the fact that its current location was designed for Level 180 players, Viltrius allowed himself the liberty of letting the Gray Death and her pack out for a stroll in the castle's surroundings. It's unclear how he communicated with the wolves, but the goblin managed to assign several conditions for the stroll — such as that 30% of the Experience gained from the killed mobs would be channeled to the castle's account, while the loot would be delivered to its treasure vaults. The Gray Death agreed and several days later, an enormous area around the castle had been entirely cleared of any monsters. And I mean entirely — even the frogs and crickets, to say nothing of the bears, elks and other fauna. Moreover, several new wolves joined the pack. The Gray Death found them in the forest surrounding the castle. And on top of it all, several of the she-wolves in the pack bore cubs. Thus the overall level of the pack had increased to 240, while the Gray Death herself had become a mature Level 280 she-wolf. Here it hit me that I had effectively acquired a substantial and quite powerful army of NPCs, which unlike my guards, wasn't bound to my castle. Vimes, my head of security, and his warriors were assigned to the defense of the castle, which meant that using them as mercenaries on raids was a risky and expensive venture.

Viltrius also surprised me with the news that it had been three weeks now that Spiteful Gnum was in my castle. The gnome had appeared before the cataclysm and was currently driving the vaults keeper insane. Cataclysm was the term the Corporation had assigned to the period that Barliona had been down. The updated lore explained that a strange meteor had passed near our world and in so doing had stopped time for an entire two weeks. For the living creatures as well as for all the phenomena and events. I'm not sure why they did this, since they could've easily resumed the game from the moment the servers had gone down, but the meteor was necessary for their internal goals I guess. Thus, Spiteful Gnum had made good on his promise and repaired the gates of my castle, expending basically all of my reserves of Imperial Oak for the purpose, after which he locked himself in his workshop and remained there for the last two weeks. At times, you could hear his muffled laughter, explosions, curses, laughter again and periodically, one of the demons would emerge from the workshop to hand Viltrius a list of all the ingredients the gnome needed next. Very high level ingredients, at that. Considering my direct order to supply Gnum with everything he needed, the majordomo couldn't say no to the gnome, but you could tell just by glancing at the goblin that he was entirely against this new tenant.

Vimes' merry band of guards did its job to a T. During the three weeks since my last sojourn in my castle, nothing of note had happened. Mr. Kristowski had come by with some unknown persons to visit the storage vaults, after which new contracts appeared in our clan. At the current moment, our storage vaults were at 70% of capacity, of which only 30% was taken up by my clan's assets. Everything else consisted of items that other clans had entrusted to the Legends of Barliona under the storage contracts. Viltrius concluded his report, but did not hurry to leave me. Judging by the way he keeps fiddling with that lapel of his, he's clearly expecting something else from me.

"We should hire some hobgoblins!" Viltrius blurted out what was eating at him. "Without the hobgoblins, the castle's empty. There's not a soul in it. Nor is there any defense against the almighty beings of this world. Master, couldn't we reach an agreement with Lady Anastaria to have her remove the alganides?"

The goblin gave me such a pleading look, that I couldn't refuse this trifle and called Stacey then and there. We'd entered the game at the same time, so she had to be somewhere in Barliona.

"Darling, I'd like to remove the alganides from Altameda."

"Not even a question. Are you in the castle right now?"

"Yes. I'll summon you."

"Hang on a minute, I'm talking to my dad. Actually — I formally grant you access to my room and to my personal chest. You can remove them yourself. By the way, let me know when you're done with the castle and I'll summon you to our location. There's a matter to discuss here."

"Has something happened?"

"Yes. War has been declared on our continent. Haven't you checked your mail?"

"War? Who?! No — I haven't had time to get to my mail. What's in my mail?"

"If I understand correctly, you should have several offers in your inbox. Dan, we opened Pandora's Box. Everyone wants the Tomb of the Creator. And everyone wants you, the owner of the Original Key as well. We've been issued an ultimatum...I don't want to overload you right now, so deal with your business and then head our way. I'll send you the coordinates by mail, and my dad's granted you access to his castle."

"Viltrius, I'm granting you access to Anastaria's room and her personal chest. Remove the alganides from the castle," I said automatically, still in shock from the news. Was the Tomb of the Creator really such a vital game object that an entire continent had decided to attack ours? Didn't they have enough Dungeons of their own? There's no arguing that the Celestial Empire was full of absolutely amazing players — the average level of their top clan was 380 and the highest-level player in Barliona played there too — a Level 433 Warrior with a difficult to pronounce name. And in view of the fact that two of our Level 300+ players had been sent to the mines — I mean Hellfire and Donotpunnik — our position was an unenviable one. To try and stand up to monsters like that amounted to nothing short of throwing away Legendary items. Meanwhile, trying to battle them with any other items was pointless — they'd crush us without bothering to figure out what our names are. The only factor that could help here was that generally players in the Celestial Empire weren't much interested in PvP. If I recall Plinto's words correctly, anything that doesn't earn XP is viewed as worthless in the Celestial Empire, and players who specialize in killing mobs might encounter some difficulty fighting players experienced in PvP. And yet, it doesn't matter one damn bit what a player specializes in when the level disparity is 100 Levels! They'd blast us out of existence in a matter of moments and head back home! Why did the Tomb attract their attention? Do they know something we don't? The Celestial Empire certainly could...

"Master! Master!" Tearing me from my burdensome cogitations, Viltrius appeared before me glowing with happiness. The joy the goblin radiated was so contagious, that I couldn't help but crack a smile myself. "We can hire hobgoblins! Four of them! No, five is better! Master, the alganides have been tossed from the castle! Nothing is keeping us from installing a defense worthy of a Level 25 castle!"

Understanding that if I don't hire some new employees for my castle this very instant, the goblin might suffer a fatal shock, I got up from my rocking chair and sat down on my official (and uncomfortable) throne. Hardly had I stuck the crown of the Owner on my head, when the castle management interface appeared before me. The first thing that caught my eye was the castle's 'green' status and a note indicating that the castle's durability was currently at 100%.

I switched over to the personnel tab, cursed silently at the cost of Vimes and his army and then fell into deep contemplation. It was true that I had to hire some hobgoblins — that was a given. And, yes, I already had a small staff of seven NPCs, a portal demon with his own portal, a whimsical majordomo ready to do my bidding, and yet the castle still lacked something. Some small detail, some trifle that would make this already lovely place utterly brilliant. I flipped through the other tabs, but found nothing that extraordinary for Altameda — everything had already been built and everything had already been bought. The castle's further development depended on improving its living conditions and decorations, but I couldn't buy this through the interface. The players had to do this on their own. So the idea of upgrading the castle seemed dead in the water, since Gnum alone wouldn't be able to accomplish much and inviting other high-level craftsmen required advertisement. And pretty elaborate advertisement at that...Here's a thought!

"Viltrius," I immediately voiced my idea, approving the payment for five hobgoblins, "tell me, what would a dinner party do for the castle and its owner?"

"M-master, did you say 'dinner party?'" the goblin asked with a stutter.

"Dinner party. A ball. A party. You can call it whatever you like, but the gist remains — advertisement for the castle and the clan. We'll invite the Emperor, the Dark Lord and maybe even the Lord of Shadow will deign to stop by if we guarantee his safety. We'll assemble the belle monde of our continent and hold a tournament."

"Master!" squealed the goblin and made a face as if an enormous slab weighing sixteen tons was beginning to press down on him from above. "Can you imagine the funds that this would require?"

"No, how much will it be?" I inquired, rolling up

my sleeves. The Corporation had reimbursed me my hundred million, so why not make myself a little present? I hope that Mr. Kristowski won't kill me too painfully if I spend several dozen millions.

"Inviting guests of such a level must be arranged ahead of time. Security has to be appropriately high. There have to be high-ranking officials from all the empires. If you wish to arrange a tournament, you must announce it publically and allow anyone to enter. As I recall it, there has never been an event of such a scale held on our continent, since it's simply too expensive. I couldn't even estimate a budget for such an affair, but it would certainly have to be no less than two hundred million gold."

"WHAT?!" The sum caused me to jack my eyebrows way up high.

"Inviting the Emperor and the Dark Lord would cost our treasury no less than 50 million alone. Everyone knows that. I imagine that the Lord of Shadow wouldn't say no to such a sum either. We would have to upgrade the castle, build a tournament arena, and provide food, entertainment, and above all security, since the Free Citizens might start to fight each other. Or not each other, but NPCs...Who knows what occurs to them. Either way, we'll have to hire security. All of this is very expensive and I have no idea where to begin in order to provide you with a reliable estimate."

"You don't need to estimate anything," I immediately started to argue. Had the Corp lost the plot cooking up such prices for inviting Emperor-level NPCs? Like hell! "Calm down. It was just a dumb joke. Deal with the hobgoblins — they need orders and oversight."

Viltrius dissolved defeated, while I spent several minutes considering what to do next — go through my mail or go check in on Spiteful Gnum? The castle management interface indicated that the gnome was in his workshop, so the right thing to do was to stop by and see what he was cooking up in there. But laziness won out — I didn't feel like zipping off somewhere and talking to anyone right now. I still hadn't recovered from my meeting with my majordomo and the news that I'd have to shell out two hundred million gold for a tournament. Opening the mailbox, I sighed bitterly at the insane amount of unread mail I had to deal with once again.

Goodbye the next few hours of my life. No, this won't do. I really need to do something about this! I guess one option was to hire a secretary.

Hi Mahan, you famous Scrooge!

Ten thousand for a unique map isn't even funny. It's just dumb! I can see your point — my initial letter was a bit naïve. But in that case...In light of recent events involving the Tomb, the map's price hereby grows to one million gold and 10% of the loot that you'll pick up in the dungeon it leads to. I get to come along and gain some of the Experience you earn along the way. As for the location that the map points to, it's a small cave in the Free Lands, concealed under a magical shroud. By way of stimulating your interest — this is the very cave in which Karmadont earned his power. The cave is inhabited by Level 350+ phantoms, so I can't do it on my own, but something tells me that you'll be quite interested in a location that's related to Karmadont. After all, you're the Creator of the Chess Set!

With all due respect and hoping we manage to come to an agreement,

Hunter Sabantul the Fortunate

My heart skipped a beat from my agitation, so I jumped up from the throne and began to pace back and forth across my hall. The Ergreis! The crystal that Lait had brought from a different world and which was now in the Tomb of the Creator! The phantoms that Sabantul had mentioned were the mighty Mages of the past who had died when the crystal was activated. I'm sure I'd be able to find out from them what the Ergreis was and how I could overcome it. How has Sabantul acquired the map? Where had he dug it up?! Stop! I already have Reptilis working on finding that cave!

"Listening," the kobold grunted into the amulet.

"Reptilis, this is Mahan...Tell me, please, how is your search for the Crastil coming?"

"Huh? I already sent you a letter with a report? Didn't you get it?"

"I haven't gotten through my mail yet. I just re-entered the game after the re-launch."

"I didn't find the cave you told me about. I scoured all the foothills of the Elma Mountains, but no dice. Mahan, you promised me that Pendant regardless of the outcome."

"I remember. I'll craft it tomorrow. I need your official permission to use your other half's image as well as to bind her to the item. Preferably in writing and to my mail."

"You got it. What are you going to do about the Crastils?"

"Nothing. I don't really need them anymore anyway. But thanks for the help. Write that letter and tomorrow I'll craft the Pendants. You'll get the first ones. "

I placed the amulet back in my inventory bag and went on pacing my hall. Reptilis had failed, which meant that the cave really was impossible to find without a map. My desire to simply pay Sabantul a million gold was so immense that I had to take ahold of myself, open the mailbox and go on sorting it, figuring that doing so would quench my desire to spend money. Before doing this, I needed to weigh the pros and cons, gather some information about Hunter

Sabantul the Fortunate and only then make my decision. The whole affair with Donotpunnik had been more than enough for me!

"*Stacey, I need your help. I want to find out anything there is to find out about a player named Sabantul. Who, what, where, when and how...All the way down to who this person is out in reality. He's offering to sell me a unique item and doing so at a really opportune moment. My paranoia tells me that I need to do due diligence here.*"

"*I'll do it. What's the item?*"

"*A map with coordinates to a cave where the Ergreis and the Crastils were discovered. Do you remember what the High Mage told me? Sabantul wrote me a letter offering to sell me the map for a million gold and 10% of the loot. I haven't replied yet. I need to understand how a player I've never heard of got his hands on such an item. Maybe it's a fake? Maybe it's a set up?*"

"*That a boy!*" Anastaria replied. "*I'll ask my dad to pull up all there is to know about this Sabantul. Will you be a while?*"

"*I'm just going to go through my mail and I'll be on my way.*"

Having shifted my cares about the Hunter onto Stacey's svelte shoulders, I created a new folder in my mailbox and placed all the requests for crafting the Pendants into it. To my immense surprise, those who wanted the Pendants were not only limited to our continent — there were several dozen thousand players from other locations. How'd they find out about it? I don't remember there being a third movie about the Legends and their capers...Did Mr. Kristowski advertise this item to such a degree that even players from other continents were willing to spend a week working for my clan for six hours a day? In that sense, the situation was pretty great, but on the other hand, eighty-seven thousand requests for Pendants really was a depressing thought. At four minutes per one Pendant, it would take me 348 thousand minutes to fill all these orders. And that equated to 241 days, working at 24 hours a day! I would collapse from exhaustion!

To the leader of the Legends of Barliona, Shaman Mahan!

Greetings to you, oh Creator! We wish to express our esteem of your craftsmanship and your desire to invest this our world with new colors and feelings, depth and unparalleled beauty. We know that you created the Chess Set of Karmadont for this world, opened access to the Tomb of the Creator and received the Original Key to complete it. We are interested in ensuring that our warriors enter the Tomb fist, and therefore wish to offer you the following: You shall receive one billion gold if you complete the Tomb with us. You will receive the Experience, First Kill and title of one of the wealthiest players of your continent.

Consider our offer. I await your response in a week's time. No one aside from our warriors shall complete the Dungeon. Become a unique player on your continent — join us!

Bihan the First, Leader of the Era of Dragons Clan. Celestial Empire.

I spent several minutes staring into nowhere. What's going on here anyway? As soon as I had pried the Tomb away from Phoenix, here comes a third faction trying to snatch it away from me. Well it's not happening! If this Bihan is naïve enough to imagine that I'll just throw myself into his embraces upon seeing a number with nine zeroes, then he's sadly mistaken. He should've thought about all this much earlier...

* * *

"And that's how things stand," I concluded my tale, relating to Anastaria and Ehkiller what had happened. "I received similar letters, though with different offers, from representative of the other continents. Five letters, five billion and everyone wants the Tomb and the Original status. It's stressing me out a bit, to be honest."

"Our situation isn't much better," Ehkiller said pensively, staring into the magical fire smoldering in the fireplace. "We came in last at the last inter-clan tournament, so generally the players of Kalragon aren't really viewed as equals by the others. As far as the player community goes, we're the weaklings who can be bullied at will. Phoenix has already received three ultimatums — if we don't share the coordinates of the Tomb and ensure safe passage to it, everyone else will initiate a targeted hunt after us and our resources. And it'll get underway on our territory."

"Coordinates? They haven't leaked yet?" I couldn't help but exclaim with surprise.

"No, but that's still temporary. There are too many people who know the entrance's location and it's too difficult to control them all. Someone will definitely like the idea of getting some clean cash for a few numbers. The Celestial Empire and Astrum is keeping quiet. I'd guess they already have the coordinates, so I propose we proceed on the assumption that the Tomb's location is already public."

"In that case, we have five high-level raid parties which have up to 100 players each," Anastaria began to calculate our forces. "The portal between the continents closed during the Cataclysm and hasn't yet come online. We have a week, at most two, to prepare ourselves."

"I don't think they'll come through the portal. Why risk their forces?" Ehkiller smiled grimly. "What if we ambush them and repel their invasion?"

"I get the impression that I'm utterly lost," I

confessed. "What would they be risking? If we kill them, so what? They'll respawn and head for the Tomb again."

"Players from other continents don't have a respawn point in Kalragon," Anastaria explained after a short pause. "If they come here to do a Dungeon, the game will respawn them at the nearest cemetery. But they're coming here to fight other players. In that case, their binding location plays a role — if they want to do PvP on another continent, they'll need to respawn at their bound location. And lose a level in the process."

"Hold up! What level? That's against the rules."

"If the risk of losing a level wasn't involved, than the other continents would've been conquered by Astrum or the Celestial Empire long since. The highest-level players are there after all. With the exception of scenarios, PvP on another continent is the only thing that can decrease a player's level. Unless of course he's bound to this continent. And the binding can only be obtained by two means — build a castle or bring an obelisk. I checked. Neither Malabar nor Kartoss have received requests to build a castle. And Geranika doesn't give castles away, so this option is out of the question. The only thing that remains is an obelisk."

"The more time I spend with you two, the more I realize how little I know about Barliona," I couldn't help but crack a sad smile. "What's an obelisk anyway?"

"It has a different names: The clan symbol, a mobile respawn point, a binding point. Synonyms aside, it's a big old ten-meter-tall statue that's really heavy and incredibly cumbersome when it comes to transporting it. You get it once your clan reaches Level 25. An obelisk can't be moved through a portal. It's a really fragile thing that is entirely immune to magic. The cost of an obelisk varies from between 30 and 40 million gold and a clan can only have one at a time. If they really do decide to bring one over here, I'll be at a loss. What for after all? Would they really do this to get to the Tomb?"

"Not only the Tomb, although it served as the trigger for the activation," Ehkiller sighed sadly. "While you two were resting, the enemy was leveling up. The departments of the Corporation responsible for developing the other two continents didn't have any new Empire launches or treacherous employees, nor did they have to create a new enemy like Geranika. As a result they spent their time making their age-old dream a reality — the conquest of Barliona's oceans. In a word, Mahan's already managed to visit one of these locations when he was hunting the Squidolphin — the Oceanic Abyss. At the moment the ocean is turning into an enormous game location with all its monsters, dungeons, islands, scenarios and events. The Corporation decided that it'd be dumb to forego such an excellent game space.

Why do you think the pirates have shown up in our continent? We haven't been able to find a quest for them in five years, and suddenly you and Mahan became captains. They're the defenders of our continent against an invasion. I looked it up. Currently, forty-two players followed in your footsteps and that's just the beginning. It's not only the battle for the Tomb that lies before us, but dominance over the seas. If the borders between the continents are erased, the high-level players of the other locations will wipe us from the face of Barliona."

"The sea," Anastaria said quietly. "They'll bring the obelisks over the sea, erect a beachhead on our continent and then head for the Tomb. But how can they be certain that the Tomb will remain uncompleted?"

A silence ensued and I realized with surprise that both Anastaria and Ehkiller were waiting for an answer from me.

"No need to look at me like that!" I objected. "I never sold anyone anything and...Oh, blast it all to hell!" I exclaimed when I recalled the updated quest list. Stacey's eyes instantly narrowed in suspicion, so I had to explain my reaction: "The highest-level player is currently at Level 433, correct?"

Having received the nod of confirmation, I went on:

"My quest for the tomb was updated. From now on the level of the Tomb Dungeon is equal to the highest-level player on the continent. If you're right and the Celestial Empire installs its obelisk on Kalragon, then the Tomb's level will shoot through the roof."

"In that case the final boss of the Tomb will be Level 483," Stacey muttered at a loss, realizing the significance of what I was saying. "We won't have anyone who could beat it. We'll need to stop the transport ships. An obelisk can only be renewed once a month. If we destroy the ship, we'll get a chance to complete the Tomb first."

"We have to do it," Ehkiller smiled bitterly again. "But how are we going to do it? Where are we going to intercept them? Where will they try to land? What kind of fleet do we need to destroy a single ship? And is it just a single ship? The Celestial Empire is the only one that consists of a player union. The other continents might send us several clans with their own obelisks. How are we going to intercept them all? How are we going to monitor their landing sites? I don't have answers to these questions. Don't forget that the sea is a new frontier for us, while for the other continents it represents a familiar and almost native location."

"We'll need a fleet," Anastaria began to generate ideas. "The north is well-defended, since the players up there are seafarers. The south is covered by the pirates, assuming we can come to an agreement with them. Daniel and I have the quest. All that's left is the west and the east."

"Geranika's out west with his shades and shadows. We can't do much there. The invaders will skirt around closed locations like Skyfoal, since the Corporation won't allow them to enter that territory. In a word, the north is inconvenient — our continent is located in a way that only make it vulnerable from the south or the east. Stacey, we need the fleet of the north. We need to meet their captains and arrange a defense of our coast. Start thinking about what we can offer to get them to fight under our flag."

"In the best case scenario, no battle will be necessary," I spoke up. "If we destroy the transport with the obelisk then the rest of the enemy fleet will be harmless for a month. Let them cruise around all they like..."

"The transport will be sailing in the center of an entire armada. No one's going to let us get close to it just like that. We could of course sneak up to it under water, but there aren't any submarines in Barliona. Or rather, there aren't any anymore, since I was forced to order Stacey to destroy your Squidolphin."

"So that was your idea?" I echoed surprised. "Why?"

"Because upgrading a ship takes time that you didn't have," Ehkiller explained. "If you hadn't opened the Tomb, Donotpunnik would've been forced to 'close' you. So I made the call and ordered Stacey to destroy your Squidolphin. It's true that it would come in handy right now, but at the time it was the right move. It's too late to cry over spilled milk — the Squidolphin won't be coming back."

"Well..." I began, considering the politically vital decision of whether I should mention my Giant Squidolphin Embryo or not...On the one hand, Phoenix and I were on the same side now. On the other, my memory of Ehkiller's words and deeds was still fresh in my mind.

"Dan?" Stacey started forward and stared at me with curiosity. "Don't tell me that you have another Minor Squidolphin."

"Unfortunately not," I shook my head and looked earnestly at the girl, who immediately became crestfallen. She leaned back in her chair in deep thought about how we would have to proceed and therefore paid no attention as I produced my mailbox, found the letter I needed, produced its attachment and placed it on the table that was so enormous that even the Emperor could have used it. Phoenix really does seem to get by just fine. "I don't have a Minor Squidolphin, but I do have the embryo of a giant one..."

Anastaria's bombastic laughter filled the main hall of the Phoenix castle.

"Was that the surprise you promised me?" Stacey asked after she'd caught her breath. "The one you told me about before opening the Tomb?"

"Basically...yeah."

"Dan, you're so wonderful..." Anastaria went on happily — and yet even a bystander who didn't know her would've caught the note of something unspoken in her voice. What's there to say about a person who knew how to read her mind?

"There's some 'but' here, isn't there?"

"Assuming that the leveling up of a Squidolphin is analogous to that of, say, a griffin," Ehkiller explained, "we'll only be able to use her in combat operations no sooner than in a half year — and that's with our most intense grinding regimen. Remember your old ship. At its first level, she was sunk in mere seconds. In order for this embryo to have a chance against the invading armada, we'll have to level her up to between Level 10 and 12. That would take half a year."

"In that case I'm not sure why you just said you were sorry for destroying the minor Squidolphin."

"If she had remained alive, by this time, you could've leveled her up to at most Level 6. And in that case we could've used her as a diversion. We could do the same thing now, but the result will be the same and the Squidolphin will be destroyed. And as you know, ships don't respawn in Barliona. So let's get back to our initial plan — we need the fleet of the north. Stacey, I want you to work on this problem. I'll go speak with the pirates and ask..."

"You said that magic doesn't work on the obelisk," I interrupted Ehkiller unceremoniously.

"What about simple physics? If a high-level player makes it onto the transport, how long will it take him to destroy the obelisk?"

"About three minutes," Stacey replied, trying not to look at her father, who had fallen silent and fixed me with his stare. Someone clearly didn't like it when I opened my mouth.

"In that case, there's the option of using the griffins..."

"The airborne approach, my young friend," said Ehkiller, not passing up a chance to interrupt me in turn, "is impossible for several reasons. The enemy will field veteran players and it would be daft to think that the armada won't have flight jammers deployed around its perimeter. So basically imagine an enormous fleet of ships surrounded by a no fly zone...Tell us again how you were planning on flying into it?"

"Dad!"

"Hang on, Stacey," I said. For the first time in many months of my acquaintance with Ehkiller, he appeared before me as the ruthless head of a leading clan, instead of a kind and generous father figure — and this caught my attention. His look, his tone, the scorn on his face — I couldn't say exactly what annoyed me, but I wanted to argue and prove my point, even if it was obviously a losing one. After all, this was my opinion and I needed to defend it. It was like something had bit me — the idea of flying over the sea was dumb? Okay, I'll approach the issue from another angle:

"I can fly in no fly zones while in my Dragon form. I can carry two people. I could take a dps, say, and a tank. I'd be the healer. I think the tank and I could give the dps three minutes to destroy the obelisk."

"I see. Daniel," Ehkiller, switched to a semi-formal tone, "try and fly up to the ceiling."

"Dad!" Anastaria objected again, yet Ehkiller was unshakable.

"Hold on, Stacey. Come on, Mahan! Turn into a Dragon and touch the ceiling. If you do it, I'll hand you the crown of the castle owner right here and now! And I mean right this instant, I swear on the Emperor!"

A bright, white cloud momentarily enveloped Ehkiller, confirming his words, so I had nothing left to do but change into my Dragon Form and fly up. Or rather, I mean try and fly up, since nothing came of it.

"Did they ban flying inside buildings or something?" I inquired, returning to my human form.

"Let's just say that if a certain someone had bothered to read the patch notes, he would see that flying for all creatures, even those that can fly without special means, has been blocked where flying's already blocked for the others. Thus, this certain someone will no longer be able to fly over cities or castles or whatever else. And, again, he is welcome to read all of this in the update notes."

"The flight jammers should only work around the outer perimeter," I just about dropped my hands from the demonstrative destruction that Ehkiller had visited on my side of the argument, but at the last moment a mischievous thought popped into my mind. "There has to be a flying area inside the armada. These are players we're talking about here!"

"Agreed, they wouldn't prohibit flying between the ships," Stacey came to my aid. "The players would be outraged. A hole in the center should remain open, but how would it help us? The radius of the outer ring will be several hundred meters. You won't be able to build the inertia to glide that distance. Don't forget that, inside the no fly zone, the system actively decelerates you and tries to make you plummet as soon as possible. It doesn't matter what speed you come flying in at, you won't have much of a chance."

"On the one hand you're right," I continued to develop my thought, having encountered support, as odd as it was. "I won't have enough velocity or altitude to cover the prohibited area. So I will need your help. Don't you have a fast ship, Stacey?"

"It's not that fast," Anastaria narrowed her eyes, unsure of what I was getting at. I love that look of hers — when she knows that she doesn't understand something and it drives her insane. "If we really need it, we could get it from the pirates. But what for?"

"Since the airborne option doesn't, erm, fly, I had another idea — we'll take a fast ship. Just one. We put a catapult on it. Just one again. We sail up to the enemy armada, using maybe like some kind of stealth or something, but maybe without it too. We get as close as we can, but in some way that keeps us relatively safe. Then we load the catapult with the tank, the dps, and me...Should I go on, or will your imaginations fill in the rest?"

"Hmm," Ehkiller replied, cocking his head pensively and finally ceasing to drill me with his gaze.

"You're a real wonder, you know? I owe you dinner tonight and then some!" Anastaria's joyous thought popped into my head, as the girl before me reclined with a look as satisfied as that of a cat that had eaten its fill of cream.

"Tamerlane the Wondrous will be our tank. No one will manage as well as he," Ehkiller said after a short pause, more for his benefit than for ours. "As for the dps, that'll be have to be Plinto...or...Well I don't see any other option really. Plinto's the only one who could pull it off in the timeframe we need. It's decided then!" Ehkiller shook his head, making some decision and almost instantly reverted back to the kind generous uncle. Like at the snap of his fingers — snap and you're looking at an entirely different person. I wouldn't want to find myself on Ehkiller's bad side.

"Tomorrow I'll receive information about our enemies' movements and figure out the course they'll set on their journey. Stacey, you owe us a ship. Mahan, you need to make several test flights. You'll have to train turning into your Dragon Form in midflight as well as catching the other players in midair. Get this part down pat. What else? I think that's about it. Let's get to work then!"

"I still have a question that I haven't gotten an answer to." Even though Ehkiller and Stacey had already jumped up from their seats, wishing to get to work on the plan we'd just concocted, I remained sitting. "Why couldn't we complete the Dungeon during the next two weeks? No one will be bothering us right now, and the Dungeon level is still manageable for Plinto. Surely we can handle this in two weeks. It'll be a cinch!"

"The Ergreis," Anastaria answered simply. "That's the entire problem."

"I don't understand," I shook my head. "What does a crystal from a different world have to do with it?"

"That's the point — that until I figure out precisely this question, it's a really bad idea to set foot into the Tomb. Can you imagine what'll happen if that crystal has similar effects to the Tears of Harrashess? After all, no one knows what kind of scenario has been attached to that crystal and why any time anyone mentions it, they also mention the other world? I'd really rather not risk it. So the first thing we need is information and we need time to find it.

And it's time we don't have if we start trying to complete the Tomb right this instant."

"If our plan with the catapult fails," I began — it seemed that today was my day because the ideas were just pouring out of me like from a horn of plenty — "the players from the other continents won't wait another month to buy a new obelisk. Why? It'll be faster for them to just conquer some nearby castle. Something tells me we need to prepare the Emperor and the Dark Lord against this idea."

"Let's assume that we'll get an audience," Ehkiller sat back down in his chair, though he remained in his avuncular form. "It doesn't seem to me that the Emperor will be happy to hear that we wish to keep him from selling someone a castle. We won't be able to keep other players from spending money on our continent."

"Why not? Of course we can." The next idea came tumbling out of my 'horn of plenty.' "Everything depends on how we frame the problem when we pitch it to him. Any way you spin it, the inter-clan competitions will get underway soon. If I remember correctly, in two or three months. Doesn't matter. If we really wish to protect ourselves from our enemies acquiring castles, we'll need to arrange a tournament of the clans of Kalragon. We need to assemble a team of the highest-level players. Why is Phoenix always participating in the competition anyway? What we need is some kind of dream team with representatives of all the clans. And when we organize and hold a tournament like that, neither the Emperor nor the Dark Lord will have any reason to deny our minor request — that is, not to sell castles to anyone for several months. After all, we would have united. We would be one whole. Doesn't the Corporation love single wholes? We'll give them just that, merely requesting a small favor in exchange — the chance to complete the Tomb. If we don't achieve anything in three months, then we'll have to give up on the Tomb — it'll be too much for us."

"A tournament..." Ehkiller muttered. "We need to hold a tournament..."

"And make sure that Kartoss and Shadow participate as well," I nodded in agreement.

"What do we need Shadow there for?"

"For ornamental purposes as well as for the unity of the entire continent. They'll be responsible for providing us with monsters to kill. Or at least that's one option."

"Shadran!" Ehkiller said quietly and a phantom materialized several steps away from me. The majordomo of Phoenix's main castle was a phantom orc. "I need a cost analysis for holding a tournament which would be attended by three emperors. Draw up a tournament ladder that resembles last year's continental competitions. Limit the number of entrants to ten million."

"Shall I factor in the costs of building the

venues?" the phantom inquired immediately. Unlike my Viltrius, this majordomo performed his orders professionally and without any unnecessary handwringing. Perhaps I should tweak my goblin's settings a bit? Although, I kind of like him the way he is. "The location of the tournament will play an important role. If you plan on inviting all three emperors, we'll need a castle in the Free Lands. It's simply not possible to use a location in one of the empires."

"Altameda's in the Free Lands," I offered. "I'll provide a portal for anyone who wants to come."

"Accepted," Ehkiller echoed. "How's that cost analysis?"

"According to the input values, the cost of holding a tournament is assessed at between 300 and 420 million gold. Prizes and rewards are not included in the cost analysis."

"What would we have to do to submit a request to hold a tournament like this?" The calm voice of Phoenix's leader did not suggest that he would regret parting with such an astronomical amount.

"The request has been drafted. Please confirm it."

"So what's next?" Making several passes with his hands, Ehkiller first looked at me, then at Anastaria, who had arranged herself in her chair to more comfortably observe this expenditure of crazy sums of money. Stacey barely managed to shrug her shoulders before a shimmering portal appeared beside us. Even hobgoblins couldn't restrict a Herald from doing his job.

"The Emperor wishes to see you!"

CHAPTER TWO

UNFORESEEN DIFFICULTIES

RESIDENTS OF KALRAGON! In three weeks' time, the Phoenix and Legends of Barliona clans shall hold a tournament to determine the best players of our continent. This tournament's winners shall defend the honor of Kalragon at the global inter-clan competitions. During the preparatory period for the tournament — and until its conclusion — Free Citizens shall no longer be permitted to kill other Free Citizens! The tournament shall be held in the Free Lands. Free tele-transportation shall be provided by the sponsoring clans: Phoenix and the Legends of Barliona. Become the best! Enter the tournament and show your worth! Information about the various contests and categories will be posted to the official Barliona site in four days. Make sure to check the news!

The enormous system notification blotted out everything in sight, including Ehkiller's pensive face.

"I'm assuming it's too late to back out of this?" he asked the Emperor who was looking majestically down on us from his throne. Once every blue moon, the audience seems to take place in the palace's throne room instead of the typical round table of the Emperor's study. I'm not even sure if I should consider this an honor or not. As soon as we appeared before the Emperor, he asked us if we were sure about our decision and, receiving our affirmation, sent the above message to the entire continent. And yet, he'd never said anything about blocking PvP mode, and this condition came as a sudden and very unpleasant surprise to us.

"You can always back out," Naahti replied. "Even despite the fact that the continent's residents have already been notified of the upcoming event. Judging by your shocked faces, you have some doubts. What are they?"

"The Tomb of the Creator," Anastaria replied cautiously, carefully choosing her words. "There are other players from the other continents sailing in our direction. Their objective is straightforward — they want to take away our right to be the first to complete the Tomb and solve the mystery of the Ergreis. Now, with this condition you've set, we've effectively lost our ability to defend the Tomb from the other Free Citizens, which was why Ehkiller inquired about the possibility of calling off the tournament. We weren't ready for this."

"I have spoken my word and my word is not subject to revision," the Emperor clattered off implacably. "All duels between the Free Citizens have been blocked until the culmination of the tournament. Sooner or later, the mystery of the Ergreis will be solved and it doesn't matter who'll do it — you or the newcomers. The power of the Ergreis is so great that we cannot afford to send favorites or unworthy sentients to face it. Only the truly mighty Free Citizens will be able to deal with the secret of the crystal — anyone else will be annihilated, along with all of Barliona and all its continents. I can still cancel the tournament — you only need to request it. Do you truly wish this?"

Ehkiller and Naahti locked eyes and froze in place. The air between the clan leader and the Emperor seemed so charged that if any sentient stumbled between them, I imagine it would be sent to respawn immediately regardless of whether it was player or NPC. The heavy gazes of the two self-assured administrators would have destroyed it in a blink of an eye.

"We would be happy to arrange the tournament!" Ehkiller gave up after an eternity that lasted an entire minute. The icy glow vanished from the Emperor's eyes and the head of Malabar added:

"I knew that I could count on you. As for the Tomb, consider how you can safeguard it without resorting to force. It's not up to me to tell you that any problem could be solved in a number of ways and the forceful approach is not always the best way out of a difficult situation. The prohibition against combat will cover all the Free Citizens, regardless of their territorial origin. But enough about the Tomb. Since we've decided that the tournament will go on, I'd like to discuss the concessions that the Phoenix clan expects to receive for rendering such an enormous service to the Empire."

"Not just Phoenix," Ehkiller corrected the Emperor. "There are two clans organizing this tournament..."

After thirty minutes of negotiations, I understood only that I had ceased to understand anything at all. Ehkiller bartered and haggled with the Emperor like a cook at a market, and Naahti for his part didn't budge an inch, wringing his hands and complaining that Phoenix was trying to bankrupt his Empire. Literally a few minutes ago, they were ready to incinerate each other with their eyes, playing the parts of spoiled princesses who look down proudly on this poor world, but as soon as it came to eking out an extra gold piece, it was like Ehkiller and Naahti had been replaced by two strangers.

"I have an idea," Ehkiller said suddenly, smirking at my bored face. What else could I do? I simply wasn't very interested in what province could help us with what resources, in what amounts, how the logistics would be arranged, what bonuses were best exacted from Kartoss, what villages and even towns would be handed over to our control, what percentages from the selling of attributes would trickle to our treasury...This just wasn't in my wheelhouse! "In order to make our discussion more productive, I suggest we invite Serart — the treasurer of the Legends of Barliona — as well as someone from Kartoss. I'm sure that the Dark Lord's representatives, or perhaps he himself, would be happy to discuss how to organize the tournament. As for Anastaria and Mahan...I suggest we let them go. Negotiations aren't really their cup of tea."

"Agreed," the Emperor said, and several moments later the Heralds had delivered Mr. Kristowski to the main hall, while a Magister of Kartoss emerged triumphantly from his portal. The preparations for the tournament began to burble with renewed force.

"What'll we do about the Tomb?" Anastaria asked pensively as soon as the Herald had delivered us to Phoenix's castle. "Surely we're not going to defend it using NPCs? Suggestions?"

"Well," I muttered, "unfortunately nothing's coming to me except for the most obvious and simplest option."

"What's that?"

"Since PvP is blocked for everyone, then no player will be able to squeeze through a tight wall of other players. It's one of those situations where a crowd of newbies can stop a crowd of Level 400s. The important thing is to hold the line and block any flying. The entrance to the Tomb is pretty small, so we can hire some minnows, arrange them in several chains and make them work in shifts. The downside is we'll have to arrange a round the clock watch. And plus we'll need some device that jams flying...which they could break, so we'll also need..."

"Daniel, you're a genius!" Anastaria interrupted me happily. She jumped up and began to pace back and forth with undisguised impatience. "I'll work out the details and we'll find the right people either in our clan or from dad's, I'll talk to Serart this very day. Damn it! This really is the simplest option and, what's stranger, the most obvious one! Even the Emperor was hinting at it! This is what happens when you get used to playing at the higher levels. All right, we've settled this issue then. I'll set up the guards this very day. Send me an invite to the Legends. It's no good when the husband and wife are in different clans."

Player Anastaria has joined the Legends of Barliona. Current rank: Deputy Head.

"Congratulations on your return," Plinto instantly wrote in the clan chat. *"Are you going to be here for a while, or are you just stopping by for another fling?"*

"Baby, I'm planning on going to see my trainers

and teachers, and then I have to go see Nashlazar," Anastaria went on, leaving the Rogue's quip without a reply. Adjusting her already perfectly-arranged hair, Stacey embraced me, placed her head on my chest, shut her eyes in pleasure and forced me to embrace her.

"What do you think — can the teachers wait a half hour?" I asked her in a hushed voice. Despite the time we had spent together in the game as well as in reality, when Stacey was so close to me, my breathing locked up treacherously, my head filled with noise, and a warmth spilled out in my chest, filling my whole being.

Quest completed: 'Tight-knit family. Step 1.' Speak to the High Priestess of Eluna to receive your reward and the next step in the quest chain.

"How about later tonight, Dan?" Stacey gave me a cunning glance and slipping playfully from my embrace. "I just knew that there's no reason to wait all thirty days! It's enough to prove that we're together again. Shall we go see Elsa tonight?"

"So that was all for the quest?" I almost choked from outrage, but Anastaria instantly reappeared in my embrace, her hazel eyes shining in triumph from yet another victory.

"I love you too, my darling," she meowed in my ear, giving it a nibble in the process. "Will you drop me off at the Paladin's training grounds? In the evening I promise to suffer my deserved punishment!"

Grudgingly fulfilling Stacey's wish and still upset by her trick, I decided to busy myself with chores. Since I'd been so suddenly promoted in levels, it makes sense to find out what this gives me. The time had come to become a real Shaman.

"*Hi, Fleita! What're you up to?*" I began by contacting my student to determine her progress. Something told me that if I show up in front of Kornik or Prontho without this quest, I'll get an earful.

You cannot communicate with your student telepathically without first establishing a private bond.

WHAT?! I sent the request to Fleita again and again, but received the same answer over and over again — our telepathy was blocked. The system didn't tell me that my student wasn't in the game — it told me that I wasn't allowed to speak with her without an amulet! How was this possible? Coming to grips with the futility of making further attempts to contact the Shaman, I decided to ask Kornik to explain what was going on...

You cannot communicate with your teacher telepathically without first establishing a private bond.

It's a good thing that this here wall is right here so I can lean against it in my shock. I'm sure that the spectacle of a Shaman Harbinger collapsing to the ground with his face contorted in amazement would make the rounds on the Barliona forums. My telepathy had been blocked!

"*Stacey?!*" Panicking, I sent a thought to Anastaria.

"*What happened?*" came Stacey's immediate reply and I relaxed a little. Only now did I notice that I had tensed up like a coiled spring in expectation of the answer. Even though everything had worked fine just that morning, the Corporation could easily put an end to something like telepathy whenever it felt like it.

"*Hmm...Never mind, I thought the Corp had blocked my Shamanic powers...!*"

"*Not all of them. I get the impression that all the undocumented features that we've been using before the update have been disabled now. For instance, I can't speak with Eluna without first getting permission from the Priests or simply asking them to do it for me. Despite the status, a warrior of the goddess isn't supposed to speak to her directly. I'm sitting here trying to figure it out as we speak. What about you?*"

"*So far all I've discovered is that I can't speak with my student or my teacher. I'll start testing everything else.*"

"*Let me know what you find tonight,*" said Anastaria and disconnected. Here I discovered that even the act of disconnection was now so palpable that I had even gritted my teeth: Before the update, Anastaria's thoughts would appear in my mind suddenly and leave it just as unexpectedly, but now it seemed like everything was happening according to strict protocol: 'Do you wish to speak with your second half?' 'Your second half has terminated your conversation. Please rate your telepathic exchange...' What's that Corporation up to with this update?

I made my way to the shamanic training ground and opened the Spirit summoning interface. My heart skipped a beat. The panel was empty. Entirely empty. All eight quick slots were utterly bare, as if I'd never used them before! The spellbook icon was blinking conspicuously, drawing my attention. A bad premonition — I opened the spellbook and cursed one more time. At the moment, I could only summon two Minor Spirits — of healing and of lightning. And that's it! Even though I was still learning an enormous number of summons, the spellbook contained nothing at all.

"Our failing apprentice has decided to honor our humble abode?" Kornik's wry voice sounded beside me, forcing me to look up from the book. "What doth his Harbingerness require of us?"

"Teacher," I bowed my head deferentially, slipping on the mask of the student. "Please explain to me what has happened with my powers?"

"What about them?" the goblin asked with

mock surprise. It was obvious that he knew what was going on.

"I can't get in touch with my student, I can't get in touch with you, I don't have any..." Patiently and methodically, I began to itemize all the 'bugs' I had encountered up till now. Perhaps they were 'features,' if you looked at them in the right light.

"Of course you can't get in touch with us," smirked Kornik. "Have you established a private bond with me or your student? Nope. Did you inscribe the Spirits you were taught into your spellbook? Nope. Did you do any of what every other ordinary Shaman does at all? I'll give you one chance to guess the answer. I wouldn't be surprised if you have no idea what your student is doing at this very moment. 'Oh woe is me! I can't reach her telepathically!' How about just calling her on the old amulet? And you call yourself a teacher..! Be thankful that you still have the power to jump all over Kalragon like some interdimensional flea. I'd take that away from you too, were it up to me. How can you summon Spirits if you give no thought to your elemental? The Supreme Spirit of Water doesn't even remember you anymore. No — things can't go on like this. You, my remedial student, will have to learn how to be a true Shaman instead of the strange paradox you were before the Cataclysm. It doesn't do after all to go about summoning Rank 50 Spirits while still at Rank 1."

"If I had done everything like an ordinary

Shaman, I would've never become Harbinger." I wasn't about to let this NPC berate me unanswered. "According to you I'm not acting like an ordinary Shaman? So what? Every Shaman has his own Way, and I have traveled mine to its end. According to you, the Supreme Water Spirit's forgotten about me? Do the Shamans have rules that they must follow in their practice of shamanism? Or is there some ideal Shaman out there somewhere that I have to compare myself to? The Shaman I was before the Cataclysm is a very real Shaman! If someone wants to destroy him in some manner, then I'd prefer to hear the truth, so do me a favor and quit telling me this nonsense. I've heard plenty of that over the last few months."

"Oh, oh, you're scaring me!" Kornik continued to mock me. "He doesn't like nonsense, he's so no nonsense — no sir, no nonsense for him! You're my student! If I tell you that you need to relearn something, then that's what you have to do. It doesn't make sense to do whatever you like and then later scour the Free Lands in search of a problem you should've solved months ago. You have to be like everyone else and follow the rules!"

"Geranika offered a deal," sounded Prontho's voice behind my back. I turned and bowed my head respectfully before the head of the Shaman Council. I guess it's some holiday today because it's not every day that you see the head of the Council outside of his office. "He agreed to destroy the Heart of Chaos if

Eluna and Tartarus adjusted the abilities of all Free Citizens to conform with the standards of their chosen classes — that is, to the main class template. The Battle of Armard demonstrated to Geranika how unpredictable the Free Citizens could be, so he decided to do this."

"And the gods agreed to this?" I asked surprised. As I recall it, Renox was supposed to sacrifice himself in order to destroy the Heart of Chaos. Did the Corporation really revise this scenario? What did they not like about nonstandard players? The entire game was built on our shoulders after all! The most interesting part of Barliona was the option to improvise some unexpected power or solution. Maybe the Corp had gotten tired of constantly correcting the scenarios to account for all the things we came up with?

"Don't you see the consequences?" Prontho raised an eyebrow inquisitively, managing thereby to demonstrate his immense dissatisfaction with my all too obvious question.

"But why?" I sighed, trying to ignore the orc's reaction. "Why do the gods want the Free Citizens to be...average?"

Prontho didn't bother to give me an answer. Turning triumphantly and losing all interest in me, the head of the Shaman Council headed toward the only building on the training ground. Our audience had ended.

"Kornik?" Realizing that I shouldn't expect anything more from the orc, I turned on the goblin.

"What do you mean, 'Kornik?' Anytime anything happens, it's always Kornik, Kornik, Kornik," aped my teacher. "You've learned all there is to learn! And much more than everyone else, I might add. I'll say it again — you need to act like everyone else and avoid trying to change anything. I doubt that Eluna or Tartarus would leave a loophole for their favorites. Why would they? I'll be waiting for you tomorrow. We're going to learn how to summon Spirits all over again...Pshaw! Now I've seen it all! A Harbinger who hasn't a clue about how to be a Shaman! What a nightmare!"

Still muttering into his nose, Kornik stepped a few paces away from me, gave me another glance, smirked and vanished. The air around me filled with the buzz of other Shamans, many of whom had never seen Prontho in the flesh before. For my part, I tried to detach my mind from it all. Kornik had basically told me outright that it was possible to go on summoning the Spirits in my accustomed manner, so I had to now consider this matter in the proper manner. I didn't feel like becoming an average Shaman.

* * *

"Mahan, it's been so long!" Favaz, my Jewelcrafting teacher — who had become first among the masters of Anhurs — welcomed me with sincere happiness. The workshop that had been destroyed during the blooming of the Ying-Yang had long since been restored. The gnome had added several floors to it so that now the pitter-patter and bustle of the craftsmen housed up there descended down to us. Over the last half-year, the Jewelcrafting profession had undergone a renaissance. The popularity of this profession now rivaled that of Smithing or Tanning, and consequently had affected the costs of the ingredients and prices of the finished products. Even before the Cataclysm, Mr. Kristowski had begun sighing about the bygone days when a simple Gold ring of +5 to some old stat cost a mere hundred gold. Now, however, the price of a ring like that was lower than the cost of the ingredients you needed to craft it, which was making the crafting of low-level items prohibitively expensive. On the other hand, the gathering and mining business was on the up and up — players were buying up stacks of ingredients by the thousands, wishing to become the next exquisite jeweler and dazzle Barliona with the craftsmanship.

"Teacher," I bowed my head as per custom, greeting my senior. The Barliona NPCs really get off on subordination, and bowing your head or curtseying one extra time never hurts. "I am pleased to see your workshop is prospering."

"It's all thanks to you!" In a fit of gratitude, the gnome placed his hand on my shoulder, pouring oil on the fire of my vanity. If I had any vanity, that is. "It's no small honor to say that I taught a Jeweler who managed to cause the Ying-Yang to bloom! Every new Free Citizen who comes to study with me first asks whether Shaman Mahan studied here at some point. Even if you did not learn the basic skills from me, the polishing and faceting of your trade was the work of my hands!"

The gnome called over one of his assistants, issued a curt order and then ushered me into the next room which turned out to be a reception room.

"I saw your recipe," Favaz went on, offering me some tea. "A very curious solution — giving lovers a chance to speak telepathically with one another. Have you made one yet?"

"Only one set," I replied, sipping the tea and noticing the temporary boost to my Jewelcrafting stats. Even if it was only +10 for sixty minutes, the important thing was that Barliona now had drinks that would boost your profession. A welcome feature for players who had dedicated themselves to crafting. "I need to create several thousand Pendants but I have no idea where I'll find the time to do it. Three or four minutes per item is too much. Much too much. And that's why I'm here. Figured you might have some useful advice for me."

"Why, what could I possible advise you..." the gnome spread his arms. "The only thing you can do is sit down and get to work. You can't transfer the recipe. You can't not do the work. So the only thing that follows is work, work, and more work. You have to work even when you're taking a break from working. There's no other advice I can offer."

Suddenly, the sound of shattering glasses resounded overhead.

"Why that no good, useless, armless thing!" Favaz yelled in anger. The gnome cast me an apologetic look, then glanced up at the ceiling, then back at me and, trying to speak calmly, added, "Mahan, please wait for me here. Feel free to read the books or have some more tea. I'll be a second. I had told a certain dunderhead to wash the windows, and what do you know, the oaf's shattered them instead! Why is it that some Free Citizens can create unbelievable things, while others can manage to break even a cast iron sphere? With their bare hands! How do you all manage to be so...so...different?"

Despite his young age, the Jeweler got up with a creak and shuffled over to the ladder — to issue his punishment to the hapless player. I even grew curious who it was who'd messed up so badly, but since the gnome had asked me to wait for him in his room, it was better for me to stay put. It's hard to believe that Favaz doesn't have the information I need about how to create the Pendants, so risking my Attractiveness with him right now would be a bad idea.

I heard the sounds of argument come from upstairs, mixed with a girlish sobbing — the dunderhead turned out to be female. My desire to go take a look grew to such a degree that I even stood up from the table and approached the staircase. Right at the last moment and by sheer force of will, I managed to change course and stopped beside a small bookcase. Since Favaz had granted me the permission to read the volumes on the shelf, then there wouldn't be anything valuable or useful among them, and yet — in the hopes of overcoming the desire to go upstairs and have a laugh at the hapless girl with the other players — I picked up the first book I came across and began to read it. *Myths and Legends of Jewelcrafting.* The update had not affected the mechanic of reading literature in Barliona — until you'd read the entire book, it would forever open to the first page and the only way to flip to the next one was to read the entire text. The Imitators were real sticklers for ensuring these rules were followed.

To my immense surprise, I liked the book. Either Favaz selected the books for his modest collection very carefully, or this work simply resonated with my current state...All I knew was that it was really interesting to read about the great jewelers of the past, who created true masterpieces with their cunning and artistry. How many amazing items had been created only to be lost to the ages! Marvels such as Borgia's Ring, which the oppressed gnomes presented to the head of the orcs, thereby earning their liberty. Or the Chain of Desires, created by the elves and presented as a gift to the king of the dwarves. To make a long story short, the Chain of Desires only made the desires of the elves come true and as a result the poor dwarves spent several years serving the long-eared folk. Nowadays the dwarves deny this simple historical fact, but a legend wouldn't lie now would it?

I had to catch my breath when I saw an illustration of a whimsical ring with a green stone. Tourmellorn — a ring of tourmaline with the symbol fashioned from the mellorn mineral. A ring created by Karmadont for the lord of the elves, who in the end never did accept the dominance of men. It's only in the present day that the kingdom of the light and dark elves occupies the north of our continent. In bygone times this people lived throughout all of Kalragon, exceeding humans both in terms of population and their artifice. Not wishing to conquer the elves, Karmadont created the Tourmellorn in the hopes of demonstrating that humans could not only fight but create as well — and do so at a level that surpassed the elves. The elves never did get their ring — the caravan that was transporting this artifact was ambushed. The Tourmellorn was lost, forever vanishing from Barliona and becoming one of its more vivid myths.

I didn't remember the moment that design mode enveloped me. Simply, a moment came in which I realized that I was in a large, well-lit room, filled with shelves, workbenches, various jeweler's tools, two furnaces, copies of the items I'd already created and many other things which would make the process of crafting items in Barliona much more pleasant and effective.

Looks like along with my updated character, the Corporation had also presented me with the official design mode. After all, I never did complete the quest chain that unlocked it...

Like hell!

My sudden desire to craft the Tourmellorn vanished on the spot. I don't know why, but I became so used to working in my old, gloomy design mode that now I felt incredibly uncomfortable in this well-lit room. It was like I was naked and on stage in front of a large crowd. No doubt there are some who like to show off their bodies, especially if there's something to show off, but I'm not one of them. This brightly illuminated workshop had everything I needed to create efficiently, even a separate panel for making sketches, but I didn't actually *need* any of that. Opening my mailbox (without even having to leave design mode), I began to compose a letter. Let them figure out what to do with me on their own — I want my old design mode back!

Dear admins, I'd like to bring to your attention that I have stumbled upon a rather embarrassing design mode, now active for my character. I understand very well that it would be a pleasure to do my crafting in such an environment. However, I would strongly prefer that you return my old, dark design mode to me. It is highly unpleasant for me to realize that I have been stripped of the chance to complete the quest chain for becoming a creator. Thank you!

Re-reading my letter, I sent it to the admins with a mean smirk. Now, whoever's responsible for me only has one way out — return everything to the way it had been. The Corporation can't ignore my letter — they're the very reason that I had become a 'certain Shaman Mahan.' If I begin to voice my displeasure, heads might start to roll. And who needs that? No one. And in the same way, they couldn't disable my design mode in general and force me to complete the quest chain. Who knows when I get around to doing it? Maybe in a year, maybe in two. When there's time. At the same time, I — as a Jeweler — have the only recipe in Barliona for an item that allows couples to communicate telepathically. Here, the Corp would have to either toss the recipe and inform its playerbase of this, or agree to my conditions. And both options suited me just fine. Anyway you spin it, the Corp didn't have much of a choice, so they'd have to give me back my initial design mode. After all, I'm ready to fight for it to the bitter end!

"That's a good book," sounded Favaz's voice, snapping me back to the game. I looked around with surprise and realized that during my cogitations, I had managed to leave design mode and was now standing beside a bookshelf, holding the volume of the Jewelers' fairy tales in my hand. "It's too bad that the items described in it are merely the stuff of myths. I would happily study the structure of several of these artifacts and attempt to make a recipe."

"Teacher, this book speaks of the Tourmellorn. Where else may I read of this ring?"

"The Tourmellorn?" the gnome echoed with surprise. "What do you need it for? This ring is useless to humans — oh, I beg your pardon — Dragons. Besides, it's just a myth, a pretty tale about a master Jeweler of the past."

"Experience shows that when it comes to Karmadont, the myths tend to be true. I'm interested in this sentient. Both as an individual who existed, as a Hunter who became an Emperor, as well as a Craftsman who created the Chess Set, the Altarian Falcon, the Tourmellorn, and the three Emperors. What other miracles did Karmadont's hands conjure?"

"The Altarian Falcon?" Favaz furrowed his brow, trying to remember something, but then shrugged and muttered: "I'd never even heard of that before...Mahan, I understand your desire, but I have to disappoint you — I don't have the quest you're looking for. Perhaps the hermit has the answers you seek. One of our masters told you about him, I believe. Have you visited him yet?"

That's right! How had I forgotten about that quest? According to my initial understanding of it, the hermit could be Karmadont himself, since no one knew where the Emperor's grave actually was. Or whether it exists at all! But, let's leave these hypothetical theories stand — both of the hermit and of Karmadont — while we continue to pump Favaz for all the info he's got.

"Unfortunately, neither before nor after the Cataclysm, have I managed to visit him, but thank you for reminding me. Teacher, I'd like to return to my initial question — is there some way of accelerating the production of the Pendants? Are there perhaps some elixirs, such as your tea, that will increase not only craftsmanship, but the speed of crafting as well?"

"Elixirs?" The gnome rubbed his chin pensively and stared at the ceiling. "There's one elixir...but, no, that won't do...a bit of nonsense, a fairy tale, no more....No, I really don't think that anything will help."

"Please forgive my rudeness but I heard something about a fairy tale. What did you mean?"

"A perfectly ordinary fairy tale. The Alchemists have spent the last several millennia trying to recreate Merlin's Potion...to no avail. According to those legends that you hold so dear, this elixir has miraculous effects on craftsmen. What exactly it does remains unclear, but the only documented case of someone quaffing Merlin's Potion led to the creation of the current Imperial palace. By one man alone. In one day. No one remembers what his name is, but everyone knows that he used Merlin's Potion — which was given to him by Karmadont."

"Again Karmadont?" I blurted out.

"Hmm, I guess so...yes. Again him," the gnome said thoughtfully. "The man was an Architect, so the Jewelers didn't really pay much attention to the affair, but...You know it really is interesting. There's never been any other mention of Merlin's Potion, whether before or after. I wonder how the first Emperor acquired it..."

The gnome fell quiet, following his thoughts into nirvana. I tried to continue our conversation, but Favaz answered me in monosyllables, indicating that it was time for me to get going.

Trying not to bug the gnome, I again picked up the book about the legendary jewelers and opened it to the page with the Tourmellorn. The ring seemed perfect to me. The desire to enter design mode and try and recreate this masterpiece again began to smolder in my chest, but I made an effort and pushed it away — I didn't want to craft in the illuminated design mode. Returning the book to its place with a sigh of disappointment, I began to make my exit. However, as I was passing through the workshop, something held me back, something stopped me...The players around me were diligently crafting rings taking no note of their surroundings. Almost all the workbenches were filled with laboring craftsmen — but only almost. Right next to me, an empty workstation winked and nodded at me like some solitary nymphomaniac.

Realizing that I needed to go meet the hermit and figure out who and what was going on, I approached the table hesitantly, sat down on the wooden bench and placed my hands on the well-scratched surface. The Tourmellorn? No, not right now.

Design mode almost consumed my mind, turning the surrounding environment into an illuminated room, but I did my best to concentrate. Barliona is a very interesting game. If players are allowed to unlock a skeleton design mode without completing a hundred quests, then it stands to reason that you could use it whenever you felt like it. Even despite the newly unlocked functionality. I simply need to imagine that I'm surrounded by darkness. They couldn't have cut it off completely!

But at some point, instead of the dark design mode, the Lovers' Pendant appeared before my eyes. As I understood it, my subconscious was feeling guilty, reminding me in this manner about the letter that Mr. Kristowski had sent me with a list of the fifty couples who were first in line to receive their Pendants. He'd already arranged with them what they'd do for my clan. The only thing that everyone was now waiting for was the actual item. Only a single Diamond fit in my mail. Serart offered to take the rest into the clan storage vaults. Indeed, my CFO had several times reminded me in the letter that the order had to be filled urgently. What I liked most of all was that I hadn't received a single call on my amulet. Serart understood perfectly well that if I didn't feel like doing anything at the moment, then forcing me would be pointless, and so he treated me very specifically. His was a considerate approach.

Using the advantages of the new design mode, I opened the mailbox and projected the letter with its list of fifty pairs. The first group. The player couples who'd decided to grow so close to one another that they were prepared to work for my clan to do so. Fifty pairs — that's like 150 minutes of office work. Damn it! That's too long! That's really too long!

I opened my mailbox once again, messed around with the settings of the mail daemon and a long list of 87 thousand lines appeared (and vanished in the distance) before my eyes: the complete list of everyone who wanted a Pendant. The enormity of my predicament stunned me. The first lot was but a drop in the ocean in comparison to the main torrent. I had to do something. But what?

Creating the Pendant was an entirely standard process. I activate the recipe, create a projection of the Diamond, the system processes the stone on its own, breaks it in two halves, polishes it and generates a window with two entry fields for the lovers' names. Once I enter the names, the Pendants are bound to the players. Then this virtual projection is combined with a real Diamond and the Pendants are complete. There's no tricks or difficulties here — a rote and lengthy process of forming the binding that takes up three minutes. And the entire time, the Jeweler is little more than a spectator — the system really does everything on its own. It just takes forever to do it!

Sighing and trying to calm down, I decided to brainstorm the various ways I could solve this problem. The simplest solution was to expedite the binding process. For that I'd need Merlin's Potion, which I didn't know how to come by. What else could be done? Start one process and somehow move on to the next one while it's running. In parallel. The interesting question is how to do this? Or is it even possible? I need to ask Favaz. I think that's about it. There's nothing else that could be thought of — the sequence of creating the Pendant was simply too regimented and...Hold on...

Regimented!

My heart skipped a beat with anxiety when I swiped aside all the projections that remained before my eyes, trying to bring my idea to fruition as quickly as possible.

Who said that I first had to form the stones and then apply the images to them? Why not try to do everything in reverse? For instance, form a huge pool of virtual names, and then apply the image of the stone to it? I have no idea how to do this, but I liked the idea. I had to try it.

Complications popped up right off the bat. The first question that I hadn't an answer to was how to visualize the name? It's a simple name, with no attributes regarding gender, class, appearance, race — a name that is associated with a player only due to the fact that's it's always hanging over their character's head. How could I make the system understand that this player was closely entwined with another one, of whom I knew nothing but his or her name, even if that was a unique one in Barliona? And Barliona as a whole? Was there a chance that the names were only unique as far as the continent went? A good question. I'd need to work it through carefully. But something else was important at the moment — how?

Hmm...Maybe, I'm posing the wrong question? Maybe instead of asking 'how?' I need to be asking 'why?' Why do people decide to be together? Why are people prepared to spend a week of their time in-game to be able to communicate with another person more intimately? Love? A pretty answer — perhaps even the correct one — but one that bore no relation to an item. For some people, love is being constantly beside each other. For others, it's a minute-long meeting once a week or a fleeting glance of two passersby on the street who may never speak with one another — or even some common activity, common thoughts, common interests. The individuals who want the Pendant are incredibly different and it's impossible to come up with some universal principle that ties each one with a concept of 'love.' In that case, we'll return to the original question — is love really the matter here? Is it simply for love that the players want to be able to communicate telepathically? The chance to be closer to one another? The option of using a channel of communication that remains closed to everyone around them? The desire to share not only words but also emotions with the other person?

Despite the fact that I was surrounded by design mode and Barliona, shivers ran along my body. Physiologically speaking, a game avatar doesn't have something like 'shivers,' and yet no one had removed the nervous system of the real person — I suddenly realized what unites those who wanted the amulet! My first thought had been accurate — it was love after all — but that was also the tip of the iceberg. If I hadn't had Anastaria, it would've been really difficult to reach this conclusion.

The first batch of fifty orders was sent to the trash can. The bright glow of design mode no longer bothered me — I didn't pay it any attention. If I was going to work, I'd work with the full list and nothing but the full list. What's the difference whether one couple needs a Pendant or eighty-seven thousand couples? In its current formulation, the number of Pendants played absolutely no role.

What mattered was something else — unity!

We'll take that as an axiom — that two people love each other. What does this mean? The manifestations of love, as I already understood, could be diverse. Even though Stacey loved me, before the Cataclysm, she did absolutely terrible things to me. But that was still love, as odd as that may seem. Why did she do this? Because she simply likes masochism? Yeah right! She did everything in order to protect me from an external threat. And she did it the best way she knew, but she did it. The question that follows is 'why?' but I already have an answer to it: because a person in love doesn't feel whole without the other half. The very expression 'second half' suggests that only together does the new, single whole form. It's referred to differently — a couple, a family, partners — but the gist of it doesn't change. At a certain point in time, people who love each other feel like a single whole. Why 'at a certain point in time?' Because you can't ignore the possibility that people might fall in love with someone else. Anything is possible, but this has no effect on the creative process.

I need to split the Diamond into its parts, polish them, and combine them with the names...This approach could work too, but it's not the right way to do it. I need to learn how to work with the names. I need to take any two names (as if reading my thoughts, the names of a couple appeared before me) and create a single union from them. Intertwine them in such a manner that only the High Priestess could untangle them and with her might tear the bonds between the players. They want to be together? Let them be together then!

Without understanding myself how I did it, I associated Rosgard the Annoying with my right hand — and Cyree the Defender with my left. I brought my palms together, and intertwined my fingers, locking them. Forever and anon, I declare you a couple! The two names before my eyes clashed together, mixed, forming an indescribable mixture of letters and colors and formed a shining sphere. The Pendant for one couple was ready.

Looking up at the list before me, I already knew what to do. Associate with the right, then with the left, form the lock, the mixture, the shining sphere and…

"MAHAN!" Favaz's hysterical shriek reached me even within design mode. "HOW MUCH MORE OF THIS?!"

I guess I'd done something terrible, but I could look at what had happened because the 'Paralysis' debuff blocked this for the next 48 hours. At the same time I realized that I was lying on something cold and terribly uneven, as if someone had piled a bunch of stones on the ground and then dumped me onto them.

"Shaman Mahan! You are under arrest for destroying the Jeweler's workshop and sending 52 Free Citizens to the Gray Lands!" The gnome's shrill outburst was joined by the menacing growl of the Anhurs City guard.

"*Stacey, I need help!*" I managed to think as the cold, iron collar clapped around my neck. They were about to escort me to jail in chains. *"The guards got me, they're taking me away…"*

Barliona jail is a fun place. On the one hand, I didn't see a thing beyond the darkness — the 'Paralysis' debuff kept me blind. On the other hand, I'd been in here before as a Hunter, so I could imagine my surroundings just fine. Stone walls that blocked not only all chat communication and Mage summons, but even my telepathic link to Anastaria. A small window with a rusty grate that could somehow stand up to a battering ram. A wooden door that separated the player from the outside world. Everything as usual in other words and I was even grateful that the debuff kept me from beholding this dour place.

No matter how hard I tried to bring it up, design mode didn't work in jail. All I could do was sit there and wait for Stacey. If she paid my bail in a half hour, I'd leave the jail, exit the game and go dig around the forums to find out what the hell was going on.

* * *

"Come on out, Mahan!" Twenty minutes later the door slid aside. The guard regarded me grimly, scanned me up and down, and added with barely-disguised contempt: "You've made bail this time around, you murderer! Be grateful that our Empire has such lenient laws."

The two points of Attractiveness I had with this fellow suggested that the guard could barely keep himself from sending me to the Gray Lands. What'd I do to him? Had I killed an NPC with my accident? That couldn't be the case — they'd never let me go to begin with. Anyone who killed an NPC within city limits was punished with the full weight of the law. All of Barliona was built on this principle. Although...What killing? The rules forbade it!

"Criminal!" growled the guard, delivering me to the jail warden. Right then, my vision returned to me — the system informed me that Anastaria had dispelled my debuff. I found myself in a small office, with a grizzled NPC behind the desk. His black mustache appeared like a target against a white background. Stacey was standing a bit to the side, watching me with a wry expression. I knew this smirk — it didn't bode anything good for me. It looked like I really had managed to cause some trouble.

"How many times do I have to tell you, sergeant," said the NPC warden wearily, "criminals stay in their cells. As soon as a sentient is set free, he or she ceases to be a criminal. You're dismissed!"

"Shaman Mahan," the old man began as soon as the guard had left the room, "in the name of the Empire, I hereby offer my apologies for your detainment. We had no right to take you under guard. The Herald and Anastaria already explained everything to us. You may go now."

"I don't understand a thing," I muttered in surprise. "Why did you detain me then?"

"You, my darling, managed to destroy the workshop. Again," Stacey explained.

"I destroyed it last time but there wasn't a punishment!"

"Last time you didn't destroy 52 Free Citizens along with it."

"But killing other players is blocked. I couldn't do anything physically! Barliona should've barred me from harming them!"

"And yet you did it anyway. You have a PK marker on you. Or at least you had it when you entered the office. But there's no penalty as such for your murders. It seems the Emperor himself didn't understand how you managed to do it. They wanted to imprison you for something else."

"For destroying two squads of the Anhurs city guard," the warden spoke up, entering our conversation. "By your hand, twelve worthy warriors were sent to the Gray Lands and only half of them bore the marks of death. Six recruits hadn't yet earned their marks and now never will. This is what we wanted to punish you for."

"Two squads?" I whispered surprised. "But how?"

"One of the recruits was the brother of my sergeant," the warden went on, ignoring my question. "They grew up fatherless and their mother asked the older brother to look after the younger one. He was recruited into the Anhurs city guard, one of the safest possible stations to serve, and yet Shaman Mahan showed up and proved the opposite. You should be proud — your name has entered the annals of Anhurs city history."

"Stacey, what's going on? What's with the guilt trip?"

"I think everyone's just in shock. No player has ever managed to kill a guard before. Typically they collapse to the ground with 1 HP, but in your case, as always, the typical outcome didn't happen. Send me your logs — I want to see what you were up to."

"Could I help in some way?" I asked the jail warden carefully, sending Stacey the logs of my Pendant crafting. The next time I begin combining them with the gems, I should first go somewhere far outside of any populated area.

"With what? His widow shall receive gold. She'll never know hardship again, but that won't bring back her son. You, the Free Citizens, only know how to do one thing — kill. Those who bear the mark of death cannot understand the grief of a mother who has lost her son."

"Stacey, here's a global question for you that stuns me with its novelty — is there heaven or hell in Barliona? A place where dead NPCs go? The Gray Lands are only for the players, aren't they?"

"Erm...Every god has a different set-up. This guard was probably a follower of Eluna, so after dying he should enter Erebus. It's a place of non-being — where the souls mix and dissolve into one another, ceasing to be individual entities."

"Is the transition instant? Do the souls immediately dissolve, or does it happen over a period of time?"

"Please don't tell me that you're thinking of going after the guards, Dan. It's not possible."

"An amazing woman once told me: 'There are no impossible things. There are only the fetters of your consciousness that forbid you from doing what you wish to do."

"I never said anything of the kind!"

"Who said anything about you? I was talking about my mother...When are we going to attempt the Tomb?"

"We're starting tomorrow."

"So I have an entire day. Excellent!"

I sighed deeply, gathering my strength and then blurted out:

"The death of your sergeant's younger brother is my fault. I won't ask for forgiveness, I won't act like nothing happened, and I won't promise the impossible. I can only tell you one thing — I will do everything in my power to bring him and the other guards from Erebus. I give you my word as a Shaman!"

Stacey shook her head as if deciding which mental clinic she had best check me into, but as she did so the following notification appeared before me:

Quest available: 'Who will guard the guards themselves?' Description: Bring back the Anhurs guards from Erebus...Time limit for completing the quest: 24 hours. Quest type: "I knew you'd choose this option!" ~James. Reward/Penalty: Variable.

CHAPTER THREE

EREBUS

"**M**AHAN AND ANASTARIA!**" Elizabeth said in a surprisingly cold voice as soon as we appeared before her. The completed quest allowed us to avoid a long waiting line and we were ushered directly into the office of the High Priestess of Eluna immediately. "To what do I owe the honor of beholding the Harbinger and the Paladin General?"

Reward received: +2000 to Reputation with the Priests of Eluna, +1000 to Reputation with Goddess Eluna.

"Your highness," Stacey and I said at the same time as soon as the reward notification appeared before us. We bowed at the same time too as if we'd been practicing all this for a long while, exchanged surprised glances and burst out laughing.

"I can see that the time you've been spending

together has done you good," Elsa remarked in the same chilly tone of voice, ignoring our happiness. The astonishing thing was that I'd never encountered such a frosty attitude from Elizabeth before. I was really trying to stop laughing, but nothing was helping — the pressure of having been imprisoned earlier was now channeling into my laughing fit.

"High Priestess we have come to see you on business," Anastaria was the first to get a grip on herself and, sighing several times to dispel her laughing fit, addressed Elizabeth. "We've completed the first part of your assignment and proved that our family is a strong one."

"So strong that you interrupted your studies with my priestesses and ran off to pull Mahan out of jail?" Elizabeth raised an eyebrow eloquently. "A couple hours were so critical for you that you decided to disregard my gifts?"

"Dan, we've got to get out of here immediately! My Attractiveness with her has fallen to 50 points already. There's something off about her," Anastaria's urgent thought flashed through my mind.

"Elizabeth, it's my fault that..." I began, but the High Priestess cut me off:

"Of course it's yours, who'd even argue that point," Elizabeth turned to face me. I noticed with astonishment that my 100 points of Attractiveness with her (which I had always been quite proud of) had dwindled to 70. This was still a pretty hefty number for an average player, but for me it was entirely unacceptable. My laughter quit me in a flash. What happened?! "What upsets me the most, is the instability around you. If there are any problems, then there's always a high probability that Shaman Mahan is right in the middle of them."

"High Priestess," I continued stubbornly, despite Anastaria's best attempts to pull me out of the office. "We have lived through many trials, both good and bad. We've watched each other's backs and saved one another again and again, so please explain to me what has caused your displeasure..."

"Explain?" An expression of false surprise appeared on the NPC's face. "Why are you so suddenly interested in explanations? Especially those of others and not your own? Isn't your motto: 'Onward and only onward!' Without ever looking back?"

"It seems like you've confused me with someone," I parried. Anastaria failed to budge me from where I stood, so she muttered something but remained standing beside me. "During the duration of our acquaintance, I haven't once done anything without good reason. No one can accuse me of that."

"Oh really? Literally two hours ago, a Shaman sent six future guards to their eternal rest. They were young, inexperienced, untrained! Of course this was done completely consciously and with full awareness of your impunity. Good work, Mahan! You barely even noticed it! And you're going to tell me that you can always justify your actions?"

"That's exactly why I'm here," I began to explain, but Elsa interrupted me again:

"You're betting on my kindness and understanding? You wish to escape your deserved punishment? That shall not be…"

"Why, I couldn't give a damn about my punishment or who metes it out!" No one thought I knew how to yell. Most of all myself. Elsa went quiet with a look of surprise on her face, allowing me to go on: "I'm prepared to suffer any punishment right this instant! But before you make any decision, tell me how I can enter Erebus!"

Elizabeth collapsed in her chair, as if her legs had failed her, and a deep silence descended on the office.

"You cannot bring back the dead, Shaman," Eluna's melancholy voice let me know that a new visitor had appeared in the Priestess's office. "Even a mourning mother, like Elizabeth here, cannot allow that to pass."

"WHAT?!" Stacey and I blurted out at the same time and began to turn our heads from Eluna to Elizabeth and back in stunned amazement. Elizabeth was the mourning mother? Something had happened with Clouter?

"Avtondil hadn't yet received the mark of death," Eluna went on, as Elizabeth stared grimly at the empty sheet on her table. "He was so eager to be of service to the Empire that he signed up to be an assistant guard. The explosion, which you accidentally caused, happened precisely as Avtondil's squad was passing alongside the workshop. Six dead. Six young and inexperienced subjects of the Empire. And among their number, the son of my High Priestess. There is nothing I can do, Mahan. Just like you."

"I have twenty-four hours to bring them back," I said stubbornly. Eluna's authority in these matters weighed on me with the weight of a stone slab, forcing me to reject this venture, flee to some remote corner of Barliona, delete my Shaman and generally forget what a capsule even looked like. If the goddess says that it's impossible to bring back the dead, then there's no sense in getting myself into this. However, the quest entry in my quest list forced me to go against one of the most powerful creatures in Barliona and, clenching my fists, insist on my position. Clouter had to be returned to this world and the quest suggested that he could be too.

"Erebus is off-limits to the living," Eluna went on.

"Then I'll go there as a dead man," I refused to concede. "The longer you restrain me, the less time I have."

"Mahan, this is not possible," Elizabeth tore her gaze from the empty sheet and looked up at me, her eyes brimming with tears. I could've killed those damn devs! Gazing into the eyes of a mother who had lost her child because of me, the sense of irreality evaporated. A sense of disgust I had never experienced before filled my inner being. I wanted one thing only — to help this woman regain her child. For me Barliona had become real again, and the NPC with the codename 'High Priestess of Eluna' became a mother who had lost her child. Not some bit of software code.

"Elsa, this world has something called hope. As long as it exists, Clouter lives. As do the other five guards. Eluna, what must I do to enter Erebus?"

"You must die," the goddess said pithily after a short pause. "You must die and forsake the Gray Lands. Be aware Mahan, you might never return."

"In that case, consider me a democrat," I managed to say before my head exploded into a million tiny bits. Eluna had personally sent me to respawn.

Loading...

Please confirm that you wish to enter the 'Erebus' location.

Please read the rules...

I was forced to read a huge chunk of text, which would ordinarily have caused shivers to zip along my spine. It turns out that Erebus is one of the closed-off locations and if I fail the quest here, my

Shaman might remain here for all eternity. That is, not for all eternity, but until the Corporation permits his lost spirit to return to the game. Smiling to myself, I pushed the 'Accept' button that appeared only after I had read the entire text, and my surroundings snapped into motion.

A fog formed around me, smoothly transforming into darkness several meters away. I got the impression that I had become a little lamp that was trying to scatter the dourness of this world but lacking sufficient power to do so. I was sparkling and sputtering but not very convincingly. Nevertheless, there was enough light to see the cobble-paved path receding ahead of me into the fog and the precipice plummeting away into the same fog on either side of the path. My legs wavered beneath me, forcing me to squat. Who knows what the depth of this precipice is — it could be two meters or it could be endless. The path before me was about fifty centimeters wide, so it wouldn't take much but a breeze to misstep and plummet into the depths.

Forcing myself to get back up to my feet and take a first step turned out to be a fairly nontrivial challenge. My mind understood that I was surrounded by a game, but my wild fear of the unknown and the height fettered my movements, turned my legs to cotton and forced me to lie down on the path to ensure I wouldn't fall. I had to struggle with myself for several minutes, even exiting to reality several times to prove to my sub-consciousness that the world around me was merely graphical. It seemed to help and I managed to creep along the path.

As I expected, my connection with the external world had been cut off — neither the clan chat, nor mail, nor the amulets, nor my telepathy with Anastaria. Nothing at all. The only good news was that the quest timer before my eyes stopped every time I exited to reality. I had to complete this quest in 24 game hours, not real ones. This pleased me because it meant I would have time to talk to Anastaria when she yanked me out at the end of the day to tell her everything I'd see. By the way, about the things I was seeing...Damn it! I can't record video here either!

"STRANGER!" all of a sudden a drawn out, malevolent whisper tore through the silence. It sounded like some giant snake had forgotten how to hiss and learned how to speak and scare the crap out of wandering Shamans. "WHAT DO YOU SEEK IN THE LAND OF THE DEAD?"

"Greetings!" I yelled just in case, noting the debuffs that blinked and instantly vanished, taking with them 10% of my HP. The voice didn't merely scare me, it also hurt me. "My name is Mahan and I come in peace!"

"YOU DID NOT ANSWER THE QUESTION," whispered the unknown creature, after which I lost control of my character: my hands and feet began to contort themselves, their joints creaking from the strain, my Hit Points raced my Energy to the bottom, and yet I remained watching this chaos of my Shaman from the side and suddenly realized that I wasn't feeling any pain! My character's sensory filter was set to maximum! If I had ventured into Erebus even a couple weeks ago, I'd be a ball of pain right now, tearing muscles and burning nerves without even a hint of consciousness. After all I still recall the 'pleasure' of cracking joints. But now...

"I have come for the six dead guards of Anhurs, who died several hours ago! Erebus is not their place!"

In keeping with what was happening to my body, my voice emerged high pitched and pierced with notes of panic and shock, yet I succeeded in the main thing — the spasms stopped.

"DEATH FOR THE DEAD, LIFE FOR THE LIVING!" whispered the voice at the level of a kitchen stoic who had spilled a pot of boiling water onto himself, leaving me on my own on the narrow path with 5% HP.

The Shaman has three hands...

I reflexively summoned a Spirit of Complete Healing, forgetting entirely that all my unlearned summons had been blocked, and so wasn't particularly surprised when instead of the desired result I beheld a notification. What drew my attention was that, even though the notification was completely ordinary, it was also illogical:

You may not summon Spirits in Erebus.

If I was prohibited from summoning Spirits that I hadn't yet learned, then the system should probably first check whether I can summon a Spirit at all and only then evaluate the location I'm trying to do it in. After all, I could simply sing a song of the Shaman mutant without even hinting at a summons. Why waste system resources tracking every word and checking whether it's a summons or not? It's dumb and unprofessional. Things like that are discouraged in the most introductory programming courses. The conclusion is evident — the restriction against summoning 'unlicensed' Spirits is superimposed and in the main world it might be difficult to summon them, but it's possible. The important thing was to figure out how to do it.

The good news was that health potions worked just as well in Erebus as anywhere else. Quaffing four bottles and making a mental note to replenish my glass stocks (which had been calculated for a Level 160 player), I cautiously moved further along the path as the quest timer continued to creep mercilessly towards zero.

The path seemed endless. I was no longer paying attention to the precipice at its edges, moving forward at a fairly brisk pace when suddenly I came upon a fork. More precisely, a second path that joined mine at an acute angle and which boasted a lumbering, half-transparent orc with a sour mug. Wearing a burlap sack, the orc moved slowly, shuffling his feet unwillingly, as if something was prodding him onward. The paths evened out, allowing me a closer view of the orc. Not a single emotion, not a single look to the side — the face of the creature lumbering beside me displayed utter disinterest, mixed with weariness and submission to his fate. Judging by his muscles, the orc was a warrior, perhaps even a good one, but this hadn't saved him from Erebus. I guess he came across someone stronger. I couldn't help but touch the shoulder of the trudging creature. That is, I wanted to touch it, but my hand passed straight through the orc as if he was a projection. A ghost. At the same time, the ghost didn't react to my lack of tact and slowly continued to approach the point where our paths joined. I didn't exist as far as he was concerned.

Like hell!

The system again glibly informed me that Erebus was no place for Spirits. I was passing through the ghost like a supermodel passes through a crowd of geeks — meeting no resistance. The orc didn't react to a single gesture I made, neither to my hands waving in front of his face, nor my shouts, nor my expletives. The Imitator couldn't care less that I spun like a top through him, trying to scatter his form. He walked towards a goal only he knew, somewhere far ahead, reducing all my attempts to naught.

Like hell squared!

Design mode greeted me with its light and the happy recognition of upcoming work to be done. Finding the Blessed Visage of Eluna among my recipes, I combined it with an ingot of Imperial Steel, since I didn't have any Marble in my bag or in my mail. My idea was as simple as a Barliona penny — create an Amulet of the Junior Novice and pin it to the ghost. I didn't see any other options for having a word with the orc.

Insufficient resources to create 'the Blessed Visage of Eluna.' Make sure that you have 1 unit of Marble in your inventory bag.

Here's where I really got angry...I don't have the resources?! How am I supposed to craft if the Corporation blocks any attempt of doing something out of the ordinary? Am I supposed to look for recipes for everything? Like hell cubed!

I can't create a Pendant because I don't have any Marble and, looking ahead, Copper ingots. I can't create a new visage of Eluna out of, say, Imperial Steel because I simply won't have time to do so. Yet I can do something else!

I caught up with the ghost who had managed to get ahead of me in the meantime, opened design mode again and with a malevolent grin created the projection of an orc. If they want to force me to work by the rules, then let it be so — I'll follow the rules. Only, the rules will be mine!

Using the 'Alter Essence' ability, I inserted Eluna's Visage into the orc's chest, thought a bit, opened my Smithing recipes, found the most basic sword I had, added its projection to the orc's hand (since it does no good for a warrior to die without a sword), shut my eyes and imagined what this entire arrangement would look like in reality. Were I in the normal gameworld, these actions would have created a simple statue — fragile and short-lived, since a Sculptor wouldn't be involved in its creation. But Erebus should have its own laws...

"Nooo!" the savage plea of the creature tore the silence around us to shreds. I opened my eyes and beheld the embodied orc, on his knees with his eyes shut, bellowing like a herd of elephants. A light as bright as a supernova burst from within him, but it didn't blind me in the process, and I could see as the fog left the surrounding environment. Everything went cold inside of me: There were hundreds, no, thousands of paths here, all uniting and intertwining and headed towards an enormous cliff that loomed on the horizon. Animals, monsters, two-legged creatures, even fish — all trudged along the paths — an enormous army of those whose time in Barliona had reached its end and who were now heading in the direction of their last stop — the point of complete rest.

The light went out, allowing the fog to flow back in and with it, the orc stopped screaming. Falling from nowhere, the sword clattered upon the stones, but the orc snatched it up with a quick motion and stood up, turning in my direction.

"Freemie Cur!" he spat out with undisguised hate and his hazel eyes began to fill with blood. "The gods had mercy upon me and granted me a chance to have my revenge!"

Before I could say anything, the orc lunged at me with his sword over his head, wishing to cleave me into two, smaller, symmetrical Shamans. On one hand, he was at Level 120 and not particularly scary to me. On the other hand, his fierce demeanor alone was enough to cause trepidation.

"Damn it all, you're a ghost!" the embodied orc spat when his sword passed through my arm, which I reflexively held out to protect myself. Wishing to make sure that I was a projection, the orc pushed me and then kicked me — but the result was the same. We were in two different planes of reality. But at least we could talk!

"Who are you anyway?" I asked what seemed like an obvious question, which however led to unexpected consequences.

"A talking ghost!" The orc's terrible face cycled through a gamut of feelings, beginning with shock and ending with fear, after which he hopped high into the air, vanishing momentarily in the fog. Returning back to earth, the orc collapsed heavily onto the path and began to crawl away from me, scattering stones and with every moment getting closer to the edge.

"Stop crawling!" I roared in a terrible voice, betting on the assumption that the orc was a soldier who was accustomed to following orders. "Atten-Hut! Ready, front! At ease! Report: Who, What, Where and Why? On the double!"

A notification that my Charisma had gone up by several points flashed before me, but this didn't bring me much joy:

"WHAT?!" roared the orc, jumping to his feet. "No Freemie Cur shall order me around!"

"Calm down, soldier." I held out my palms in supplication, turning off my officer mode. "No one's trying to give you orders. If you had gone on crawling, you would've fallen over the edge. Who are you anyway?"

"The lies of a Freemie Cur shall find no audience in my soul!" Paying me no attention, the orc again tried to stab me with his sword and again confirmed that we were ghosts to one another.

"All right, do whatever you like." Once I realized that I wouldn't be able to chat with this creature, I waved my hand and continued along my path. I needed to find the guards.

"Wait!" I had only walked a few meters when the terrible stamping of the orc sounded behind me, and he ran through me, stopping and turning to face me several steps ahead. "Where am I? And what is this creature?"

"Actually, I wanted to ask you the same thing," I replied with surprise to the warrior who was pointing at a round monster covered in sores who was crawling along the path beside ours. I figured that the revived warrior could help me figure out how this Erebus worked as well as its rules, but it looked like the orc didn't know anything himself. "Tell me, what is the last thing you remember?"

"Fire," the orc seethed. The warrior's face filled with an internal struggle between his hate of all 'Freemie Curs' and the thirst to communicate with this strange creature. It was a thirst strong enough to quench the fire of fear before the unknown. And it won the day. "A Freemie Fire Mage incinerated me and my men. We were garrisoning a village. Then you appeared, this fog and this path. Where am I?"

Ah! So this isn't just a warrior but a commander? In that case, his Imitator must be fairly advanced to try and fight for survival. If that's even permitted to the local AI.

"We are in Erebus." At these words, the orc's face once again filled with utter despair and resignation, so I had to think of something to cheer him up. "I came here to retrieve six dead souls and return them to Barliona. If you like, I can take you with me. Will you be able to overcome your loathing of all Free Citizens?"

I'm not really sure why I'm even dealing with this fellow. He's an orc; he doesn't like players; he's only a Level 120...You could find a dozen of orcs like him in any village for the cost of a couple gold pieces. Heck, you could even ask for change. However, there I was, standing before the orc, awaiting his response. As one ancient author once said: "You become responsible, forever, for what you have tamed." Or in my case...created. Or embodied. It doesn't matter.

"You don't seem like the other Freemies," the orc remarked after a some consideration. "You're different."

"Can I take that as a 'yes?'" I asked. The orc didn't respond, but his eyes turned hazel again, indicating that he had already made his choice, even if he hadn't voiced it. Looks like someone wanted to protect his pride.

In order to safeguard myself in the future, I selected the orc and offered him to join my group. What if we had to fight? He'll go berserk and start crushing the enemies left and right and accidentally nick me in the process. At the moment we're in different planes of reality, but who knows what awaits us up ahead?

"A Dragon?!" the orc's astonished voice

resounded throughout Erebus, drawing a smirk from me. Yup, I'm a Dragon. Tremble before me and all that. For the first time I recall, I actually regretted that this locale didn't allow me to record video — the vivid expression of astonishment on the dark-green mug really was picture-worthy. The orc's facial muscles were dancing so rapidly that I was beginning to be afraid his jaw might lock up.

"These are all the creatures that once lived and are now dead," I waved my hand in the direction of the path along which the round monster had passed crawling who knows where. Even if there wasn't anyone there anymore, the orc should've understood whom I meant. "They are following their path to non-being as you were just now. There's an enormous cliff up ahead which might not even be a cliff, but an enormous magnet drawing the souls towards itself. That's where we need to go."

"In that case, will we be able to return to Barliona if we head in the other direction?" the orc asked, confirming my hunch that his Imitator really was an advanced version. He wanted to survive.

"It's possible, but I can't go find out. First we have to search. We'll decide how we're going to get out of here later, after we've found everyone I'm looking for. Are you with me? Or are you going to go back?"

"Gerdom Steelaxe doesn't betray his allies, whoever they may be!" The orc puffed out his chest proudly and directed his gaze in the direction of the fog-covered cliff. If I understood what the NPC was saying, we would be going together after all.

I'll remember our journey to the cliff for a long time. Not so much for the terrible sight of monsters and creatures we passed along the way, as for the resignation imprinted on their faces. The ghosts trudged bleakly to their unknown goal and, the closer we got to the cliff, the more worried I became about Gerdom. What if he's sucked into the cliff? Then reviving him would've been in vain. As his creator, I don't want to see my creation destroyed.

"Mahan?!" A familiar voice exclaimed in astonishment, causing the orc to adopt a combat stance. I automatically tried to place my hand on Gerdom's shoulder, intending to calm him, but yet again only encountered thin air. We remained in different planes of reality.

"Slate?" I asked cautiously, disbelieving my own ears. Several moments later, a shade appeared in the fog and slowly gained the form of a bear.

"I thought you became human?" I blurted out when I realized that the enormous bear and the Prince of Malabar were the same entity. An entity several heads taller than my orc, who stood frozen with his sword.

"That's right," the bear confirmed, transforming back into his human form. The fur along the hide withdrew into the torso, revealing an entirely nude and wrinkled bear, after which the body began to withdraw into itself, forcing the joints to twist in an unnatural manner. Not a very pleasant sight, especially for someone unprepared, so I wasn't surprised when Gerdom bellowed a war cry and leaped on the werebear with his sword. Sparks went flying from where the sword struck the stone, the orc was flung around by his own inertia and he barely caught his balance at the edge of the path, halfway 'inside' the body of the Prince. These two were in different dimensions as well.

"Your friend is a bit touchy," Slate remarked, completing his transformation. Paying no attention to Gerdom's sword flashing before him and piercing his torso, the werebear approached me and offered me his hand as greeting. The gesture was so natural, that I automatically shook his hand.

"You don't belong in Erebus," noted Tisha's husband, smiling at the shock on my face. Slate was real for me!

"What the..." I said the most articulate thing that came to mind.

"The dead don't linger too long in the Gray Lands either," the werebear understood the gist of my inquiry and began to explain. "Anyone who bears the mark of death enters Erebus in a month. We spend the rest of the time here, in the form that we arrived in. I'll become human when I return to Barliona. There's not much time left. How is Tisha doing?"

"Okay, I believe," I muttered, still out of sorts.

All of this was just too unexpected. "Geranika returned her mother, so Tisha is catching up on lost time with her and is getting used to having two parents again."

"Her mother was alive?" Slate asked with surprise, forcing me to recount the recent events in the living world.

"I can see you're not sitting around idly," the Prince smiled when I had completed my tale. "In that case, let's get down to business. I've been sent to negotiate with you."

"Negotiate?" I echoed surprised. "Who?"

"The boss of this entire mess," Slate gestured at the fog all around us. "The one who consumes the souls of all the dead creatures. The one who wishes to snatch a crumb of his deserved treat. The son of the High Priestess of Eluna is a very great delicacy. I am even afraid to ask how you've managed to involve yourself in this affair. The Servant of Chaos has sent me to you."

Given that Slate couldn't contain his laughter looking at my face, its expression was quite telling. If I relate to Anastaria everything that's been said here word for word, she'll eat me alive! Why doesn't my damn camera work?!

"As you know, Barliona isn't unique. It is but one of many world spinning in eternity. Every world has its own Creator and often several worlds have the same one, but haven't you ever considered the question of who created the Creator? Who was the primary cause of everything that is? Now you know the answer — it was Chaos. Self-sufficient, whole, joining everything within himself, eternal, Chaos decided to play a game and structure certain parts of himself, fettering those parts with certain laws. This being of absolute power created the Creators, who were granted the power to create worlds, and then Chaos began to wait patiently when these worlds would eventually return unto itself. Each dead creature that does not bear the mark of death, returns to it, bringing with it the pleasure and joy of reunion."

"How do you know all this?" I asked surprised. I'd never had a reason to delve so deeply into Barliona's history, and my mind was now absorbing the new information like a sponge.

"The portal of reclamation is located several kilometers from here. A piece of Chaos that the deceased enter. The portal takes all creatures aside from those that bear the mark. We who bear the mark can only wander around and talk to each other, sharing information. Five months of doing nothing will drive you crazy unless you speak to someone. But there are some lucky ones whose time of revival is short. I recently met one of them — a Dungeon boss named Gigantic Mantis. He comes here every week. He told me that after revival, we won't remember a thing about Erebus. Death, darkness and new life —

that is all that our memory retains. However, once we return here again, we will remember everything. Such is the lifecycle of information."

"What did the Servant want from me? And why does he seek negotiation instead of making his demands? By the way — this might be a dumb question — but why you? Did this entity appear before you and order you to go find the Shaman and hold talks with him?"

"I...No, everything was..." Slate hesitated, blinked his eyes, trying to understand why he had appeared before me, and even backpedaled several steps from me as if I was about to attack him.

"YOU CANNOT SPEAK TO ME FOR VERY LONG!" came the reply, forcing me to my knees. All of my stats plummeted towards zero, pausing at the 10% line, and almost for the first time in my time in Barliona, I wished peace and fortune to the unknown technician who had set the sensory filter on my capsule to maximum.

"I understand," I creaked, pouring my quickly diminishing supply of HP potions into myself.

"The Servant of Chaos knows what you seek. Six ghosts are slowly yet surely moving in the direction of their last point of rest. There is almost no time. You are being offered a deal — you will perform two tasks and you can take the ghosts with you."

"...?"

"Mahan, try to understand, I didn't come up

with this. Moreover, I won't remember a thing when I return to Barliona, so you have to decide on your own. The first thing you have to do is sacrifice this creature," Slate pointed at Gerdom, who tensed at the words. "Simply knock him off the path. He will return to the same place you plucked him from. If you adopt your Dragon Form, you will be able to touch him."

"Got it," I drawled. "What's the second assignment then?"

Slate breathed a deep sigh as if gathering his courage and then blurted out:

"You have to compensate Chaos for every soul you take. You must make a sacrifice. A thousand deaths for each soul you seek to retrieve."

"What?!"

"To make this task easier to perform," Slate went on, shutting his eyes, clenching his fists and spitting out the words unwillingly, "the Servant will give you the coordinates to the Annihilator. You must adjust it to destroy the required number of cities. The Mages aren't expecting another attack for two years, so you won't have any problems."

The Annihilator... Mages... Two years... Cities... As if at a click, the mosaic came into sharp focus. The Annihilator was the device that once every fifty years generated the black fog of which the High Mage of Anhurs had spoken. A device to destroy cities. Sounds fun — I was being offered the chance to be remembered as the Destroyer of Barliona.

"So what do you think?" asked Slate, opening his eyes. "Is that a fair price for rescuing six sentients from the land of the dead?"

"Here's my counteroffer. Ten for one," I gibed, knowing full well that I wouldn't be able to send even one sentient to Erebus. Otherwise, I could go ahead and delete my Shaman right now — Eluna, the Emperor and the Dark Lord would never forgive something like this. Perhaps only Geranika would welcome it. Hmm...Geranika, eh?

"A THOUSAND!" the bombastic voice boomed, taking my words seriously. Maybe I should make a little '/s' sign and hold it out at the right moments.

"Mahan!" Slate exclaimed angrily, but I was off and running:

"Fifty! I mean, I'm not asking for Karmadont here — and he's the only one who could be worth a cool grand. Everyone else is spare change. We're talking about town guards here! They've all got arrows in their knees! Fifty is the most I'll do."

"FIVE HUNDRED!" the Servant of Chaos rejoined after a thoughtful pause. Slate and Gerdom were staring at me with pure loathing, like I was the vilest creature in the world. But by this point I had already formed a plan and I wasn't about to abandon it.

"A hundred — but only out of my respect for a representative of the creator of life, the universe and everything. A hundred souls for one guard!"

Pause.

"TWO HUNDRED!"

"Deal! But I have two conditions," I yelled, barely concealing my glee. "The first is that I have to see the guards to make sure that the goods are in good condition. And the second is that I get to take Mr. Steelaxe here with me."

"WHAT?!" I was forced to the ground once again. "HE SHALL BE DESTROYED!"

Begone smile! We're haggling again!

"I don't understand why you sent Slate to see me, if you're the one doing all the talking," I grumbled, quaffing the last of my potions. "If all your yelling kills me right now, there won't be anyone to make a deal with. Gerdom comes with me. Twelve hundred souls is a completely reasonable price for seven. Now let's see the goods, er, guards I mean."

"You have changed," Slate spat, while the master of Erebus made his decision. "The Mahan I knew would never do this."

"It's a good thing that you won't remember anything then. How do I use this Annihilator thing?"

"Two hundred more souls for Gerdom." Slate ignored my question. A map icon was flashing alluringly, inviting me to check the updated map. Swipe that aside. Now's not the time.

"Sure," I agreed. "And so we agree on one thousand four hundred souls. Where are my guards?"

"Look." A passage formed in the fog leading into

infinity. Several silhouettes appeared on its other end. The distance between us was so enormous that the figures did not seem to move. "Are you satisfied?"

"What is this?" I asked with surprise, when the corridor disappeared. "Where is that anyway? All you showed me were some strange silhouettes, nothing I could make out. Is that even them? Are you trying to pull one over on me?"

"Try and think about what you're saying!" Slate exclaimed. "You're dealing with the Servant of Chaos, the progenitor of all that is!"

"Which includes lies and deceit," I parried. "Didn't he create that too?"

"What do you want?" The Servant asked through Slate.

"I want to see them at arm's length. To make sure that they're the ones I'm looking for. Then we can keep talking."

"YOU ARE INSOLENT, SHAMAN!" the master of Erebus couldn't contain himself.

"I'm merely looking out for my interests."

Skill increase:
+2 to Trade. Total: 21.
+2 to Charisma. Total: 82.

"WATCH OUT!" Erebus went spinning around me, Slate and Gerdom disappeared and once everything had calmed down, I saw the six guards trudging along at arm's length from me. With Clouter in their midst.

"One thousand four hundred souls, Mahan. You have eighteen hours," said Slate appearing beside me. Gerdom didn't trail far behind and again tried to stab me with that sword of his that I gave him. What is wrong with the orcs anyway? Why are they so stabby?

"How do we get out of here?" I asked, reining in my anxiety. James knows me very well, and he'd never come up with a quest like this for me. I had to think!

"If you walk from the portal," Slate explained, trying not to look at me, "then you'll get tossed out of Barliona in ten seconds."

"And Gerdom?"

"Is he somehow different from you?" Slate spat out once again. "Ten seconds in the other direction and he's free of the Servant of Shadow. What do you need him for, murderer?"

"He'll bring me my slippers!" I couldn't help but quip. Those silly NPCs are going to try and teach me how to live my life!

Slate fell silent, clearly considering his next speech, so I addressed the orc:

"Are you ready to obey my orders?"

Flaring his nostrils and trying to restrain his anger, the orc merely raised his head and boomed:

"Gerdom Steelaxe shall never carry slippers! I

shall be happy to return to Chaos with my honor intact! Better you kill me somehow!"

"YOU! WILL! OBEY! MY! ORDERS!" I didn't even yell this so much as growled it, expelling the words through clenched teeth. Swiping away another notification about +2 to my Charisma, I caught up with the guards who had left us behind with one giant leap. Opening design mode as I flew, I created the projections of all six guards. The outward appearance of the guards had been a mystery to me until now. In order to foil the Servant, I had to see them, including Clouter, who had grown up and changed a lot since the day we had met. I needed to act quickly, while the Imitator responsible for the Servant hadn't understood what I had in mind.

All that I needed was to come up with ten seconds somewhere.

"Nooo!" six throats screamed in unison as the blinding light shattered the fog of Erebus to pieces. No time to lose! I opened my wings and only now realized that I had already become a Dragon. Hell with it! Leaving the path, I glided at the guards and grabbed them in my arms. All six of them. Gerdom was a dozen meters away, so I flapped my wings, grabbed the orc by the leg with my teeth, biting down to the bone or perhaps even through, and then darted away from the center.

One second!

"Mahan!" Slate's shout faded behind me. To

hell with it!

A third second!

"WHAT?!" The Servant of Chaos came to much too quickly, beholding my flight with astonishment.

The sixth!

"SHAMAN, YOU ARE VIOLATING OUR AGREEMENT!" the orc's and guards' life bars fell halfway. They were little more than dangling dolls, allowing me to carry them away from the center of Erebus. In my Dragon form, the voice of the master of Erebus had no effect on me. A little consolation, that!

The ninth second!

"OUR DEAL IS OFF! YOU SHALL BE PUNISH..."

The tenth!

You have left Erebus against the will of its master. From now on, this location will be off limits to you.

Scattering benches, candles, players and other dross in every direction, I landed heavily in the hall of Eluna's temple. The guards, who still had no idea what was going on, fell out of my grasp and rolled along the floor. I spit out Gerdom and grimaced: The orc's HP was practically at zero.

"*Stacey, I need help!*" I hollered telepathically, sending a summons. I urgently needed a healer.

"What do you want me to do?" Stacey appeared

instantly, still in her Siren form. The players around us gasped in awe at seeing the Siren and the Dragon in the flesh for the first time. I pointed at Gerdom, who had somehow still avoided returning to Erebus. The orc was fighting tooth and nail for the chance to remain in Barliona.

"Who's this, Mahan?" Anastaria exclaimed with astonishment. Her actions weren't doing any good — the orc was wheezing on the floor, his Hit Points had waned to 3% and went on waning, the auras and flashes around him doing nothing besides making the orc groan more hysterically. "What the hell?! He's a Zombie!"

WHAT?!

"What's going on here?" Elizabeth's ringing voice forced the temple into silence. I stared dumbly at Gerdom's properties and didn't know what to do: A Dark Zombie Warrior. Level 120 and with every passing moment burning away under the light of Eluna's temple. Anastaria's healing had done the opposite of what I wanted.

"Have you returned, Mahan?" Elizabeth asked, surprised. "So quickly? Did you fail to..."

"Mother!" sounded Clouter's barely audible voice.

"Son!" The High Priestess immediately turned into a mother. Elizabeth rushed to one of the guards. Falling to her knees, she pressed him to herself...and immediately pushed him away.

"NO! Anything but this!" Elsa whispered in despair. I looked up from the creaking Gerdom, peered closely at Clouter and couldn't help but blurt out:

"Oh goddamn!"

The properties of the High Priestess's son were more telling than any swear words: 'Clouter (Level 250). Zombie Priest.'

CHAPTER FOUR

THE HARBINGER

"**D**AN, WHAT HAVE YOU DONE?" Anastaria asked quietly, looking over from Elizabeth who was frozen in shock to me and back.

"I brought them back from Erebus," I grumbled, checking and seeing that all the guards were now Zombies. "The way I see it, it's better than nothing."

"Okay, we'll figure out what to do with them later. What's with the orc?"

We looked over at Gerdom who was still spasming on the floor. His Hit Points had fallen to 2%, he was foaming at his mouth and his eyes had rolled back, but the orc continued to cling on to life.

"I'm pulling him out of here. Deal with Elizabeth. I'll tell you everything later," I grabbed Gerdom by his legs as Anastaria looked on in puzzlement, opened my 'Blink' input box and blinked right into the center of the Nameless City. If the orc is suffering from Eluna's light, perhaps, he'll feel better in the murk of Tartarus?

What I liked was that as soon as I set foot on the cobblestone street of the capital of Kartoss, the orc stopped groaning and foaming and his Hit Points froze. However, the good news ended there. The bad news took over from here — the orc's green mug turned gray and lesions began to appear on his skin.

"The enemy has breached the walls!" A squad of the Nameless City guard appeared beside me and leveled its pikes at the graying orc. What in the living hell! If these Minotaur guards didn't treat Gerdom as one of their own, the Priests of Tartarus may have a similar issue.

"Stop it!" I yelled, shielding the orc. "I need help!"

"We don't help the minions of Shadow and their lackeys!" boomed the guard captain. Nevertheless the pike tips ceased their advance on my orc.

"Dan, where are you? Elizabeth has locked herself in her cabinet and isn't letting anyone in. The Priests are all in shock."

"You have to buy us some time, Stacey. I'm in the Nameless City. Get Fleita, she's a Zombie and maybe knows what to do."

"I'm no minion of Shadow! Nor am I his servant!" I shouted at the guard.

"We're not talking about you, Shaman! You brought this creature to our city." The Minotaur pointed at Gerdom. "It must be destroyed! The Nameless City is no place for the minions of Shadow."

I swore out loud. Today was clearly not my day. Not only had I turned the guards into Zombies, but now it turned out that Gerdom was aligned with Shadow. No wonder Eluna's light has a negative effect on him. I'm amazed the orc even survived those few moments in the goddess's temple!

Understanding that there was no point expecting a miracle in the Nameless City, I blinked toward Altameda. There was one last thing I could try to save Gerdom. The healers of Malabar and Kartoss couldn't help — it wasn't in their line of work. They'd be more comfortable throwing my orc on a pyre. The only other option was one I really didn't like. It was fraught with the peril of punishment from Eluna and Tartarus. And it didn't promise anything other than further problems. But I had managed to snatch the orc from the jaws of death and my pride prevented me from allowing those same jaws to have him after all. Especially, mere minutes after I'd saved him.

"*Master, the enemy is here with you!*" The Gray Death's thought flashed in my mind and we were instantly surrounded by a pack of wolves. My wolves. Who, it turned out, knew how to speak to me! I'd need to get to the bottom of this.

"Save him, don't attack!" I ordered, again shielding Gerdom. I cast a longing glance at Altameda, stepped away from Gerdom just in case and exhaled several times, clearing the air from my lungs (though really I was just delaying the inevitable). Finally, I yelled:

"Geranika, I summon you! I require your assistance."

Practically speaking, nothing happened. Flaming arrows didn't rain from the sky; the earth didn't cleave asunder; the woods didn't cease to be green nor the sky blue. Only the wolves tucked their tails in and dashed away like hurt puppies, leaving the Gray Death bristling and rearing on her own. In her pride, she didn't abandon her master! I imagine someone in her pack is going to get it tonight!

"THE ENEMY!" the local Guardian yelled somewhere barely within earshot, after which his heavy, receding steps indicated that the ruler of these lands was indeed wise and experienced: After all, who would willingly enter battle against a stronger foe? The tactically correct decision is to retreat to a safe distance and apprise the situation. Which is exactly what the Guardian is doing at this moment as fast as his legs can carry him. If he has legs that is...

"You called me, my failed student?" Geranika asked in a tone so neutral that it seemed more appropriate to friends or coworkers than two sworn foes as we had been before the Cataclysm. Geranika arrived dressed in his finest garb — a black, velvet suit, polished shoes, a red tie, a cane, a flawless coif. His appearance elicited sympathy, but not fear. If you told someone that he was one of the scariest creatures of Barliona, they'd laugh you out of town.

"I managed to rescue your warrior from Erebus," I pointed at Gerdom. "My acquaintances can't heal him — no one knows how to work with Shadow. I need your help."

"How curious," Geranika circled Gerdom, paying no heed to the Gray Death's growling. "What do you need with one of my fallen soldiers?"

"When I was rescuing him, I didn't know that he was one of your own. In Erebus, all the shades are gray."

"I understand. Does it upset you to destroy a creature that you yourself created?" Geranika guessed. "I won't lie to you. I'm not going to heal him. I don't need him. A mere Level 120 Zombie...He's nothing. But we can make a deal."

"About what?" I furrowed my brow.

"You can heal him yourself," grinned Geranika. "I'll teach you!"

"I won't become a servant of Shadow!" I cut him off.

"Pff...Shadow, light, darkness," Geranika scoffed indignantly, "they're all just names really. Names for one and the same thing. You were in Erebus — so you know how it all ends. Chaos spawned us and to Chaos we shall return."

"I won't become a servant of Shadow," I said again, although my voice was a bit gravely this time.

"What the heck do I need you for? I'll show you how to heal my minions and you can figure out the rest yourself. Use my gift or don't use it...If you want to save this Zombie, heal him. If not — let him die. What a princess you are — 'this but not that and this way but not this way.' Make your decision, Shaman! Are you going to the end or are you stopping right here?"

New ability acquired: Summon Minor Shadow of Healing. You are temporarily renouncing the Spirits of the Ancestors and calling on the Shadows, tearing reality and being to fragments. Cost of summoning...Cost of healing...May be used anywhere except in Imperial palaces. -50 to Reputation with all Kalragon factions for each summon of the Shadow. Upon reaching Hatred status with any faction, a hunting party will be sent out after you.

New faction unlocked: 'Lord of Shadow.' Current Reputation: Hatred.

The first summon of a Battle or Healing Shadow is a test and does not have an effect on Reputation.

"You can figure out when and why you should use my gift on your own," smiled Geranika, noting my long face with satisfaction. Along with the Healing Shadow, I also received a Minor Battle Shadow and now I didn't know what to do. What did I need any of this for? I hadn't asked for it! After a few seconds, Geranika hiked his eyebrows and asked:

"So are you going to revive my warrior or are we going to go on acting like two young and inexperienced lovers on their first date?"

The spellbook appeared before my eyes with a thick red line that split its pages in two halves: A top section for my Spirits and a bottom section for the Shadows. A vivid and sparkling Spirits icon occupied the top half of the first section, while the bottom section featured a gloomy and grim Shadow icon, resembling a spit stain. A standard game mechanic, the book's pages, even the empty ones, were divided in two halves. The grim conclusion I drew from this was that the Corporation had granted the players a chance to play with the Shadows. This meant that Barliona would soon see an enormous army of Shadow, assembled from Free Citizens. And this, in turn, would cause an outbreak of PvP battles. The players would start massacring each other left and right. These were Shadows after all: They could be used anywhere. Even in a city...

I heard Gerdom groan as his Hit Points dipped to 1%. A timer appeared before me: 60...59...58...

I had a minute to make my choice.

It was painfully easy to use a Shadow — all it took was stretching out your hand in the direction of the patient, casting the summon and enjoying the result. No dances with a tambourine or Intellect requirements. Just your hand and a summon.

34...33...32...

Geranika was examining my castle with a bored look on his face, demonstrating his utter disinterest in my decision. There were no signs or omens from the figureheads of the world, not a peep from my premonition, as if nothing important or fateful was taking place, so I swore, stretched my hand at Gerdom and pushed the Healing Shadow icon. The first summon is harmless...

The world vanished. Images began hurling past my eyes, replacing one another at an unimaginable rate. No sooner did my eye latch onto some item than it vanished replaced by another. An alabaster throne. A scowling green monster. A falling meteor. An explosion. A bloodied and charred creature, standing on two legs and leaning against some kind of stick. Fog. A cave. A crystal.

The whirlwind of images ended. An enormous, semi-transparent, red crystal appeared before me. It hung in the air, emitting a wondrous light. If the Cupid faction, which busied itself with Barliona's Valentine's Day event, saw this wonder, I bet their personal menageries would go mad with the desire to acquire it. A crystal in the shape of a heart, the form that enamored girls so loved to draw. What could be sweeter?

The apparition vanished just as abruptly as it

had appeared. I stared with surprise at my own hand, from which a Shadow resembling a thick snake was coiling in the direction of Gerdom. As soon as it touched the orc, the world around me was pierced by his savage scream — the Shadows reached the orc even in his unconsciousness. The scream was so piercing, so overflowing with emotions and pleas for help that I barely managed to keep myself from jerking my hand away and interrupting the summon. The Shadow enveloped the orc slowly, as if relishing his agony. At last it reached his head and the scream choked and sputtered out. The orc drowned in the Shadow, turning into an ugly cocoon.

"The Shaman decided to summon the Shadow," Geranika said with bemusement, approaching Gerdom. The summon ended, yet the orc didn't even think to stir. He didn't seem to be thinking anything at all actually. The cocoon rose one meter off the ground and began to bend in various directions as if the creature inside of it was struggling in agony. Only now did I notice that the Gray Death remained standing beside us, scowling at Geranika.

"Let's see whom you snatched from Erebus' clutches," Geranika went on in a business-like tone, touching the cocoon. A sharp clap followed and the orc's body plopped heavily onto the ground.

Your Reputation with the Lord of Shadow has changed. Current status: 'It's complicated.'

"Mahan, I don't even know how to thank you for such a present," Geranika drawled with satisfaction, examining the listless body. I stepped forward. The creature lying on the ground was about twice as massive as the former orc. Its Hit Points were full, its properties hidden and in general it was unclear to me what I had created. I needed to take a closer look.

"*Master is joining Shadow?*" the Gray Death's telepathic question was so unexpected that I froze for a moment.

"No," I said aloud after several attempts of answering her telepathically. It was clear as day now that the she-wolf was sentient.

"*Master has revived a warrior of Shadow.*"

"I know. That doesn't make me a minion of Shadow."

"You know, Mahan, talking to yourself is a symptom of several mental illnesses," Geranika didn't let the chance to score a cheap point slip away and butted into our conversation. "I have a nice white shirt with really long sleeves that I'd be willing to give you if you like."

"Very funny. Take your orc and get out of here," I snapped.

"How would I simply go without first thanking you for my new General? You just gave my army a senior officer. Now it's my turn to repay the favor."

As soon as Geranika said that, Gerdom's

properties became visible to me and I could barely contain my feelings. And my feelings made me want to start cursing the entire world, with the choicest expressions reserved for the devs and James. The players would kill me.

Gerdom Steelaxe (Level 750 Shadow Orc). Shadow Army General. Creator: Mahan.

"There's no point in offering you items; you won't take them," Geranika went on. "Titles, honors, lands...That's all dross. I know!"

"I am ready to serve, your lordship!" the orc boomed, interrupting Geranika's exclamation. Gerdom staggered to his feet, swayed, leaned against an enormous two-handed scimitar, which the cheap short sword I'd given him had turned into, swayed again, caught his balance and breathed deeply. The orc hadn't the strength to take even one more step.

"Oh you shall serve, don't you worry." Geranika made several motions with his hands and Gerdom vanished in the portal. "All right, one's been dealt with, now it's your turn."

"I don't need anything from you!"

"Not even information?"

"You want to tell me how we can best capture Armard?" I couldn't avoid a gibe.

"No, Shaman! Why would you need Armard when you have Altameda? Everything is much more interesting than that. You have six Zombies on your hands, correct?"

"How did you...? Yes," I switched off my emotions and tried to apprehend the Lord of Shadow's speech as an old movie that I'd seen a hundred times already. 'Cause I just knew something really crappy was coming.

"In Kartoss lives a creature named Knucklear. Once upon a time he was a Troll Monk, a mad ascetic, one of the radical patriots of Kartoss. Fate, however, played a mean trick on him, turning him into a Zombie. Knucklear didn't abide this and turned back into a troll. Then into a Zombie. Then again into a troll. After that he got tired of transforming back and forth and he became a Zombie again. Now he teaches the Monk adepts. If you find a way to see him, you might be able to discover how you can turn six fresh-baked Zombies into living creatures again. That's enough information to pay you for my General.

Quest updated: 'Who will guard the guards themselves?'

"And that's about it," Geranika concluded, leaving me in stupefaction for the third time. This entire story had been pre-planned by James? He knew that I would summon Geranika and accept his conditions? "In a few weeks, we shall meet at the tournament. Gerdom will show you what he is capable of. Until we meet again, my future ally!"

"Dan, Elizabeth has emerged from her cabinet. She refuses to acknowledge her son." Anastaria's thought occurred in my mind. *"She says that her son has died and the creature that you brought back isn't Clouter."*

"Summon me, Stacey! There's been some new developments."

"...and banish them! My decision shall enter force and effect right this...Ah! Mahan! You too shall be..." In the form of the Ice Queen, Elizabeth was looking down on the surrounding world, not noticing, or not wishing to notice anything around her. Clouter was sitting on the floor bawling, his hands covering his face. The five guards that I'd pulled out of Erebus were standing grimly in a clump beside the far wall, glancing at the High Priestess from under their brows. About fifty players had crowded into the main hall, not wishing to miss the spectacle. We were separated from them by an invisible line that the players didn't cross. Either the game didn't allow it, or they were afraid of incurring the wrath of the High Priestess. The resulting clearing served as a good site for the trial that Elizabeth was now putting on — the punishment of six inadequate guards and one insolent Shaman. The only problem was that the Shaman wasn't about to take the NPC's wrath silently. I had other plans for this evening.

"I know how to bring them back to life," I cried,

interrupting Elsa. "Clouter shall be human again!"

A silence ensued. Elsa froze with her hands still akimbo, absorbing my words. The guards trained their grim eyes on me and even Clouter ceased crying, unveiling his tear-stained face from beneath his hands. What kind of a guard was he? He's still a child!

"How do you plan on doing this?" Anastaria asked after a short while. The pause was drawing on and neither Elizabeth nor the servants nearest to her were about to speak, so Stacey began to rescue our situation.

"There is a Monk teacher who lives in Kartoss named Knucklear..." I related the story of the troll, without mentioning the source of my information. "Those whom I returned from Erebus shall live once again!"

Silence reigned.

"Clouter, we need to go. We don't have much time," I approached the boy and offered him my hand to help him rise. The timer was still hanging before my eyes, counting down the time I had to complete the quest, so I needed to hurry. There were only about 20 hours left.

"Is that possible, Mahan?" Clouter asked sniffling, wiping his running nose.

"What a question. Everything is possible in Barliona. Do you men need a personal invitation?" I turned to the grim-faced guards. "Company at attention!"

The reflexes embedded in the Imitators triggered flawlessly — all six, including Clouter, ordered themselves in two ranks of three. The guards cheered up noticeably — their faces acquired meaningful expressions, their backs straightened, and their hands stopped shaking. If it weren't for their chalk-white faces, set off by their gilded cuirasses, you'd be hard pressed to recognize that they were Zombies. Assuming, you couldn't read their properties, that is.

"High Priestess," I addressed Elsa bravely, heartened by the guards' reaction. "Permit us to leave the hall without any further remarks."

"Permission granted. Oh!" Elizabeth exclaimed and blushed deeply.

"Company, right face! Straight march!"

The players clumped at the passage and blocking it, dissolved as if a magic wand had been waved at them, yet I didn't need that. Why use your feet to walk when you pay a portal demon? I got out an amulet and ordered:

"Viltrius, send me a portal. We have guests coming..."

* * *

Upon reaching my castle, I ordered delivery from the Golden Horseshoe, collapsed in my rocking throne, shut my eyes and sighed deeply. Viltrius took care of the Zombies, taking them on a tour of the castle. The guards' eyes sparked with excitement — not everyone got a chance to visit Altameda. Maybe I should keep them? Vimes would come up with something for them. They'd fit right in...No, all that later. Right now I need to rest a little. It's crazy to think that I returned to Barliona only ten hours ago. Any other player would take a month to accomplish this! Right this instant, I should probably speak with Mr. Kristowski to determine how our clan should proceed in the wake of the Cataclysm, but he was still over in the palace hammering out the details about the tournament. Why the hell did I come up with that idea anyway?!

"Dan, we've started working on the Tomb," Anastaria's voice yanked me from my sweet slumber. I believe I fell asleep.

"Who is 'we?'" I asked puzzled, at a loss and still half dreaming. Here it struck me — Phoenix! "How's it going? By the way, I thought you wanted to start this evening? Why'd you change your mind?"

I need to approach the game more calmly. I don't have the resources to complete the Tomb. Only Phoenix has the raid parties to do that, so there's nothing odd about them starting earlier.

"It was just a test run. We weren't planning on killing anyone. We needed to see what was inside."

"Judging by your face there's something unusual in there. Don't keep me in suspense. Out with it."

"We can't use ordinary methods of illumination in the Tomb. Neither torches, nor magic lanterns, nor fluorescent moss work in it. No one can see anything. The Tomb is completely dark. The floor is made of stone but we couldn't feel any walls, as if we were in an open space. One of the Rogues crawled ahead but a slab fell on him, killing him instantly. We lost a second Rogue to a pendulum that knocked him into an abyss — it's looking like the first level is a stone labyrinth. Both Rogues lost a level upon dying."

"WHAT?!"

"When you enter the Tomb, you get a notification that it's a different kind of Dungeon. Each death costs the player a level. But only within the Tomb — as soon as the player exits to Barliona, he's back at the level he entered at."

"And if he reenters again, the level goes to what it was in the Tomb," I guessed.

"That's why I was in my Siren form when you summoned me. There are a ton of pendulums in the Tomb. They're constantly threatening to knock you off. My raid party held on to my tail while I crawled ahead, feeling the way. But that's not even the main thing. Sooner or later we managed to sketch a map of the Dungeon — we got the newbies who don't care about levels so much to do the work. We promised to level them up out in Barliona in exchange. The main thing is that the Tomb's floor is constantly shifting.

Changing. And so are the pendulums and the falling slabs. It's a really horrible labyrinth. I have no idea how to get through it. We'll have to think hard about how to proceed."

"There's no light at all in there?" I clarified.

"None whatsoever. I tried everything I could think of, even lit a bonfire. Nothing."

"Maybe there's no light in the Tomb because you guys were doing it without me?" I suggested.

"That's got no effect on it," Stacey snapped annoyed. "The Original status only extends to the loot. Trust me — you're not the first 'Original' that I've had to deal with in this game. You're the third actually. We managed to make a deal with the first, but not with the second. Still, we completed both Dungeons in question. So it's not about you. I'm missing something. Something important...We won't be going anywhere this evening. There's no point in entering the Tomb until I figure out how to complete that first area."

Stacey collapsed on the throne, shaking her head and muttering something to herself. I was at a loss. I realized that the girl before me wasn't some iron maiden or a powerful neural network that could process hundreds of possible actions in a minute, but an ordinary girl who didn't know what to do. The change was so striking that I unconsciously got up from my chair, walked over to Stacey and took her hands, trying to warm them. Overwhelmed by the beauty of Barliona, I'd somehow forgotten that Stacey was human — and that therefore she could lose to, as seldom as that happened.

"Everything will work out," I began to assure her automatically with foolish platitudes. Then, I took her in my arms and suddenly we found ourselves in the real world. The cocoon's lid slid aside, the wires disconnected, we jumped out of our capsules and...How nice it is that the quest timer stops when the player is out in reality.

We didn't stay there for very long...

"You have a pretty castle," Clouter said excitedly. The sorrow, bitterness and resignation had left his mind, like all the useless information leaves the mind of a student who's passed his exams. Clouter again resembled our old companion from Beatwick.

"There's this bit of business," I tussled the fidget's head as Clouter, in turn, began to stroke and scratch the Gray Death, causing the she-wolf to slit her eyes and almost purr like a cat. She'd never encountered such friendly attention before.

"Mahan, tell me, why did I become a Priest?" Clouter left the she-wolf alone with difficulty and looked up at me inquisitively. "Mother said that there's nothing divine about me and that the goddess does not hear me. I even considered becoming a

Warrior, and then this thing happened..."

"What thing?" I asked carefully.

"Well...I don't even know how to explain it. There wasn't anything in Anhurs, but here, when I met Viltrius, it was like I found some bit of truth. I could see the goblin as if he was in the palm of my hand — his torments, his desires, the deep esteem he felt for his master. I also realized the Viltrius has a very negative relationship with his god. I don't know whether you can see it or not, but there's a negative relationship emblem hanging over the head of your majordomo. It's simply screaming that you are dealing with a creature who is not loved by his god. Or a creature who doesn't love his god, I'm not quite sure. I have no idea why I only see it above him. Neither you, nor my guard friends have an emblem above their heads."

"An emblem? What does it look like?" I asked baffled. If an NPC can suddenly see the bars for Hit Points or Reputation, then something's really broken somewhere. And I had better notify the admins about it.

"Well...An emblem is simply the name I've give it, since I don't know what it is," Clouter backpedaled, dispelling my worry. Back at the very dawn of full-immersion games, the learned scholars fought pitched battle, tearing theirs and each other's beards out, trying to prove their points of view. Some said that humans would fall over the edge and completely relocate their consciousnesses into the game. Others claimed that nothing would happen and their mad colleagues should seek qualified help. There were pickets, rallies and protests. But that was twenty years ago. I was still young and ignorant and didn't understand why we couldn't simply enjoy the immense quantity of fantasy literature that appeared in response to the new technological leaps. Dmitriy Rus, Ruslan Mihaylov, Andrei Vasiliev — the works of these men had embedded themselves in my consciousness, engendering a deep affection for computer games. It's a good thing that the future they predicted hadn't come to pass. "I simply don't know how to describe it correctly. Viltrius' emblem is kind of like...well...it's all whorls, red, all intertwined and decorated with scary images, skulls and teeth. It's very difficult to concentrate and get a long look at it. It's constantly shifting and moving like a mirage. The only thing I'm sure of is that only Viltrius has it."

"Does Vimes have one too?" I ventured. Viltrius is a goblin. A creature that's incredibly uncommon to Malabar. On the other hand, in Kartoss, goblins are a dime a dozen. What if upon turning into a Zombie, Clouter had become a Priest not of Eluna, but of Tartarus?

"Who is that?" Clouter frowned cutely, trying to appear more mature.

"The captain of my guard. A huge and terrible Tauren."

"You have a Tauren in your castle?!" Clouter hopped up with excitement, glanced several times at the door, wishing to get away from me as quickly as possible, and then rattled off impatiently: "Where is he? Will he let me touch him? Does he look like a cow? Does he have real horns? What about hooves?"

"Viltrius, call Vimes in here," I asked the goblin, interrupting Clouter. I'll confess that I was quite shocked when I first laid eyes on my guard captain — Taurens were considered extinct. But I'm a player who's prepared for the twisted fantasy of the developers. Clouter however is an ordinary NPC, and everything in Altameda is a wonder for him.

"Oh mommy!" Clouter's eyes went round and he clapped his hand over his mouth, stifling his scream. Proud and dauntless, Vimes thundered through the doors. Clad in steel like a tank, the Tauren instilled fear and trepidation, as any high-level NPC should.

"Master!" Vimes boomed, inclining his head respectfully. Only now did I realize that Vimes was playing to the audience. In the presence of Clouter and the guards — I noticed the new Zombies in the doors — the captain of the castle guard had appeared in his full splendor, demonstrating who enforces order in Altameda. One glance at a guard like that is likely to banish any sinister thoughts from your head. Aside from maybe getting out of the vision of this monster as quickly as possible.

I looked at Clouter and barely contained a satisfied smile. Along with the hand clapped over his mouth, the boy looked completely shocked. It was like he'd seen a ghost. It's nice to be the owner of things so unique they cause such trepidation. Even if it's only among the NPCs. And even if it's only in a virtual game.

"Oh but he's so sick!" Clouter finally came to and looked over at me. I was stunned — his eyes were full of everything but surprise and wonder. Pain, consternation, compassion...Clouter was looking at me like I was a person who abused animals. "Why don't you help him?"

Without awaiting an answer, Clouter approached the Tauren. Vimes didn't know how to react, so he froze and looked over at me several times searchingly. The boy didn't evoke a sense of danger in the Tauren and you could see that he himself didn't feel any fear of the imposing warrior. The other guards were pressing themselves against the wall, trying to stay out of the Tauren's sight, but Clouter headed confidently towards my head of security, set on doing something known only to him.

"You poor fellow." The fledgling Priest shook his head, placing his hand on the Tauren's shoulder. "Don't worry. We will figure something out."

Mandatory quest available: 'The Pain of the Captain of the Guard.' Description: Vimes, the

guard captain of Altameda, executes his duties perfectly, concealing from the world the sorrow of his loss: The truth is that Vimes' love has been abducted by the son of his tribe's chieftain. Vimes could not oppose the will of his tribe and so left his tribe to be a guard, seeking death in battle. Solve this problem. Quest type: Mandatory, castle-related. Reward/Penalty: Variable.

Two impossible things appeared before my eyes basically at the same moment. The first was a mandatory quest, which were so rare in this game that you could count them on the fingers of one hand. The second was that Vimes sank to his knees, covering his weeping face with his hands like a small child. Clouter began to console the Tauren, stroking his head, and here the third impossible thing happened — Vimes collapsed to the floor entirely. At first I thought that my guard had taken ill and I even lurched in his direction; however, Clouter stopped me. Vimes was merely asleep.

"Did you know that he hasn't slept in three years?" Clouter looked at me. He didn't resemble a happy fellow anymore, but rather an old man wizened by life, who had just solved another difficult problem and was now scolding a poor student. In the given case, me. "Or do these things not interest you?"

"How did you learn all this?" I asked.

"I don't know. I simply saw it. You can't not see

it. It's a flaming fire. A hope cornered in a tight corner. The desire to die. Mother told me that Priests can see through other creatures, but it was off limits to me. I was a Warrior. But now I am a Priest and therefore...Don't force me to explain what I don't understand myself, Mahan. Let Vimes get some sleep and then help him. It doesn't matter how, just help him. Even if it's just ordering him to forget about his beloved once and for all. Vimes respects you; he won't dare ignore a direct order. Promise?"

"I will make sure to help Vimes," I confirmed, discovering an entirely new appreciation for the phrase 'resolve this issue.' The quest didn't tell me that I had to rush to save the girl, even if she was a girl with two horns and hooves. Who knows, maybe she's happy and returning her to Vimes won't actually solve anything. I need to resolve this issue the way the owner of a castle would do it. Damn! I am getting the distinct impression that there's a trap here somewhere!

"We must travel to Kartoss," Clouter went on sadly. "There's nothing else we can do here."

The portal demon opened the way to the central square of the Nameless City and our detachment of seven sentients set off on its journey in mournful silence. That's the way things work out sometimes — you feel like everything's okay, that you're happy, and then you speak with an NPC and everything changes. Your mood plummets and doesn't even seem like it's about to return. Who asked me to invite Clouter to my castle anyway?

* * *

We found the Monk Instructor at the cemetery outside of the Nameless City, under the shadow of a great tree. Knucklear was busy honing one of the most important monk skills. He was sleeping. We barely managed to shake him awake. The stout man reeked of wine. Maybe I'm missing something, but the last thing I imagined was that this creature could be a teacher. I'm not sure what the devs were on when they came up with him...although, actually that's not much of a mystery. The mystery is something else — how did the quality control department approve this drunkard. This is a social game after all!

When a meaningful expression appeared on his inebriated face, I began to relate the gist of the problem. Knucklear scratched his belly and drawled meaningfully:

"So that's how it is! Yeaaaaah...Sounds like work...Ah-ah-ah-hrrrrooo..."

When it finally dawned on me that 'ah-hrrrooo' was not the continuation of a meaningful phrase, but a simple old snore, I exploded. I guess it wasn't Knucklear's day since it had begun with Elizabeth's unexpected anger and ended with Vimes on his knees bawling and Mars ascending in the Taurus constellation. I never imagined I'd feel so angry about an NPC, but Knucklear really got my goat. He managed to accomplish what even Prontho hadn't. He made me lose my temper.

The Shaman has three hands...

You are attempting to summon a Spirit beyond your rank. You are summoning a Spirit you have not mastered. The summon is impossible.

...and behind his back a wing...

You are attempting to summon a Spirit beyond your rank. You are summoning a Spirit you have not mastered.

...from the heat upon his breath...

You are attempting to summon a Spirit beyond your rank.

Shining candle-fire springs...

For an instant the candle's flame flared around me with the full intensity of the sun — only to be snuffed out and give way to the coolness and gentleness of water. Reality slipped away from me as I found myself in a liquid environment. I was filled with feelings that I had never felt before. How do you describe the way a fish feels, able to change direction at any moment in three dimensions? Freedom? Independence? The opportunity to make a choice, that only it will be responsible for? Who knows? Fish are pretty strange creatures when you think about it. How can you stay silent when you're surrounded by such beauty? Such grandeur? Such might?

"Remember brother, the water is deceptive. Don't let it drown you," I heard a faintly familiar voice, forcing the thoughts in my mind to turn over limply. Someone was trying to accuse my beloved, darling water of doing something illegal, so someone was really asking for it. Water is the source of life! How could it be deceptive?

"Shaman — these aren't Spirits and dances with the tambourine. This isn't petitioning the ancestors and appealing to their wisdom. A Shaman is a guide between the worlds. Not a bridge. As soon as a Shaman becomes a path between those who remained and those who wish to remain, he loses himself. A Shaman may guide someone but he cannot pave his own way. The time has come to decide who you are — a guide or a path. Don't let the water deceive you, Harbinger. Feel."

The heavy voice grew heavier with each word. I scowled with displeasure — not only was this jerk accusing my beloved water, but he was also forcing

me to do something, to think about something! Me —
a Harbinger of Malabar!

The desire to find out who considers himself
immortal grew so intense that I tried to push away the
pleasure that had gripped me and concentrated. And I
do mean tried because nothing came of it — the water
remained inside of me, around me, I was the water
and I wasn't about to leave this state.

"A powerful and cruel element. It has claimed
more than a thousand fools, who thought they were
stronger than it. You cannot fight against the element.
You must agree with it. You must pacify it. Feel."

The obnoxious voice continued speaking to me
like to a small child that had gotten its hands on an
electronic device and was now trying to figure out how
it worked by means of a hammer. The rage and
irritation that the unknown creature's voice evoked in
me were much more vivid and intense than the desire
to dissolve and vanish in the water's gentle hands. It
had been a long time since I had to make a decision
like this — I had to choose the type of pleasure I
would receive. Either the pleasure of the water, or the
pleasure of smearing someone's face across the floor.
Kornik would have a fine smirk if he learned this...

Kornik! The Shaman! Barliona!

An electric shock ran through me. I
remembered who I was! Player Daniel Mahan, who
had found himself in a strange scrape with water and
somehow forgotten, even if temporarily, his own self.

What were these strange experiments that the Corporation was conducting? The 'Exit' button appeared before me for a second, offering me an escape to reality where I could dig deeper into these humans experiments, yet something held me back. My mind understood that what would follow would be an illegal action, since my faculties of feeling were too excited, and yet something inside of me demanded that I go on. It wasn't the water's flirtation, but the desire and chance to extricate myself from this situation and understand why all of this had happened.

"Return to me." As soon as the 'Exit' button vanished, another wave of pleasure engulfed me, with its pleasant and barely perceptible whisper. The water was insatiable. I was soaring in weightlessness, watching the play of light, whole beautiful creations appeared and vanished around me, beckoning into some dark distance. My mood was improving, my objectivity was waning, so with my last crumbs of consciousness, I shut my eyes and tried to concentrate. The water was all around me in all its majesty and beauty. If I allow it to engulf me, maybe something bad might happen, something that might influence my future existence in Barliona. If I don't allow it to engulf me — the opposite will happen and I will receive bonuses. All that remained was to decide what to do…

"What do you need all these cares for, Shaman?

Renounce your doubts and sorrows and return to me."

When it became clear that I could resist the caresses and gentleness of the water, I brought the heavy artillery to bear. The voice. So gentle, so inviting, so mesmerizing that for a few moments I forget everything that existed. There was only the voice and its calling. Leave everything? No problem. Forget it all? Right this instant! Return to the voice? Of course! I'll only have to think of what to say to Anastaria, since...

Anastaria! Barliona...Damn it all!

The hallucination vanished as if it had never been. The 'Exit' button appeared before me again and it was only through sheer will that I managed to keep myself in Barliona. If initially my premonition had whispered quietly that I couldn't leave, now it was screaming and waving a red flag. Something powerful was coming, something that I would like, though I still had to earn it. I had to remain. I had to hold on.

Suddenly the water's gentleness and care vanished. Along with its mesmerizing whisper. In their place came cold and abrupt currents which eliminated all the pleasure I had experienced earlier. The abrupt change in environment caused me to open my eyes and see the water around me roiling in motion. Several meters ahead of me, as well as all around me, the water began to embody itself, gradually adopting the form of a semitransparent water elemental. Thirty seconds elapsed and I found myself surrounded by a dense ring of nine Level 300 monsters. With eyes as red as oxygenated blood. Aggroing mobs! Progress bars were glimmering above the monsters' heads, steadily approaching 100%. If I understand the elmentals' transformation correctly, the bar reflects the final formation of the creatures. Right this instant, the monsters were at 82% of readiness, and with every passing moment, the distance between me and the Gray Lands was growing smaller. Dealing with nine mobs would be too much for me.

Like hell!

The Shaman has three hands...

This time I didn't bother singing out loud. The water surrounding me didn't keep me from breathing, but it did keep trying to get into my mouth as soon as I opened it. I had to resort to doing my summoning mutely, like Kornik had taught me. The system again informed me that I'm not allowed to summon a Spirit that was beyond my rank, yet I swiped away both the notification and the system itself. I am a Shaman! The only limitation to which I would agree was my own unwillingness to do something. Everything else had to be intercepted and cut out at its root. Since I'm not allowed to work with the Spirits directly, I'll have improvise. And how can I improvise, being a Shaman Jeweler? That's right — only in design mode.

Without even considering how foolish my actions were — spurred on by my sharp feeling that I was doing everything correctly and the way it needed to be done — I opened design mode. Finding myself in the middle of my well-lit creative chamber, I mentally bound one hand to one edge of the room and the other to the other edge and then abruptly brought my hands together. I'd done a similar thing when I was crafting the Pendants, so my mind didn't bother resisting the novelty of this action. Since a completely reasonable precedent already existed — one which had caused me to end up here to begin with — then there wasn't much to think about or consider. I needed to act.

The room began to waver; it contracted and collapsed with a clap into a formless lump like a tablecloth that had been whipped from the table and crumpled. I was plunged into my customary and longed-for darkness, punctuated by the shelves bearing my former creations. My old design mode. I kicked the illuminated interface away from me with revulsion, causing it to roll along an invisible floor and vanish in a bright flash, and created a projection of the Water Spirit. Kalatea had once told me that Spirit summoning and crafting have nothing in common. That these things exist in different planes of reality. Well...Let's see which one of us was wrong — the insolent Shaman who lets his premonition guide him at all occasions or the experienced ideologue and creator of our class. After all, I intend on working with the Spirits through my crafting.

Damage taken...
Damage taken...
Damage taken...

A litany of notifications began to flash past my eyes, telling me that I was taking damage and trying to distract me. Once again thanking the unknown technician who had turned off my sensory perception, I completed the creation of the Spirit and looked him over critically. Outwardly he looked like an elemental, but he was quite different — my creation had appendages. Six appendages in his lower portion, which served as his legs and about seven-eight flexible appendages throughout his body, variously appearing and vanishing along his barrel-like torso. Due to his warped face, my elemental was more of some monster than a Spirit, but to my untrained eye, the result was excellent. The Spirit should scare his enemies. If not with his actions, then at least with his face.

The most important thing remained — I had to force my Spirit to do what I told him to. Simply put, he had to defend me from the rabid elementals who had by now managed to take my HP down to 60%. This, despite the insane amount of armor and all the magic resistance that came with it. If I had been wearing my old gear — the cocoon's lid would long since have slid aside, releasing me to my own devices for the next twelve hours. By the way! I should really pay to shorten my respawn time. A million gold isn't the kind of money that you're sorry to lose six hours of gameplay over.

Embodying the Spirit didn't work. Whenever he acquired the required density, I realized that I had created a simple statue which would fall apart in a few seconds due to my lack of the Architect or Sculptor professions. Try as I might, design mode only created lifeless items, since that was all it knew to do. But that didn't make me happy. I needed a result...

You have entered the unity.

Since nothing else occurred to me, I completely shut off my brain and began to act on pure instinct. I can't embody the Spirit? No problem — I'll be the Spirit myself!

"Greetings, brother!" A ringing voice sounded instantly in my head. At first I was taken aback, then I understood who was speaking: Spirit-Me. I was hearing those whom I had summoned! *"I can't activate your creation. Give me a way to reach it."*

"He is weak, take me instead!" another Spirit-Me yelled from some other part of the Universe. *"No one but me will be able to control your elemental!"*

"Me! Only me! The rest are too weak!" Dozens,

hundreds, thousands of Spirit-Me's hung over me, offering their services. All I had to do was reach out my hand, touch the entity I wanted and allow it to soak into the created Spirit through my essence. All I had to do was serve as a bridge between the world of Spirits and my world of real things...No! I won't be a path! I am a Shaman!

I was about to dispel the unity, since I wasn't seeing anything useful to me here when suddenly a question occurred to me that I couldn't answer.

"Who are you?" I asked, since the opportunity had presented itself. *"Why can the Shamans summon you? Why weren't you destroyed in Erebus? Why don't you return to Chaos?"*

Like at the wave of a wand, the noise and clamor disappeared. When I began to think that the Spirits had fallen silent because of my insolence, a thousand throats spoke in unison:

"WE ARE THOSE WHOM THEIR ANCESTORS REMEMBER! THOSE WHO EXIST BECAUSE OF OTHERS! WE ARE THE DEVOURERS OF THE ESSENCES!"

As the Spirits spoke, each word cast me deeper and deeper into a state of utter shock. The entire logic of the Barliona afterlife I had believed in, collapsed like a house of cards. Completely and irrevocably.

The Spirits were basically vampires. Like all mortal creatures, they had once died and their souls had been consumed by Chaos. However some essence

(I didn't really understand what it was) had remained in Barliona. Every time that someone recalled a deceased creature, he would give it a piece of his life force. In a word, if a sentient begins to live only in the past, it dies very quickly. Barliona seemed very strict about this. Furthermore, the more renowned the creature was during its life, the more life force its essence received, to the point that eventually it would become conscious. Yes, it could no longer return to Barliona as a living creature, since its Spirit had already died, but the stronger essences received the ability to inhabit a dead body, turning into a Zombie. Some become Spirits for Shamans to summon, acquiring this or that power in the process. Others become phantoms, others Astral demons, and others great heroes of the past who could temporarily embody themselves in the living world. Basically, there were many options for what could happen to an essence. The main problem was to remain consistently remembered and thereby receive this life force...even if doing so meant having to kill living creatures. The main goal was to live at the expense of the living. Thence the devourers of the essences and hence...vampires.

I couldn't help but draw an analogy to the real world. We too remember our ancestors...And even today, people believe in ghosts, strange voices, odd howls...Blech! Enough! I didn't come here for this!

"In other words, you can't become living because

your souls have been absorbed by Chaos?" The idea struck me. *"What if someone managed to steal a soul from Erebus? How can it come to life in that case?"*

"THIS IS IMPOSSIBLE! IN ALL OF HISTORY, ONLY TWO CREATURES MANAGED TO ESCAPE EREBUS."

"If there were two, there could be more," I refused to surrender.

"NO! THE DIRECT DESCENDENT OF HARRASHESS — AND THE SON OF TARTARUS AND ELUNA WHO DECIDED TO BECOME MORTAL — ARE TWO VERY UNIQUE CREATURES."

As Alice once cried: "Curiouser and curiouser!" What an enormous, elaborate world Barliona is! If you just look around a little, there's no limit to what you can find...

A lightning bolt of epiphany pierced me through my head to my toes. I understood! A Shaman cannot be a bridge or a path between two worlds. If he is, he must surrender himself and eventually he'll cease to be a Shaman. An NPC will die; a player will lose his powers. A Shaman must serve as a guide. To guide the Spirit to the correct place and sacrifice this other creature. Until the Shaman becomes a Harbinger, he must give his own life force to summon Spirits. I was always surprised by the cost the Shamans had to pay for each summoned Spirit, and only now did I understand where my hands and feet were. As soon as a Shaman becomes a Harbinger, he is granted the ability to figure out himself and decide what is more important for him: to engage in sadomasochism, giving up his own life force for each summons, or to become a conduit, allowing the Spirits to devour other creatures. Warriors, children, animals...whoever...as long as it isn't the Shaman himself. What a nice little class I chose to play!

I looked at the created Spirit and yet another realization dawned on me. It wasn't for nothing that I had entered a unity...

I was told that the water is deceitful and tricky. Dangerous and unreliable. Pitiless and senseless. Naïve and foolish creatures! Water is the source of life! No creature can exist without it. How can someone call it terrible? No. It is the way it is. All-consuming, multiform, embracing and gentle. It's stupid to resist this. Water can only be limited by some other form, figure or vessel. For example, the Spirit I had created...

You have subjugated the Supreme Water Spirit. Duration of subjugation: 31 (Crafting) seconds.

The eyes of the elemental I had created filled with a bright light as, simultaneously, my unity and design mode vanished into non-existence. I was again surrounded by enormous sheets of water — the nine elementals trying their best to kill my character —

and yet a new challenger had appeared: the Spirit I had created.

"Let them have it!"

The system hiccupped one more time about how I had to work within the rules, but I wasn't paying any attention to it. The battle had begun...

"Q.E.D." Kornik's mocking voice tore the surrounding space in twain and suddenly I realized that I was standing in front of a great tree. The elementals and my Spirit had vanished, as if they'd never existed. Beside me stood the six Zombie guards, cautiously examining the graves at their feet, while right before me, in a lotus pose, sat Knucklear satisfied and smiling. Behind the monk's back stood a whole detachment of Barliona's finest NPCs: Kornik, Prontho, Nashlazar, as well as another dozen or so Shamans that I hadn't yet met. What's this all about?

"I won't waste time on pretty words," Kornik went on. "I'll be brief — good job and all that. I'm sad to admit it, but I no longer have the right to call you my student, just as you can no longer call me your teacher. Welcome to Barliona, Harbinger!"

Harbinger class confirmed.
The 'Water Spirit Rank' restriction has been lifted, as you will no longer need it.

CHAPTER FIVE

THE HERMIT

"GREETINGS, OH NEMESIS! Please accept my gift, Harbinger!" Nashlazar slithered over to me on her enormous tail and held out a small branch. The item was thickly decked with white berries which were as large as good-sized pearls and which hid the green leaves and the green stalk from sight. I accepted the gift automatically and immediately opened its properties. This should be a nice present! The greater my disappointment when among the properties I encountered about the most mundane thing I could have:

Branch of White Mistletoe. Description: A present from Nashlazar. Durability: 20. Item class: Common.

Not even a hint of some function, hidden bonuses, possible quests or other little tidbits that I loved so much. An ordinary piece of wood that even had Durability. No doubt it would wither away in the next few days. What kind of a present is this anyway?

"Greetings to you, Dragon! Please accept my gift, Harbinger!" An elf I'd never met before followed behind Nashlazar, handing me a fern. Again no bonuses or powers. A simple branch.

One after another, the Shamans began to come up to me, greet me and deposit their bouquets in my hands. Kornik's was pine, Prontho's was oak. Really quite symbolical of them — one as prickly as a hedgehog, the other as impenetrable as an oak. Is that to say that Nashlazar is actually a white and fluffy Siren? Like hell!

"What is going on?" I exclaimed when the Shamans arranged themselves in a line, nodded one more time and vanished, leaving me one on one with a very smug-looking Knucklear. "*Kornik?! What in the hell?*"

"*Phew, what a dreadful lack of manners!*" the voice of the Harbinger Elf appeared in my head. It sounded so disgusted and outraged that I couldn't help but wince. The odd thing is that I'd never imagined that Elves could be Shamans. It seemed to me like they were usually Druids, Hunters, Mages, but never Shamans. But no! Not only was there at least one Shaman among the elves, but he was a Harbinger too!

"*A cursing Shaman, what could be worse? Kornik, haven't you told him about the Harbinger channel?*" The Dwarf Harbinger echoed the Elf.

"*What do you expect from a savant who's become Harbinger in only a year?*" the Elf spoke up again. "*He's got neither stature, nor experience, nor an ounce of respect for his senior and more experienced colleagues. A Dragon through and through!*"

"*I hereby strip Mahan of his ability to communicate with Harbingers for one day. Let him reflect on his behavior,*" Nashlazar announced and the other voices fell silent. A notification flashed by, announcing that my telepathic link with the Harbingers had been blocked. All I could do was raise my eyebrows in puzzlement and ask myself: What was that? Why'd they just toss me out like some unruly kitten? What'd I do anyway? No, Shamans are definitely strange people. Their communion with the Spirits really does come at a price — some part of their sanity is lost in the process. And lost for good.

"Are you done playing with your Shamans?" A mocking voice inquired, forcing me to look up from my examination of the horizon in search of universal justice. Knucklear. The monk was sitting in a lotus pose, slowly running a toothpick through his teeth. Once he was sure that I was looking at him, the fat man nodded to the guards, "What'd you bring these thugs here for?"

"I want to bring them back to life. I've heard that you know how to do that," I blurted out honestly, unwilling to beat around the bush.

"You want it?" The monk aped me. "Did you

ask them? Do they actually want to become living?"

"Of course!" replied the six guards as if on cue, while the one who was the jailer's brother added: "We have families to return to!"

"All right, all right! You don't have to yell," Knucklear frowned unhappily. "Let's assume that you really believe that you want to return to the living, return to your previous service as guards and only remember this entire affair as some terrible dream. Am I right?"

Six guards began to nod their assent, forcing another smirk from the monk. What did he want? NPCs never use sarcasm just like that, so there had to be some reason here. Yet I hadn't the slightest idea what it could be!

"Okay...Let's do this differently. Tell me, kid," the fat man turned to Clouter, "how do you like being able to see the affinity of other sentients? How do you like seeing their fears and secret desires. Understand what bothers and unsettles them? What's it like being a Priest?"

Clouter was taken aback by such a question and stared at the monk blankly. Here it is! Someone else had joined my clan of stupefied creatures. I no longer feel alone in my stupefaction.

"You will remain a Priest as long as you remain a Zombie. I have no idea how this happened, but if you return to your previous condition, you will become a Warrior again. Are you ready for this?"

Clouter's eyes grew as large as saucers, he staggered from the monk, shaking his head, tripped over a root sticking out of the ground and collapsed. The fear and shock at the danger of losing his newly-acquired class, was so immense that Clouter paid no attention to the fall, trying to crawl away from the danger before him.

"That's what I'm talking about," Knucklear remarked philosophically, grinning as he watched Clouter take cover behind a tree. "What are we going to do then? Six Zombies returned from Erebus, so six Spirits have inhabited our world. In order to make them living, we'll need six bodies — and here it's looking like someone's getting cold feet."

Clouter peeked from behind the tree. The guards were staring dumbly into the ground and it was looking like the opportunity to return back to the land of the living was zooming away with the speed of an express train.

"Are you saying that if I don't agree then none of us can be living again? No one will return to life?" the boy asked in a voice so plaintive that I couldn't help but feel a twinge of pity for him. Was being a Priest really so alluring to him that he was prepared to give up his mother for it?

"Six Spirits, six Zombies," Knucklear replied implacably. "And you need to make your decision now — the longer this takes, the weaker your Spirits will be."

"Mahan, what am I going to do?" Clouter glanced over at me. "I don't want to be a Warrior."

Quest updated: 'Who will guard the guards themselves?' Time remaining: 60 minutes.

"What's with you?" the boy asked after I had done cursing. Whatever choice I made right now, I'd end up paying for it with Attractiveness and Reputation. If I ordered them to turn into people, I'd lose Clouter who'd begin to blame himself and blame me for not remaining a Priest — causing Elsa to be upset as well. If I tell him to remain in his current state, the other five Zombies would suffer and blame me, which would make a good portion of the Anhurs NPCs really upset with me and my clan as well. There was danger all around and yet I had to resolve this in short order.

"All right, boys, what do you choose?" I addressed the guards as a way of starting. Having received a monotone mutter in response (the guards preferred their old lives in Anhurs but would accept any decision made by the master Earl), I frowned: The current situation looked like it might affect my social status as well. Clouter meekly asked me to keep him a Priest, if that was possible, but refused to speak out against the will of his colleagues as he considered doing so wrong.

"What do you say?" Knucklear asked me only a

minute later, clearly prodding me to make a decision. "Are we going to turn them or not? Six Spirits — six Zombies. There's no other way."

Ignoring the monk's question, I was about to call Stacey for help when a mad idea buzzed into my head, dodging any of my attempts to swat it out of there. Once the idea had grown tired of buzzing, it settled on my brain like on a sugar cube and began to gnaw at it with smacking noises, demanding immediate action. A wondrous picture took shape in my imagination — the hamster and the toad were standing shocked, their eyes popping out of their sockets, while the fly, blinged out like some famous rapper, was sitting on a sofa in oversized sunglasses scarfing down pieces of my brain like popcorn and calling for the show to go on. The idea had buzzed in to see the show and now demanded I go on.

The amulet of communication appeared in my hand like by magic.

"Speaking!" Came the response, evoking a sigh of relief from me. There had been no guarantees that my student was in game.

"Fleita, this is Mahan. I have a..."

"MAHAN!" The squeal in the amulet drowned out everything around me. "WHERE ARE YOU?"

"Don't yell like that," I barked unhappily. "At the moment, I'm with the Zombie Monk teacher in Kartoss and I..."

"Don't move, I'll be there in a jiffy! Five

minutes! Don't go anywhere! I'll be quick!" roared the little monster, hanging up. I stared dumbly at the dead amulet. What was that?

"So what do you say?" Knucklear asked again, forcing me to return to reality and ticking off another minute of my time limit.

"If it has to be, I'll become a human again, Mahan," Clouter too was prodding me to make a decision, just like the guards who'd stay Zombies until the end of time for their beloved colleague.

Like hell!

"Mahan!" A mere three minutes passed before an insane whirlwind enveloped me, almost knocking me off my feet. Once the dust had settled, the whirlwind embodied itself as Fleita, hanging on my chest and bawling her eyes out. "You came back! I was watching that terrible trial and thinking that you'd never come back! How could they do that to you? Mahan! They all said that you were done, that you'd never show up again, but I went on believing! I really did believe! But I couldn't find a way to get in touch with you! And Kornik refuses to teach me. He says that the Zombies now have new teachers coming from other continents, let them deal with the Shamans! Mahan, where'd you vanish to? And also someone..."

A river of words poured out of Fleita. The girl didn't even think of letting me go, her arms still clasped around my neck, all the while chattering at a thousand words a minute. Along with the theoretical pails of tears. On the one hand, players can't actually cry in Barliona, unless it's in a scenario, on the other hand, a dry crying is even more terrifying than an actual one.

"...and the Emperor doesn't say anything, since the update has now taken effect and it's not clear anymore whether I can join your clan or not. Sally from the other continent told me that..."

"Hold up!" I shouted, placing Fleita down on the ground. Among the general noise emanating from Fleita, I couldn't find the information I needed. "What did you say about the clan?"

"They don't want to transfer me to Malabar!" Fleita tried to throw herself on my neck again, but I stopped her.

"What exactly did they say?"

"Nothing! Nothing at all! I already wrote the devs two letters. They don't say anything. Or rather they replied that the issue is being processed, and that they'd figure out the exact dates and stuff as the situation develops," Fleita said these last words in a semiofficial and contemptuous tone as if mocking the Corporation officials. "No one wants me to join your clan!"

"I do," I reassured the girl, "but for that to happen you'll have to adjust your character a little bit. Are you ready?"

"Adjust my character?" Fleita stitched her

brows together in puzzlement. "How?" And why? And where? Will you let me join your clan afterwards? What'll be my rank? And how..."

"Stop!" I interrupted the girl yet again and in several words related to her the difficult quandary of Clouter and the guards, slowly and steadily working my way to the main reason for why I had called my student to begin with.

"I don't understand," she muttered with surprise. "You need six Zombies. They're already here. You need six Spirits. They're wandering around somewhere. At the same time there's a difference of opinion about whether it's worth turning back or not. What do you need me for?"

I stayed silent, looking at Fleita the way Kornik used to look at me. Wryly.

"OH COME ON!" Fleita somehow managed to yell with her whisper so loud that I expect they could hear her even in Malabar. "You want me to be the substitute Zombie?!"

"Knucklear, I have six Zombies who need to be turned into people," I told the monk, having assured Fleita that everything would be okay and I would take her into my clan. After which I turned to Clouter and added: "My dear Clouter, what are you still doing here? Shouldn't you be on your way to meet the Priest trainer?"

"Mahan, I..." Clouter began, but I cut him short.

"Write a letter to your mother, please. Explain everything to her, but in your words, don't overthink it. Here," I offered the boy a pen and granted him permission to use stationary at my expense. "Good luck to you, Priest!"

You have made your choice.

Quest completed: 'Who will guard the guards themselves?'

Reward: Friendly status with Tartarus.

"I accept your sacrifice, my daughter," boomed an ample and powerful voice, forcing goose bumps (which didn't actually exist in Barliona) to appear all over my body. I turned around and beheld one of the most powerful creatures of the game world — Tartarus. The god of Kartoss. A humanoid creature, with two legs and two arms and a head that resembled a terrible combination of a dark sphere which had something roiling within it that I couldn't quite focus my eyes on. Tartarus was terrible indeed.

"I accept your decision and take you under my banner," Eluna appeared beside Tartarus. The sudden concentration of divine creatures in one tiny area began to warp reality. The only thing missing was...

The space around me went dark, becoming two bipolar worlds as the Astral consumed me.

"WE ARE PLEASED WITH YOUR STUDENT!" growled the Spirit of the Lower World. "WE ACCEPT

HER DECISION!"

"SHE SHALL BE THE CONDUIT AND PERFORM OUR WILL!" added the Spirit of the Higher World. "YOU DESERVE A REWARD, SHAMAN!"

"FROM NOW ON WE SHALL USE HER TO DO OUR BIDDING!" added the White Spirit. "YOU MAY TELL KORNIK THAT HIS DEBT HAS BEEN REPAID!"

Control over your character has been temporarily blocked. At the moment, your character is possessed by the Supreme Spirits of the Higher and Lower Worlds.

To say that I was surprised would have been an understatement. I didn't even bother swiping this message aside, reading it again and again and trying to figure out its secret significance. And on the face of it, the significance was terrifying — this very instant, some highly advanced Imitator was controlling my Shaman. What the hell was this?!

My inquiry to tech support wrote itself on the fly. Trying to use the proper legal jargon, I inquired in pure curse words, what the hell they were thinking when they took away control of my Shaman from me? How was I supposed to know if at the moment all my funds weren't being transferred to strangers or my personal information wasn't being downloaded?

+1000 Reputation with the Spirits of the

Higher and Lower Worlds. Current status: Exalted.

"Mahan, this is impossible!" Fleita whispered in rapture once I'd been returned to the game world. I looked around and apprised the situation. I'd never seen such astonishment on my student's face before. Once upon a time, I happened across a video in which a child who had lost his sight in infancy regained it following a surgical procedure. I'd never seen such a sincere and incommunicable elation and, simultaneously, shock, and I imagined I'd never see it again. Things like this are unique and you can count yourself lucky to witness them even once in your life. But I was wrong — I was lucky enough to see it a second time, and in person. Giving Anastaria her due for forcing me to always keep my in-game camera running, I checked Fleita's properties and swallowed hard. Nothing in this game had prepared me for this.

Draco the Decembrist. Great Shaman. Dragon of Light.

"You changed your name," I said astounded, refusing to believe my eyes. "And your race..."

Fleita — or rather — Draco — didn't say anything. Damn it! How am I supposed to tell her apart from my Totem now? Suddenly there were too many Dracos in Barliona.

"All right kids, that's quite enough of staring at

each other and not knowing what and how and when and where," Knucklear scattered the lingering silence. "Girl, don't you have to start performing the Supreme Spirits' tasks as urgently as possible?"

"I...Yes, I'll be just a second," muttered Fleita-Draco, still in shock and staring at a text only she could see.

"Hang on!" I managed to cry before my student dove into the portal that had just opened up. She hadn't cast a scroll which meant only one thing — the girl had received some curious scenario. If that was the case, I'd need to make the most of this opportunity. The brand new Draco glanced at me with her enormous gilded eyes, glinting like polished gold in the sunlight. Muttering something about changes for the better, I opened the clan management interface and invited her into the Legends of Barliona. I wasn't about to let a Dragon (whose powers and abilities still remained a mystery to me) go off freely in the unknown.

"Thank you!" A smile bloomed on my student's face. "Mahan, I will complete all my quests and then tell you about what happened here. Thank you! And...Thank you!"

Fleita-Draco looked away, blushed and then glanced up at me again, appeared beside me and I didn't even have time to blink when her lips alighted on mine. The kiss was initially so clumsy and strained yet so insistent and unexpected that I, unwillingly, replied at last, lowering my face to meet the girl's desire.

"I understand everything, but I couldn't help myself," the girl said after the sweet moment, which seemed to last thousands of years, ended. Sparkling from happiness like a Christmas tree, the girl entered the portal, leaving me in a state of happy shock. Even though what had happened had been unexpected, I can't say that I didn't like it. Damn it — I did like it. Fleita was an attractive girl and it'd be dumb to pretend that I never wanted to get to know her better. So I did. And I can't say that I didn't like what I discovered either. Something tells me that I should edit the video of what had happened in Kartoss before showing it to Anastaria...

"All right, you five don't have patrons of that level." Knucklear's voice reached me through my fog, reminding me that I was not alone. I had to concentrate and dispel the lovely stupor, to see that he was speaking to the five guards who were still Zombies. A note was lying right at my feet, which I guessed had been written by Clouter. The boy himself was nowhere in sight. "Gather your belongings and follow this student. Turning back into a living creature is a difficult and tedious venture. You'll have to work hard."

Somehow entirely unnoticeably, I remained completely alone in the middle of a forgotten cemetery in Kartoss. The guards were ushered out by the monks, thereby preparing a new batch of exciting quests for the players — from 'Bring 100,500 crab whiskers from crabs killed in the second harvest moon' to 'Sing a song of those who fell in battle against the Mages of Malabar.' In other words, gather some stuff so that the Zombies could return to their living selves. The only upsetting thing was that I wouldn't get a crack at it. Only Kartossians were allowed to participate.

I mourned this fact a few moments until I recalled that I already had an interesting quest to do for the next few hours. The hermit! Stacey was occupied, Fleita was taking a stroll somewhere, and Mr. Kristowski was still cooped up in the Imperial palace discussing the future tournament, so I had the unique opportunity to find out who the hell this hermit was. Why were there so many loose ends tied up in meeting him? And, furthermore, he was an Artificer who knew about the Titan Armor...

Shivers ran down my spine — I had promised Kreel that he would kill the Dragon. Damn it! Not only had I managed to spoil that quest, but I had broken my word.

Squelching my urge to get my amulet and arrange a meeting with Kreel, and making a mental note to be more conscientious about my own promises, I opened the map and entered the hermit's coordinates into my 'Blink' input box. An elephant is best eaten bit by bit.

A new territory has been discovered: 'Silvan Plateau.'

Quest available: 'Artificer. Stage 1. Prepare for the meeting.'

Do you wish to start the quest?

I found myself at the foot of one of the many mountains in the Elma Range — a sierra that ran like a terrible, winding scar from the north to the very south of our continent. The hermit's location may have been in the South, but the area around me didn't resemble a tropical resort in the least. I could make out the forest among the heaps of ice and snow, but the area immediately around me may as well have been Antarctica. The fragments of wood and frozen leaves that poked up through the ice here and there indicated that there had recently been a leafy forest here — like the one I could see in the distance. But something had happened and nature here had changed. Or to the opposite — everything had happened the way it was meant to. Shrugging my shoulders, leaving the mystery of this glacier's sudden appearance in the middle of the tropical South unsolved, I pushed the 'Yes' button. The time had come to meet the hermit...

Ten minutes elapsed before I realized that the meeting would have to wait. My character received the unpleasant 'Frozen' buff, as well as 'Chill' and 'Frostbite,' my movement speed dropped by 90% and I was informed that I could no longer summon a flying pet, yet still the hermit didn't appear. As bitter as it was to admit it, I was forced to open the description and read what I had to do to prepare for the meeting. Another ten minutes in this freezing cold would kill me. Opening my quest log I stared grimly at the description and realized that I had some entertaining minutes, hours and possibly days waiting ahead of me. The description promised me nothing else:

Prove that you are worthy of meeting the master...

* * *

"And there aren't any caves or portals or signs or anything?" Anastaria asked, offering me a mug of steaming coffee. Even though the game was above all just a game, and my sensory perception was turned down to zero, I had grown so cold morally that I really felt a chill when I crawled out of my capsule. It was warm, comfortable and light in our apartment but I was shaking as if I really was in an icy forest. In a few hours of scouring up and down the glacier I hadn't managed to accomplish anything but freezing myself and my character to death — at which point we'd been sent to respawn. Cute — I wasn't killed by some terrible mob or a Dungeon boss, but by a huge pile of snow and ice that had appeared who knows where from.

"Nope," I replied, wrapping myself in the quilt and exhaling the stunning aroma of freshly-brewed Jambi coffee. I glanced over at the roasted chicken that Stacey had ordered in the nearby take-out place. My spouse had emerged from the game an hour before me, and had arranged our food, drink and comfort. "There's nothing there at all."

"As you can imagine, it's pointless to ask on the forums. I don't have this info either. Head over to the library, maybe you'll find something about the Artificers there," Stacey had initially been interested in the hermit until she realized that this NPC was made for craftsmen and would be useless to her. The girl sighed heavily, looked at the wall that had some drawing on it and blurted out: "Dan, I talked to my dad. The Celestial Empire will be in Kalragon tomorrow night."

"What?" I almost scalded myself with the coffee. "You said that we have a week?"

"Our informant turned out to be a double agent," Stacey smirked sadly. "They were leading us around by our nose, like a bunch of lambs, slowly leaking the info we were looking for. The Celestial fleet will land on our continent tomorrow evening and they're bringing an obelisk."

"One thing on top of another! What'd you decide?" I was certain that Phoenix would have decided on a plan of action by now.

"Remember our meeting with my father this morning? He was checking to see how well you understood the situation. He wanted to see whether you'd understand that there are 'specially trained' people whose job it is to develop strategy or whether you'd begin to spout off one idea after another. This morning, my dad was disappointed in you, yet our analysts now believe that the option of attacking the obelisk transport in your Dragon form is the only possible way to stop the invasion. And you managed to come up with it in mere seconds, on the fly...You don't have any desire to study statistics and data processing by any chance?"

"Thanks, maybe later. So in other words, we need to attack the Celestial fleet tomorrow? Will it be you and I or will Plinto join us?"

"We need someone who can destroy the obelisk. Plinto is the only one who could do this quickly and completely. Dan, tell me, what was the kiss with your student all about?"

How in the...?! I understand very well that poker is not my thing, since I blushed from head to toe. No one's ever caught me so handily before.

"A spontaneous friendly kiss as a sign of gratitude for inviting her to the clan and helping her become a Dragon," I blurted out the first think that popped into my head.

"Can I see the video? You were recording, weren't you?"

Everything turned upside down inside of me. Stacey was asking the questions so calmly that I got scared. Lying would be useless, as would be wheeling and dealing, I felt in my heart of hearts that it would only make things worse. I was desperately trying to remember how long the kiss had lasted and where my hands had been, yet I managed to reply in a relatively calm voice:

"Yes, of course. I'll bring it up on the screen right now."

Both of our capsules were connected to our home AV system — such was the symbiosis of a powerful computer, a smart home, a multimedia center and god knows what else, all intended for the single purpose of extracting as much money as possible from the consumer. Stacey had set up the capsules so that the footage from Barliona was immediately recorded by the computer — to make it easier to analyze it, according to her. Today's kiss was there too.

"Didn't I tell you — a simply formality!" I said, sensing all the pressure leave me. Without expecting it, I had turned into an athlete before the final burst — every muscle was tensed to its maximum and then some. My kiss with Fleita-Draco had lasted only eight seconds, I counted, and my hands remained hanging at my sides, while my generally shocked appearance only suggested one thing — I had no idea what was going on.

"Mmm..." Anastaria hummed significantly. "A friendly kiss, you say?"

"Of course!" I reassured her and trying to change the subject, asked: "Why don't you tell me what you dug up about the guy with the treasure map?"

"Basically nothing. Hunter Sabantul the Fortunate, Level 85, just over a year total play time. There's nothing about him that stands out. He doesn't post on the forums, the Hunter trainer doesn't remember him, and he doesn't even have a rare pet. An ordinary mediocre player. There's an endless number of players like him in Barliona. His current whereabouts are unknown, but my people are on it. That's all the info I have from today's efforts."

"Weird," I continued trying to put distance between me and the kiss. "How would such an ordinary player have a map like that?"

"The weird thing is something else," Stacey corrected me. "He could've found the map. Barliona's full of coincidences. The question here is how would he know that you'd be interested in his offer? How does he know that you're interested in Karmadont and anything related to him? He wrote two letters and yet they're so different that in my view, they were written by two different people. The style's different. The approach's different. The gist is different. Everything's different! Only the sender's the same."

"Then let's meet with him and get to know him

better." Stacey had piqued my interest. Really, how did this person find out this info?

"First we need to solve the Celestial situation, then we can get back to Sabantul. He's not going anywhere, that's for sure. For the moment, my dear husband, the time has come to figure out how you react or don't react when someone kisses you...Is there something you want to tell me?"

I was forced to expend my full arsenal of words and explanations to prove to Stacey the most evident thing — that she was my one and only love on the entire planet. Embracing the girl quietly sobbing on my shoulder, I swore to myself that there would be no more kisses! I'd exhausted all my arguments this time around and I wouldn't survive a second one...

I looked dejectedly at the glacier and cursed the developer who had come up with it...Or perhaps (just as likely) the player who had caused this chaos. Over the twelve hours of my temporary absence, the ice had receded from the trees. Not much, only a few meters, but the burbling brooks were glibly informing me that this anomaly had come into existence recently and would soon vanish. This was no natural phenomenon and I could even guess who had caused it. Kreel the Titan had the ice affinity, so I could bet that his big old paws had something to do with ice popping up this deep in the hot and smarmy South. It couldn't have been anyone else.

Stacey had been kind enough to grant me six

hours to figure out the issue with the hermit, after which she explained to me that I would be "grabbed by the scruff and sent to save the continent from the invasion." Six hours of which I'd already spent twenty minutes sitting here meditating on this ice, unable to understand what I was supposed to do. To prove that I was worthy of meeting the master...The most logical outcome that followed from this phrase was that I had to craft some pretty and preferably unique thing — here and now. To prove that I was a cool Artificer and all that. The one problem was how that would help me solve the problem. It remained unclear. Besides, I was certain that creating an artifact was just too banal to earn a meeting with the hermit. He wouldn't even notice such a trifle. I needed something more large-scale. But what?

The shadow from the nearest mountain shielded the glacier from the sun's rays, slowing its melt. Various beasts would periodically emerge from the forest, look at the obstacle that had appeared on their customary paths with surprise — their Imitators would begin to compute new paths, while the model froze in an entirely unnatural pose. I especially got a kick out of a Level 83 wolf who began to update his pathing while standing still on one paw. I figured that even a Shaolin monk would have envied his technique.

Once the wolf had vanished back in the forest, I shuddered — the tautology notwithstanding, the ice was freezing, forcing my thoughts to move slower and slower. Eventually it occurred to me to call Kreel and ask him about the hermit — an intelligent and worthy idea — however, to my immense surprise the Titan wasn't available: I could not communicate with a player who was in the divine chambers.

In a burst of irritation, I kicked a hunk of ice beside me. A small piece broke off of it, rolled along the ground, encountered a spot of sunlight and vanished in an instant. It didn't even leave a wet spot behind it. A wry smile unfolded on my face — so they had used Kreel to create an ice trial for me? Excellent! I'll deal with it like an ordinary player!

And what do ordinary players do when they encounter a problem? They ask for help!

For the first time in a long time, I opened my clan management screen. Yeah...It was time to scratch my head in bemusement — the clan membership counter was growing without pause, incrementing by one or two members every couple seconds. At the moment, the clan had just over 30,000 members, of whom about a third were currently online. It took an effort to look away from the statistics — all the various classes, races, primary professions, secondary professions and their levels that were in my clan. There was so much diverse information about every clan member that, just for laughs, I tried to find the 'real address' and 'real name' data tables. Damn, these were there too! No one had entered their addresses, and yet more than eight thousand players had entered their real names. I hummed. Clan management was turning from 'let's run around together' to a serious enterprise that demanded time, energy and resources. I had an outsourced manager who dealt with the clan's financial issues. I had recruiters who looked for people to join the clan, but no actual leadership. There weren't any raid leaders, treasurers or officers. There were thirty thousand people who wanted to get their projections. I looked at the little dragon whirling around me — I had grown so accustomed to him that I barely noticed him anymore — and I realized a terrible fact. I needed one more deputy. I needed someone who would play the role of the head of the Legends of Barliona. Someone who would make the decisions, organize the raid parties and act as the clan's representative at various events. Shaman Mahan had to step back into the shadows and do what he did best — craft. Managing people wasn't my thing.

When I made this final decision, it was like a stone had rolled off my shoulders. I sent my current coordinates to Viltrius, returned to the clan settings, found the mass mailing tab and sent out a letter to everyone in the clan:

Hello everyone! People, I need your help. Right here and right now I need players who can cast fire spells. *Anything they can — lava, fireballs, bonfires — hell, if you've got a lighter, if such a thing even exists, I can use it. I need to melt a huge mass of ice in a few moments. But I need organized help — I need groups of players. I need raid groups that will become raid parties. And the people who organize them will become Legends of Barliona raid leaders with all the attendant privileges and powers. The raiders that come with them too! I need people within the hour, whether they're our own or strangers — it doesn't matter. The groups need to be sent to me through the Altameda portal — my majordomo has my coordinates. Feel like taking a chance and becoming someone in this clan? Then make it happen! You have one hour. The countdown begins now.*

I didn't really have another choice. Stacey had placed really tight time constraints on me. Swiping away the notification that had appeared before me just like any other member of the clan, I kept an eye on the clan chat. A minute after my letter, things were still quiet, and then the chat exploded. Dozens if not hundreds messages began streaming in every second, announcing their services as officers as well as footsoldiers.

"*Why?*" Stacey's thought popped into my head. "*The hermit?*"

"Not quite, but close," I related the current situation to Stacey and the decision I had made about dealing with the glacier. To my surprise, Stacey didn't approve of my sudden initiative. She explained that since only a third of the players were in-game, the chances of there being good organizers among them were minimal. There would be no consideration for the players' level distribution, nor a common pool of resources. Only she, Mr. Kristowski, and I had access to the clan statistics, so in a word there was nothing here but my urge to melt the glacier. Things just weren't done this way and this was no way to determine clan leadership...in clans that take themselves seriously at least.

"What do you want me to do?" A pretty female voice jolted me from my prostration. When she really wants to, Stacey can still artfully place everything in its right place, leaving whoever's talking to her with the certain feeling of his personal insignificance and foolishness. I checked the time — five minutes had elapsed since my message and there were already five hundred players standing before me with an elf at their head, waiting for my orders. The clan management screen displayed all the information I needed about this long-eared girl: Marle Regina, a Level 155 Elf Priest. Real name: Stacey. Clan membership: 14 weeks. That was it.

"I need to melt this crap," I pointed at the glacier. "Turn it all into a lake of magma."

"I need clarification. You want us to melt the ice or melt the ground and stones into a lake of magma? That would require different resources."

"The latter." I became curious whether terrain in Barliona could be terraformed. Would the game allow such drastic changes to the terrain? Would the Guardian's Imitator permit it? I wanted to check it out!

"Lucca, I need fire mages. Lots of them," Marle called a friend on her amulet and then looked back at me: "Mahan, do you know any geomancers? Or do I need to find those too?"

"That's an odd profession, but it rings a bell..." I liked Marle's approach to the problem at hand. The only thing that interested her were clear, laconic, pointed questions.

"Geomancy is terraforming. The geomancer's spells allow her to change the Barliona terrain to her wishes. We won't be able to create a lake of magma unless we use players that have such powers. At the moment, I don't know anyone who can do this, which is why I'm asking you whether I have to find them too."

"I see. Wait a second," I reached for an amulet and called Svard, one of the independent players of Barliona who dealt with crafting.

"If this isn't pizza delivery, I have nothing further to say," barked the voice in the amulet.

"This is way cooler than pizza," I replied in kind. "I need a specialist who can vandalize Barliona terrain."

"Is that you, Mahan?" The tone changed immediately and completely.

"Uh-huh. Svard, I need a high-level geomancer. And I need him now."

"What am I, a recruiting agency?" The answer came in such a tone that without seeing Svard I knew he was already deep in thought. "Do you need someone from Malabar, or will Kartoss do too?"

"Could be from the Celestial, for all it matters," I gibed. "I'll send you the contact to my new raid leader. She'll get in touch with you."

"So it's true and Stacey is with you again?"

"Yes, but this is isn't Stacey. That is, this one's called Stacey too but she's not the Stacey you're thinking of. The girl's in-game name is Marle."

"Hmm...interesting. Give me ten minutes. Over and up."

"You heard me, here are the contacts," I sent a copy of the amulet to Marle.

"Raid leader?" The girl's face displayed an emotion for the first time. Trying to act precisely and accurately, as if she had some military past, Marle wasn't ready to receive the third rank in the clan from me just like that. Without any test. Well, this will let her know the kind of crew she's running with now.

"Welcome and all that," I smiled, making the necessary changes in the clan settings. "You are the first to bring me a combat-ready group. So you're a raid leader already. No point in wasting time. You have your orders. By the way! If any new groups appear, you're in charge. I need complete coordination among all the raid parties, senior raid leader!"

I made the last remark as the portal opened and players began pouring out of it. Raid party number two had arrived. Excellent — it'd only been have ten minutes. If I understand correctly, Marle had managed to assemble her raid party within the clan, without advertising it to Clutzer or Magdey. She had players between Level 80 and 160, who clearly posed no interest to the other raid leaders. No big deal! Low levels is something everyone has to reckon with. The important thing is that the players have the desire, the opportunity and the ability. I'd take care of the rest.

"The time has come. Everyone's in position. We are ready," said Marle exactly an hour after I had sent my letter to the clan. By this point in time, a huge crowd of people had gathered at the glacier — three fully-equipped raiding parties with fifty fighters in each, about a hundred Mages, Necromancers, Druids and other magic classes who could cast fire, as well as Svard with a trio of taciturn players, Spiteful Gnum who had climbed out of Altameda for the occasion, Anastaria (astonished by such a gathering of players), and the chief raiding parties of Phoenix. There was a host of people. Marle's amulets didn't fall quiet for a second, but the girl didn't even think of complaining. Her quick replies, eagerness and demeanor made it clear that she was relishing the responsibilities that had been entrusted to her. Perfect! The important thing was that she didn't wither under the pressure. I'd need to make sure to issue her some nice bonus as compensation and incentive to continue in this vein.

"Let's begin. Let me see a lake of fire instead of this ugly glacier!"

I didn't really know myself why I needed a branch office of hell here in the foothills of the Elma Mountains. But to be honest, what drove me to invite all these people here remained a mystery to me as well — as well as why they'd all agreed to come. In my view, there was only one correct way to reach the hermit: craft a fire artifact. And yet my premonition, stubbornness and desire to do everything my way, all demanded their own course of action. A course of action that would go against all reason and logic — just the way I liked it.

When the ice began to melt, I turned into a Dragon and flew up into the sky. The spectacle the players had effected was hypnotizing and I didn't want to miss a single moment. Red streams of lava from the Mages, golden fire elementals from the Shamans, the Druid's phoenixes sparkling with all the colors of the rainbow, the Necromancers' dark and grim demons...Thanks to the game's physics engine, the ice was melting without any heat or steam, so nothing kept me from enjoying the show.

"Your turn, Svard!" Marle commanded when not a shiver of ice remained. Svard, Gnum and the three taciturn players Svard had brought, stuck a staff into the ground. The top of the staff looked like a gnarled root with other roots sticking out of it. Then the geomancers joined hands and began to circle it. At first I couldn't help but smile, but when the staff's roots began to emit a green fog — a thin snake that darted towards the flaming section of terrain — my smile vanished. The wisps of fog was at once beautiful and terrifying. On their way they pierced several fallen trees as if they didn't notice them. Only the embers that flared up in their wake suggested that the wisps were real and not at all harmless. After ten seconds, the geomancer circle began to slow down, the players' faces grimaced with pain, and yet they went on spinning, performing a ritual only they understood. Reaching the area the glacier had occupied, the tentacles of fog began running its course back and forth and interweaving until they formed a fine grid that looked like a net superimposed over the varying slopes of the terrain.

"Burn it!" wheezed Svard when the net of fog had been completed. He collapsed to the ground as did the other members of the ritual circle. The healers rushed over to heal them, but everything was in vain — all five geomancers had been sent to respawn.

"Revive them and...FIRE!" I'd never imagined that a small girl could scream like that, but the game didn't care about what I imagined. The raid leader's order should have been audible to everyone, so it had to be loud and so forceful that no one would think of questioning what they had to do. Even I tried to spit some fire, but the system helpfully reminded me that Dragon's Breath was unlocked only at Rank 50. At my Rank 16, I had nothing to contribute here. This wasn't a scenario, after all.

"*What's next?*" came Anastaria's thought, returning me to the issue at hand. At some moment I had even forgotten to flap my wings, staring mesmerized at how the stone and ground burned beneath me and as a result almost fell into the pool of fire. I don't know what game mechanics came into effect when the terrain began to change, but an unbearable heat was emanating from the lake of lava, knocking off my HP as fast as an express train. I even had to fly up a little higher to avoid burning up. The lake that had appeared was bubbling and roiling, emitting heat and threatening to incinerate anything living within itself. And yet still, the spectacle was wonderful.

As I was about to answer Anastaria and tell her that I had no idea what to do next, my eyes caught one unexpected phenomenon. A whirlpool. Right in the center of the lake. It wasn't very large and you couldn't see it from the shore due to the constant bubbling, yet it was clearly funneling the lava somewhere inside Barliona. It looked so misplaced in its surroundings that for a moment I didn't know what to do. This thing had no place being here. My epiphany came right away — I realized what I had to do next. Trusting my premonition and the speed of Stacey's reflexes, I flew for the center of the lake, folded my wings and, just before plummeting into its depths like a stone, said telepathically:

"Stacey, a bubble..."

The flaming lake accepted me into its embrace like its own child. At the same time, the countdown timer indicated that I would be treated like a child for a very short time. Just 10 seconds.

Inside, the lake of fire was completely red. I swam as hard as I could deeper and deeper, wishing to reach the end of the funnel in the allotted time, but after five seconds it was clear that I wouldn't make it. Maybe I was just treading lava and the liquid's density didn't allow me to keep diving. Maybe the lake didn't have a bottom at all. In any case — I was staring at the same homogeneous red mixture below me as above and to the right and to the left of me. Stop! The mixture ahead of me looks much lighter! It's like there's a void there!

Stopping my descent, I made several broad strokes forward and, right at the last moments of my bubble, flew out of the lake of melt into some kind of room. A quick glance backwards let me know that this room had no wall: only magma that slowly crawled to fill the space. A shimmering force field I hadn't noticed, was slowing its progress.

"Tell me, esteemed Artificer," sounded an irritated, female voice. I turned to see a raven-haired woman sitting in an ancient armchair that resembled a throne. She was wrapped in a Mage's white shroud and was of indeterminate age. Between 25 and 50. Make up, particularly in-game, is a scary thing. "What made you disfigure my already ascetic abode? Are you really so daft that you couldn't figure out how to reach me by the normal means? Why couldn't you just craft the most barebones of artifacts?"

I was about to open my mouth and ask where the hermit was when my eyes automatically scanned the woman's properties — and promptly got stuck in my throat. The answer to my question was sitting on the throne right in front of me and drilling me with her angry gaze.

The Hermit (Level N/A)

That's impossible! The Hermit had no level! This isn't possible in in Barliona!

CHAPTER SIX
A FRIENDLY VISIT

"**I**S THAT YOUR best imitation of a telephone pole?" the woman inquired with irritation, and waved her hand in the direction of the wall of fire. "You ruined my abode, you invaded my sanctum, caused a bunch of noise on your way in and now you just stand there? Now you're stiller than water, lower than grass — now you're no longer you?"

The Hermit waved her hand one more time and the wall of fire vanished, turning back into ordinary masonry.

"*Dan, what's going on?*" I heard Anastaria's whisper in my head. "*The Lava has stopped moving. You're still alive...Perhaps you should summon me over to you?*"

"*No way!*" the Hermit butted into our conversation shamelessly, shocking me even further. "*You've got no business here!*"

"*Who's that, Dan?*"

"*A nightmare that flies upon wings of night!*" The Hermit sounded like she meant business. "*Stop *distracting your husband. I still need to figure out a punishment for him!*"

"Why a punishment?" I went on the offense, once the system glibly informed me that telepathy doesn't work from inside the Hermitage. Stacey had been blocked. "I'd been ordered to find the Hermit. I did as ordered. There wasn't any requirement about how exactly I was supposed to do this, so I refuse to accept your punishment. As for destroying your abode...Where?" I spread out my arms as if I weren't sure what the lady was talking about. "And by the way, why is it so dusty here? You're a lady and yet you live in such filth...Since when do real players play the roles of NPCs? Is this a scenario?"

"I can send you back," the Hermit muttered angrily and the recently rebuilt wall turned back into the fiery lake. I wonder if this happened only here at this location or if the rest of the lake had turned to lava too. I bet Stacey and the other players are scratching their heads trying to figure out what's going on.

What really stunned me was that I was facing a real NPC. I'd never seen it with my own eyes, but there were all kinds of rumors among the players that Corp officials act the roles of NPCs in certain scenarios, especially if they fall behind on an Imitator's development and behavioral heuristics. At the same time, they have to provide a truthful answer if asked whether they're an NPC or a player. An NPC will hear the question, but won't assign it any significance. They generally don't know anything about the existence of the real world. Over my eighteen months of play as a Shaman and three years as a Hunter, I had only encountered one NPC who knew that something lay beyond Barliona — Prontho, the boss of Pryke Mine. But even he had lost his knowledge once he had entered the wider world. Stop! Pryke! I had huge plans for it! Sakas, the convicts, the desire to hire some people. Why had I forgotten about all of this? My own experience teaches me that in the larger game world, no one's happy to see a player with a red band. I had to take care of this problem as soon as possible.

"I get the impression that your thoughts are far from this place," said the Hermit, still unhappily but now without the notes of anger. "A terrible punishment threatens him yet he's off daydreaming among the clouds. Do tell why you didn't create an artifact like every other creature?"

"It was too obvious," I confessed honestly, shaking my head at the sight of the wall once more returning to its typical brick-based composition. A game's a game, but no one had circumvented the standard game processes — transformations like these would have cost immense amounts of Mana. Or the direct intercession of some divinity that I hadn't yet noticed around me. Or...?

"Standard, you say..." The Hermit interpreted

my pause in her own way, thought a little longer and then quickly said: "All right, we'll assume you've passed the trial and appeared before me. What do you want, Shaman?"

"Honestly, I have no idea what I'm doing here," I blurted out. To be honest I was no less surprised than the Hermit. For a moment her eyebrows began crawling upwards, but she quickly took a hold of herself and put on a mask of implacability, allowing me to continue my thought. How many times have I told myself that I need to watch my tongue, but every time I seem to forget..."I guess the right thing to do right now is to claim how great of an Artificer I am, the hope of this world and simply an ideal student, but I think that those'll just be words. There's no substance behind them."

"Explain," the Hermit sat down on her throne and stared at me with curiosity. "The way I see it, you've reached the peak of Artifact crafting. The Cursed Chess of Balance, the Cursed Dog, the Blessed Visage of Eluna, the altered color of your Artifacts, the Holy Ring of Driall, the Unicorn Horn of Eluna's Blessing, the Lovers' Pendant...This is a very interesting path for an Artificer, so I'm unclear as to what you mean when you claim that there's no substance to your words."

I inhaled and exhaled loudly. I didn't have anything to say. It was odd, but even though a moment before I plummeted into the lake of melted rock I understood perfectly well that I needed the Hermit, now, appearing before her, doubts appeared deep inside of me. Did I really need to step onto the way of the Artificer?

"You're very articulate and so convincing that I bet you've never been rejected," the NPC remarked sarcastically, forcing me to check her properties one more time to make sure that the Attractiveness stat was indeed still among them. I was still facing an Imitator instead of a player. Only it was some kind of a strange Imitator that I'd never encountered before. Even Geranika wasn't this harsh.

"I don't have anything to say," I shrugged. I looked around, noticed a small stool and took a seat without awaiting an invitation. If the Hermit sits in my presence, why should I stay standing? "Until I reached this place, I was entertaining the thought of setting out on the path of the Artificer. I need to complete the Chess Set."

"The Chess Set?" the Hermit frowned. "What Chess Set? You wish to recreate the Cursed Chess Set?"

"What's the Cursed Chess Set have to do with it?" It was my turn to be surprised. "I'm talking about these."

As I said this, I drew the dwarves out of my inventory bag and held them out to the Hermit.

"The Chess Set of Karmadont..."

The Hermit's eyes grew as large as two saucers.

Then, I found myself imprinted into the wall. I didn't even have time to notice what happened. There I was standing a little away from the Hermit offering her the chess pieces — and here I am pressed by some mysterious force into the wall, so hard that I can't even move a finger. And between these two moments, there seemed to be nothing.

"YOU DARED TO BRING THIS KEY HERE?" the woman's voice resounded so loudly that the cave around us trembled. And, I mean, there was a mountain over our heads! "YOU WISH TO REMIND ME OF MY DEFEAT?!"

The hundreds of debuffs that suddenly appeared on my character caused my HP to plummet towards zero with a purpose. The Hermit didn't give me a chance to reply, suggesting that her questions had been entirely rhetorical in nature. She had already decided that I had to be destroyed.

LIKE HELL!

Despite the unbelievable number of status effects, no one had prohibited me from changing into a Dragon, which I decided to do now. I needed only a moment to slip the dwarves back into my bag. My premonition was no longer screaming but rather wheezing raggedly that this entire assault was triggered by the Chess Set and the Hermit wouldn't calm down as long as these remained in my hands. She really had something against the dwarves. I should've shown her the orcs instead...

"A Dragon!" the Hermit whispered pressing me into the ground. I was instantly hit with debuffs blocking any transformation, yet I managed to accomplish the thing I wanted to do in the brief seconds the transformation afforded me — the dwarf pieces that had been plastered to my hand by some game mechanic were now simply in my hand. The offending item had been removed and now I had to establish some kind of civil channel of communication with the enraged woman who had apparently once suffered some great defeat. "How did I fail to guess this from the very beginning?! Who else could craft two cursed items in the very beginning of his way? Who else has such a mind so defiled, so corrupted that he could never imagine something holy? Of course! A follower of the Tarantulas! It was a mistake to show me this key, Dragon! You shall never leave this tomb until the end of your days. Even after that I won't hand you over to Chaos! I shall immure you just as your master did to my husband!"

The Hermit's voice was so steeped in loathing and cruelty, that for several moments I forgot I was in a game and began to panic. My mind succumbed to the horror! The only thing that brought me to my senses was the game interface that continued to sway and waver at the edge of my field of vision — and the 'Exit' button which, thank Eluna, no one could block. I could calmly slip out into reality, make a cup of coffee and return relaxed to deal with the Hermit later.

LIKE HELL! Ain't I a Shaman, or what?

"Kornik, I need help!" I yelled telepathically into the ether, understanding perfectly well that Nashlazar had blocked my ability to do this — a fact that the system helpfully reminded me of. Well I don't give a damn! My teacher should hear me! *"KORNIK!!!"*

No this won't do, I'll need more volume!

The Shaman has three hands...

Long long ago when I was still only setting out on my Way of the Shaman, I happened to get in touch with Kornik while he was in Geranika's captivity by using a Spirit of Air Communication. After I unlocked telepathy, I forgot about this Spirit and the capabilities it offered, but now the time had come to cash it in again. All of my Spirits had been turned off, including this one, and I still hadn't managed to learn them all after returning to the game, but my premonition was telling me that I was moving in the right direction.

...and behind his back a wing...

I was compelled to sing my song in my mind, once and again ignoring the system notification about my inability to summon a Spirit that wasn't in my spellbook. I knew what I wanted, I knew how to do it and all I had to do was keep bashing my head against the system.

...from the heat upon his breath...

The system refused to be bashed by my head. The devs had done a fine job blocking the Shaman's secret skill of ultimately being able to summon whatever Spirit he wished to. Following the update, my class has once again been turned into a humdrum nothing, which no one wanted to play! How are you supposed to live a peaceful Shamanic life in Barliona if you're constantly boxed in and kept from exercising your imagination? Who even needs this kind of treatment...?

Blast it all to hell!

Design mode!

I shoved away the well-lit room that appeared before me like some old and obsolete piece of junk. I needed my native, dark version of design mode that no one would ever forbid me from working in. I can't summon a Spirit — that's a fact that I'll have to abide by. But no one can keep me from crafting one!

In design mode, the Spirit of Air Communication appeared without any questions, as if he had been standing at the entrance to my mind, waiting for his chance to slip through the erected barriers. I created the simplest ring that I could from the materials I had in my bag, unwillingly shoving one of the Diamonds intended for the Pendants in it and using the 'Instill Essence' skill combined the Spirit of Communication with the Diamond. This done, I examined the outcome: Under the rules of item crafting in Barliona, any new creation had to undergo a period of adaptation to the game world. Over several days, a recipe is generated for the item that permits the crafter to craft the physical item in the game. Only then can a player claim to have invented the new item.

I didn't need that right now.

My goal right now wasn't to create a ring. My goal was to get in touch with Kornik. Therefore, if I create the item here in design mode instead of out in reality, then...

Shining candle-fire springs...

You have created a virtual item. You may use it for 31 (Crafting) seconds. The item does not exist in the game world at large.

"Kornik! I need your help."

"Mahan?!" The goblin's surprise was evident even in telepathy. *"How? This time you're definitely barred from communicating telepathically."*

"I'll explain later. I'm sending you my coordinates. I need your help."

"You're with the Hermit? What the hell do you need with that lunatic?"

"At the moment it looks like I'm about to be enslaved forever."

"I need twenty seconds to get ready. She won't give you up without a fight! Hold on!"

The time expired. The ring with the Spirit that I had used to call Kornik turned into a cloud before my eyes. It had performed its purpose in Barliona and no longer needed to exist. Twenty seconds!

Kornik knew that the Hermit wouldn't give me up without a fight. Odd, but that was the way it was. That means I needed to help him. What can an incapacitated player who can't even turn into his human form do? That's right! Only a diversion that no one expects! How I cherish you, Mr. Kristowski! The first group of players seeking their Pendants had already supplied me with Diamonds and all the necessary ingredients. All that was left was to find the time to embody the template in-game. What had happened when I was creating the template? That's right — a big explosion! I'm certain that it won't be any weaker now. The Hermit wants war? Excellent! She will get it! She wants me to take a normal approach and craft some artifact? I'm about to bury her in artifacts! I call on you, oh Pendants! On the count of three!

One!

Two!

Just sign on the dotted line!

Skill increase:

+1 Reputation with the Hermit. Current status: Enmity. Points remaining until Mistrust: 11999.

"Oh mother of our earth!" Kornik's voice seeped through the light that filled the room and plunged it into a haze. "I beg you not to be angry with my student and allow him to tell you his tale."

WHAT?! This is the battle?!

"Don't worry, Harbinger, your student just explained everything to me," the Hermit replied in a satisfied voice. The lighting returned to normal and I saw scorched walls, Kornik on his knees, and the Hermit twice as large as she had been earlier with her eyes closed in pleasure reclining in the throne that was now too small for her. She opened her eyes with visible effort, looked over at me and then at Kornik, then at me again and sighed heavily.

"A follower of Karmadont and his masters is incapable of creating an item of such purity."

"In that case I'll leave you two alone," Kornik got to his feet, smirked and turning to me, added: "I'll be waiting for you tomorrow in Anhurs. You will have to pay a penalty for a false summons. Can you imagine! Summoning me like some errand boy...! Oh the people a poor goblin will have to work with..."

It looked like Kornik couldn't care less that among the Shamans he and I were of the same rank and he had no right to punish me. For him, I had remained the errant student who bungled everything he touched. And who needed to be punished...

"Allow me to see the key one more time, Shaman," the Hermit asked once the goblin had vanished. I retrieved the dwarves and offered them to the tensed up woman. I wonder what is eliciting this reaction in her...

"Yes, this is he..." The cave's owner said after a short pause. "Marvelous...You are following in Karmadont's footsteps and yet you are crafting holy artifacts. How is this possible?"

"Honorable Hermit," I tried to be as respectful and polite as I could. The woman's question was clearly rhetorical, requiring no answer, so I decided to ply my line. "Please explain what you're talking about. Unfortunately, I don't seem to understand and..."

"Enough!" The cave's owner cut me off with notes of anger in her voice. "I have absorbed the energy of your creation and now know you much better than you know yourself. Deep inside, you are anything but well-intentioned and polite. Don't try to appear dumber than you are in actual fact. Call me Linea."

"Okay. In that case, here's what happened..." The Hermit's status was unclear to me, so I decided to simply tell her what connected me with the Chess Set of Karmadont. Beginning with my desire to create the orcs, demonstrating them to Linea there and then, and ending with my realization that I wanted to create the Chess Set as I was crafting the Tourmaline War Lizards. Wishing to develop the topic of Karmadont, I told her everything that I had managed to find out about him — the great Emperor who united the empire of humans, the great creator who crafted unique items among which only the Imperial Throne of Malabar survived to this day. A Hunter who managed to survive where everyone else fell. Linea didn't interrupt me, listening attentively and smiling to herself as I listed Karmadont's achievements. Finally I concluded my monologue. After a short pause, Linea said pensively:

"Human memory is a strange thing. It wishes to remember everything bad and evil that ever happened in history, and yet it is afraid to enter the very source of this darkness. And for this reason, it idealizes it, whitewashes it, imbues it with heroic qualities, while everything good and holy that fought against the darkness is tainted and blackened. I'm afraid I have to disappoint you, Shaman. Karmadont was never a kind and generous ruler. To the opposite! He was the Head Priest of the Tarantulas and really did unite the human tribes into a single empire, massacring everyone else in the process. Learn the true history of this man and then you will understand my reaction to the chess pieces you created..."

Karmadont really was a great man; however, just as with the Dragons he was a great man on the wrong side of history. Linea didn't know how the simple Hunter had earned the power of an Emperor and where he encountered the Tarantulas, to whom he bowed his knee. But one fact was clear — Karmadont gained his power after he returned from his search for the Ergreis. I smirked thoughtfully. There was simply too many signs pointing to the cave whose coordinates some random player was trying to sell to me. My premonition insisted that I wouldn't be able to avoid going there. After he returned, Karmadont assembled an army of followers, seized power in a small kingdom and began to methodically annihilate his neighbors, feeding the souls of his captive foes to the Tarantulas. At the same time Karmadont began to create, wishing to demonstrate to the world the perversity of his essence.

"But the Imperial Throne is not an unholy object!" I cried surprised.

"True. Except that an Emperor who sits on the throne must die in order to leave it. He cannot live even six months without it. Could you really call this a holy object? And keep in mind that Eluna worked on the other aspects of the throne, removing many of them from memory. Even she did not manage to destroy the lifelong bond. Despite his immense might, the Emperor remains a slave of the throne. He loses his freedom the same instant that he places his crown on his head."

In general, Karmadont turned out to be a fairly interesting craftsman. For example, the Altarian Falcon — the scepter of power he created and Geranika's most desired item — turned out to be a banal device for mind-controlling others. The wielder of the scepter could bend the will of any creature and force it to do his bidding. Or the Annihilator, the coordinates to which I received back in Erebus. Karmadont created this item in order to butter up his masters — the Tarantulas. This last bit of news came as an utter surprise to me, since I had figured that it had been Chaos who had created the Annihilator. Everything turned out much more interesting and convoluted. If it weren't for the story with the Dragons — who had in the span of an hour gone from the guardians of Barliona to one of its most terrifying nightmares — I would have never believed Linea. Yet she spoke with such a melancholy smile that I couldn't really doubt her for a second. I needed to review history.

"Therefore, when I saw a piece of the key, destroyed by Karmadont himself, I thought about his return to this world. Want me to tell you something only you know? When you were creating the Chess Set, your Artificer level didn't change. For, this is not an artifact. It is a key."

"The Tomb has already been opened," I said carefully, trying not to stir any unnecessary emotions in Linea. Practice showed that the woman was mercurial and belonged to the tribe of shoot-first-ask-questions-later.

"That's what you think," the Hermit shook her head sadly. "You opened the passage, but you didn't open the Tomb itself. The point of the Chess Set isn't to open something — to the opposite. Karmadont created them with a single goal in mind — to inter the Creator inside. Even if you complete the full set, you won't get inside. The entrance to the Tomb does not exist in Barliona, nor the Tomb itself. I'd have discovered it long ago. Trust me — mountains do not pose much of an obstacle to me."

"Then where does the opened passage lead?" I asked in shock.

"That doesn't interest me. Enough about Karmadont. In my view, Shaman, you are not yet ready to set out on the path of the Artificer. Before moving forward, you must fulfill your duties to the other Free Citizens. Complete the Pendants. Give them to the lovers and then return to me. Then I shall show you what it means to be an Artificer. And now go, you still have much to do."

Quest updated: 'The Creator of the World.' Description: Complete the Pendant quest, fulfilling the orders from players up to the current date. Then, return to the Hermit for further instructions.

I had a hundred questions for the Hermit, but as soon as I opened my mouth, my surroundings wavered and a moment later resolved into the familiar sight of the Elma Mountains, a huge number of players and a tranquil lake of lava. Linea cast me out of her cave like some naughty kitten.

Who was she anyway?!

My return was accompanied by various special effects — there was no other way to explain the attention I received from the crowd of players. They were expecting revelations and explanations from me — such as, for example, why I'd brought them all there. So I had to take a breath and come up with an excuse on the spot.

"A big thanks to everyone! We accomplished what we needed to and got everything we were planning on getting. The Imitator will distribute the rewards among the participants, Marle is hereby named the official leader of the raiders of our clan and you may address any questions you have to her. Thank you again for your quick response time and work. I am confident that we will all see each other soon. I have many plans for further adventures together! By way of an additional bonus, I'd like you to know that our castle portal will be available for your use free of charge for the next week! Viltrius will send you wherever you like whenever you like!"

Judging by the hubbub that ensued among the players, they'd been expecting something more concrete from me — accompanied by a demonstration of unique items I had acquired — and yet I concluded my speech and dissolved among the crowd. Before telling the world the true history of Karmadont, I needed to discuss this news with Stacey. Did it even make sense to do this?

"*Will there be a video?*" Her thought instantly occurred to me.

"*No, it was blocked. I'll tell you everything this evening. What's the news with the Celestial Empire?*"

"*They're coming. They'll be here in two hours. Grab Plinto and let's go. We don't have any time.*"

"*It's a dumb questions, but still — do you have a mole in their clan?*"

"*Just as they do in ours. Don't let the small stuff distract you. We need to stop our guests in their tracks.*"

* * *

Were I a bit more sentimentally disposed, I would say that a crisp sea breeze tussled my hair, while one of the most beautiful women in the world was pressed up against me, her eyes shut in bliss. But the fact was that we had clambered aboard Stacey's ship (which had sailed ahead of time to meet us at the likely landing site of the Celestial Empire fleet) and were now intrepidly rushing athwart the waves and away from the continent, clutching the rigging and trying not to topple overboard from the violent rolling. A storm had settled over the seas.

"Visual contact in ten minutes!" yelled Calran, who had somehow become the captain of Stacey's vessel. I don't even want to imagine what my wife had promised Grygz's right-hand man to entice him over to her 'Freemie' vessel.

"Mahan," Plinto gibed sarcastically, getting comfortable in his catapult basket, "I'll bet anything that your depraved mind is responsible for coming up with this mode of conveyance! Who else could think of shooting players at enemy ships! Tamerlane stop screwing around and hop on board. This ride's about to take off!"

Tamerlane the Wondrous, a tank from Phoenix, tied a rope around his waist that was supposed to keep us tethered together as we traveled through the air and then climbed up to join Plinto in the basket. I couldn't help but crack a smile — the Warrior who was as huge as a buffalo clad in plate armor, crushed the Rogue completely under him, pressing him into the catapult's depths. Plinto uttered a taut grunt and proclaimed a choice, unkind oath against all tanks including Tamerlane. It didn't seem like the Rogue frequently had the opportunity to press up against a large male body. Even if just in the game.

"Visual contact in five minutes!" Calran reminded us spurring me to join the pile. Tying the rope around me, I crawled on top of Tamerlane — who didn't even notice my insignificant addition to his mass. To Plinto's advice that I lose some weight please, I blurted out something prickly, trying to conceal the trembling of my hands: Even though I enjoyed flying a lot, right now I didn't feel like myself. It's not every day that you get catapulted by, uh, a catapult.

"We have visual contact! We're entering the no-fly zone!"

"Ten seconds!" Anastaria commanded immediately. "Nine...Eight..."

The Celestial armada didn't bother trusting fate and destiny, and therefore set up its no-fly zone to be as large as it possibly could be — as far as we could see. The horizon was quickly growing darker with the hundreds of approaching ships. My heart tightened — if we assume that each vessel is carrying a hundred players, then a truly terrifying force is moving against Kalragon. Thousands of ships with a hundred players in each...Stopping an avalanche this immense would be an impossible task.

"Three...Two...One...Blast off!"

My chest compressed, locking in the last breath I took, and my heart collapsed into a point and crawled down to my heels, causing an unpleasant sensation beneath my stomach. And all of this was caused by my own emotions and phobias, since I was still playing with my sensations turned off.

"Wheee!" Plinto cried happily. Forcing my way

through the thick wind, I turned my head and saw the Rogue dangling at the other end of the rope tied to Tamerlane's waist, his arms stretched out as if they were wings. Plinto was savoring the act of flying, something you could not say about our tank. Tense and contorted like an embryo, he was muttering something under his breath. I'm sure that if we would be doing this out in reality right now, a head of broccoli would have envied the green on the Warrior's face.

The Celestial armada was approaching us as fast as a bullet. We hadn't even reached the apex of our trajectory when the first enemy ships began to pass beneath us. The system notified us that there were players (with difficult to pronounce names) targeting us and every second there were more and more of them. Our arrival had not gone unnoticed.

The Celestial Empire was sailing to Kalragon's shores in a broad, expansive formation, in the center of which three solitary ships were moving on their lonesome. Our mission objective. I was happy to discover that I had been right to assume that there would be an area where flying was permitted within the fleet's perimeter. Players mounted on the Celestial analogues of our griffins were darting in barely perceptible dots between the ships below us.

"We need the right one!" yelled Plinto, pointing at the largest ship of the three. How he managed to spy the statue from this height remained a mystery to me, but I wasn't about to argue with him. Turning into my Dragon Form, I pulled the Warrior and Rogue over to me, placed them on my back, spread my wings and barely avoided an uncontrolled fall. Our flight velocity was so great that my wings were almost torn off! Cursing several times for not having found the time to practice this maneuver, I folded my wings and began to extend them little by little, in the hope of lowering our speed. We had almost reached the far side of the armada when I finally managed to open my wings without hurting myself and adjusted our bearing.

"Heh, suckers," smirked Plinto. I didn't share his glee however. The entire perimeter of the armada was littered with Mages who were already summoning help. Appearing on the decks of their vessels, they immediately began mounting pterodactyls and soaring up into the sky. Judging by the number of pursuers now after us, the trajectory of our fall had already been calculated and we'd encounter a warm welcome in another minute or so. Quickly, robustly and professionally — and were we ordinary players, we'd go plummeting to our deaths in the cold waters. But I was a Dragon, so thanks for playing and until next time! Like, subscribe, and all that jazz.

"Tune in next time for the exciting adventures of the Lone Ranger and Tamerlane!" The Rogue was entertaining himself, spurring me like a jockey on a racehorse. I couldn't see behind me, but I'd bet he was waving his arms imitating a lasso. When we're back down on the ground I'll kill that bastard. "Come on, Scout! Put a little more into it! Those flying chickens are gaining on us! Have you forgotten how to fly or what?!"

It only took me several flaps to tear away from our pursuers and smash into the sails of the ship Plinto had been directing us to. I didn't have the time to slow down for a gentle landing. The only thing that I managed to notice before getting tangled up in the rigging was the immense statue of a man with his arm raised upward. The statue was in the middle of the four-masted vessel and the question of how Plinto had noticed it became even more mysterious.

"We're in position! Summoning now!"

We didn't try to risk it. If the choice is between two healers, one of whom is a Level 300 Shaman with a single unlocked Spirit of Healing and the other is a Level 352 Paladin who had several hundred raids under her belt, the choice of the latter is more than evident. Stacey couldn't fly with us, since I didn't have the capacity to carry her; however, we had the unique ability of summoning each other to the other's location, which is what we now used to great effect. While I was dealing with the cordage and canvas that had wrapped me like a cocoon, three high-level Kalragon players rushed at the statue. It had to be destroyed at any price!

"Bravo!" sounded a low male voice to the

accompaniment of clapping. Someone was applauding us. Only now did I notice that there was no other sound aside from my grunting as I struggled to free myself from the rigging. Neither Plinto striking the statue, nor the sounds of spells, nor the cursing of the Celestial defenders. There was no sound at all. I was about to be surprised when I noticed the 'Sphere of Negation' debuff, which blocked all sounds. No one could hear me wheezing besides myself, so nothing bad had happened. But the very fact that there was a sphere around me disheartened me — it takes some time to cast one of those. It would already have to be on the vessel at the time of our arrival.

"They were waiting for us! There's a mole in Phoenix!" Anastaria confirmed my hunch. I became even more disheartened. Are they about to send us to respawn?

"Help the Dragon!" sounded an order and the white canvas shrouding my vision slid aside. I couldn't help but curse when I beheld what was going on around me — our intrepid commandos, Anastaria, Plinto and Tamerlane, were alive and well and standing several meters in front of me, unable to move a muscle. And this was not due to some spell — there was nothing affecting us beside the Sphere of Negation. Everything was much simpler — like a boyband cornered by its fans, the trio was surrounded by Celestial players in an impassable stockade of bodies, arms, legs and other body parts.

The displeasure on Plinto's face demonstrated that he wouldn't be able to rescue us in this situation — after all PvP was disabled here too.

The ship's crew heaved me to my feet and surrounded me. No one even thought of doing damage. In fact our captors generally treated us like esteemed guests, as if this wasn't a game but reality — where human life actually means something. Strange.

One of the players — a Level 389 Warrior named Bihan, brought a hand to his mouth and his voice resounded across the deck:

"We welcome our dear friends from Kalragon to the ship of the Era of Dragons clan! We are especially happy to see a Dragon in their midst! I had heard rumors that one of your players earned the ability to transform into this legendary creature, and today I have seen this miracle with my own two eyes. Please accept my sincere apologies for your inconvenience, but I cannot allow you to destroy my obelisk. We need the Tomb and we shall have it."

I raised my head and beheld another shocking detail — right over my head, my new 'dear' friends from the Celestial were stretching out a net. Even though I had only just now thought of turning into a Dragon and toppling the statue, our continent's guests had eliminated any chance of my suddenly taking flight. We were being outplayed and our opponents stayed several moves ahead constantly.

This was something I really didn't like one bit.

"I invite our guests to my cabin, where we can discuss all these matters in the appropriate setting. No need to struggle, Vampire. As you have already guessed, the PvP ban affects all of Barliona, not simply your continent. Thank you for arranging the tournament!"

Stacey glanced over at me with surprise and immediately lunged forward from a jolt to her back. The Celestial players began to use their bodies to push our trio in the direction of the cabin doors. A bald Level 313 Warrior who had been standing behind Anastaria was trying hardest of all. I didn't hear what he said, but the expression on his face made it clear that he was enjoying pressing up against my wife and letting his arms run free along her body. Stacey couldn't do anything to him — she couldn't even turn around and show this bastard that what he was doing was wrong — so she pursed her lips and took a step forward, and then another. And another. And another.

"Dan, it's okay, he's barely touching me!" Before a white film descended over my eyes, I managed to hear Anastaria's thought. It's too bad that it appeared too late. The bald Warrior was working the crowd, closing his eyes in ecstasy, sending virtual kisses and casting meaningful glances at his neighbors to show what a Casanova he was — and this ugly pantomime was finding a favorable reception among the crowd too. However, there was at least one noble spectator among this clown's audience — me. Anger fogged over my mind, so when the system notified me that I could not cast a Spirit of Lightning at this jerk, I resorted to extremes.

Minor Battle Shadow...The power that Geranika had granted me and which allowed me to summon the enemy of all that lived — the force that sought only to cast Barliona back into Chaos. I'll be a ballerina in a provincial theater if the developers hadn't made the players vulnerable to Geranika's gifts! I selected the Warrior and pressed the Shadow icon with pleasure. The moment of truth had come — was I a ballerina or a Shaman?

When the world vanished, a thought flashed in my mind — I'm not much of a dancer.

Images flickered. The Alabaster Throne from the previous vision. The blackened creature sitting upon it. A crystal in the form of a heart on his knees. Flickering. A laughing man standing before the throne. Flickering. The crystal vanished but the charred creature remained on the throne — impaled on its own staff. The creature was alive! No corpse ever had eyes so filled with pain. More flickering. Geranika, pensively regarding the throne and the creature on it. Flickering. There was neither throne nor Geranika. Only the charred creature surrounded by a hundred small orbs. Crastils!

When Barliona pushed the hallucination out of

my head, the first thing I saw was a thick Shadow coiling like a snake around the Warrior. A look of astonishment filled his face when his HP began to fall — yet this was almost instantly replaced by a malevolent gloat. The Minor Battle Shadow was consuming him only at a rate of a tenth of HP per second. At this rate, I'll be killing this Warrior over the course of several years. The bald player met my eyes and with his laughter showed everything that he thought of me as well as what he was planning on doing to Anastaria.

Bad move on his part...

"Geranika, I require your assistance!" I whispered in an icy voice. My emotions left me as if they'd never been. I felt nothing at all as I looked at the Warrior, eyes rolled back, laughing. Neither hate, nor the desire to kill him, nor wrath. Only cold and ice. Stacey's thoughts were sounding in my head, but my condition didn't permit me to assemble the sounds into meaningful words. At the given moment, I didn't care about anything at all — Reputation, Empires, the game in general and Barliona in particular. The thug was pawing my wife right before my eyes. The thug had to die. There was no other way.

"I am listening attentively, oh Shaman!" Geranika's voice sounded right above my head. The entire deck of the ship had gone quiet. All the players had their faces turned up. They could hear Geranika despite the Sphere of Negation.

"I would like to cast into the Abyss all Free Citizens on this ship that do not belong to my clan." I raised my head and saw the Lord of Shadow standing several meters from me on the taught net. Geranika was again dressed in his typical navy suit — which seemed as natural to Barliona as a submarine to Ancient Egypt.

"Nice request," smirked the former Shaman and, ignoring the net, descended through it to the deck. He pushed away the Celestial players surrounding us with an invisible field, to keep them from interfering with our conversation and getting underfoot. "What would you give me in return?"

"What do you want?" I answered his question with mine. At the given moment, I was ready to agree to anything.

"Two months of service to Shadow," the Lord of Shadow replied, as if he'd been waiting for this moment.

"A week." To everyone's surprise, especially mine, I began to barter by reflex. Geranika shook his head.

"Two months, Mahan. Two months. You will do my assignments, as strange as they might seem to you. No questions, no demands, no explanations. In return I will grant you the ability to destroy the Free Citizens on this ship here and now."

"I don't need the power to kill them," I cut him off, understanding that having to respawn wouldn't hurt the bald player one bit. "I need to send them to the Abyss."

"Oh! The Shaman knows his way around punishment!" Geranika said, surprised. "Everyone's used to seeing you as a docile little lamb, and here it turns out that you're a real bad apple! I have a condition. You..."

"What's going on here?" Bihan roared emerging from the hold. I suppose that someone had told him through the chat that something was going off plan, so the head of the clan decided to personally dispense his punishment. "Who dared enter my..."

"Silence," Geranika barked with irritation. He waved his hand and everyone on the ship turned to statues in the manner I'd seen back in the Dark Forest. The Lord of Shadow had not lost any of his powers.

"As I already told you, I decided to change the terms of my assistance to you," Geranika turned to me, as if nothing had happened. In my peripheral vision I could see dozens if not hundreds of players on flying mounts smash against an invisible sphere that had appeared around the ship — slipping along its circumference into the sea, unable to reach their goal. Summoned by my call, the head of the Empire of Shadow made sure to keep us safe. "I will send everyone on this ship, aside from your clan mates, to the Abyss. In exchange you will take part in the tournament under the banner of the Empire of

Shadow. What do you say?"

"*Dan, what the hell are you doing? What Shadow?*" Anastaria broke through my stuttering mind, but before I could find something to reply, Geranika got ahead of me and demonstrated that an NPC of his level has no problem reading telepathy:

"What Shadow? Why the finest Shadow in all of Barliona, I assure you," he said. "There are several Free Citizens who have chosen the way of the Shadows, but they are singular and aren't capable of organizing a tournament. I need Mahan precisely to show all of Barliona that the best fighters fight for me. Everything else is a cheap imitation."

Quest available: 'The Shadow Warrior.' Description: During the tournament, you will fight for the Shadow faction. Lead its players at the tournament! Reward: Friendly status with the Lord of Shadow, the Emperor of Malabar, and the Dark Lord of Kartoss.

"I agree. Send them to the Abyss," I cut off all ways of retreat and agreed to a catastrophic drop in my Reputation with the monarchs of the two empires. Given that I had Exalted status with the Emperor and the Dark Lord, agreeing to a decrease in this status...To hell with it! This is a game after all! I can always win it all back! And if not, to hell with it again!

"Wonderful!" Geranika smiled sincerely, and

unable to contain himself rubbed his hands like a pawn shop dealer. "Very nice doing business with you, Mahan! Until we meet at the tournament! And, oh yes, I am very sorry about Tamerlane..."

I froze, unable to understand the meaning of these words, yet when the ship emptied as at a wave of a magic wand, I cursed earnestly — the Phoenix's tank had been on the ship and yet wasn't in my clan. In accordance to our agreement, Geranika dragged him down to the Abyss too.

Ehkiller will, eh, kill me.

If Stacey doesn't do it first.

"What happened here?" Bihan asked menacingly, once he'd regained the ability to speak.

"Plinto, the statue!" I ordered, trying to avoid looking at Stacey, who was standing still now due to my own actions rather than Geranika's orders. I'd figure things out with her later. In the evening when she eats my brain. At the moment only two things concerned me — the obelisk that Plinto needed ten minutes to deal with and Bihan, who for some reason had stayed on the ship. I didn't have anything against the NPC sailors staring at us anxiously from the masts. But the player should have been sent to the Abyss!

"Deal's off, Geranika! You left one of the Free Citizens on the ship!" I shouted into the air, understanding that under the game mechanics he'd hear me even on the other end of Barliona.

"The Lord of Shadow made no mistake, Dragon," said a dark-haired woman emerging from the hold, demonstrating a fine understanding of Kalragon's geopolitics. I did a double take — the woman had bare appendages that resembled spider legs or wings that had been picked clean sticking out from behind her back. Azari the Patient (such was the name of the Level 400 Priestess) watched closely as Plinto set upon the obelisk. I shuddered even more — the appendages were alive! This player could actually control the spindles on her back! "Every player *was* sent to the Abyss."

"These two are golems. Perfect clones of the real players that the players can control from afar," Anastaria said without looking away from me. "Mahan, meet Azari the Patient. Race — Kumo. She's a were-spider. Her appearance should tell you as much. She likes artifacts. She's the deputy head of the Era of Dragons clan. And she's also a proper bitch."

"The great Anastaria. A Paladin Healer. Siren. The brains of the Phoenix clan who abandoned it all for her husband," Azari didn't remain in Stacey's debt. "A hysterical and useless doll that has nothing aside from a cute face and her daddy's money."

Azari smirked and as she did so the obelisk collapsed from a pretty statue into a pile of rocks. Got it!

"Two minutes! Fascinating!" Azari hummed,

nodding her satisfaction. "I was hoping to occupy Plinto for five minutes, no less."

"*Goddamn it!*" Stacey cursed telepathically. "*This is a set up!*"

"Judging by your calm face, you've already understood," smirked Azari. "I suggest we head down to the hold and discuss the terms of your capitulation. I don't think anyone has anymore doubts that our clan will be able to entrench itself on Kalragon territory. By the way, what is the Abyss? Where did you send our players?"

CHAPTER SEVEN

BETRAYAL

"**P**OLARIUS LIQUOR, highly recommended," Azari decided to play the role of the welcoming host, offering us a drink. Understanding that there wasn't much else to do, we passed into Bihan's captain's cabin and took our seats around a small round table. In doing so, the head of the Celestial Empire took the only armchair, allowing us to choose from a red and green chair. Even though the round table made everyone equals, someone wished to show that he was more equal.

"*Stacey, why weren't they sent to the Abyss?*" I was still beset by the mystery. Geranika couldn't avoid fulfilling our agreement to a T; otherwise the system would've already punished him and freed me from the stupid quest. As soon as the bald Warrior had vanished, my ability to think clearly returned to me and with it the shock of my forthcoming drop in Reputation. But there was nowhere to run — I would have to represent Shadow at the tournament.

"*Because these aren't players. Or rather, these*

aren't the players' characters."

"Erm…"

"Judging by your furrowed brow, I'm sure you two are having a fascinating exchange on the telepathic channel," Azari didn't bother concealing that she knew all about our ability to communicate without speaking aloud. I was about to freak out that the Priestess knows too much when her next words put everything in place. She didn't know a damn thing! "I received a notification that you've already crafted my Pendant, Mahan. When will you send it to me?"

"Speak to my manager," I replied, sighing in relief in my mind. This spider needed a Pendant and that's what she thinks we're using to speak to one another. This means that if something goes wrong, she will try to block the item and not a unique ability. That alone was good news. By the way! "So why aren't you two in the Abyss? Any player who isn't in my clan should have been sent for a time-out in that closed location, and even Mages wouldn't be able to get you out, so you simply shouldn't be here. Yet you're still here!"

"So that's what the Abyss is," Azari smiled. "I'm even curious about the penalty you had to pay. Sending a hundred players to a closed location through an NPC…Your karma should have taken a hefty blow."

"You didn't answer my question," I insisted

once more. "Why aren't you in the Abyss?"

"Because I'm not here to begin with. Neither I nor Bihan are on the ship at the moment."

"And we're speaking to ghosts?" I gibed, though Plinto's eyes made it clear that there wasn't anything funny about my joke.

"Not quite ghosts. Didn't your lovely girlfriend tell you about the singular and unparalleled beauty — I mean myself here — who has been crushing her in every possible and impossible battle for the last four years? Raid tactics and strategy, improvisation in the face of evolving situations, decision-making accuracy, an actual social life outside of the game. She's only second. Everywhere and always! The one time that she surpassed me was the one time I didn't compete — I mean the Miss Barliona contest. Nature must compensate for a lack of intelligence, so it granted her a homely appearance. But even there, this doll only managed to earn second place. Habit, I suppose. She's just so..."

"Maybe you'll stop demonstrating to the whole world how much you envy my wife?" I interrupted Azari's fascinating monologue. "You didn't answer my question."

"Why should I answer it at all, Shaman?" The Kumo asked surprised. "You're not in a position to dictate terms. This ship is surrounded by thousands of players who want nothing more than to tear you into little pieces. Only the will of my master keeps them from doing so. I'll be the only one doing the talking here, while you agree to my terms and sign on the dotted line. Do you understand?"

Azari decked the last question in so much ice and charisma that if we'd been out in reality I'd already be a piece of ice sitting in front of her and trying to make myself even smaller and less noticeable. But we were in Barliona and this silly girl had permitted herself to say some bad words about my wife. So I have the full moral right to forget about decorum. I'm really getting sick of everyone walking all over me today!

"Big words," I began to work myself up. "Dictate. Master. Dotted lines. Capitulation...Do you even know how to speak normally? Are you like this in real life or are you just taking this roleplaying thing too seriously? Personally, I understand one thing clearly — if you don't tell me why you stayed on this ship, you can forget about the Pendant. It's like you're trying to frighten a porcupine with the sight of your bare ass. Don't you need that item, or what?" Using the search filters, I quickly found the Pendant pair in question, which I had created in the Hermit's cave. Making their properties accessible, I went on:

"It just so happens that I couldn't give a damn about what a certain Azari the Patient and Niaz the Triumphant thinks of me. I'm even ready to compensate them if you don't end up receiving the Pendants in exchange for the work you've done for my clan. You do remember that you're going to have to work for me, don't you? Practice shows that you can't quite pick me apart at the moment — it's just not the right time of day — so you can take all your players, restrained by this windbag that, in your feeble mindedness, you call your master," I pointed at the grimacing Bihan, "and shove the lot of them into a location whose name is currently blocked by the profanity filter. And now that we've measured and established who's longer and thicker, I suggest we get back to a more constructive conversation. I'll repeat the question — why did you remain on the ship?"

"Dan, you're really asking for trouble here..."

"Hell with it. Who are they, Stacey?"

"Golems. Dolls that the players can control. At one of the competitions..."

"Why do you need this information?" Bihan asked calmly, interrupting Stacey.

"So that I can understand how I can kill you next time," I replied with befuddlement at having to explain something so evident.

"Your position is not entirely clear to me, Shaman," Bihan went on. "Or your demands. You can read all about the golems in any Barliona FAQ. Anastaria will explain to you why I am only at Level 389 when practically all my warriors have passed the Level 400 milestone. There's nothing left but to consider that you have found yourself out of your depth and wish to provoke a conflict. Correct me if I am mistaken."

"You're absolutely right," I nodded. "This situation cannot be resolved by anything short of a conflict. You wish to gain access to the Tomb. I don't want you in there. As for my position and demands...I am still waiting for an answer."

"Azari, be so kind as to satisfy our guest's wishes," Bihan was so calm and reasonable that I began to feel out of my element. I'm behaving like a quarrelsome newbie who'd first stepped into Barliona and decided that this game world owed him everything. And everyone else is speaking to me accordingly.

"As master wishes..."

As difficult as it was to admit it, the information wasn't worth a half-eaten egg. At the second intercontinental competition, the subject of the crafting contest was a recipe for golems — an avatar's in-game clone. Depending on the Engineering skill and the 'Golem Control' parameter that was unlocked the first time a golem was controlled, a player could substitute his avatar with this golem for six hours a day. A golem's death didn't affect the avatar or its stats, so Bihan made a very interesting decision — he deleted his character and created a new one from scratch. Using his clan's resources he leveled up to maximum at the training grounds and through the use of quests and mobs without dying a single time. When the time came to enter the larger world — since even the training grounds have their limits — Bihan entered as his golem instead of his actual character. The player only received half of the XP that the golem earned, but even this was enough to level Bihan up to Level 389 at the current moment and he was thus the only player who was higher than Level 200 and who hadn't ever once had to respawn. Each hundred levels without death endowed Bihan with insane bonuses and the higher he was above Level 100 the greater the bonuses were. There wasn't much remaining until the next milestone — a mere 11 levels — at which point Barliona would be in awe of the reward that the Corporation would grant to Bihan.

"This information isn't secret and is accessible to any player who is even slightly curious," Azari concluded, smirking sarcastically. "However, the Shaman wishes to match his spouse in intelligence as well as behavior."

"Here's your Pendant," I slid the item over to Azari, maintaining a poker face as I did so. Despite my inner displeasure with my own behavior and the current situation in general, I had to ply my line to its conclusion. "It's too bad that I had to insist on Bihan's assistance to remind you of your position in your clan's food chain. I mean, serving the drinks, telling the fairy tales and pleasuring master between the sheets. Everything else should be left to the big boys. I thought that the East was big on subordination. When a woman goes too far and begins to show off the sting of her tongue, don't they immediately cut it short? Either I'm wrong, which is unlikely, or you're really a man who's somehow convinced the Corporation to let him play with a female avatar. By the way, that would explain why you weren't at that beauty contest. Who would allow you to..."

"How dare you?!" Azari screamed jumping up from the table. Her face acquired a strange gray hue and it suddenly became very crowded in the cabin. There was the sound of splintering planks, Bihan's surprised grunting, I was pressed into the wall and two enormous yellow eyes appeared before me. A Dragon!

"I think I should take some lessons from you," Plinto wrote in the clan chat. *"No one's ever pissed her off this much. Not even me!"*

"Danny boy, you've just earned yourself a terrible enemy!" Stacey echoed Plinto, telepathically. *"Oh how I cherish you!"*

"KILL! DEATH! HUNGER!" Somewhere deep inside my mind, I heard the thundering voice of the Dragon that had pressed me into the wall. At first I decided that Azari had transformed into a Dragon, stripping me of my status of the only Dragon in Barliona, and became upset. Then I recalled that Fleita too was already a Dragon and I became upset even more; however, checking the creature's properties raised my spirits. A pet! This was only

Azari's pet, though how and where she acquired it remained a mystery. But either way, this beastie can't do anything to me. PvP is forbidden. And that's a good thing because I wasn't certain about the battle's outcome — judging by the size of this mug, this guy's dimensions could even give me a run for my money, to say nothing of Draco.

"KILL THE ENEMY! EAT THE ENEMY!" The Dragon continued to amp himself up, after which he opened his enormous, toothy mouth and spat a stream of flame at me. I didn't even manage to shut my eyes from surprise when for the second time I found myself in the middle of a lake of fire. And if the first time I had Stacey's bubble to protect me, then now I was simply standing in the center of a fire tornado and looking on with surprise as Durability bars appeared on the cabin's walls and rushed as quickly as a boy to his first date toward zero.

"Why?" I managed to ask the Dragon before everything suddenly stopped. Never responding to my question, the Dragon vanished in an instant, leaving not even a slight wisp of smoke in his wake. I pried myself from the wall and looked around — the cabin had turned into a large, charred chamber. Stacey and Plinto were standing next to walls that had been burned through in several places, looking around bewildered. Neither Azari nor Bihan were with us. The fire had incinerated their golems.

"As for how we can kill them," muttered Plinto,

critically examining his daggers, "we could simply burn them. Tell me, oh my beauty, why was there an ambush here? Did Phoenix acquire another Hellfire?"

I frowned, not quite understanding Plinto's implication, but Stacey's answer cleared it up for me: He was talking about the mole. Someone in Phoenix was spilling info to the Celestial Empire.

"I propose we step over to the neighboring ship and continue our conversation there." Utterly unfazed, Bihan appeared in the cabin's door. "Unfortunately, this seafaring transport will soon have to be scuttled. And just so we don't have to waste time negotiating an answer to the question that Mahan is clearly forming in his head, I'd like to state that each of the central ships has three golems. Esteemed Vampire, you may naturally kill them, but I would like to conclude our conversation on a positive note for everyone. I don't see the sense in fighting, considering that Ehkiller and I have already agreed to everything."

"WHAT?!" I'd never seen Anastaria so shocked. Even outside of Beatwick when she was trying to use the Siren's venom on me and failed, she had managed to control herself. Now, however, her shout had burst from her so naturally that it was clear that she wasn't aware of what was happening.

"I will repeat my offer — let us please move to the neighboring ship where we can discuss everything..."

Azari did not join us this time. Either she didn't

have any spare golems or she was on another ship bawling and sobbing and unable to come visit with us, since Geranika's sphere didn't disperse, or maybe Bihan simply forbade her from appearing before him. After all, despite the constructive conversation ahead of us, I wouldn't let anyone speak ill of Stacey. Even someone some mega-epic winner of everything and all.

"What do you think the Tomb of the Creator is?" Bihan began in a roundabout manner. "Why did I decide to invest so many resources of my clan in order to reach it? We're sailing to another continent after all. We've even picked a fight with a very interesting trio — a Dragon, a Siren and a Vampire. Why would I try to explain all this to you? What did I need any of this for? Do you really think that it's all over a simple Dungeon? That I would seek Mahan's collaboration to complete a Dungeon just so I could sell some Epic or Legendary items for a profit?"

"*Stacey, is he trying to muddle us or something?*"

"*I'm afraid not...Let's listen to what he has to say.*"

This is when things got interesting. When I opened the Tomb of the Creator in Kalragon, the High Mages of all the other continents beheld a vision: The Tombs on their continents were fake. The Corporation had eliminated the doubles and to ensure that we'd still have fun, resorted to the trick of Prophecy — our

Tomb had to be sealed.

Bihan even showed us a unique quest that the heads of the three leading clans of the Celestial Empire received from the Emperor. If I skip the boilerplate, the gist was simple — search, destroy, seal. Under no condition could they kill the Dungeon's final boss. Even approaching him was forbidden. For, the Tomb of the Creator is the heart of all evil in Barliona. There sure is a lot of evil wandering around on our continent lately.

"Several days ago I contacted Ehkiller with an offer and today we've come to terms about all the main points of our agreement. The Era of Dragons and Phoenix have become allies and shall work together to defend the Tomb from the other clans. The plan is to slay the first two bosses with your cooperation, earning whatever rewards we can, and then detonate an Armageddon Scroll in the Tomb, sealing it for all eternity. No one will ever reach the center of this Dungeon. Victor, please confirm this."

"That's right," came Ehkiller's voice and only now did I notice a comms amulet in Bihan's hand. "The Tomb must be sealed...I have information that the Dragon of Shadow that Geranika is currently raising as quickly as he can will be an utter lamb compared to what the Tomb might unleash. The Corporation has been looking for a chance shake things up in Barliona for a long time. We cannot allow it to do so."

"So why didn't you stop us?" I blurted out. "What is all this masquerade with the raid on the obelisk for?"

"Bihan knew we were coming," Stacey began to figure out with barely concealed anger. "They wanted to test their warriors. Three central ships is bait for an Armageddon Scroll. All of Barliona knows about how much you love to set off fireworks. They chose a sacrifice, created a statue and sailed forth to see who's worthy of the raider rank. I didn't see any of their main guys. There wasn't any particular information about PvP being banned on the seas, so they placed the ships in the center and..."

"It was edifying to see what the Vampire and Dragon are capable of," nodded the head of the Celestial clan. "In view of the coming tournament, this is very useful information."

"What's our tournament to you?" Stacey frowned, yet there was another question bugging me.

"In that case, where's the obelisk?"

"I imagine somewhere right near our continent," Plinto spoke up. "On an ordinary merchantman, with a basic escort of three to four ships, no more. To scare the pirates away. You borked your Squidolphin and there's no other in these waters, so..."

Attention: Tomb of the Creator level has increased. New Level: 483.

"I see..." I drawled sadly, seeing the fateful notification.

"I'd like to point out," Bihan smiled, "that in the next eight hours, members of another twenty clans from our continent will land on yours. As for the tournament — Ehkiller as the organizer offered us to take part as invited guests. The Emperor liked the idea so much that he sent invitations to all the leading clans of Barliona. Including, as it now turns out, to Geranika, who will be sending Mahan. Does that answer all you questions?"

"You made a deal with Ehkiller, not with me." The rabble rouser in me awoke. For some reason everyone decided to make decisions for me again. I hate that. In this case, the time has come to express my displeasure. Even if the decision that had been forced on me was the right one. "If you don't remove your obelisk and your ships from our continent, Level 400 without respawning will remain a fantasy for you."

"You are threatening me?" Bihan arched an eyebrow in surprise.

"Calm down, Mahan," Ehkiller's voice said from the amulet, but I decided to go to the end. This is my Way!

"No, I'm not threatening anything. I'm promising you," I said curtly, shrugging my shoulders. "If you decide to take the Tomb from me, I'll take your achievement in exchange."

"I'm curious how you'd do that," Bihan smirked. "Will you throw slippers at me?"

"Why waste slippers?" Plinto interrupted, twirling his stilettos. "He's got me. Several weeks of work and I'll find whoever. It's strictly a technical problem."

"Think about it. And make your decision." It took all my self-control to keep a smile from plastering across my face. Plinto was with me! "We're going to go. Killer, where are you right now? We need to talk...Plinto, send this dud back to maintenance," I pointed at Bihan and a second later the golem collapsed in a pile of pebbles on the floor. I didn't have to ask the Rogue twice.

Putting aside the question of why we still had the ability to kill golems, while they couldn't hurt us in return, I blinked into Phoenix's main castle. Before leaving the ships, I managed to notice some wispy essence resembling a Shadow flit out of the golem and zoom away through the side of the vessel. Why look at that! If we assume that this is the gaming version of the golem's spirit, which the player controls and this spirit just flew not to another golem but back to its owner, then...Something tells me that a very curious job awaits Plinto shortly.

"I'm going to go for a stroll," said the Rogue when we reached Ehkiller. Whistling a cute tune, he set off for the doors with a slight jig, unwittingly attracting attention to himself. I shook my head in wonder. Who would think that this person is far older than 30! Plinto was so unfettered and unrestrained in the game that the only thing that occurred to you when you met him was whether he was a kiddo or a student.

"Ehkiller, do I understand correctly that you just betrayed us through and through?" I asked a minute after the door shut behind Plinto. Stacey and her father were playing the staredown game, without making a single sound, so I had to remind them that I was there too.

"Dan, he and I need to speak alone," came Anastaria's thought and immediately, without looking away from his daughter, Ehkiller added:

"We need to speak alone. Mahan, go join Plinto."

I froze. On the one hand, Stacey had asked me. On the other hand, Killer was tossing me out like an errant kitten. Go have a walk, boy, while the adults have a chat. What am I supposed to do here? To hell with all this! I sat down in the nearest chair, smiled widely and shut my eyes.

"I'm not going anywhere, Stacey. Cast a shroud of silence. I'm not a dog."

The shroud was cast in short order. All I could do was watch Stacey and her father calmly listen to each other in turn and then argue their case. But soon, the 'in turn' part was forgotten and both began to talk without listening to the other. After that the 'calmly' part went too, first on Ehkiller's part and then Anastaria jumped to her feet and began to gesture with her hands. When the two began to scream, it became clear that the negotiations had reached a dead end.

"Come on back, Plinto. We're leaving," Stacey's message appeared in the clan chat. I looked at her with surprise. Inhaling deeply with her fists clenched, Stacey was listening to Killer who was waving his hands almost in front of his daughter's face.

"Mahan, teleport us to the Tomb." As soon as Plinto entered the hall, Stacey stepped out of the shroud of silence and headed toward us with her head held high. Pursed lips, clenched fists, a straight back, narrowed eyes — I'd give so much to have heard what they had discussed. Or rather, what they had yelled about. I'd never seen Stacey this angry.

"Magdey, step aside please," Anastaria growled in a whisper when we appeared at the plateau before the Tomb. Or rather on the only path that led to it. The teleport had worked as it should have — it determined the coordinates of the location, checked to make sure that it was possible to teleport us there, discovered that the given coordinates were occupied and began to search for the nearest available egress point. It so happened that the nearest location for three players was a hundred meters from the entrance and not even on the clearing itself. The path to the Tomb was cluttered with players from the

Celestial and Phoenix clans, who were now acting as living shields.

"Direct orders from the head of the clan — not to let anyone through, especially you," Phoenix's chief raid leader replied with a shrug. "Speak to Ehkiller if you have questions."

"Kid, it looks like you forgot who hired you," Anastaria's voice was so cold that I took several steps back. Even if PvP was disabled, it's still hazardous to stand next to an angry Siren. And I have to see her *in reality* later.

"Direct orders from the clan head," Magdey reiterated. "I can't let anyone through to the Tomb without his personal permission. And I don't have that."

"I love mortals," smirked Plinto, stepping up beside Stacey. "Are we going to break through Stacey?"

"Direct orders from the clan head," Magdey parroted, stunning us with his impassivity. "In a word, flying over the plateau is forbidden."

"Bastards!" Anastaria whispered/growled again and her avatar dissolved in the surrounding world. The girl had exited to reality.

"You know, Mahan," Plinto looked up at the sky and made a face like he had a toothache, "my advice is don't leave the game for a few hours. We've been betrayed and Stacey needs to cool off. If you get in her way right now, you'll both be sorry later. Have you and Serart figured out the clan's future yet? I think it's a good time to deal with that issue."

It was hard not to agree with Plinto. I'd never seen Anastaria in such a state before. I really didn't want to exit. It wasn't that I was scared of the girl's ire, rather I really didn't want to yell and argue with each other. Stacey needed time to decide for herself how she felt about her father's decision to betray the Tomb to the Celestial. Under no circumstances should I interfere in that process.

I spent four hours with Mr. Kristowski and by the end, my brain had gone to a fine organic gray mush full of numbers and charts. The most stupefying thing was the situation with the tournament. Arranging a teleport into Altameda for an immense number of people would cost me an insane amount of money that neither the Corporation nor Phoenix were about to compensate me for. At the same time, I couldn't back down — direct orders from the Emperor, that stuffed windbag. I hope that my monopoly on all commerce in Altameda's vicinity — which I had as head of the region — would somehow cover these costs.

On the whole, the clan's economy was stable, thanks to the labor force of players wishing to receive their Pendants. Manufacturers, craftsmen, gatherers, hunters — the clan was enjoying unbelievable opportunities for development, even if temporarily. Mr. Kristowski even managed to find several Sculptors among the lovers and send them to help Spiteful Gnum — another personal headache of mine. As a craftsman, Gnum was unparalleled — he had repaired Altameda's gates, added new defensive works to the castle, made several extra defensive statues and slowly inched Altameda up to Level 27. But at the same time, Gnum was a black hole in the ledger. Or a red hole if I'm permitted an accounting pun. Under orders from me to provide the gnome with whatever he required, Mr. Kristowski had summoned and paid for the transfer of three players with insane Engineering stats from a neighboring continent, doing so without blinking an eye. After all, according to Gnum there were a bunch of klutzes working on our continent who had arms growing out of their...Serart didn't bother pumping the gnome for information, but it was clear that this player had decided on some new improbable venture. Svard and his team began to show up in Altameda like it was their home. Gnum had outfitted an elaborate workshop for himself and it was already the third week that he was in it without emerging, passing his instructions through the amulet and not allowing anyone but Viltrius to come in. Even the invited Engineers and Svard with his gang were forced to work in a neighboring building, a second workshop. Or — what bothered me the most

— the former armory. A minus to defense. In general, I needed to figure out as quickly as possible what Gnum was up to in there. For, two and a half million gold a week over some possible fancy of his was too steep a price. Even for a high roller like myself.

And yet, Gnum notwithstanding, the Legends of Barliona clan was enviably stable in the financial sense. There wasn't some crazy growth, but we were in the black in the ledger — two million clean profit a week with our salary costs, property taxes for the castle and payments for the NPCs being made flawlessly. If it weren't for the tournament which promised to consume all of the liquid capital we had at the moment, we would grow and grow.

At the end of our meeting I received a new list of Pendant orders from Serart — and reclined wearily back in my chair. It would be too wasteful to deal with the 'financial red hole' later, so I asked Viltrius to summon the manic gnome to me.

"He won't come, master," the goblin drawled apologetically. "His Craftiness is occupied."

"His who?"

"His Craftiness," Viltrius repeated dutifully. "His Craftiness ordered that he be called 'His Craftiness.' Your orders to me are to aid His Craftiness in every endeavor, so I didn't bother running this question by..."

"Enough!" I interrupted the goblin. "Remember: His name is Gnum! Nothing else! Got it?!"

"Yes, master," a smile appeared on the goblin's face. "No more 'Your Craftinesses,' no more concubines and no more orgies — is that correct?"

"ORGIES?! IN ALTAMEDA?!" Viltrius managed to do exactly what Ehkiller had done to Anastaria several hours ago: Yank me from my relaxed state. "WHERE IS HE?!"

Viltrius reached out and touched me and the castle walls wavered, dissolved and reformed into a wooden door from behind which I could hear moans of pleasure come filtering in a steady stream. Someone was getting his rocks off and all that was happening in my castle! I'll kill that scumbag.

"GNUM!" I completely lost my temper and kicking down the door, barreled into the workshop. This is my castle! I'm the owner around here! "WHAT THE HELL?!"

"Oh! Mahan! Hello! Just the guy I was looking for!"

I froze in the doorway, shocked by what I saw. Gnum hadn't simply arranged a workshop for himself — he'd created a monster! Several of the walls had been demolished, turning the space into one giant hall, in the center of which stood an immense heap of machinery. An army of succubi roiled all around it, diligently hammering and screwing various parts to its body, moaning in pleasure as they labored.

"Mahan, I'll need a Squidolphin," Gnum went on unfazed, tearing himself away from his examination of various schematics, a portion of which was hanging from his work table. Tossing his hair, Gnum went on as if nothing odd was happening: "When are you going to go catch one?"

"What is this?" As soon as I saw that there wasn't an actual orgy happening in the workshop, I began to regain control of my temper. Externally, at least. What the hell did Gnum bring all these succubi here for?!

"Scram, you little green rat!" Gnum hissed at Viltrius who had peeked from behind my back, causing the goblin to flee with a squeal.

Once he was sure that we were alone, Gnum continued:

"This is the *Valor of Gnum I*. I have to admit the name isn't the best. So you still have the option of changing it. The options are *Valor of Gnum I* or *Gnum, Craftsman Inimitable* or..."

"I'll ask you again — WHAT IS THIS?!" I began to lose the temper I'd regained.

"What do you mean?!" Gnum asked surprised. "Didn't I tell you? This is the first ever airborne-transport-assault vehicle of Barliona. And what's more is that no-fly zones don't apply to it. This little sparrow can fly wherever you like — in Malabar in Armard, even in another world! It has cargo space for up to 300 players, ballistae and its own flight jammers, active magic absorbers, and a full set of dishware and silverware that I had to order bespoke from a guy named Beaux. Look, I even pinstriped the nose..."

"Gnum, did you just introduce military aviation to Barliona?" I cut off the gnome who was beginning to lose himself in his babble.

"What do you mean introduce?" Gnum reproached me. "I invented it! Though I need an engine for it. Without it, this thing won't fly. The Squidolphin. A half-living creature that plays the role of a ship. If I place it in the middle of my power unit, the energy created should be enough to..."

"Stop! What the hell do I need this thing for?"

"Erm...What do you mean what the hell for? To fly around."

"I can fly around as it is!"

"There's a difference between flying and flying! When you fly, can you attack anyone? Aha! See? With this sparrow you'll be able to..."

"Gnum, hold on," I drawled, sighing deeply and dispelling my irritation. "Tell me, why are you doing this?"

"Erm...Well to do it. This is a flying ship! There's never been one like it in Barliona! If we equip it with weapons, we'll be able to capture any castle we like. Their defenses aren't calculated for something like this! Or..."

Gnum began to expostulate all the advantages of having the first aircraft in the game, while I stood before him unsure of what to do. Punishing the gnome and stripping him of funds would strip my own clan of a very useful member who could repair anything as well as create new items from scratch. But to allow him to spend money on...well, 'junk' was the only word that came to mind...WHY would I need this?

"...And so that's why I need a Squidolphin," Gnum finished his thought. "When are we going to go find it?"

"Are you going to kill it?" I asked wearily.

"Pff! What am I, a moron? To the contrary — it's all going to revolve around the Squidolphin! This is Barliona after all — you can do anything in it as long as you have a good foundation. So the Squidolphin will remain herself. Only she'll be inside my power contour. She'll still level up, gain experience, grow. Only inside a shell. I was going to use the tentacles to..."

"Here," I pulled the embryo (that had basically been covered with non-existent dust) out of my bag and handed it to Gnum. "And it better fly. You have a month. Are there any questions?"

I couldn't explain my sudden largess. Was it premonition? No, I didn't feel any sense of right or wrong. Logic? Like hell! Logic and I don't gel...Prophecy? Don't make my slippers laugh. There wasn't anything but my own foolishness that could explain this. I just wanted it!

"This is perfect, Mahan!" exclaimed Gnum,

slipping the embryo in his bag. "Listen, I'm going to make one more call right now — we'll need more workers. Come by in a week and I'll show you what I have."

"By the way, what the hell do you need succubi for?"

"Well, the project's a secret but someone's got to do the work. So I have to work with what I have. Can you imagine the surprise in Barliona when my sparrow appears over Anhurs?! Or over some castle? We'll have to work on the bombs. There's already countermeasures to magic...we'll see how my absorbers handle what those Mages throw at them!"

I didn't bother explaining to Gnum what his experiments were costing us and I didn't inquire what would happen if the ship didn't fly or what would happen if...A million 'ifs' that I kept to myself as I looked at the gnome who'd forgotten I was even there. He had already dragged over some tub and the succubi were filling it with water, so that even now a gestation timer was ticking away over the tub with the Squidolphin embryo in it. In two days, there'd be a new monster in this world.

Lifting the fallen door in silence, I closed the entrance and pensively headed toward the central building. Despite all his zaniness, I really liked Gnum. I respected his drive, his confidence in himself and his puzzlement at how other people thought differently from him. You couldn't say he didn't belong in this world and he was an entirely reasonable young man — only he lost all control when he began to work. He became mad in the best sense of that word. And I envied him in this regard. I would very happily forget everything and focus entirely on crafting new items. Even the same old Chess Set of Karmadont. But no, I have to manage, administer and run around here and there finding solutions to various problems. Blech!

Damn it! Maybe I should give it all up and take on some quest to complete to the end? Revisit the days of my youth when there was no clan, no problems with the Celestial, no Tomb. There was only me and a cloud of Experience hovering over me, just ready to rain sweet XP on me...But I have a clan to lead and a tournament to organize...And I need to make the Pendants I promised to Mr. Kristowski...

To hell with all this! It's decided then!

Hello Sabantul! I'm ready to buy that map from you. We can meet in an hour in the Anhurs Central Square.

CHAPTER EIGHT
LAIT THE REBORN

LOCATION UNLOCKED: 'The Cave of Feeris.'
Quest available: 'In search of the truth.'
The cave is defended by three hundred and
two Level 330 Mage phantoms and twelve Level
350 High Mage phantoms, headed by Feeris, the
High Mage of Anhurs. Clear the cave. Reward:
+100 Levels, evenly distributed throughout the
raid party. Penalty for refusing/failing quest: 0 XP
for slain phantoms.

"I just knew that I shouldn't let you two in here
without me," Sabantul rubbed his hands eagerly,
accepting the quest. "All right boys. I'll be standing
here to the side while you figure things out with the
phantoms. And hurry up. I'm a busy man with many
busy plans."

I shook my head in astonishment at the Level
85 Hunter. Sabantul belonged to that very narrow
circle of people that I hated from first glance. Though,
to be honest, I never even knew this circle existed.

Even Bat, one of my old acquaintances from Pryke Mine had initially seemed like a kind and pleasant person. Not Sabantul, however. Not only had he hugged me fraternally when we met, like he was some close friend or something, not only did he refuse to sell the map, offering to sell his services as a guide instead, but on top of it all he acted in the most careless, outrageous and rude manner — just begging to be sent to respawn. A single question of his ("How's Anastaria in bed anyway? Should I order an Imitator of her next time I'm in the Date House?") almost made me lose my head and destroy the idiot right there in Anhurs. If it hadn't been for the Celestial players who'd let me blow off some steam earlier, Sabantul would have been dead meat. Although, he's dead meat anyway, since even though I don't hold a grudge, we definitely didn't make any deal that I wouldn't kill him at the end of the quest. I'll hire some PvP aficionados who'll ensure that this scumbag can't get out of respawn until he's learned some lessons. Nothing personal, it's strictly...well, personal.

"Mmm...yeah," mustered Plinto, screwing up his face in displeasure. "Mahan, I'm uh not sure we should go in there without backup. Are you sure that you and I can handle it? Maybe we'll call in a raid and..."

"No raids!" Sabantul exclaimed angrily. "I'm not about to lose out on 33 levels because y'all are too scared. And there's XP to be had for the kills! In short, grab your knives and get on with it! You owe me for inviting you to this quest!"

"Mahan, let me kill him a couple times, what do you say?" Plinto's message appeared in the clan chat. *"The boy's confused and needs help. I shall make him see the light."*

"Sabantul, you do understand that we can't do anything against these mobs?" I began carefully, unwilling to make things worse, but was cut off immediately:

"You want to screw me too? No problem! Pay the damages from the fraud clause and go wherever you like! Either we do the Dungeon together or you pay me!"

I frowned like a tooth had been pulled — I'd found my way into this situation and now didn't know how to get out. The Hunter had insisted that we add a 'fraud' clause to our contract — as soon as we learned the coordinates to the Dungeon, nothing kept us from sending Sabantul to respawn and doing the Dungeon on our own. The clause had seemed overzealous to me, since I had no intention of tricking anyone, so I agreed without a second thought. Who knew that the situation would turn out this way...?

And yet, on the whole, I had to give Sabantul his due — he had managed to find the entrance to the Dungeon which was invisible even when we were standing within three meters of it! It was only when he pushed aside the branches of some bush that was luxuriating in this region that we saw the shimmering entrance between two small trees. I even flew up into the air to make sure — the Dungeon could not be seen from above.

"All right..." It was my turn to buy time as it had been Plinto's earlier. "If we don't have a second choice, I suggest we kite the phantoms in one at a time. We'll deal with them at the entrance. Plinto, stop acting dodgy. The time has come to prove to everyone that you're not simply number one for nothing."

"If only..." grumbled Plinto, going into stealth mode. "First they let a bunch of Celestial players onto the continent, and then they cry about it. Hang on — I'll take a look and see what's up."

"Can you do it without whining so much?" Sabantul gibed carelessly in Plinto's wake. Plinto stopped for a moment and *"This puppy's doomed"* appeared in the clan chat, after which the Rogue vanished around the corner.

A minute passed. I was getting tired of waiting and Plinto's green frame let me know that he was still okay, so I tried to chat up Sabantul.

"Listen, here's the million dollar question for you: How'd you find the coordinates to the Dungeon? This is a location for Level 300 players. At your level, there's no way you found them by accident. That means you got them somehow. I'm even curious — where?"

"Five million and I'll give you an answer,"

smirked Sabantul.

"Like hell," I smirked back. "Five million to learn that you read them in some book or killed some mob that dropped the map...No thanks — you're costing me plenty of money as it is."

"Whatever. You'd definitely want to know. Didn't I write you that Karmadont acquired his powers in this cave? So then, didn't it occur to you how I know you'd be interested?" Sabantul made an enigmatic and smirking face (which just begged for a well-timed left hook). "You sure would be surprised to learn the reason..."

"I reckon three hundred thousand is a fair price," I offered, trying to mask my sarcasm and my appraisal of Sabantul's intelligence. Does he really think I'll pay? That I'll rush to spend enormous sums of money to know how he discovered this cave? Considering that I'm already here..? Yeah...That'd be well received in Barliona. I can already imagine the conversations that would take place:

Alice: "I need money. But where can I get it?"

Bob: "Let's sell Mahan information about how there are three empires on our continent! We can get five mil easy!"

I mean, kids these days! Sheesh...

"Nah, Mahan," Sabantul drawled contentedly, assuming that I was haggling. "Five...Five sweet, ripe, juicy millions. And not in-game either — I don't want to flash that kind of money in front of Roxanne. What city do you live in?" The question was so unexpected that I answered before even thinking about it. Hearing the name of the city, Sabantul exclaimed with surprise: "Why, we're neighbors! I'm just three hours' drive away from you! Anyway, I'll make an anchor point — you two can figure things out without me — and I'll head in your direction. We can meet at 11pm at the Bluebird Diner. Oh and bring Anastaria — I want to see what she looks like in real life. All right, I've set the anchor point — I'm out."

Sabantul's avatar froze and went transparent but didn't vanish entirely — the anchor point was working. I stared at it in shock, still unable to find the right words to describe the situation to myself. What the hell just happened?

"I have a couple acquaintances," said Plinto, examining his manicure and stepping out of the shadows. "They live in your city. Nice people. Reliable people. The best people. My point being — maybe I should exit to reality too?"

"Erm...what?" I asked, still stumped. Plinto was saying something, but the sounds just didn't make sense in my head.

"I'm saying there aren't any strays around the corner. The Mages are all clustered in groups of five. You and I can't handle one group like that...Pretty name by the way...'Roxanne'...or was that just a handle?"

"It's a name like any other," I grumbled, coming

to my senses. "All right, I'll take a look myself and we can figure out what to do later. There's no one around the corner?"

"It's clear. Hang on, I'll throw up a shroud of stealth."

A barely noticeable shimmer appeared around us. Plinto had activated one of the Rogue's spells, granting stealth for other players in a certain area. Useful tool, but a bit unreliable. If even the hem of your shirt sticks out of the shroud's AoE, the mobs will aggro you instantly. As a result the Rogue tried to use this spell in the most delicate of situations, and preferably only with individuals of the opposite gender. It's nice when a girl has to press herself up to you...Damn! I had to talk to Anastaria immediately!

Despite its odd location among the trees, the Dungeon's layout was fairly canonical — a winding corridor hewn by some mysterious forces from sandstone, three meters wide by three meters tall and illuminated by smoldering torches. As soon as we turned the corner, we encountered a huge cavern, the far end of which vanished in murk. At the very edge of the visible space, I made out a massive throne of a dark material. I cursed to myself once again — Shamans can summon a Spirit of Far Sight, which would help me see the creature sitting on the throne. But someone (let's not point fingers here, particularly at one careless Shaman) once again forgot to stop by his trainer and learn the summons available to him at his level. I still had the same two basic Spirits in my spellbook and slots that I'd received back in the mine — minor Spirits of Lightning and Healing. Would I have to resort to design mode again? Not an option — it would take too long.

"Basically this is it," Plinto summarized, nodding in the direction of the group of phantoms standing nearby. The five half-transparent figures — all Level 330 and wrapped head to toe in phantom shrouds — stood several meters from us beside a pile of Crastils. Leaning against their whimsical staffs, the Mages were staring at the orbs like they were trying to hypnotize them.

"Five is too much for you?" I asked just in case, already knowing the answer.

"If they were at Level 300, it'd be worth a shot," Plinto admitted honestly. "But here, I'd have to deal with each one separately — my mass spells won't affect them. They're immune. I can't handle five — you'll have to heal me and, as a result, take damage from the ones to the side. Their dps isn't scary to me, but they'd eat you alive."

"How many can you take at once?"

"Two for certain. Three...Yeah, I could do three too. The fourth is a question mark and the fifth is definitely on you. You didn't stop by your trainer, did you?" Plinto hit me where it hurt. "So you don't have mind control. All right, there are several options..."

"Maybe Thunderclap?" I interrupted Plinto. "I'll

turn into a Dragon and freeze them all to hell."

"Uh-huh. What's the AoE on your Thunderclap? About forty meters? In a minute I can kill ten, maybe twenty phantoms. But there's more than a metric crap-ton of them here. What are we going to do with the others? The ones your Thunderclap aggroes? That's what I'm talking about...Like I was saying, there's two options here. No, three. The first is we go to Anhurs and you learn some normal Spirit summons. We come back and it's Shaman time. Mind control and all that good stuff. The second option is we say the hell with it all and get into a fight. We can figure out what's what once we're in it. The third is I step aside while you blow this entire place to Kingdom Come. We pick up the loot and go home happy."

"Erm...What are you on about?" I asked, puzzled by the last bit.

"I'm on about you, Shaman Mahan! You're the guy who slew Geranika. Wiped out an army of players. Caught a Squidolphin. Married Anastaria. In game, at least. By the way, when are you going to invite me to the wedding?"

"What wedding? Have you seen what's going on with her? Stacey's generally been crazy this last week. Either she's giggling without any reason or she's sad or she's quarreling with her dad."

"You're a big boy. You should know that women get this way once a month," Plinto smirked.

"If only! She's fine in that department. Nothing's going on there at all."

"Mmm..." Plinto drawled ambiguously. "Nothing going on, you say...Ho hum. Generally crazy, you say...Well, well."

"What do you mean 'well, well?!' What do you mean, 'ho hum?'" I exclaimed, growing irritated. "You're laughing but I have to go home and listen to a lecture about how harmful smoking is in public places!"

"Oh my poor darling. Everyone's so mean to him, no one loves him, everyone just wants money from him," Plinto was openly laughing at me, shaking his head and tisking. "And his wife's at home, waiting for him with a battledore."

"With a what?" I grimaced, hearing an unknown word.

"What an uncivilized child you are — don't you know basic things? A battledore! It's like a piece of wood. An implement for manually increasing the localized level of education. A very useful thing in your case. I should recommend one to Stacey. All right, experience is the child of difficult mistakes. You have some phantoms to deal with, so don't relax. In a word, I'm for the third option. So — well — oops!"

The shroud of stealth protecting us vanished. With a smug look on his face, Plinto went into stealth and dashed back up the corridor, managing to wave at me from behind his back as he did so. I turned around and gaped — five phantoms stood a step away from me. Their shrouds turned to reveal scowling skulls whose hollow eye-sockets — to my utter horror — began to fill with fog.

Red fog.

My hands began to move on their own, not waiting for orders from my shocked brain. They pulled my long-forgotten tambourine with its mallet from my bag and a monotonous rhythm resounded through the cave: Boom...Boom...

The Shaman has three hands...
...and behind his back a wing...

-50 to Reputation with all Kalragon factions.
+10 Reputation with the Lord of Shadow.

I didn't have any Spirits. That was a fact. I had Shadows. That was a fact too. My reputation with the Emperor and the Dark Lord would be wiped out in a few days anyway when the tournament started — I'd go from Exalted to Friendly status. So there was nothing to lose.

Except for the fetters restricting me!

From the heat upon his breath
Shining candle-fire springs...

"D-E-E-E-A-A-ATH," sounded a drawn out

whisper that resembled relief more than threat, and the five phantoms beside me spiraled up into the air like smoke. And yet I was totally sure that the dps from my Shadows was laughable.

Quest updated: 'In search of the truth.' 5 of 314 phantoms expelled from Barliona.

My tambourine fell silent. Lifting my head, I couldn't contain a deep sigh — a vast crowd of phantoms stood all around me. They stood there quietly, as if they were relishing my momentary triumph — right before tearing me to little pieces. Damn it! Would I be sent to respawn after all? I definitely wouldn't be able to handle all of them.

"GRANT US DEATH, SERVANT OF THE FOE!" As if to demonstrate that I have no idea what's going on with the quests around here, a Mage that looked markedly different from the rest stepped out of the crowd. Instead of a shroud, he was wearing a luxurious robe from which one bony hand decked out in rings reached out toward me. A massive chain with a dark stone that looked more like an abyss than a stone let me know quite clearly that I was speaking with Feeris, the High Mage of Anhurs.

"GRANT US DEATH, SER...THE FOE HIMSELF!!!"

I don't know how the Corporation programmers manage it, but what followed was pretty spectacular

— the indomitable Level 300+ phantoms started away from me in terror like vampires from sunlight. Even Feeris, an advanced Mage, took several steps back. I looked on in puzzlement — until Geranika's pensive voice behind my back let me know that it wasn't me who had startled the phantoms.

"Mmm...yeah...So there I am sitting in my castle, contemplating my next plan for taking over the world when all of a sudden — someone's using my Shadows. And not just kind of here and there, but quite confidently, with self-assurance, panache — in a word with a complete understanding of what he's doing and why he's doing it. And he's doing it in a place that has the status of 'kill any trespassers first and ask questions later.' Shaman, you never cease to surprise me! I'd never imagine that you would be the one."

"That's how it worked out. Is this your doing?" I nodded over at Feeris and his gang.

"Are you talking about the phantoms? My grandfather hadn't even been born when they were sacrificed. But they definitely were sacrificed to Shadow. And yet, they weren't here the last time I stopped by this place. Which begs the important question: 'What the hell?'"

"Surprise!" I drawled with a note of sarcasm. "You're only a runner-up! Someone was using Shadow before you? Will you release them?"

"Me?!" Geranika hiked his eyebrows in

surprise. "Mahan, when did you decide I was charitable? You dug them up, you should send them to Erebus yourself. My dear fellow," Geranika turned to Feeris, "will you be so kind as to tell us your story? It would be very curious to hear who is behind this. And after that, Mahan can kill you lot. Correct?"

Quest updated: 'In search of the truth.' Description: Listen to the story of Feeris, the High Mage of Anhurs and afterward banish the phantoms from Barliona.

Attention! Using Shadows to complete this quest will incur a penalty of -15950 Reputation with all factions of Malabar and Kartoss. Make the right choice.

"I'll think of a way to banish them," I agreed, accepting the quest. Something tells me that Shadows aren't the only way to solve the problem of the phantoms. Otherwise the reward of thirty levels would be really pricey.

"WE BELIEVE YOU, FOE AND SERVANT OF THE FOE!" roared Feeris and began to tell a highly fascinating story from Barliona's past...

Once upon a time, there lived a Hunter named Karmadont, an ordinary person who thirsted for power like no one else. He constantly tried to sneak into the palace to no avail — the guards tossed him headfirst time after time. Eventually the Hunter began losing his mind — unable to attain the Imperial throne, Karmadont began to don a crown that he'd fashioned from whatever was at hand. He began to take self-important walks through the capital. As if he really were the Emperor. Everyone looked on in contempt, figuring him for some fool. He didn't cause any harm and he made the citizens laugh. Feeris was only a Mage adept back then and he would often give Karmadont money for food to keep the Hunter from starving. No one paid any attention when the Hunter vanished; people had enough problems of their own to worry about the town fool. Ancient human civilization was pretty disjointed as it stood. There were dozens of empires and kingdoms, all of which fought with one another over scraps of land that had been generously granted to the humans by the Elves or the Minotaurs or the Dwarves or other 'ancient' races. Even the Tarantulas only viewed humans as nourishment in the most extreme of cases — the brief human lifespan didn't permit enough time for their Souls to fill properly with the Barliona energy that the eight-legged rulers hungered for. For the Tarantulas, humans were like hay is to cows on a sunny day in the center of a grassy meadow — sure you could eat them, but why would you when there are Elves, Minotaurs, Titans...? Human Souls were an acquired taste.

Several years after Karmadont's disappearance, a black cloud appeared and wiped out several cities.

Fifty years later the cloud appeared again, then again after another fifty, each time taking a terrible toll. Even the Tarantulas hadn't done as much damage to the humans as this dark scourge. Thus began the endless search. The Mages' towers took up their present-day positions — the northernmost point of every city where they could be the first to meet the black cloud. Feeris, who had by then become the High Mage of Anhurs set forth to find a means of salvation.

They found a cave. Within it, surrounded by Crastils, they found an alabaster throne — and in it Lait — an alien being, charred past recognition. Only the odd inhalation and exhalation suggested that this creature was still alive. In his hands he held a stone in the shape of a heart — the Ergreis. Feeris followed his orders diligently. Having carefully studied the figure without touching it, he recorded the information he had gleaned onto a crystal and sent it to Anhurs with a Mage. As soon as the portal closed behind the messenger, Feeris crossed a hitherto invisible boundary, approaching the Mage. The Ergreis had to be studied.

A malevolent laughter filled the cave. Karmadont stepped out of the shadows. The same village idiot who had hundreds of years ago wandered around Anhurs. Time had not altered him — he was the same ebullient young man. Only his laughter boded nothing good to the Mages.

Their magic did nothing against Karmadont —

he absorbed everything as though he was a minion of the Tarantulas. Their portal spells ceased to function and then Karmadont sacrificed everyone. But not to his Rulers — he sacrificed them to the unknown god of another world. The sacrifice gave him the strength to cross the protective barriers around Lait, but there wasn't enough time — Karmadont barely touched the Ergreis when something threw him away. Twelve Mages only managed to hold him for a second.

Karmadont did something with the throne and Shadows began to pour from it. The Hunter was drinking them in. He vanished, leaving the phantoms by the throne — the god of the other world hadn't accept the sacrifice. For whatever reason, they wanted the Ergreis. Karmadont lured another 302 Mages to the cave and then did the same thing to them as he had to Feeris, sacrificing them. Then the protective barrier collapsed completely, allowing the Hunter to snatch the crystal from Lait's hand. At this point, Feeris's memory ended — their essences began to be drawn away by another world's god. What happened after this and why they again returned to the cave, Feeris didn't know. By the time they returned, the Alabaster Throne had vanished — Lait, still living albeit pierced by his own staff was sitting on a black stone that resembled a throne. Various creatures would periodically find their way into the cave, but they couldn't do anything to the phantoms. Locked in the cavern, the phantoms were stumped until I appeared and began to destroy them with the same power that had possessed the Alabaster Throne.

"Okaaay," Geranika drawled pensively when Feeris had fallen silent. "Let's assume I'll be able to explain why they returned — the throne is in my possession and the earlier covenant with the foreign god was broken. But how did Karmadont manage to activate it? A mystery...Mahan, do you have any Bard friends? We could summon Karmadont's Spirit."

"Bards?" I echoed stunned. "What do Bards have to do with this?"

"Okay, I see. Then everything's clear to me here," Geranika summarized, hesitated, twisted his head here and there, weighing all the pros and cons and then simply evaporated. The Lord of Shadow had decided that everything that would happen here now wasn't worth his time. I get the impression that Geranika's changed since the Cataclysm. And I'm not sure whether it's for the better or for the worse. At least I could make deals with him earlier. Nowadays he's too withdrawn, occupied with his thoughts, and never wants to chat.

"WE HAVE PERFORMED OUR PART OF THE BARGAIN, SHAMAN! GRANT US DEATH!" Feeris roared, yanking me from my contemplation of the Lord of Shadow's behavior.

"Is Lait still here?" I asked, buying time and feverishly racking my brain for some way out of this situation that didn't involve a penalty.

"YES! IN THE HEART OF THE CAVE! WE HAVE PERFOR..."

"Wait!" I interrupted the phantom. I'd like to see him before throwing Shadows at you lot. What if he vanishes along with you? I'd like to know what happened between your disappearance and reincarna...er...reappearance. I'm sure he'll know."

There was no objection, so I headed into the center of the cave. If I told people, they wouldn't believe me. Instead of embroiling myself in an epic battle involving multiple respawns, I'm planning on leveling my Reputation to its foundations — basically to Friendly status! And all of this is happening without me being able to...Oh sweet Tartarus!

A big thanks to Barliona for not including the quite natural bodily function of showing off the contents of one's stomach to others...Lait looked horrible! The King from my Chess Set was basically unrecognizable amid the hunk of charred flesh on the black throne-stone. As I was approaching, I thought that a normal person was sitting on the throne — though perhaps with some burn wounds — but with every step, new nightmarish details struck my eyes. Lait had no legs. Or arms. It was like his torso had been gnawed, revealing pieces of bone and internal organs to my sight. A single eye remained of the face's typical features. His entire body was covered with a thick dark crust, his skin burned past recognition. A long staff was impaled through Lait's chest, but despite his overall shocking appearance, this being was still alive! The Death Knight was breathing! Slowly, with a wheezing, yet he breathed! The developers were a really sick bunch!

Heeding a sudden urge, I grabbed the staff and ripped it out of the creature's chest. A white liquid sprayed out with it, a moan resounded throughout the cave and a heap of debuffs collapsed on my avatar — everything from Stun, to Blindness to Nausea. Everything began to waver before my eyes, my consciousness began to fade, dissolving in the white fog, and then the image of a healthy and living Lait appeared before me — with a loading bar over his head. Barliona had launched this scenario for the first time. And did so on the fly. The loading bar hit 100%, blinked, and the world regained its volume spawning me under a protective magic dome...

"We'll break through!" growled Lait, shooting a blue torrent of energy out of his hand. Pure Mana...Lait was channeling it to a dome held up by a nameless man, squeezing the last bits out of himself, but everything was in vain — the defensive sphere was wasting away before my eyes. It seemed that neither Lait nor his nameless companion had the strength to maintain it. I glanced at the limits of the dome and smiled — a heap of creatures from various races, from demons to angels, mages to archers, from humans to elves — all trying to break through the dome and wipe their enemies from the face of the earth. Hell roiled all around us and it was only thanks to Lait's and his nameless companion's strength of will that we were still even alive.

"You need to leave, Lait!" the nameless man moaned more than wheezed, falling to a knee.

"We set out together," Lait answered him in a growl, quaffing a flask of some blue liquid. "We'll go down together too. The gods are dead, the Dragons are dead, the castle's gone. Where shall I go? No! We will fight a little more!"

"Fool! My heart won't be enough for them! They'll only want more power! Take it away! I will cast a portal to another world and send you out! Don't let them take my essence! I don't want to be an eternal slave to these bastards!"

"But..."

"Get to it!" the nameless man somehow found the strength to straighten himself and the dome increased by threefold. The creatures amassed on its other side were scattered, broken, skewed, giving the god (for, as I understood it, this was the god of another world) more power.

"Take your staff and cut my heart out!" the nameless god added, now in a normal tone of voice lacking any strain. The blood seeping from his nose made it clear that this exertion had not come freely — the god was consuming himself. "You will only have a moment to dive into the portal, I won't be able to hold the dome any longer. Do it, Lait! We can't accomplish anything else here."

To my astonishment, Lait didn't argue or object, trying to appeal to reason. The same staff I had just yanked out of his chest now appeared in his hands. He lurched towards the god and sank the blade deep into his breast. When Lait's hand reached into the god's chest, a portal appeared beside them. Lait pulled out his hand and in it the Ergreis, shining as bright as the sun. He clasped it to his chest, cast one last look at the god and in this instant the protective dome vanished. As it did so, a vast avalanche of fire, lightning and ice collapsed on the tarrying Emperor, turning him into a charred stump in an instant. And even though he no longer had a heart and was little more than a charred stump himself, the nameless god kicked Lait sending him flying into the portal.

A loading bar.

The cave in which I encountered Feeris. The Alabaster Throne upon which both sons of Barliona's Creator had once appeared. An old man with sad eyes, kneeling before the throne. Crastils forming several concentric circles and radial lines around the throne. A portal opened and Lait tumbled out, wheezing and clasping the Ergreis to his chest with his only remaining hand. The old man looked up in surprise, examining the creature, yet when he saw the Ergreis his astonishment knew no bounds — his bright blue eyes became two enormous saucers. He made a gesture with his hand and Lait, who had been lying on the ground, was lifted into the air and wrapped with a white foam, putting an end to his groans.

"YOU WILL FEEL SOME PAIN," sounded a bombastic, caring voice. The old man placed his hand on Lait's head and a terrible scream of pain filled the cave. "AAAAH!"

"HMM..." smiled the old man, taking a few steps away from Lait. I refused to believe that I was looking at the Creator of Barliona — or rather his representation by the game's developers. However, the voice that made my entire body vibrate, the Alabaster Throne, the general surroundings and the ease with which the old man manipulated Lait's body told me the opposite. I was looking at the virtual projection of the Creator of Barliona. Recording video was, as per usual, blocked. Stacey would kill me.

"THE DARK EMPEROR OF THE HUMANS, DECIDING THAT HIS TRUTH IS THE ONLY TRUTH. WITH THE HEART OF THE GOD OF LIGHT, WHOM EVERYONE BELIEVED TO BE DARK. CURIOUS. I WILL NOT BANISH YOU — TO THE CONTRARY, I WILL GIVE YOU TIME TO CONTEMPLATE EVERYTHING YOU HAVE DONE IN YOUR LIFE. FROM NOW ON — YOU SHALL BE THE GUARDIAN OF THE ALABASTER THRONE. THE ETERNAL GUARDIAN! AND I NAME THE HEART OF THE GOD THE ERGREIS! FROM NOW IT SHALL SCREEN THE

SHADOWS!"

A scream resembling a hoarse wheezing tore from Lait's throat when the white foam began to seep into his skin. The old man sat the charred creature on the throne. He carefully placed the Ergreis on what was left of Lait's lap. Then, waving his hand he raised the Crastils and heaped them around the throne. They were no longer necessary. So does this mean that the Crastils were jammers that blocked the powers of the Alabaster Throne? Three perfect circles, eight radial lines...Okaaaay. Looking around one more time, the old man vanished. Still another loading bar appeared before me. The cutscene had ended...

I was returned to the cave with the phantoms and the charred Lait. He was still quiet, unable to summon the strength to utter a word. The white liquid that the Creator had gifted to Lait, coagulated over the wound in his chest as if the Emperor was a kind of Prometheus. Only in this case I was the eagle.

Despite the cutscene I'd seen, I still had no answers to the questions that interested me — what had happened after the phantoms had disappeared. What did Karmadont do? Was the High Mage of Anhurs right when he claimed that the Ergreis was located inside the Tomb of the Creator? And what was the purpose of the heart of a god of light from another world? What was its power?

Still unsure of the answers to these questions, I looked at the properties of the staff that I'd pulled out of Lait's chest and could barely contain my agitation. I cursed. I looked at the properties one more time. I cursed more elaborately. What the hell kind of an unlucky day is this?

Lait's Stinger. Description: Like any child of another world, Lait's staff has its own will that not everyone is fated to master. Charges: 0 of 1000. Properties. Hidden. Unique weapon. Limitation: Only for Death Knights. Requirements: Must be Level 400+

"SHAMAN! GRANT US DEATH!" Feeris reminded me right away. Damn bodiless spirit! According to the scenario he waited thousands of years! Is it that difficult to wait another five minutes?

Understanding perfectly well that I was holding a worthless stick with a pointy metal end, I swatted at Feeris with it like at an annoying fly. I knew well enough that it was time to wrap it up here and move on. For...

Quest updated: 'In search of the truth.' 6 of 314 phantoms banished from Barliona.

+1 Charge to Lait's Stinger. Current value: 1 of 1000.

Description: 1 of 20 of the staff's abilities has been unlocked — Absorb Soul. The staff's crystal is inhabited by the spirit of a Black Mage,

which absorbs the Souls of sacrifices and draws energy from them. Requirements: The absorbed creature's level must be lower than the staff's by more than a hundred levels.

Attention! In this scenario you are permitted to use the Absorb Soul ability of Lait's Stinger.

The new notification interrupted my train of thought, diving deep into my sub-cortex. I froze, turning and staring at the place where the phantom Mage had just been. There wasn't even a light phantom cloud left. Wow! Who said that the Mages had to be killed? Let them rather do some more work for my clan! All I had to do was find a worthy Death Knight who could use this staff!

To my immense surprise, I had to chase the phantoms around the entire cave. For whatever reason they weren't very keen on exchanging their cozy and ample cave for a tiny crystal and slavery to some strange dark Mage — but who was asking them anyway?

+1 Charge to Lait's Stinger. Current value: 309 of 1000.

Quest completed: 'In search of the truth.'
Level gained!
Level gained!
Level gained!

Level gained...

Attention! Lait's Stinger's Absorb Soul ability is now unavailable.

"The third option always works," smirked Level 395 Plinto, appearing beside me. "Are you aware that Stacey will definitely kill you now? You just earned 33 levels without her when all you had to do was pop out to reality and tell her. Nah, Mahan, you definitely shouldn't go home tonight. Where am I going to find another like you? Have you considered what we should do with that fellow already? Will we contravene the will of the Creator and send him to his rest?"

Only now did I understand that Plinto had witnessed the same thing I had. He had also been in the other world under the dome, he had also seen the Creator, he had seen the quest update and understood why I suddenly began dashing around the cave after the phantoms. He had watched, understood but stayed silent. I guess he relished the sight of this scampering Shaman!

I swung and with a quick motion tried to behead Lait. But only tried — Lait and his staff now occupied different dimensions. For the rest of the world, the staff in my hands was little more than a pretty projection. After all, I'm no damn Death Knight!

"Heh," sounded Plinto's giggle. He dashed at the charred Emperor and set upon him. His green daggers moved so quickly that an impenetrable sphere formed around Lait. But to no avail — for Plinto, Lait was in another reality as well.

"I see. The Creator decreed that Lait shall be smoked for all eternity and that's the way it must be," the Rogue remarked philosophically, sheathing his daggers. "It's not our place to challenge this. By the way, did you notice that Sabantul has vanished? Did he disconnect his capsule or something?"

I turned around and hummed with surprise. Really — the Hunter wasn't anywhere to be seen. If I recall how an anchor point works correctly, it requires a network connection to stay in place. Considering that capsules are always connected, there shouldn't be a problem here. Capsules have their own uplinks, a primary and a secondary. Capsules also have their own requirements for a constant connection as well as their own...Well, they have their own everything! It was practically impossible to disconnect a player from Barliona, especially in the newer, recently updated cocoons. If a capsule was disconnected from the net, all its settings were reset. Then you'd have to go through initialization and calibration all over again, which would keep the player out of the game for a good while. Who would enjoy lying around a metal tube instead of zooming around Barliona's expanses?

"He did get the level bonus though," I noted, looking up at Sabantul's gray frame. The red '+33' on it indicated that we had performed our part of the agreement and that now I was well within my right to kill that bastard as many times as I wished. As soon as PvP is unlocked I guess.

Shrugging my shoulders in puzzlement, and failing to understand what Sabantul had done, I gathered all the Crastils intending on conducting an experiment. I had remembered the figure they had formed. If I assumed that the Crastils blocked the Shadows emanating from the Alabaster Throne, then they could easily block other objects of Shadow. I remembered the figure that had been arranged around the throne. Considering that there were 302 Crastils dispersed around Barliona, I wouldn't be able to screen an item of such size. But I didn't need to either! For example, this will be more than enough for Geranika's dagger that he's so fond of leaving in all the wrong places. Then we wouldn't have to use the Stones of Light.

With this thought in mind, I disbanded our group, sent Plinto to Anhurs and exited to reality. The time had come to speak to my wife.

We have guests. Dress yourself.

The note in Stacey's hand was pinned to the door. Given that we tend to walk around our home naked, unwilling to spend extra time on getting dressed unnecessarily, this warning was a very welcome one. The mystery that remained was who the guests were — guests aren't permitted in our building without proper authorization. After one incident in which some crazy game addict broke Stacey's leg, attacking her in the middle of the street, she stopped going out without a bodyguard. Ehkiller even forced us to set up several lines of security around the building. "You can't have too little security," he explained when I began to mention that I could take care of my family's safety on my own.

"Hello, Daniel!" To my immense surprise, our guest turned out not to be Ehkiller, like I had first assumed, but rather the individual I'd grown accustomed to calling Clutzer. Deputy Head of the internal security service of the Barliona Corporation, Major General Alex Hermann in the flesh. "You really did take your time. Really."

"Alex," I nodded, sitting down in an unoccupied chair. Deciding that no one would be killed for another five minutes at least, I used one of the marvels of modern-day technology and ordered a Tom-Yum soup from the kitchen Imitator. I never imagined that I'd develop a taste for spicy food. Until I met Stacey, I never even suspected that Thai food existed — a pile of red, spicy chili with odd bits and pieces of nourishment. Trying the soup for the first time at Stacey's advice, I almost lost it. Despite my respectable age, I was weeping like a child. Tears rushed from my eyes uncontrollably, my mouth and stomach were an inferno, my jaw was twitching — yet I couldn't stop. The sour taste kept me coming back. I don't remember how much liquid I had to drink to extinguish the burning in my mouth, but since then I'd become a slave of the soup. Stacey called me a gustatory masochist, but I didn't care — Tom-Yum became number one for me.

"And to what do we owe a visit from such a highly-placed guest?" I asked, finishing my food. Stacey and Alex hadn't fallen behind me, ordering desserts, so I didn't have to eat on my own. Not that that would have embarrassed me — my stomach was grumbling and I was ready to swallow everything and everyone around me.

"I covered the boilerplate chatter about the weather and the politics with Anastaria, so let's get right down to business," Alex nodded agreeably. "Daniel, tell me, do you know a person named Andrew Mazey?"

I shook my head — I'd never heard the name before.

"You may have met him under an alias — Sabantul the Fortunate."

"Sabantul?" I exclaimed surprised. Exchanging a puzzled glance with Stacey — she too was familiar with this name — I went on: "Of course. We just met several hours ago in Barliona. Tell me, why are you interested in this player? Has he done something? Did he acquire the map he sold me in some underhanded way?"

"Hold up!" Alex frowned from the torrent of

questions. "Let me ask the questions initially. Tell me, do you know why he wanted to meet with you?"

"Mahan?" Stacey looked at me in surprise. "Did you want to meet with him?"

Alex sighed deeply, as if saying to himself 'look at these people I have to deal with' and continued with resignation:

"Okay, I'll lay my cards on the table. About three hours ago, the man that you know as Sabantul exited the game. A preliminary analysis of his last hours in Barliona suggests that he was going to travel to meet Mahan in order to tell him the story of how he received the coordinates to a cave whose existence is an enormous question for the developers. Right now, we're looking for documentation about this location. It does not exist in the standard repository. Two hours ago, an ordinary Imitator, tasked with cleaning Sabantul's residence, discovered his lifeless body. The first responders discovered a mangled gaming capsule that had been disconnected from the network. Someone did not want the police to know what Sabantul was up to the last two hours he was in game. One of the detectives happened to be one of my close acquaintances. He asked me to review the game logs and you can maybe imagine my surprise when I saw the painfully familiar name: 'Mahan.' Sabantul was killed by a shot to the head. Even his eyes were cut out to prevent us from scanning them for a trace of the assassin's image. Having superficially familiarized myself with your venture into the Dungeon, I would like to ask you 'how,' 'where,' and 'why.' Mahan?"

Two pairs of eyes fixed on me. Alex's piercing look and Stacey's surprise and shock. At first carefully, choosing my words cautiously, and then emotionally, remembering Sabantul's stupid behavior, I began to tell the story of our relationship, trying not to skip any details. After all, you-know-who is in the details...

A cold sweat struck me through and through — if Sabantul was killed because of his planned meeting with me, then I should be very worried. There was only one way I could be associated with Sabantul in Barliona — when Stacey, using her dad's security service had tried to figure out who Sabantul was. These were the only people who knew that I was interested in the Hunter — there was no other link.

I met Stacey's eyes and realized that she was thinking the same thing. Cursing the fact that we couldn't speak telepathically out in reality, I decided to stay quiet about our investigation. At first I need to discuss this with my wife...Hmm...girlfriend...Damn it! We need to talk about our status — who are we to one another anyway?

"He dropped an anchor point and exited the game. Now the anchor point is gone too...I can't say anything about this. You need to look at the logs. Plinto mentioned it when we'd completed the

Dungeon."

"Mmm...yeah..." Alex drawled sadly. "To be honest, I was expecting to hear something I hadn't heard from you. This location had been built by the same team that kept you in virtual space, during Donotpunnik's manipulation of Barliona. The project remained frozen for a long time, so no one noticed it during revision. Sabantul obtained the coordinates outside of the game — an analysis of the logs shows that no one told them to him. In fact Sabantul himself only appeared nine months ago, after he'd leveled up at the training grounds of the Azure Dragons. As you see, I'm revealing currently confidential information to you, hoping that you will meet me halfway. Mahan, I need to learn at least something from you. A gesture, a hint, a name."

"A name!" I recalled the phrase that Sabantul had mentioned in passing. "Or at least a handle. I didn't really understand. 'Roxanne.' You can check the logs. Sabantul mentioned her."

By coincidence I was looking at Stacey as I uttered the name and as I did so, her eyes went wide with shock. The name Roxanne meant something to her!

"There are almost two thousand different Roxannes in the game," Alex grimaced. "There are even more out here in reality — lately the name's become popular among young families. By the way, what'd you decide to name your kid?"

A pause followed. The stone mask on Stacey's face cracked, showing a universal melancholy to the world. She even moaned a little as if saying 'who asked you?' and then reclined in her chair, tucked in her legs, nuzzled her chin between her knees and began to whimper quietly.

"Your capsule's medical indicators are showing unambiguously that..." Alex began, but noting Stacey's reaction, hesitated, looked from Stacey to me and back and then asked baffled: "What, doesn't Mahan know?"

The only thing it occurred to me to ask was:

"Stacey, you're pregnant?!"

CHAPTER NINE
THE BARD OF SHADOW

"THAT'S WHY I DIDN'T SAY ANYTHING," Stacey concluded sadly, reaching to the end of her 'engrossing' (in all senses of that word) tale. "The doctors still refuse to guarantee anything. I hope you understand why I..."

"You're such a little scaredy-cat, baby." I embraced the girl who was on the verge of tears and pressed her to myself. "Everything will be okay. We'll be okay. We've been in worse situations and we've made it through!"

When she was still a child, Stacey was diagnosed with a rare disease that, effectively, made it impossible for her to conceive or have children. Her father took her to the best doctors in the land, but they simply shook their heads in puzzlement. Since in our world, time and money can accomplish if not everything, then quite a lot, eventually a solution was found: In order for Stacey to become pregnant and bring a healthy baby to term, she either required in vitro insemination or some miracle. Stacey put off medical intervention up until the last moment and resolved to tell me everything right after the wedding so that we could decide together how we would deal with this problem. Because of all this, imagine her surprise when upon entering Barliona one day, her capsule notified her that she could spend no longer than 8 hours in the game — the maximum time limit for pregnant women. She instantly went to see her doctor who confirmed the capsule's diagnosis while scratching his head in puzzlement — what had taken place was nothing short of a miracle. And yet, the doctors advised her to wait in order to see how the pregnancy would develop. For the last three weeks she had been seeing the city's best gynecologists and obstetricians, without telling me or her father a single word. Scary. What if all of this is simply a dream?

We had finally reached the moment when it was time to talk about our relationship. Not merely in the 'I love you; let's be together' sense, but as a conversation that would place everything in its right place: what, where, why and how. Starting with the wedding and what it would look like, where we would go for our honeymoon, and ending with all the financial questions. Stacey's family — especially following the Donotpunnik affair — had become one of the wealthiest in our region. When I asked how much the Corporation had paid for Ehkiller's silence and understanding, Stacey named a figure with so many zeros that my jaw clean fell off. Numbers like that don't exist! This was why Stacey was incredibly happy with our independent financial position and my ability as the future head of the family to provide the level of comfort she'd gotten used to, doing so without turning to her father for help.

I had to give Alex his due. Realizing that his further presence has become inconvenient, he had left us on our own for a few hours. And yet we still had to ride with him to the police station in order to sign our affidavits. This incident really had been utterly out of the ordinary — the mysterious killer had not only left no trace, but he'd managed to wipe clean the recordings of all of the cameras in the vicinity. To make absolutely sure that no one could even get close to him. The police Imitators huffed and puffed, growled and smoked, but they were unable to reconcile the bits and pieces of information into one big picture. It simply didn't exist. The corpse existed but the information about how it got that way, didn't.

"Stacy, tell me, who is Roxanne?" Once all the formalities had been dispensed with, I decided to relax a bit and ask the question that had been bothering me. "When I mentioned that name, you started as if it's connected to unpleasant events in your mind."

"Roxanne," Stacey said unwillingly, hesitated, gathered her thoughts and then began to tell her story while staring into the 'nothing' outside of the car window. "Roxanne and Alexander Vecchi are the people I suspected of your abduction. They've been my father's main competitors for a long time. A huge error on my part. If I had taken into consideration both options — them as well as Donotpunnik — everything would have worked out otherwise. But I got fixated on Roxanne as being the mastermind."

"Why?"

"If I only knew! I simply...I never liked her. She is rude, irritating and revolting. Several times she visited my father on business, and every time she left nothing but disgust in her wake. You mentioned Bat the other day — well, imagine Bat in a skirt. She's happy to smile at you, while she holds a knife behind her back and bides her time for the most opportune moment to stab you. I don't like people like that...Listen, Dan, I had a big fight with my dad."

"He wants us to do the Tomb with the Celestial?" I guessed.

"You're giving him too much credit. He's already made the deal. While you were chasing the phantoms, I spoke to him one more time. He knows that the Ergreis is in that Tomb. And he knows what it does. He wants to hand the heart over to the Celestial Empire. According to the prophecy that Bihan saw, the penultimate boss has the heart. And he'll only drop it if you're there with the Original status. Dad promised that you'd take part in the raid. Phoenix's raiding parties, Plinto and I will come along as reinforcements. The contract's already been drawn up, so dad doesn't have a way out."

"Whoa..." I managed in shock. What a pleasure it is to live among the elite. While you were breaking your back, doing your job, they managed to sell you out, buy you back and sell you out one more time for a slightly higher price. Real bunch of capitalists these guys. They've been doing the same thing for ages.

We reached home in complete silence. Stacey was still hypnotizing her reflection in the car's window, while I did my best to gather my thoughts. Here, if I filtered out all the profanities bouncing around in there, I was left with a single clear thought: 'Ehkiller isn't right.' Really not right. It's even strange that he decided to surrender the Tomb to the Celestial players without putting up a fight. Considering the amount the Corporation had compensated him with, money shouldn't be an issue for him. That means that something else's at play. But what?

Attention, everyone! Everyone! EVERYONE! The first Kalragon inter-clan tournament has begun!

EVERYONE TO THE TOURNAMENT!

During the tournament, killing other players has been disabled across the continent.

Furthermore, to ensure that nothing distracts from such a momentous event, during the tournament, access to all Dungeons on the continent has been disabled as well!

GOOD LUCK AND MAY THE STRONGEST

AMONG YOU TRIUMPH!

(Teleportation services to the tournament location are being brought to you free of charge by The Legends of Barliona Clan)

The next morning was sadly ruinous for my clan — two days remained until the tournament and the entire continent was changing. Festive banners and posters were plastered all over Anhurs. The guards were dressed in their parade uniforms and even their pikes were festooned with tricolor ribbons — a symbol that during the tournament, all wars had stopped around the continent. Three empires — Malabar, Kartoss and Shadow — were united under the eaves of my castle, revealing my coordinates to every thief and brigand in Kalragon. I'm sure that among the tournament participants there'll be plenty of those who'll plot to rob my castle. After the tournament, I'll have to change my castle's location. Mr. Kristowski will again complain about my spending of sums with seven zeroes. What the hell was I thinking when I offered them Altameda anyway?

A player dashed past me, handed me a paper and ran onward. I glanced at the text and couldn't restrain a smile — the Corporation had already cooked up a bunch of social quests for the tournament. For example, I had just triumphantly and with great honor received a summary for the 381st Tournament with a schedule and list of all its events.

Day 1

10:00 Tournament Opening Ceremony

14:00 Individual Archers Competition. Distances of 100, 200, and 500 meters. No level caps.

15:00 Group activities. Number of participants: 20–50. No level caps.

15:00 Kalragon's Top Chef. Qualification phase.

19:00 Arena (2 vs. 2). Qualification phase. All participants scaled to Level 100. All personal items scaled to Level 100.

20:00 Battle of the Bards. Qualification phase.

Day 2

...

...

Day 7

10:00 Last Man Standing. Individual competition for the title of Tournament Hero.

21:00 Tournament Closing Ceremony.

My eyes almost rolled up into my head when I saw all the events that had been invented for the tournament. Forget two birds, the Corporation had decided to kill the entire flock with one stone — there were individual competitions here as well as contests for duos, groups, chefs, sculptors, bards and every other gaming class that was committed to crafting. It's scary to even imagine the size of the crowd that'd show up at my castle walls.

Please confirm the withdrawal of 30,000,000 gold from your clan account.
For: Initial payment for the tournament's opening.

With a feeling of utter emptiness, I pushed the 'Accept' button and entered my digital signature. Mr. Kristowski didn't have the authority to transfer a sum of this size, so I had to approve it personally. The Corporation was getting on my nerves yet again — when someone other than you spends money like this, you tend to take it more calmly. Ehkiller was about to spend three hundred million on this tournament. Well done, I applaud you, have a pie as a reward, or something. But when you have to give someone 30 million with your own hand, understanding that your return will be insignificant, your inner menagerie, long since in hibernation, will surely start dusting off its torches and pickaxes in preparation of a protest: 'Animals against Financial Ruin!' 'All Paws to the Barricades to Oppose Corruption and Largess!' 'Down with the Tyrant Shaman!' and other motivational slogans flashed past my eyes, when the clan budget had once again plunged to unacceptable levels.

Why is this happening to me?!

"Look guys, it's Mahan!"

"Get out of here, you Corporate lapdog!"

"Thank you for the tournament!"

The other players milling around the Anhurs central square had noticed me and immediately began to harass me. The most surprising thing was hearing them berate me — I didn't think I'd given them any reason to be upset...and yet a large part of the players were pouring all their choice words on me, screaming that not only was I the Corporation's creature but that I had abandoned 'free crafting' for easy money. Over the last three years, many a hunter of wealth and fortune had studied my biography.

Seeing that I had nothing to do in Anhurs, I blinked to Altameda. I wanted to see what had happened to my castle.

"Master!" squealed Viltrius as soon as I appeared. "The hobgoblins wouldn't let him in, so he...he...he killed them! The m-monster!"

I looked around and almost swore. None other than Geranika sat reclined in my throne, sipping some wine from a wine glass. Five furry spheres lay at his feet — checking their properties I discovered that the hobgoblins were still alive. Geranika had wrung them, dried them, emptied them, but kept them alive. Spiteful Gnum was muttering grumpily to himself, wandering around the defensive statues he had crafted and glancing unhappily in the Lord of Shadow's direction. The only thing I could make out clearly from his grumbling was 'I'll get my hands on you yet!' and 'I'll show you what happens when you hurt my girls!' I guess the statues had attacked Geranika as soon as he appeared, but he simply froze them. As he did to Vimes, whose horn I could see protruding from behind one of the statues.

"Curious boogers," drawled Geranika once he noticed me. "I'll need to get some of my own. I'm surprised I actually had to concentrate so as not to kill them while ensuring that I could speak with you. I wonder where they draw their power from...But all right, that's for later. Get your stuff. I need to introduce you to your future army."

He didn't have to repeat himself. Emptying my personal inventory as much as I could and throwing anything I didn't need into the bank, I left only some Diamonds for making the Pendants, healing potions, elixirs of Mana, ten scrolls — and then swore at myself one more time for not having gone to see my Shaman trainer. Nodding to Geranika that I was ready, I held out my hand to teleport when a surprising exclamation sounded from the front door:

"Halt!" shouted Plinto, bursting into the hall, disabling his acceleration as he went. "Running off to Shadow without me? As Mahan likes to say: 'Like hell!' I'm coming with y'all!"

Video recording worked perfectly in the castle and thanks to Stacey's demands and an updated capsule with a memory upgrade, it would turn on anytime it could. So now I was imagining how great of a screenshot I could obtain later, and most importantly, where I would hang it: Geranika, stunned and still, his mouth half-open, his eyes foggy and his Imitator trying desperately to resolve the most optimal course of action to take. I have to confess that Plinto had shocked me as well. I hadn't expected this from him, but Geranika shut down entirely. Geez, I sure hope he doesn't like reformat himself or something...

"Do you comprehend the consequences of this decision?" It took the system an entire 30 seconds to generate the appropriate behavioral algorithm.

"A bonus for being one of the first players to visit Armard as a guest and not as a conqueror. The first and only who'll enter and exit the 'Cellar of Betrayal' without having to bash my head against a wall to leave. The first and only, even if just for a short while, Shadow Vampire. I doubt the Patriarch will object if I do some recon work about how to best fight Shadow. Within Shadow itself. Do I need to go on? Or are you suggesting that my Reputation will drop and all that? Pfff...That don't scare me. I'm going with y'all."

I had to concentrate to understand what this 'Cellar of Betrayal' that Plinto had mentioned was — the player Musubi had set up a hundred of the best players from the Heirs of the Titans and the Azure Dragons clans, sealing them in a room inside the city. They were forced to kill each other to get out, but...Here I ceased to understand the point of going to that 'room.' There wasn't anything there, after all. Why would Plinto need this?

"I accept your choice, Right Reverend Plinto the Bloodied," Geranika uttered in an official tone and even bowed to the Rogue noticeably. "You are not bound to me by anything, so you shall have a reward once the tournament is over. Whether you accept it or not shall remain up to you. Do you need time to get ready?"

Plinto smirked and shook his head, while I looked at the Vampire with entirely new eyes following Geranika's words. When had he gone from a Cleric to a Reverend? Attaining a new rank, as I well know, isn't a matter of scratching your head. You have to put in an effort. Does he live in Barliona, or what?

Geranika told Viltrius to soak the hobgoblins in water to restore them, then appeared beside Plinto, touched him, appeared beside me and the world around us lost its volume transforming into the special effects of the inside of a portal.

"Welcome to Armard!" Geranika said triumphantly, when reality regained its substance. I barely managed to look up to see how the palace had changed since the Cataclysm, when a long litany of notifications began to stream past my eyes with the speed of a bullet train:

Achievement unlocked: 'Too good to be

true.' Description: **You have joined the first fifty players who have visited all three palaces of the three Empires. +2 Attractiveness with all Kalragon NPCs.**

Quest available: 'Secret Recon.'

Quest available: 'A Friend among Strangers.'

Quest available: 'Mata Hari, Ames, Fuchs, Julius & Ethel Rosenberg, you...'

Quest available...

The system offered me a dozen quests for various factions and Empires of the continent — beginning with a basic reconnaissance and mapping of Armard and ending with a quest to assassinate Geranika. The reward for each quest was so attractive that everything contracted inside myself when I pushed the 'Decline' button again and again. My Reputation with the various factions — even ones I'd never come across before — plummeted, but I couldn't care less. I didn't come here to spy.

When the quests ceased appearing — or perhaps when the system decided that I wasn't about to take its bait — the flickering before my eyes ceased. I was about to look around and enjoy the work the developers had put into the continent's third palace, when Geranika suddenly said to me:

"Check them."

For about ten seconds nothing happened and I even managed to exchange puzzled glances with

Plinto when a painfully familiar voice sounded from behind me.

"They're clean, brother. Neither Malabar nor Kartoss sent them to us."

Your reputation with Geranika has grown. Current status: Respect.

You have gained access to the Palace of Shadow. Current access level: 38%.

Your reputation with the factions of Malabar and Kartoss has fallen to Friendly status.

You have lost access to the Palace of Malabar.

You have lost access to the Palace of Kartoss.

You have lost...

A dozen notifications popped up informing me of all the locations I had lost access to, but my full attention was concentrated on one tall person dressed as a High Shaman — the red cape, the hat with horns, the staff, and a mallet and tambourine hanging from his belt. Shiam's dark hazel, almost black eyes were drilling into me like he wanted to incinerate me where I stood. I doubt there was an NPC in this game who hated me more than Shiam and I doubt there's an NPC in this game that I'd be happier to dispatch for a good long rest. The Corporation had managed to concoct a program that I really disliked. And that was putting it mildly.

"Jeepers!" grinned Plinto, deciding that the silence had drawn out for long enough. "You two are staring at each other like a husband and wife who've been at it for a decade!"

"Theirs is a complicated relationship," Geranika chimed in glibly, then turned to his brother and in an utterly different voice — one that radiated might and the impossibility of disobedience — uttered: "I forbid you from hurting Mahan or Plinto for the next ten days. He shall represent Shadow at the tournament. Are there any questions?"

Shiam's face twisted itself.

"I have no questions, brother," he all but spat out, turned on his heels and quickly walked out of the hall.

"My how serious everything is here," Plinto went on mocking. "Searches and orders and prohibitions and questions. What was all that?"

Geranika decided that Plinto's question was a rhetorical one and didn't bother to answer him. Instead, a portal flared to life, dissolving the space all around it. Geranika had made sure that we were serious in our intentions and was now prepared to lead us onward. By the way! So it turns out that Plinto also refused the unbelievable bonuses for establishing a spy network in Armard. I will have to ask him why.

"What the hell!" Plinto blurted out when the

game returned to its prior density. Geranika didn't bother to take us around the various parts of his palace to show off its wonders. The Imitator was playing the part of the head of an enormous Empire who didn't have time to spare whatsoever.

"Your first warrior," Geranika said curtly, impassively staring at a player running through an obstacle course. In the form of an enormous cat shrouded in tattered fog. No — not a cat but a puma! A Druid? I tried to check the properties but couldn't catch the puma in focus, as there were constant pendulums, axes and blades flashing between us. I shared Plinto's shock entirely — the Rogue's obstacle course in Anhurs, which I had once traversed a hundred meters of, was a playground for children no older than two in comparison to the monster we were looking at. I blinked and tried to get used to the rhythm of the pendulums, when a shiver ran down my spine — their movement was not subject to the physics engine! They moved so chaotically that a reasonable question occurred: How is the puma still running that course?

"All right. I'll give it a shot. Doesn't do to leave the girl on her own," Plinto transformed in a flash. The chain mail vanished revealing a taut leather armor. Or cloth armor. It was difficult to tell what Plinto had donned, but one thing was clear — the Rogue had ensured he would have a full range of motion. Even his feet were now shod in moccasins instead of his customary combat boots. Looking at the Vampire's gaunt torso, the only thing that popped into my head was — 'a fly.' He was basically a weightless gymnast, capable of performing miracles at athletic competitions.

"Anscenica, meet Mahan. He will lead the Shadow raid at the tournament," said Geranika, offering his hand to the Elf who had managed to encounter a sharp pendulum blade after all. I smirked — an Elf Druid and she's playing for Shadow? Whimsical combination. Not only are there too few Elves in the game, but they're also playing for Geranika!

"What's up? I'm Anna," the girl smiled blindingly and offered me her hand. I shook it with pleasure, earnestly examining her. A pleasant, pretty face that was a little scary and fitted with incredibly deep, saturated gray green eyes which seeped fog and cute little elf ears living a life of their own. I realize that everyone tries their best to look like they're in a fairy tale in this game, but even in this context Anna could easily be considered one of the prettiest girls I had ever seen. Eh, forget that, she was the fourth prettiest! Anastaria, Raniada, erm, that Mage chick who was always bickering with Stacey whose name I no longer remember...and now Anscenica. I sure am lucky with pretty women!

"Tell him about your abilities," commanded Geranika. "Don't forget to mention you lunar bind. A part of your trials will be this evening."

"Okay. So...Where should I begin? Well, in general...Damn!" Anna began to stammer and vacillate. "Sorry, I'm nervous. It's the first time I'm speaking to such a famous player. I'm afraid I'll say something stupid. Stop! What's got into me? Oh that's right! My abilities..."

Having a conversation with Anscenica was quite the pleasure. She was a mad blend of competence, childishness and carelessness — all diluted with happiness and sincerity. Clearly, with substance and examples but at the same time so whimsically that a smile appeared on my face, she began to recount all her abilities. Plinto — who had failed out of the obstacle course in the meanwhile without having even reached the spot where we had first seen the puma — joined our conversation and began to ask all kinds of technical questions: the time it took to cast her spells, how long they affected the enemy taking into account Shadow Alignment, character properties, and development specifics. Naturally a great portion of these questions were quite private in nature, and yet the Level 155 Druid answered everything we asked her.

The day went by in a flash. Even though officially Shadow wasn't an Empire that players could play for, there were plenty who did so anyway. Geranika introduced us to twenty-five who were, in his words, the most notable of the Free Citizens in his

Empire. I was particularly pleased to meet a Paladin/Mage couple — a guy and a girl who decided to switch sides to Shadow with their entire clan...of two. On the other hand, now, joked Shadow Paladin Endiga Mizradin, the Silver Moon clan enjoyed the same status that Phoenix had in Malabar and the Dark Legion in Kartoss: The number one clan of its Empire, even if unofficially. To my astonished question of how a Shadow Paladin was even possible, Endiga explained that Eluna remained his goddess. She still hoped that he would return to the one true path and therefore hadn't stripped him of his powers. Along with Geranika's gifted Shadows, the Paladin's powers were such a mishmash of entries that I got lost in his description after a few minutes. One thing was clear — we had a Level 247 tank and a Level 212 Shadow Fire Mage named Eyrie. The girlfriend or wife (I never did figure out what their status was) provided fire support under the principle of 'even if the entire world is against you, I'll stand beside you and feed you ammo.' One provides the cover, the other pours Burning Shadows on the enemy. A volatile mixture.

"Finally, the last member of our team," said Geranika, teleporting us to...a library! I'd gotten accustomed to not being surprised by anything in this game, but the creature that now appeared before us forced me to relive that forgotten feeling. Scorning all rules of decorum, I opened the properties of the girl (who was too engrossed in a book to notice us) to see who I was even looking at: A Profaned Biota. The system immediately offered I familiarize myself with this new race, projecting the image of a 'typical' Biota, but I swiped all that away. Not right now. Although...If the 'typical' specimen is what a Biota is supposed to look like, then Lorelei (as this player was named) looked quite atypical to her fellow Biotas. And not necessarily in a good way — but, well, different. Through her bluish-green skin, which resembled more that of a pickle than of a human, small and sharp thorns protruded — sometimes forming ornaments and sometimes simply chaotically. The black veins along her skin indicated that some disease was rapidly spreading through this creature's circulatory system. And all together this looked both visually interesting and revolting. When Lorelei looked up from her book and over in our direction, I had to make a great effort not to start back — her eyes were perfectly green without even a hint of whiteness, an iris or a pupil. It was impossible to tell where the girl was looking, which stressed me out. I'd never considered the fact that I'd grown accustomed to looking at the direction that the person I was talking to or arguing with was looking in. I was accustomed to seeing the eyes of any sentient creature of our world. Not for nothing the devs had endowed even the lowliest mobs with pupils, figuring accurately that players might be shocked by their absence. I suppose when it came to the Biotas, they had decided to try something else. I suppose I'd jumped the gun boasting about my luck with women. By the way, it's strange that girls typically create attractive avatars for themselves, but in this case...

"Erm...Hello!" I said the first thing that came into my head. "What are you reading?"

"As usual, Mahan is verbose and eloquent," Plinto gibed, turning to the girl. "I'm Plinto, this is Mahan. Let's assume we've been introduced. We're assembling a team here and we need a list of your powers."

"What — you're not going to make some joke about salad, broccoli, a cactus or Cippolino?" the girl asked in a mocking voice, sliding the book aside.

"Cippo-what?" I frowned, unsure of what the girl was getting at. From a technical perspective, the Biota really could be compared to a cabbage due to the various leaves that covered her, but associating this creature full of shadow and shades with a lowly cabbage...I don't know about you — but my brain isn't capable of such abstractions.

"Forget it, you weren't even born when children were watching that movie. Darling, tell me, why are you here and not at the obstacle course? At your Level 143, it'd do you good to use the grinding opportunities of the local facilities as much as you can."

"I am increasing my skills, Sergeant!" Lorelei barked unexpectedly and erupted with joyful, infectious laughter.

"Oh really? You served?" Plinto's brows rose higher.

"Something like that. One day with Paulie and Xander is worth a year's worth of service." Her reply didn't clarify anything for me.

"I see," Plinto smiled, while his face acquired a rare gentleness. "You live with soldiers?"

"What you mean, live? I survive with them!" Lorelei corrected him with businesslike irritation.

Here, I had to admit to myself that I had completely lost the thread of their exchange, ceasing to understand them just a little more than 'at all.'

"Listen, my head's hurting from this chatter, so let's just get to your powers," I asked Lorelei. "By the way, how do I pronounce your name? Is it Lo-re-LEI or Lo-RE-lei? Maybe, LO-re-lei?"

"The stress falls on the last syllable, so Lo-re-LEI, but you can simply call me Lori. As for my powers, you can look through them yourself. It'd take too long to list them."

Lori didn't waste much time and simply granted us access to her character's properties. In everyday, reality terms, the girl had just appeared before us in less than her underwear. She was completely nude! And she'd even handed us an X-ray for the sake of thoroughness. Either I'm missing something, or the people playing for Geranika are strangely naïve — no one had said a single word about us digging around the properties or attributes of the players we'd met. Trying not to look at the items that Lori currently had equipped — half of which would drop if she died — I made a copy of her current stats, opened her spellbook and got down to reading.

Shadow Shield: You allow a piece of the surrounding world to enter you and summon a Shadow to defend yourself. The Shadows surround the Bard, absorbing the damage he is taking. Damage absorbed by each Shadow: (Intellect × 10). After absorbing its maximum level of damage, the Shadow vanishes. If an undamaged Shadow receives damage in excess of its maximum absorption level, excess damage is channeled into the interior world. Maximum number of Shadow Shields: (1 + Composition). Basic time of use: 5 seconds. Cost: (Character Level × 10 Mana).

I read over the Bard's defensive ability several times until I understood that I was looking at a different version of the Paladin's bubble. Considering that the Biota race was intrinsically inclined to Intellect, her shield would be able to absorb a lot of damage. Of course Plinto in Sprint could deal ten blows in several seconds, yet Plinto was one of a kind, while there should be many Biota Bards.

"This ability has nothing to do with the Biota race," Lorelei explained to my comment that with a spell like this, a Bard is practically a Paladin with a ukulele. "And it doesn't do to call Eid a ukulele. He won't like that."

"Erm...HE?!"

"You can see for yourself," grinned Lori and pulled the strangest guitar I'd seen in my life out of her bag. In any case, it looked like a guitar to me. The twelve-stringed vegetable-thing resembled its owner in a way — clearly, it had been acquired in some Biota location. But I really was in for a shock when Lorelei began to play it. I never imagined I'd hear an electric guitar in Barliona.

The figure of a brawny warrior appeared next to the Bard, decked out in plate armor from head to toe.

"And why do we always find ourselves in some strange location?" the knight asked in a low, ample voice. "And among strange company," he added, looking at Plinto and me.

"Let me introduce you," Lorelei replied. "This is Mahan and Plinto. They will lead the raid at the tournament we are participating in. And this is Eid — the spirit of my instrument and at the same time a tank."

The ghost knight bowed his head respectfully but didn't offer his hand. I wonder if I could even touch him?

"Hey there, Iron Man!" Utterly unfazed by Eid's transparent state, Plinto slapped him on the shoulder. "What great blood flows, err, used to flow in your veins?"

"I don't believe that the word 'blood' applies to me. I was never like you. I am the soul of this instrument, created by a great luthier," Eid informed us and in one fluid motion 'flowed' over to Lorelei's right shoulder.

"All right, don't stress it," Plinto turned to Lorelei. "How long can you summon him for? And how does he tank? How does he heal? How does he..."

The questions and answers began to pour forth like a rushing river and I quickly got lost among its eddies and tributaries. Raid Leaders who know how to manage the players' best attributes are either born or formed through constant practice. I'm ashamed to admit it, but for me this role was inaccessible. In any event, at the moment — it'd be a waste not to learn how to lead a raid with such renowned teachers as Anastaria and Plinto.

"Listen, if it's not too much to ask, maybe you'll play something?" After Lorelei had answered all his questions, Plinto stayed quiet for about ten seconds, calculating something in his head, and then decided to say what was on his mind. It had really been a difficult day — of the twenty-six meetings we had, I could recall about four of the powers that had been shown to me. It's a good thing there's a video recording of the whole thing and Stacey would help me figure everything out later. "First time I've seen an electric guitar in Barliona. I'd love to hear it."

"No question about it," Lori thought a few

seconds and then strummed the strings. "I'll show you why Geranika granted me the power that you mistook for a bubble. And you'll get to see how I can buff other Shadow creatures around me."

It turned out that Eid was a copy of a guitar synth from reality. At least, that was how Plinto described this miracle. The product of an advanced technology that combined the functions of a guitar and synthesizer, which allowed musicians to imitate the sounds of basically any string instrument. Even though this was far from my wheelhouse, when they told me that the guitar synth could be programmed with basically any sound, I began to realize what was going on. Sarcastically, I inquired how it could even be possible to program a string instrument with, for example, a flute? Or a drum? An organ? I didn't really have that many words in my vocabulary for musical instruments, but I did have enough to ask this quite pithy question. And I received a very pithy response: It wasn't possible. You could only partially add separate effects and plug-ins of other instruments into the traditional game. This was precisely why guitar synths hadn't supplanted traditional synthesizers, while at the same time unlocking very interesting possibilities for guitarists.

Lorelei interwove an organ line into the guitar's melody and the library filled with a deep music full of power and latent menace. When Lori's voice joined Eid's, I shut my eyes in pleasure and submerged myself in the music — reinforced with spells, the Bard's voice literally forced the air to vibrate. Shivers ran up and down my body in packs, and a pleasant sensation began to unfold itself in my chest, as if a small sun was being born there and trying to fill me with its strength and energy. I wanted to run, fly and swim at the same time! The feeling was incommunicable — I'd never felt such an energy and desire to do something! My hands were literally shaking from my impatience to grab a shovel and start digging from the fence and until lunch. Amazing! Lori wasn't simply a genius — she was stunning and the song...What song?! This was a hymn! A real, genuine hymn...

...to Shadow...

The sound and the song ended abruptly. I opened my eyes and...shut them. For there was nothing around me, aside from a strange, dark and swirling fog seeping from my own hands. Sighing deeply and dispelling my desire to fly, I opened my eyes again. The fog became transparent. Lori and Eid, who was covering her with his shield, were slowly retreating from the boiling and bubbling brick of the library's floor. The desk that Lori had been reading at was half gone — the Shadows had consumed it. They were rushing through me trying to burst forth and destroy the surrounding world and, at the same time, I couldn't do anything to stop them. I didn't want this! All of me wanted nothing by to plunge everything into

Chaos!

Suddenly a wild and piercing shriek sounded, rising in pitch to ultrasound. The Shadows whirling around me shuddered, as if they were alive and darted to the right. I followed their motion and saw a similar moil of Shadows beside me — Plinto also wanted to destroy the world. Our Shadows touched and, to my surprise, began to consume each other. Or destroy each other.

"This is why the Hymn of Shadow shouldn't affect the Free Citizens," said Geranika's sad voice. "The power, the strength and the desire to become mighty and deadly all comes with an Achilles Heel — for some reason when the Shadows come into contact they begin to destroy each other. Lorelei, you must flesh out your song — Free Citizens should not be subject to the Hymn's power."

"It'd be nice to know what I'm supposed to do with this too," Lori muttered quietly as Plinto's whimpering sigh filled the library:

"I'll be gobsmacked!" The Rogue had really taken a hefty blow: His eyes were wide-open, their pupils immense, clearly indicating that I had been lucky that my sensory filter was still all the way up. The only thing I had felt were vibrations and emotions. Plinto, it seemed, had felt much more.

"Don't you play with the Heralds of the Horn band?" he went on, rubbing his temples wearily. "After that...Yes, it's hard to recognize you...Damn!

That was pretty cool! Like that one time in the cave with the 'Sounds of Barliona.'"

"What sounds?" Lori inquired, peeking out from the shield of the spirit escorting her.

"I'll dig up the recording and send it to you. I won't leave you alone now, my little cabbage. I'll bring you some fans too. My wife won't forgive me if I don't tell her that I met none other than Kiera White herself!"

Still struggling to come back to his senses, Plinto took on his Vampire's battle form — two enormous, black wings unfurled themselves behind his back, his eyes turned red like an aggroing mob, and auras of fear and panic appeared around him. To complete the transformation, sharp fangs extended from his upper lip. There aren't many players who could calmly look on this extravagant Rogue, and Lori backpedaled instinctively, instantly butted up against Eid, and cursed loudly.

"Keep in mind, bloodsucker, that besides cabbage my ancestry includes garlic too..." she warned just in case, without hurrying to step out from behind Eid who was covering her.

"Heh! I'll keep that in mind! Mahan, transform into a Dragon. You'll feel better," Plinto said, turning back into his human form and stretching his neck. "You should be aware, madam, that I don't eat ladies. Not for dinner, in any case. Better tell me, what's the next song? We play your masterpiece about the Fifth

Horseman all day along in our house. I never imagined that I'd like a rock ballad, but you really are something. Can I get your autograph?"

"You should have seen yourself a minute ago," Lorelei still looked a little taken aback and uncertain, but she risked stepping out from behind Eid. "Who could say no to someone as scary as you? Anyone who dared would probably find themselves in the Gray Lands in the blink of an eye. As for new songs — you'll hear them at the Battle of the Bards. We almost have a new album ready. We were thinking of using the clan competitions to do some marketing for it. But then this tournament popped up and I guess we'll have to play some of the new songs at it."

"You lot are getting too distracted," Geranika intervened. "There's a tournament ahead of you and you need to get down to business. If you've settled the matter of Lorelei's powers, you should leave her so she can work."

"Easy for you to say — work!" Lori grumbled quietly, sitting down in the surviving chair. The armored ghost immediately took up his customary position on her left shoulder. The Bard inhaled deeply, exhaled and looked up at Geranika with her strange eyes. "You can't simply up and write a song about a person you know nothing about, aside from some contradictory myths. And this library has neither a catalog nor an index nor some alphabetical organization system. The little I've managed to glean about Karmadont over the last day won't be enough for even half of a chorus. Once upon a time there was a great hunter who united the human tribe into a single empire. And that's it. No details. I can't work like this. I can't even pin down a contemporary of his to speak to. I could summon its soul and find out at least something about Karmadont that way. He may be the most famous historical figure in the Barliona lore, but there's absolutely zero info about him."

Karmadont?!

"What do you need Karmadont for?" I asked carefully. Maybe Plinto is right and I should turn into a Dragon to release this pressure that's throbbing all through me. I wonder what'll happen — will I become a Dragon of Shadow? Or simply a normal Dragon that seeps fog?

"You're right to point out that I'm not the first to use Shadows. Karmadont used them a long time before me, so I wish to summon his Spirit and ask him how he learned to do it. The Bard must find or compose a song that will summon this creature."

"That's a little more accurate," I became so interested that I even calmed down a little. "What do you mean by summon a Spirit?"

Lorelei sighed and told me an entertaining tale about another ability of the Bard, which was not directly tied with her combat abilities: The ability to summon the Spirits of dead creatures. The important thing here was to show the system that you're summoning a specific individual and for that you needed information about them. The more you specified the dead individual, the higher the probability of summoning the soul you needed. The Bard had another, more complicated way to do this by personally traveling to the Gray Lands, but even there she would need detailed information about the soul she wanted to summon.

"Mahan, don't you think that it makes sense to share some information with her?" Plinto wrote in the clan chat. The Rogue looked at me inquisitively, but didn't say anything out loud, allowing me to make the decision on my own.

"There's too little information about Karmadont in the books," I agreed with Plinto. "I tried to find some mention of him in the Anhurs library, among the jewelers, I even asked the Emperor if I'm not mistaken. But what's out there, in public sources, doesn't really correspond to who Karmadont was in real life. I don't know if it'll help you compose your song, but listen to this. Here is what really happened with Karmadont, the first human Emperor..."

I told Lori everything I knew — how the Hunter started out, who he was, who he became, what he created and what he eventually did. I'll be the first to admit that the story that ensued wasn't the nicest, but it was the most complete and accurate story of the ones that currently existed.

Lorelei stayed quiet for a while, considering

what she had heard.

"Again with those overgrown spiders," she muttered to herself. "I suppose I might manage summoning this soul out in the Gray Lands. There's already one song that seems relevant, and there's even a specialist on the Tarantulas and their followers. If I don't find Karmadont, I'll find one of his fellows."

"You know something about the Tarantulas?" I asked surprised. "Will you share?"

"I can even sing a song to you about them," she promised, "but first let me do what I promised Geranika."

"In that case," Geranika decided, "Plinto — there's no limitation on killing another Free Citizen in my Empire. So, if you would be so kind, please take care of this fine lady. Kill her."

CHAPTER TEN
THE CHESS SET OF KARMADONT

I WAS SITTING ALONE at a recently-repaired table in the Armard library, trying to understand something from what I was reading. The book was interesting and it had pictures. The letters were all familiar to me. The words that the letters composed were also well-known to me. Even the sentences carried their meaning, and yet the idea in the text kept evading me. The sentences I read didn't linger in my mind for longer than a second. Each new sentence was completely new and entirely unrelated to what had come before. It was unique and trying to escape my mind like the dozens or even hundreds that had come before it.

Reading was the last thing I wanted to be doing — the Shadow Hymn required immediate action and emotional expression.

As soon as Plinto had sent Lori to the Gray Lands, Geranika spirited him away to training, promising to show him something that would even surprise the world-weary Rogue. Plinto could not refuse an offer like that. Before leaving me, he repeated his suggestion that I turn into a Dragon to dispel the buff I'd been saddled with, but I was overfilled — I needed to transfer the effects of the Hymn on my own! Without resorting to any damn Dragons!

Tossing the book aside, I sighed deeply and paced the room, barely keeping myself from breaking into a run. I wanted to do everything at once — jump, fly, jog, swim. No! This wouldn't do! If I can't occupy my mind, I'll break down! Where's my design mode?!

Tossing aside the 'illuminated' version of my crafting interface, which kept dutifully appearing by default, I sighed with relief — the effects of the Shadow Hymn in design mode were noticeably weaker. My eyes began to wander along the virtual shelves. No, it really is easier to be here! I don't even want to...

The Orc Warriors from the Karmadont Chess Set drew my attention. Powerful, regal, indefatigable — the eight figurines represented Unique items which no one would manage to recreate in Barliona ever again. Even me. Orcs, Dwarves, Ogres, Giants, Lait, the Lizards. Six types of pieces I'd crafted facing six more that had not yet been crafted: the War horses, the Trolls, the Elves, the Orc Shaman, the Archmage, the Leader of the White Wolves clan. Although no! There was also the chess board that had to be crafted. So all in all I've crafted less than what I haven't crafted yet. In other words — I had barely begun to complete the mission of recreating the Chess Set.

Should I drop everything and give up? Forget about the complete set? Admit that it would never be recreated after all?

LIKE HELL!

My desire to act consumed me entirely. Shall I jump and jog? Shall I fly and crawl? Not in this life! I know of more productive ways to blow off steam.

The knights — or rather the two Amethyst War Horses. No doubt these are powerful monsters clad in armor, who had performed some great feat in the course of their difficult lives as animals of war. Perhaps they carried a king or emperor from the field of battle. And did so on their last legs. The design mode immediately began to waver, offering to show its customary video series about the knights' history — but I forced it to regain its customary solidity through an unbelievable exertion of will. NO! Enough tales! Enough distractions! My head began to heat up and I got the distinct impression that blood (non-existent in Barliona) was trickling from my nose, but I refused to surrender. I saw the projections of two massive horses rearing on their hind legs and thereby using their chests to shield the riders on their backs...a goblin and a Biota. Hmm...an odd combination for Malabar. Design mode wavered again, again offering me the chance to watch this story, but I shook my head, dispelling the offer. NO!

The Emerald Troll Archers. What might they be

like? Grand and mighty? Like hell! They're Trolls after all! No doubt they're two loners who like to lie in ambush and await the moments when no one expects them! Or expects them, but from the wrong direction. They're Trolls. Sarcastic, wry, smirking with long recurved bows and black arrows. Why black, I have no idea. More vivid that way. I'm not sure why but at this point, the name 'Edka' popped into my head. Odd, as far as I recall it, it was that of a Shaman...But okay! I hereby name one of the trolls Edka and the other...The system came to my aid here as through the confines of the 'wavering' design mode, I heard: *"Enough, Tany! You've already won! Tany! Stop!"* I made another effort, the taste of salt appearing in my mouth, but design mode against regained its solidity. I don't want to watch 'cartoons!' The other troll will be Tany then. Why not? Should there only be men on the board? Women, especially troll women, were a terrifying power. Just look at Stacey. And two, sharp-eared and hunching trolls appeared beside the rearing war horses. Excellent, moving on.

The Aquamarine Elf Archers. I know! It didn't matter to me who the devs had in mind for the elves. I already had my own image of an archer in my mind. Once upon a time, I had the pleasure of watching the film version of J. R. R. Tolkien's *The Lord of the Rings*. It featured a very vivid character who was very unlucky with the ladies and who never ran out of arrows. At all! Whatever he did and whoever he shot

— his quiver remained full of elven arrows. Legolas. A solitary ranger played by...played by...erm...I forgot the fellow's name. But it doesn't matter! The important thing is I remember what he looked like, so it's utterly clear to me what I need to do with the elves. The system again recommended I watch the video, this time less insistently than the previous two times, but I only shook my head. No! Placing two similar looking, but slightly differing in details Legolases beside the horses and the trolls, I moved on to the next piece.

The Orc Shaman of Peridot. I barely considered who would have the right to represent this figure on the chessboard when a bright light bulb went off over my head — Prontho! He meets all the necessary requirements and then some! He's a Shaman. He's an Orc. He's as hard-headed as a stone. And for the Shamans of Barliona he performs the same role as the queen on the chessboard! Who cares that there was no thought of him at the time of Karmadont — I'll adjust the lore of this world to my own ends! The system accepted its fate and didn't even bother prompting me to watch the video. Its feelings were hurt and it took a seat off to the side, muttering to itself unprintable words, sadly folded its arms, and allowed me to place the transparent orc beside the other projections.

The Elemental Archmage, a Human of Sapphire. Here too I had no possible alternatives.

Feeris! The Human who had found Lait. The Mage that Karmadont betrayed. A Phantom whom I had consigned not even to death so much as eternal service in the strange Death Knight's staff. I suppose using his image for the chessboard will be a worthy continuation of his service to Malabar. Not only in life, but in death too!

The Leader of the White Wolf Clans. An Orc of Green Diamond. Here I had to think. Of all my Orc friends, only Prontho fit this role, but I'd already assigned him to be a Shaman. Two Pronthos on the chessboard would be too much. Shivers coursed down my spine — the hell! A very curious idea...And why the hell not? Who said that everything should be simple? First of all I needed to create the image. An ordinary person. Two legs, two arms, a torso, a head. An ordinary humanoid. A Shaman, who else? A staff, a cape, a cool-looking hat with horns. A surprised look on his face, as if he'd seen a turtle for the first time and was asking himself: "What the hell happened to this fellow?" Blond hair. Gray eyes. An inscription over his head: 'Mahan.' Green skin. Now let's enlarge him. Now let's make his forehead wider. We'll move his lower jaw forward, and stick some fangs on it. Erm...A skirt! That's right! I had seduced the goblins in a female habit! A skirt for the orc! We'll paint his lips. And underline his eyes. Damn! The main detail — a bone in his nose! And a flower in his hair! No, I suppose I should erase the Mahan label. If

Stacey sees this, I'll be sleeping on the couch. And she'll start locking her closet and make-up boxes. I guess I'll color his hair black too. After all, the hell with it!

The chessboard. I didn't bother overdoing it and crafting anything farfetched. I needed an ordinary, standard chessboard that fit all the proper dimensions and met all the requirements. Sixty-four black and white squares. Glinting letters and digits. A special space for pieces that had been taken. It doesn't seem fair to me to remove the pieces from the board at all. They have to be together. I spent a long time considering whether I should make the board as a case that could store the pieces. But I decided that that would be too banal and ordinary. Everyone does that. Instead, I adjusted and expanded the area for the taken pieces. Green ones on one side, blue ones on the other. Nooks appeared on either side of the board, shaped to contain each piece. Even another piece of the same type — say an orc warrior — wouldn't fit into a nook that wasn't its own. They were custom tailored. Like graves.

The most important thing remained. The projections took up their places before my eyes, but they were still not alive. They had no animating force. No energy. No thought. No emotion. They had nothing but one thing — they had me. Their creator. The being that only wanted one thing — to pour the energy that overfilled him into the world around him. Plinto had suggested I turn into a Dragon to take off the pressure. At the risk of repeating myself — hah! A hundred times hah!

I recalled Lori. I recalled the song she had performed. I recalled the emotions that had filled me from head to toe like an enormous wave. I recalled my desire to act, to fly, to run, to swim and jump. I recalled the power. I recalled it all! I remembered it and passed it to the projections, breathing a piece of myself into each one. For a moment there were so many of me that my head began to spin. I was myself. I was the pieces. I was the chessboard. I was...What am I talking about, 'was?' I am!

"That was a good library," Geranika's irritated voice pierced the blinding light. "With very rare books. Unique you could say. Mahan, you're costing me a fortune! When am I going to get any use out of you?"

Congratulations! You have recreated the Legendary Chess Set of Emperor Karmadont, the founder of the Malabar Empire...
Bonuses received:

Malachite Orc Warriors	+1% HP, MP and Energy regenerated per minute; +10% to Strength.
Lapis Lazuli Dwarf Warriors	+1% HP, MP and Energy regenerated per minute; +1 to Crafting.

Alexandrite Battle Ogres	+1% HP, MP and Energy regenerated per minute; +30 Attractiveness with all NPCs younger than 18.
Tanzanite Giants	+1% HP, MP and Energy regenerated per minute; -50% to Energy costs.
Tourmaline Battle Lizards	+1% HP, MP and Energy regenerated per minute; +10% to Speed on a mount.
Amethyst War Horses	+1% HP, MP and Energy regenerated per minute; +10% to Endurance.
Emerald Troll Archers	+1% HP, MP and Energy regenerated per minute; +10% to Agility.
Aquamarine Elf Archers	+1% HP, MP and Energy regenerated per minute; +30 Attractiveness with NPCs older than 18.
Orc Shaman of Peridot	+1% HP, MP and Energy regenerated per minute; +100 to Energy.

Elemental Archmage, a Human of Sapphire	+1% HP, MP and Energy regenerated per minute; +10% to Intellect.
Leader of the White Wolves Clans, an Orc of Green Diamond	+50% chance to find an Uncommon item. +40% chance to find a Rare item. +20% chance to find an Epic item. +5% chance to find a Unique item. +1% chance to find a Legendary item.
Emperor of Malabar, a Human of Blue Diamond	+50% chance to find an Uncommon item. +40% chance to find a Rare item. +20% chance to find an Epic item. +5% chance to find a Unique item. +1% chance to find a Legendary item.
The Chessboard:	+10% Resistance to all damage types.

Quest available: 'The Prisoner.' Description: The Chess Set of Karmadont is a key. But it is not a key to the Tomb of the Creator. It is a key to the Creator, who is imprisoned in a different world. Find the place of power and destroy the Chess Set. Quest type: Unique. Limitation: Only for the

Creator of the Chess Set. Reward: Meet the Creator.

Skill increase:

+7 to Crafting. Total: 27.

+35 to primary profession of Jewelcrafting. Total: 200.

You have recreated the Legendary Chess Set of Emperor Karmadont...–42000 to Reputation with all factions of Malabar and Kartoss. Current level: Hatred.

Title of Earl lost.

Achievement unlocked: 'One versus all.' Description: You have become 'inconvenient' to the ruling houses of Malabar and Kartoss. +12000 to Reputation with all Shadow factions of Malabar and Kartoss.

Scenario activated: 'The Burden of the Creator.'

The light emanating from my hands gradually faded until I could see an enormous wall of system text as well as the cause of Geranika's irritation. The library no longer existed. Along with several other chambers that had been within a ten meter radius of my latest creative endeavor. Geranika and I were hanging in the center of a perfect sphere, twenty meters in diameter, which now represented the annihilated portion of the palace.

"Doesn't look like anything's really happened to

the library. I just nicked the reading hall a bit, that's all. All of the books are fine," I grumbled when the silence started to linger. The news that from now on Malabar and Kartoss were off limits to me was not pleasant in the least. Had the scenario designers completely lost contact with reality? Haven't they been rewarding me with reputation for each individual chess piece — only to suddenly take it all away for creating the full set? And not only take it all away, but drive me down to Hatred status! Minus 42,000 is enough to wipe out any status, even Exalted!

"Ah Mahan, Mahan," Geranika smiled sadly. "The library isn't the issue. The issue is..."

ATTENTION! EMERGENCY DISCONNECT IN 5...4...3...2...1...

YOU HAVE BEEN DISCONNECTED FROM BARLIONA!

I would give a lot to find out what the 'issue' was according to Geranika, but today, I guess, they'd decided to finish me off completely. Gifting me several lessons for the future to boot. Very unpleasant lessons.

The first was that during an emergency disconnect, the system doesn't have time to completely shut down all of its mechanisms. The player regains consciousness, yet the capsule's superficial attributes remain in place. I'd never considered that the removal of catheters from certain bodily orifices could hurt so much.

The second was that the liquid filling the entire space of the capsule doesn't have time to drain either. When the catheter began to slide from my mouth, I reflexively swallowed and inhaled — the motion of the catheter had tickled the nerve endings in my throat. It's a good thing that I still had my reflexes — when I swallowed, the tip of the catheter pressed against the root of my tongue. I began to heave and gag and this kept the liquid from passing further down my throat. Those same reflexes made me start up and 'surface,' but I smashed my head against the closed lid. Stars danced before my eyes and I collapsed back onto my back stunned.

The third was that the capsule's lid stays shut and it's very ugly from the inside.

Fourth…

"Get up, Daniel! Dan, can you still hear me? Dan?" Stacey's anxious voice tore through to me through the dancing stars and the fog of my consciousness. I heaved one more time. At long last both the lid and the bindings were gone, so I adopted a half-vertical position and trying to build on this success, coughing and gasping for air, tumbled over the edge of the capsule to collapse like sack of flour on the floor. Finally, I had a moment to catch my breath. Stacey was screaming something, stroking me, crying, stroking me again, but my unfiltered apprehension of reality took its time coming back to me.

"...you didn't answer and I decided to pull you out of the game!" At last I could distinguish a cogent thought from the roar surrounding me. Like a tumbler clicking into place, my consciousness returned to me.

"Why?" I wheezed. My throat burned and I wanted to cough, but I controlled myself. It wasn't such a big deal — it sometimes taking a few gulps of oxygen-saturated bio-liquid does you good.

"I saw a notification that you had completed the Chess Set," Stacey began to explain, still crying her eyes out. "I tried to contact you telepathically but the system said that you weren't available. Then a notification appeared announcing a quest that the Chess Set had to be destroyed. That you had to be killed! But you still weren't answering! The markers indicated that you were in Armard. What was I supposed to think? WHAT?! It took me one time to get trapped in Armard to spend a week on the therapist's couch! I got scared that you were trapped too...Dan, I..." The tears intensified. Stacey, my wonderful and beloved wife, the terror of all the living and all the dead, turned into wailing little girl, terrified that I'd been locked in the game and was being tortured. Hugging this darling wonder to myself, I looked around and barely kept from swearing — the end of a network cable was lying beside the capsule. It had been torn out of the capsule at the root.

"You're my savior," I whispered after inhaling deeply and chasing away the nervous shaking and emotions. I began to stroke Stacey, who was splattered with the bio-fluid as well, when I noticed to my astonishment that my hands were trying to reach for her throat. To her pretty and long throat. To strangle her!

In addition to the embedded player monitoring systems, the capsules had several other built-in safety layers. Among these was a 'quick exit' button — which allowed someone in reality to force a player to exit the game. Parents frequently used these to keep their children from spending too much time in game. But even if you push this button, the system takes its time pulling you out — taking up to several minutes to comfortably return the player to reality. Stacey, however, had acted rashly. Having suffered several hours in the Chamber of Pain — the Dungeon that had been custom-made to torture her, she didn't want me to relive the same ordeal even for a moment. So she did the simplest and most effective thing — she yanked the network cables out, instantly disconnecting me from the game with all that that entailed. When a capsule is installed, its cabling is routed through the wall in order to prevent even the slightest chance of interruption. But in our case, a *force majeure* had played a role — as always. I had moved to Stacey's place only several days ago — we planned a global repair, so the technicians had placed my capsule haphazardly. During its installation, the technicians and our architect had decided to put off the proper installation since both capsules would be moved anyway. This decision had to be officially sanctioned, so we signed papers about our liability about this or that...I could kill them all!

"Tell me what the quest says," I said, understanding perfectly well that there was no point in yelling or telling her off. Making a note to myself to remind her what happens when the connection is broken and why the capsule has at least three network cables, I tried to get back to constructive communication. The scenario designers really must have eaten too much of some controlled substance. Not only had they wiped out all my Reputation but they'd also sicced the playerbase on me. 'The Burden of the Creator' scenario...Damn! This is why Stacey yanked the cables out?! While we wait for the technicians to show up, while they reset the connection, do the testing and set up everything...We'll waste a day easily on dealing with this mess and I'll be out of the game the entire time. And meanwhile I have Geranika over there waiting to tell me something important. Stacey, oh Stacey...I should remember that she has markers on me. After I return to Barliona, I'll have to go see Elizabeth. I need to remove them. I don't like this spying on your spouse business.

At first tearfully but then slowly coming to and

turning from a frog into a lovely princess, Stacey began to relate to me what she knew about the Corporation's latest move. All I could do was groan in surprise and, in my own turn, tell her about the enormous wall of text that had appeared after I had created the Chess Set. And so!

The first was that a system notification appeared announcing that the Chess Set had been created. At last, the public at large had learned the name of the creator — Shaman Mahan.

The second was that all the players received a quest: Stop Mahan at any cost. Don't let him reach a location with certain, specific coordinates. That is — the Tomb. And what's important was that this was indefinite. The scenario had no time limit. For their parts, the Emperor and the Dark Lord promised to help the Free Citizens any way they could. For example, from now on portals, teleport scrolls, Mage summons and my Harbinger Blink ability were useless to me. Anything that could whisk me from point A to point B without monotonous travel on my own two feet no longer worked. It was just as possible that they had prohibited me from flying on griffins or in my Dragon form, but I'd have to check that. I'm even curious if Stacey understood all this in those several seconds that she was reading the quest description and trying to get in touch with me.

The third was the reward. He who stops me closer than anyone else to the walls of the Tomb, or to put it bluntly — sends me to respawn — will instantly receive Exalted status with Malabar and Kartoss as well as one Epic item for his class and level. Directly from the hands of the Emperor and the Dark Lord. All other, 'interceptors' will receive Respect status and a Rare item for their level and class, though from the hands of an Adviser or Magister. Again, speaking bluntly, a cute new game had been launched: 'Send Mahan to respawn and you'll get a bonus.'

Like hell!

I reached for the telephone and with undisguised rage dialed the number familiar to any player. Technical support.

"Hello on behalf of the Barliona Corporation! In order to provide the highest quality service, this recording will be recorded. You will be connected to an associate in..."

"Good day to you! This is Connie speaking!"

"Hi, this is Daniel Mahan. Please connect me with the manager responsible for setting all of the players of the continent on a manhunt after me. I'd like to hear what he has to say!"

"Thank you for contacting us and using our services, Daniel! May we offer you..."

"Oh don't start with that!" I yelled into the handset. "Again, connect me with whoever developed this idiotic scenario! Or I'll sue you all to Kingdom Come!"

"Negative emotions will not facilitate a

constructive conversation," the girl replied impassively. "Your request has been assigned ticket number..."

"Yo, Mahan, what're you hollering about?" A new voice suddenly cut in. A vaguely familiar voice, so I took a stab:

"James?"

"Your ticket has been transferred to another Corporation associate, thank you for your call." Connie held her own to the end and left us with her head held high. God I hate tech support.

"What, were you expecting, Mr. Johnson himself? Of course it's me. What are you hollering about? Why'd you scare that poor girl? What if you made her cry? This is why they never want to talk to you."

"So this is your doing?"

"Don't act like you're suffering from chronic amnesia!" said the voice on the other end with mock hurt. "You know very well that I'm responsible for any mess that breaks out in Barliona."

"Hello! This is Anastasia Zavala," Stacey joined our conversation. I looked up and saw her at the second phone blowing me a kiss. "Please introduce yourself."

"Oh! Bringing out the big guns, huh?" James replied without skipping a beat. "James Boaster, manager of the innovations department. Is that enough, or do you want my entire title?"

"That'll suffice. James, please be so kind as to explain why you are limiting Daniel's gameplay? Announcing an officially-sanctioned hunt after a player is a very dubious step on the part of the Corporation. Can you imagine what would happen if his sensory filters are lowered to 70% and the entire player base begins to kill him over and over again? Given his current Reputation — would the Heralds and Magisters bother to get involved? I request that you call off this manhunt against my husband. Otherwise, we will be forced to pursue legal action."

"I anticipated this," the manager on the other line was clearly enjoying this conversation, "so I'm ready to explain. You see, Miss Anastasia, Daniel has created something that shouldn't have appeared in Barliona at least for the next year. This kind of thing happens with him, what can you do? Understanding very well who we're dealing with, I ordered a special scenario to be designed for him. As I understand it, Daniel hasn't yet familiarized himself with it and as a result, you have formed a negative impression of what is going on. But this is only a matter of your lacking the proper information. I assure you that as soon as he returns to the game and reads the scenario description, your opinion of it will change dramatically. I can only advise you to craft Lovers' Pendants for yourselves, since your telepathic communication and ability to summon each other has been temporarily blocked."

"So then why..." Stacey began but cut herself off. "That is, are you telling us that there's no imminent danger to Daniel at the moment?"

"Anastasia, one legal conflict with your family was enough to make it clear to us that we should stay on the good side of the law when you're involved. Do you recall what the current state of the game is? If there's anyone who can hurt another player, that would only be Mahan himself as there is no PvP limitation on Shadow powers. Enter the game yourself and see what happens. I'm confident that you will be pleased with the outcome. In any case, I'm counting on it. Have I assuaged your doubts or do you need an official response from the Corporation?"

Stacey and I exchanged glances. She merely shrugged — it made no sense to be outraged until all the information was in. Thanking James for his explanations, we called the technicians to restore the connection, washed up, got dressed and ordered dinner from the kitchen Imitators. Then we sat down to spend some time together, since the technicians had promised to show up only the next morning and there was nothing better to do.

"A while back, I came across a funny line: 'I got off the web and discovered that my wife was a great conversationalist,'" I joked several hours later when we had turned to a discussion of the latest musical trends — which neither one of us really knew anything about. I had brought up the example of Lori and her band, which Plinto had been so mad about. Stacey, meanwhile, was obsessed with a trio named *Larsi*, a family band, in which the girl knew how to sing and loved to do it, while her parents hovered around her providing her with support and a rhythm section.

"I'd never imagine that the phrase might apply to me."

"Agreed. The only time you and I spend together is in Barliona," Stacey said. "I don't even remember the last time I went out to town. Not to meet someone on business, I mean, but just to take a stroll, wander around the streets, meet some new people, be a normal person."

"With a security detail of ten bodyguards," I smiled. "D'you forget about your leg, kitten? If some idiot fan like that creep decides to attack us, I won't be of much use I'm afraid."

"Yes, I know," Stacey said bitterly. "We'll have to apologize to the Vecchi, by the way."

"So what's the problem?" I was suddenly overcome with the desire to get Stacey out of the house. It's not like we had to go strolling through dangerous neighborhoods..."You said that they live in our city. Let's drop in for a visit."

"Nah," Stacey was taken aback. "Dropping in on someone uninvited is rude. It's not done. What if they're in Barliona? Or they're not home? Or..."

"Then we'll go home," I refused to back down.

"Or to the park. We can throw stones at the geese. At night, under the stars! Just imagine — you, me and some stupid geese! Pure romance!"

"Those are swans," Stacey corrected me with uncertainty creeping in her voice, which drove me to press more.

"All the better! They're not as dumb as geese, but swans make for bigger targets! Get your stuff. First we'll go see what's-her-name...Roxanne, and say a couple of kind words to her. And if she's not home, the hell with her. We'll dash off to the park! Are you with me, mademoiselle?"

Bah! It's too bad you don't get to level up your skills in real life. The system would've definitely told me that I'd gotten bonuses to Charisma, Speech and Bartering, as well as some other tasty and useful stuff for a player. Stacey smiled and offered me her hand so I could help her get up, accepting my idea of a late outing despite the late hour.

"This is their place," said Stacey, stepping out of the car and turning to face an enormous four-story castle. "Nice little mansion, don't you think?"

All I could do was grunt my assent. When we had only just left the city and headed in the direction of 'moneybags village,' I began to suspect that maybe just dropping in wasn't the greatest idea I'd had. My suspicion grew stronger when we flew past several security posts — though no one dared to stop a Zavala car. But the fact that there was so much security there at all said plenty as it was. Now, standing in front of the enormous iron gates which were massive enough to serve as a respectable stretch of railroad track, I understood that I still had a ways to go to get used to my new social stratum. For example, my personal menagerie would never permit to throw massive amounts of money to the wind only to build an almost perfect copy of the Anhurs palace out in reality. And if it did let me, then I'd bawl them out myself.

"The Vecchi's suburban residence." One of our bodyguards approached a well-hidden booth, pushed a button and was answered by a female voice. "How may I be of assistance?"

"Good evening!" Stacey walked over. "I am Anastasia Zavala. I'd like to speak with the owners. Is this possible?"

"One minute please, let me inquire." Considering that we hadn't been told 'no,' someone was at home after all.

"Please pass on through," the intercom announced less than ten seconds later. "Alexander is ready to receive you."

"Alexander?" I glanced over at Stacey with surprise.

"The husband," she explained quietly, getting

back in the car. "His profession is a mystery. Several years ago, he was awarded the 'start-up of the year' award. As you can see, his start-up is doing just fine."

"Yeah," I drawled, regarding the statues rushing past us.

"Welcome to the Vecchi residence." An elderly yet remarkably hale butler met us at the main door. Despite his advanced age, he held himself with astonishing confidence and assurance. One glance was enough to tell that the old man didn't have much energy at his disposal and yet he maintained it so carefully that you couldn't help admire his bearing and tact. There were minuses too however — with all due respect to the Vecchi, dressing a butler as an Adviser to the Emperor of Malabar is a bit too much in my view. Just a tad over the top.

Inside, this palace wasn't very original either — basically everything that I had seen in Barliona had been recreated here in reality. At one point I even tried to read the butler's properties, assuming that these adherents of 'imitation' had managed to recreate this function in our world as well. But no dice — the old man had no properties. Or else I didn't have access to them.

"Anastasia, what an unexpected surprise." A relatively young-looking man met us in an oval office that in Barliona served the function of the Imperial council chamber. At first glance, I'd give him 30 but it was unclear how old this business magnate really was. Modern medicine, money and a desire to look young can work miracles. A head, two arms, two legs and short-cropped black hair...If you ask me, an ordinary person of whom there are masses in our city. The main thing that stood out was his fitness, which one normally encounters among professional athletes. It was a good thing at least that Alexander hadn't started dressing like the Emperor and met us in an ordinary robe with the emblem of a black Chinese dragon embroidered on it. A symbol? An emblem? Something vaguely familiar which I had seen somewhere and immediately forgotten.

"Alexander, please forgive our temerity. I decided to pay you a visit," Stacey smiled, offering her hand. The master of the palace took it and elegantly kissed it and only then looked over at me.

"Daniel Mahan, if I'm not mistaken," Alexander offered me his hand. I shook it and barely contained my smile — judging by the firmness of his grip, I was speaking with a strong and confident person. I even felt some sympathy for him. The charisma of the master of the palace could be sensed not only in his grip but in how he held himself in what seemed like an ordinary bathrobe. We were dealing with an aristocrat through and through. You could strip him naked and he'd manage to appear noble.

"Tea? Coffee? Juice?" Mr. Vecchi offered as the old butler arose beside him. Almost immediately! Now it was clear how he spent the energy that filled him.

He had his own internal motor! I'll need to try to find someone like him...

"...And that is why I decided that you were the root of all our troubles. I did my best to hurt you, which doesn't do me any credit, and as a result I wish to offer my apologies. Personally and sincerely." Stacey concluded her brief monologue from her comfortable seat on the enormous couch.

"Wow," Alexander drawled, clearly flustered. "This...Hmm...This is a wow! To be honest, I have been considering for a while now why my partners seem to be dropping off one after another, but I couldn't find the reason for it. So this was your doing?"

Stacey merely shrugged her shoulders ambiguously, sipping the aromatic coffee in her hand.

"Yes, Anastasia, I have to confess that you've astounded me. Shocked me. There are few people who would find the courage and strength to come and tell the truth. And moreover, avoid insults and apologize directly. If Roxanne were home, she would not have been able to control her emotions and would surely start to cry."

"She's not here?" Stacey asked with surprise.

"She is away on business. It has already been a month, by my reckoning, and she will be away for another. I hope that..."

"I already spoke with everyone and asked them to bring everything back to order," Stacey smiled, understanding what Alexander had wanted to ask her. "I'm sure that they'll come back this very week. If anything, give us a call. You have our number."

Almost imperceptibly, the conversation transitioned to purchases and sales and how Alexander's website was doing, so I grew bored. With all due respect to the speakers, I didn't care.

"May I offer you a tour of our gallery?" After half an hour, when I had begun to yawn openly, the owner made a gesture to the butler. It looked like he wasn't planning on letting Stacey go and she wasn't rushing to get back home. Alexander was an interesting conversation partner.

The old man led me to a wide and long corridor that played the role of the local art gallery. There were many paintings. In fact there were very many. Large, small, pretty, vivid, dark — not every museum could boast such a collection. I even began to wonder whether they were all real or fakes...They could easily have been the latter to — Alexander had demonstrated his proclivity for imitation.

"The ancestors of the Vecchi," the old man began to explain, stopping before the first painting. Dressed in ancient vividly colored costumes, the man and woman stood beside a fireplace smiling at the viewer. Alexander — the painting featured none other than him — had been depicted very manfully. The proud bearing, the rapier hanging from his belt, the gaze of a thinker directed into infinity — the painter had managed to convey Mr. Vecchi's grandeur and charisma effectively. The woman, I would guess Roxanne, was also depicted...

A cold sweat swept over me. My nervous system glitched. A wind howled through my head — there was not a single thought in it. I froze like a sculpture — unable to look away from the smiling woman. The woman looking at me from the portrait of the Vecchi was none other than Marina.

The same Marina who had set me up and sent me to prison, the same Marina who had returned to betray me again.

CHAPTER ELEVEN
THE BURDEN OF THE CREATOR

"DANIEL, I'LL SAY IT AGAIN — this is nonsense!" Stacey spent our ride home fruitlessly trying to appeal to my reason. Yet I remained unshakable: Roxanne and Marina were the same person for me. In an attempt to disabuse me of my conviction, Alexander showed us photos and videos of Roxanne — which only made me dig in my heels further. This was definitely the woman who had offered to become my girlfriend during that ill-fated seminar. Alexander tried to get in touch with Roxanne in order to prove me wrong, but her phone was out of network range. As it had been that entire month — which prompted me to remind those present what had happened with the so-called Marina. She had been incinerated. This really made the palace owner lose his cool. Calling me "a milksop oaf," he kindly requested that we depart his residence and never consider returning ever again. On the whole, the entire evening ended unpleasantly with a tangle I couldn't make any sense of.

"Stacey, I can prove to you that this isn't nonsense!" An interesting thought suddenly came to me. "Turn around! We need to go to Cafe Alventa!"

Cafe Alventa was an establishment of great renown among certain narrow circles. This was where burned-out Barliona players would go to try to wait out their dependency on the game. You could arrange a secret one-on-one meeting here, even if someone was spying on you. Most importantly, this was the unofficial headquarters of the Freelance artists.

"Mahan, Anastaria." An enormous bartender nodded at us as if we were long-time pals. Despite the late hour, the place was practically brimming — the in-game pace of life in Barliona left an impression on this corner of reality. When we entered the cafe, I heard someone whisper *"Look! It's Mahan and Anastaria! What are they doing here?"* but no one tried to block our way or talk to us. This wasn't the kind of place where you did something like that.

The giant bartender had a dishtowel in his hands and was automatically drying glasses with it. His expressionless face could easily have led you to assume that he was off somewhere in his thoughts, but his eyes betrayed the opposite — the bartender's clinging gaze checked everything up and down, assessing how much danger this or that detail posed to the establishment. I didn't know the bar manager personally as I hadn't been here in a few months, but I knew for certain that anyone in his position would have earned it for good reason.

"I'd like to organize a poker tournament. I need other players. Everything by the rules." If you were to translate this to open speech, I had said: *"I have work. I need a Freelancer. Without anything illegal."*

"Why would a player who prefers to play on his own, prefer others?" the bartender asked in a bombast, still mechanically drying a glass.

"I need independent people. The outcome of the tournament might be so unexpected that the girl with me here, might not believe it. I want to demonstrate that the game was fair and within the rules."

"Will you be playing using a Barliona deck?" the bartender frowned, for the first time betraying an emotion. There were plenty of hot-heads willing to risk everything to hack Barliona but they were not allowed into this cafe. Alventa prized its reputation.

"No, a standard deck. No Barliona or other themes."

"Cat!" the bartender suddenly barked loud enough for the entire place to hear. "Take these guests to the game room! We're about to hold a tournament!"

Law enforcement agencies naturally knew all about this place but tried not to interfere with its operations. Freelancers, just like private detectives, were very useful people. Data recovery, lost passwords, information, exploits — they were frequently employed for legal as well as mostly-legal purposes. The big fish that dealt with 'dirty' as well as 'big' business, didn't hang around the cafe, but we didn't need those either.

"Dan, I don't understand what we came here for," Stacey addressed me as soon as we'd settled down at the gaming table. "What are you trying to prove?"

"I'm not trying to prove anything. I want to show you," I smirked, clenching my fists under the table. The likelihood that the data that I want to find hasn't already been wiped was around 50%. Either they'd erased it or they hadn't. I could run this search on my own — I had the skills and experience to do it — but I didn't want to give Stacey a reason to doubt me. As soon as she sees the result, she'll believe me on the spot.

"Good day, gentlemen!" The door opened and five people entered the room with a dealer behind them. They wore masks yet, despite this, I knew two of them. Our paths had crossed in the past. The other three were unfamiliar to me, but I hadn't any doubts that they were competent — the bartender didn't let people wander in off the street. It took recommendations and proven experience to get these gigs.

"Place your bets," the dealer dealt our hands. "Mahan has the big blinds. Anastaria small blinds. Take your places gentlemen."

Everyone took their seats and the 'game' got

under way.

"Here's the situation," I began, folding my hand. "Eighteen months ago, a Freelancer retraining took place. No doubt you took part in it. I need any information you can get about a girl who sat beside me at that event. Who she is, where she's from, how she got here and why. The most important thing I need is a video or photos of that retraining session. I'm certain that this data is stored for about three years, so you shouldn't have any difficulty finding it. I'm willing to pay double. I need all this as quickly as possible."

"Why do you need this, Daniel?" asked one of the masks. I recognized her — several years ago we tried to date, but nothing had come of it.

"I suspect that the girl who had introduced herself to me as Marina is none other than..."

"Let's find the girl first," Anastaria interrupted me, tossing several chips into the pot. "I raise. And I'll add that we need a full list of who was at that meeting. The female part. A dossier for each one, including a photo. You may exclude yourself," Stacey turned to the masked girl. "You were there, weren't you?"

"Determine the female participants, provide dossiers about them, including a photo and a video of the seminar," the girl replied without a hint of awkwardness. "Anything else?"

"No. Whoever does this first will get paid treble.

Everyone else will get the agreed rate."

"So everyone will get paid?"

"Yes. I need as much information as possible."

"When's the deadline?"

"Yesterday," I smiled. "The earlier, the better. But no later than within 24 hours."

"I accept the terms," said one of the unfamiliar masks, pushing his chips into the center. For him, the game had ended. "All in!"

"Call," echoed everyone else. "Your assignment will be completed."

The game ended. The dealer helped us draft the services contract in which I accepted all liability for any illegal action the people I hired undertook, and then I transferred the required money to the cafe's account and passed on my contact information for where the obtained the information was to be sent. Then I headed home quite satisfied, while Stacey followed behind without saying a word. Until we got home, at least. As soon as we had showered and gotten into bed, she turned to me and said:

"Let's assume — and I do mean *assume* — that you're right. As I recall it, you mentioned that you had looked for information about Marina after your bet. You even found something. Why then didn't you notice the resemblance between a simple programmer and one of the most famous women of not just our city, but our entire region?"

"I wasn't looking for information about a

specific person," I explained, realizing that I couldn't avoid being honest here. "I needed info about Marina's education and the courses that she had taken. Comparing her appearance to some celebrity didn't really cross my mind. Plus, I've never been interested in celebrities. The posters I had of you were more than enough. You were my celebrity."

"Don't change the topic."

"Stacey, I'll say it again — it's not just that I'm sure that Roxanne is Marina and they are one person. I'm utterly convinced of it. It's...It's like in the game when your premonition screams that you need to do something."

"So what is it screaming now?"

"That I should figure it out and understand: what, why and how? Do you understand that if I'm right, then Donotpunnik's conspiracy reached far deeper than it even seems right now? Why would Roxanne get involved in it? Would the wealthiest woman in the world really risk everything over some more money? Her status, her name, her freedom? Her very life, if you think about it! Remember what Alex said: They never did find Marina. That is, they found a heap of ash that remained of her."

"I don't understand," Stacey frowned. "What are you getting at?"

"You know," I sat up from my excitement, "I even see now what happened! Marina really does exist! Or rather existed!"

"You're scaring me, Dan."

"Look! Assume that there really was a freelancer named Marina who specialized in exploits. Some old, wrinkled, one-legged lady, obese and unable to move on her own. One-and-a-half years ago she had to attend a retraining session, but instead Roxanne showed up in her place. Under her name. If I'm right, and damn it, I feel that I am, then our search results should be pretty fascinating! The freelancers will dig up a dossier on Marina, who she is and where she's from, and yet if they find a video, well, there won't be any Marina in it. But Roxanne will be there!"

"You've been watching too many cartoons," Stacey smirked a little unconfidently, but I was on a roll:

"Alex was looking for Marina and he found her! Inside Barliona everyone knew Roxanne as Mirida, so...Stacey!" My eyes glowed. "We need to visit Hellfire or Donotpunnik. They saw her out in reality! Let's show them a photo of Roxanne and ask them whether they recognize her? I'm sure that Alex can arrange a meeting for us!"

"Did you forget that you're an outlaw in Barliona?"

"Ah the hell with the Reputation! I mean really! I had it, I lost it, to hell with it! This is a game after all!"

"Dan, forget the word 'game,'" Stacey sat up.

"For you, Barliona is a way of earning your living and providing for your family. You have a clan that earns you a stable income. What its owner's Reputation is means a lot."

"It's not an issue. Once they install the capsule, I'll make you the clan head. Meanwhile, I'll deal with Geranika and Karmadont. Something tells me that if I get to the bottom of that whole affair, either I'll get it in the back of the neck, which is where I am now anyway, or I'll end up with some exceptional bonuses. I'll transfer the clan over to you tomorrow."

"The hell with that! You're not making a clan head out of me," smirked Stacey. "I'm with you. Do you really thing that you and Plinto will get all the goodies? Like hell!"

"Hey, that's my catchphrase..."

"Darling Danny, you better get used to it — from now on we are one in sickness and in health. So, I won't be letting you go on your own, don't even count on it. Make Fleita the head."

"Who?" I almost started from surprise.

"Fleita the Decembrist, aka Julia DeCembreaux. I'll draft the contract, don't worry," Stacey paused, gauging my reaction and laughed: "I found out everything there is to find out about that girl. Don't worry. She's studying to be an economist, has a boyfriend — that is, had a boyfriend — now she's free and spends all her time in Barliona getting used to her new race. It's looking like the

Corporation has decided to turn her into a new object of 'reverence' by including her in a bunch of new scenarios. She's not afraid of responsibility despite her capricious attitude and she's intelligent and knows how to behave responsibly. She'll be a perfect clan head, believe me. Do you want me to speak to her myself?"

"Uh...Erm..." I replied with eloquent astonishment, staring at Stacey's hazel eyes. In the twilight they were so dark that I couldn't even see their whites. Two deep, dark wells, capable of consuming the mind of anyone who crossed her path — in the given instance, me.

"It's agreed then," Stacey smiled, adding a twinkle to her dark eyes. "Tomorrow I'll go see Geranika and ask to join his team. He let Plinto in, after all."

"Plinto lost all of his Reputation," I tried to object, but Stacey was unshakable.

"Darling, I remember the Dark Forest. I remember what you did and what you got as a reward when it was all over. I find it hard to believe that the Corporation will really strip you of everything you've attained. And I want to be among those who'll gain the bonuses, so I'm with you. Are there any questions? Objections? No? Very good. Come over here..."

The technicians came early in the morning. Corporate professionalism kept them from saying out loud what was evident enough on their faces and no doubt 'bunch of clumsy apes' was among the kinder of their thoughts. My capsule was moved to the wall. The networking cables were tucked neatly away into said wall and we signed another heap of documentation about our liabilities with the equipment. After we'd gotten rid of our glum guests but before going to see Geranika, I opened my mail.

> *From: Cafe Alventa Administration*
> *To: Daniel Mahan*
> *Daniel, attached please find the results from one of your tournament members. Payment has been made. We look forward to working with you in the future.*
> *Kind regards,*
> *Cafe Alventa*

"Come here, Stacey," I smiled, seeing the dossier on a Marina Corvus, aged 31. I had made a slight mistake — Marina wasn't overweight. To the opposite, she was attractive with pretty blue eyes, a turned-up nose and spiraling chestnut hair. The only problem was that this woman bore no resemblance whatsoever to the Marina I had encountered at the seminar.

"This is the Marina who is now a little heap of ash," I began to explain the files I'd received to Stacey. "And look, the actual video of the seminar has been deleted. It doesn't exist! Even though this data is kept for three years, someone with access to serious resources managed to delete it. HOWEVER! As we both know, Cat was at the same retraining session as me. She had a video of her own which is...Voila! Staceykins, I present to you the Marina that framed me and sent me to prison. Now, tell me, darling, do you still think I'm crazy?"

"What the..." Stacey whispered in shock, shut her eyes and cursed. I was right like never before — on the video, sitting beside me and dutifully writing down the citation for yet another law was none other than Roxanne Vecchi.

"We need to go see Hellfire," Stacey growled/whispered through her teeth a minute later. "Can you set it up?"

"Let's try it," I nodded and dialed the Corporate number. "Put me in touch with Alex Herman..."

"What can I say..." Alex rubbed his chin, looking sadly at the wall. It took me ten minutes to get through a hundred managers and assistant vice presidents to Alex and he, hearing my conclusions, decided to come visit us at home right away. Looking at the documents that I had by now received from all five of my mercenaries, Alex's face went grim. "Whenever it seems that everything is clear and unambiguous, Mahan rides in and turns everything upside down. Where'd you pick up this talent — or is it something you have to be born with?"

Without waiting for her answer, Alex went on:

"First of all — not a word about your suspicions to anyone. That's right Mahan — suspicions! Until you have proof of the opposite, Roxanne is innocent. We'll talk to Alexander. We'll take the documents and...Damn! Why do you need to see Donotpunnik?"

"To make sure that..." I began, but Alex cut me off.

"Again, this case is now in our jurisdiction. Meeting Donotpunnik or Hellfire might hurt the investigation. If you're right and Mari...Roxanne I mean, is really alive, then seeing Donotpunnik can only hurt. She's sure to be following anything around these people. I can't let you do that..."

"Clutzer," unexpectedly even to myself, I called Alex by his Barliona name, causing him to start as if he'd seen — or in this case heard — a ghost, "I need to talk to Donotpunnik. I have no idea why. But I need to. Set it up...please."

Once again a silence descended on our apartment; only now, three people were involved. And two of them were staring at me and thinking about something feverishly. Finally Alex sighed deeply and slowly, as if under great stress, said:

"Tomorrow you can see Donotpunnik. Daniel...You know, I spent a long time studying the code that went into your Shamanic premonition. And, well...It didn't exist. Your premonition is simply your own personal premonition. A sixth sense. A third eye.

Call it what you want. I'll arrange the meeting but I insist that you don't mention Roxanne to anyone. This is very important."

Attention everyone! Everyone! EVERYONE!

The first Kalragon inter-clan tournament begins today!

Face the best players of Barliona! In addition to the three empires (that's right, you heard correctly — three!), representatives of all of Barliona's continents will take part in the tournament as invited guests.

Become the best among the best!

The notification announcing the launch of the event filled the space before my eyes and refused to be swiped aside. I had to read it in its entirety. As soon as the system made sure that I had fully read it, the notification dissolved like fog. I looked around and couldn't help but smirk — the library had been fully restored. There was no sign that I had recently destroyed it by creating the Karmadont Chess Set.

"Oh! Has the doom of all life decided to wake up from his nap?" Geranika's wry voice sounded beside me. "Took you a good while to come to."

"I see the library's already been repaired," I ignored Geranika's barb, examining the nearest shelves. "Was it difficult?"

"The Spirit of Barliona has gifted you three

teleportations," Geranika went on. This conversation was beginning to remind me of an exchange between two deaf people — everyone's doing the talking but no one's listening. "You will be sent to Altameda immediately, from there to Pryke and then back. You know, Mahan, I'm curious what you did to attract such attention. Did you sell your soul?"

"Are you asking why all the empires have it in for me?" I decided to play his game, but to my surprise Geranika replied:

"Not all of them. Only Kartoss and Malabar. Shadow couldn't give a damn what threat you pose to the pillars of this world."

I looked at Geranika with puzzlement, causing him to burst out in laughter:

"You have no idea what I'm talking about, do you? If you get into the Tomb, you'll discover a lot of unnecessary information. Information that the Emperor and the Dark Lord would prefer to keep secret. That's why every Free Citizen has been given the single quest of stopping you from reaching that secret. They're using them like a flock of sheep that mills in front of the gates and doesn't let anyone into the village. Although, they're using them about the only way you can use Free Citizens. Brainless sheep."

"Those sheep stole your scepter," I reminded Geranika of one of the episodes of in our mutual past. It's never pleasant when an NPC insults players.

"And forced me to make concessions," he

agreed without batting an eyelid. "You can add that the same sheep made me mortal by piercing me with the horn of the unicorn. But that's in the past. You and I inhabit the present, in which you pose a mortal threat to the entire world order. Were it up to me, I'd happily help you, but...Well, it's not allowed. The Emperor and the Dark Lord have made a deal with Barliona itself. And Barliona accepted their terms."

"Why?" I asked baffled. "What'll happen if I get into the Tomb?"

"Let's put it this way — there won't be much good from it," a hoarse voice said from behind me. I turned around. A man and an orc. An old man and an...old green orc. Wrapped in torn, tattered and soiled gray capes — the kind that the homeless sometimes resort to — they looked utterly out of place even in the Spartan decor of Geranika's palace. I found myself looking at two pairs of white eyes that had faded with time, causing me to feel a bit awkward and forcing me to read the properties of the new arrivals. It's nice to know who I'm dealing with...

Darius (Level 1000 Human).
Critchet (Level 1000 Orc).

I shook my head in bafflement, trying to dispel my confusion. This simply couldn't be! Had Barliona broken down? I checked Geranika's properties just in case.

Geranika (Level 1000 Human). Lord of Shadow. Shadow Harbinger. Narlak City Guardian.

No, everything seemed okay. Who the hell are these two then? There's a dozen or two creatures in all of Barliona who are at Level 1000. Emperors, gods and their analogues, such as the Supreme Spirits and, erm, key NPCs like Renox. And that was all! There's not supposed to be any Dariuses or Critchets on this list!

"The Tomb is a secondary matter," Darius went on, arranging himself in a chair with a creak. The NPC's hands trembled noticeably as he placed his walking stick aside. I looked over at the orc and frowned — only now did I notice that he too was on his last legs. They trembled and his face periodically twisted in a grimace — the orc was suffering but he remained standing. He was supporting himself with his crutch, but he stood as if wishing to demonstrate that he had strength enough — that he was stronger than the human. Damn! These old fogeys are about to fall apart to pieces without even telling me anything interesting. On a whim, I grabbed a chair and taking several steps offered it to the orc. He sat down in it with an evident sigh of relief and gave me a grateful look. It took but a moment but it was enough to understand that I had done a great favor for him.

"Let me introduce you, Mahan," Geranika stepped between the old men. "The old tired orc is

Critchet. The old tired human is Darius. Be sure to love and honor them. They have several questions for you."

The old men wanted to know the story of Lait that I had learned in the cave. Especially as it concerned the Alabaster Throne. Surprisingly, the two NPCs began inquiring after the method of blocking the Shadows in the presence of the Lord of Shadow himself. Deciding that this was probably just another puzzle that the devs had cooked up for players who'd set upon the path of Shadow, I related everything I managed to learn in the cave without omitting a single detail.

"In that case, we must assume that the desert appeared because Karmadont took the crystal," Darius summarized enigmatically and, seeing the puzzlement on my face, explained: "Initially the Creator himself blocked the effect of the Throne. After that the crystal. Once Karmadont removed the Ergreis, it was only the power granted to Lait that blocked the Throne's effects from afflicting Barliona. And yet that wasn't enough and as a result an enormous lifeless desert formed around the cave where you killed the phantoms. Everything is dead in it."

"This may be a dumb question, but who are you guys anyway?" I decided to start figuring things out. "Why are you interested in the Throne? And why don't you ask its owner about it? I mean, he's standing right here, grinning like an idiot. I bet he knows more than me about what's going on."

"Heh, who we are, what we are, how we are..." the orc muttered to himself. "We already told you. We're old, tired creatures who have their own particular goals. As for you — it's time for you to go to Altameda. You're due for an opening ceremony of a tournament!"

The orc flourished his hand and I suddenly found myself in midair. Or rather, the floor receded from me in a whimsical way without me feeling any motion at all. If I shut my eyes, I'd imagine myself still standing on it. But if I open them...Oh the horror. The old man mimicked his partner and a brilliant, emerald portal appeared right before me. What the hell is this then?! That's not supposed to happen in Barliona — portals are either blue, white or (in really extreme and typically sinister situations) red! But certainly never green!

The orc flourished his hand again and the invisible plane that I had been standing on vanished. I went flying into the portal like an Olympic diver: graceful, without a splash and with a fancy pirouette in mid-flight. I'd give myself a 9.9 for that one without a second thought.

"Master! They're down again!" Viltrius squeaked plaintively, coddling a catatonic hobgoblin in his arms. The portal spit me out right in Altameda's main hall, wiping out the hobgoblins in the process.

Neither Geranika nor this geriatric couple had any respect or for that matter concern for my castle's teleportation defense.

"Viltrius you have one day to come up with an effective method of blocking unwanted guests from teleporting into our castle," I seethed at the cringing majordomo. "If you have to buy something more powerful than hobgoblins, then buy it. If you have to level up the hobgoblins, level them up. If you need to make a deal with the Guardian, then make it! I'm tired of whoever waltzing into my castle whenever they feel like it. Or do I need to find another majordomo who'll be able to solve this problem?"

Despite his generally green tint, Viltrius turned as white as chalk, squealed that he would resolve the problem this very instant and then vanished. I collapsed in my rocking throne and cursed for good measure. I don't know what came over me. Going off on an NPC who served me truly and sincerely was stupid and wrong, but the emotions roiling within me demanded some release. I'm not made of stone finally! I have an utter mess on my hands back in reality, while here in Barliona the devs have come up with an entirely different mess in which I'm enemy number one. On top of it all, Stacey is pregnant and I have no idea what I'm supposed to do...Argh!

"Mahan, it's such a pleasure to encounter you in the castle!" Spiteful Gnum barreled into the main hall. "I'm finished! When are we going to test it?"

"You're finished with what?" I didn't understand what was going on at first, still in my misanthropic rut.

"What do you mean?" Gnum looked at me with unvarnished surprise, shock even. "The airship. You came by to look at it yourself! I told you that I'd manage it in a week — well, it only took a few days after all! Check it out — I'm like your very own mad scientist! To get the power unit to work, you need forty chunks of azarcite which is as volatile as my wife during pregnancy. The chance of making it is one in five hundred, and it burns through resources so fast that your goblin started looking at me funny. And then bam! A few tweaks here and there, an adjustment to the alchemical processes and I got all the azarcite I needed! Enough sitting around! Let's go test this baby!"

Reflexively, I opened the Harbinger's 'Blink' input box and entered the workshop's coordinates. Who'd imagine actually walking there...Yet Barliona had a surprise for me — the Blink didn't happen.

Due to the 'Burden of the Creator' scenario, you are unable to use your Blink ability.

"Come on, Mahan! What're you just sitting there for?" Gnum refused to leave me alone, literally pulling me out of my chair. "You're not allowed to teleport, stop molesting the teleportation system. No means no! It's you and your feet, *mon ami*, so up and at 'em!"

As we emerged into an open area, I turned into my Dragon Form and flapped my wings several times. Surprise number two — I can't fly either. Unwilling to give up, I asked Gnum to summon a griffin, clambered onto its back and encountered surprise number three — the bird squeaked, thrashed its wings but couldn't get off the ground even a centimeter.

"Are you done?" To my surprise, Gnum waited out my experiments stoically. "Didn't you read? You're enemy number one and all that. You're not allowed to fly."

Then Gnum smiled maniacally and added:

"At least, not the way everyone else flies."

I had nothing left to do but follow the gnome, since he didn't bother explaining the thought behind his grin. With a mere 'you'll see for yourself,' Gnum shuffled ahead of me to the workshop, managing to stop on his way next to empty niches tisk his tongue and shake his head.

"I can see there's work upon work here," Gnum said, stopping beside yet another empty nave, and then turned to me and asked: "When are you going to busy yourself with the castle? Level 26 was impressive last year! Phoenix, as I hear it, is already almost at Level 30! We should bomb them! I already came up with bombs! I don't have a lot at the moment, but we all know that the recipe is the most important bit!"

"Gnum, sometimes I'm afraid to imagine what goes on in your mind," I replied honestly. "A hundred interconnected sentences that..."

"That arrange themselves into perfect fractal — if...if you ignore all the everyday dross!" the gnome replied in a huff. "I really have to explain everything to you...No, but okay, that'll come later. There's no time right now. Come on. I'm gonna show you my little bird! Don't you need a way to move around Barliona?"

By the time we reached the workshop, neither one of us was saying anything. The gnome's last phrase had piqued my curiosity to such a degree that I decided not to tempt fate by irritating the inventor with further talk. What if he gets upset and refuses to show me the...

"Ta-da!" Gnum yelled triumphantly, throwing open the workshop's enormous doors. "Love and cherish her — *Gnum's Valor* — a Giant Airborne Squidolphin. Or GAS for short! I came up with it myself!" Gnum added with pride. At his word, the succubi yanked off an enormous white sheet, revealing the airship.

No, not an airship...

An airborne monster!

When I had last seen the ship, she had been concealed by trussing and it had been difficult to assess the magnitude of *Gnum's Valor* or *Folly* or whatever. Now, however, I was staring with shock at an enormous steel octopus, unsure of whether I should be happy or not. The octopus's body consisted of a three-deck round construction that had ten tentacles attached over it like a steel cupola. Similar tentacles were protruding from the ship's side, giving her the resemblance of a Squidolphin. And yet the similarity ended there. I should tell Gnum to change his name to Frankenstein!

"Does it fly at least?" I managed, approaching closer.

"Come on now!" Gnum was about to get upset again, but thought better of it and suggested I climb aboard. "Hang on, you'll see!" The time had come for me to test Barliona's sensitivity. This wasn't technically a means of transportation — it was a part of Barliona that had been torn up into the sky. And therefore it shouldn't be blocked from flying with me on board!

I climbed aboard up a spiral staircase. According to Gnum, all players with access would fly in on griffins or teleport in, while the staircase was for my use exclusively. So that I wouldn't forget my roots.

Still not understanding what Gnum meant by that, I clambered onto the ship. The diameter of the central circle was so long that I even glanced over at the doors. To my trained eye, we wouldn't fit.

"Gnum, don't you think the entrance is too tight?" I asked the gnome who had stuck some odd-looking goggles on his face.

"Entrance?" he furrowed his brow and then broke into a smile. "Who needs an entrance? This baby flies wherever she likes!"

Your castle has been damaged...

Just in case I hadn't noticed that Gnum had just ripped open a giant hole in the workshop's ceiling, the system reminded me that any game action is monitored and evaluated accordingly. In this case, by means of finances, since the Imperial Stone that is required to repair buildings, costs an arm and a leg. The walls and roof collapsed inward, crushing various equipment beneath the rubble, but the ship crawled out of this conflagration unharmed — the upraised tentacles worked as conduits for a forcefield that protected the GAS. We rose slowly and through my porthole I managed to spy Viltrius, aghast and stunned, reckoning up the cost of repairs, yet the goblin's plight soon receded to the back of my mind. I felt triumph — I had managed to fly! Against all odds!

"You're not allowed to fly, teleport or use flying transports," explained Gnum. "But the GAS isn't a flying transport, it's an ordinary marine vessel that...Ah! Look — we have guests."

A hundred griffins arose into the air, surrounding us from all sides. Since we were above the castle, the players couldn't get very close, and arranged themselves around Altameda's perimeter. A moment later, the first lightning bolt came flying at our GAS, then another and a few moments later we found ourselves in the center of a Tesla Coil that was being set off by hundreds of people at once.

"The hell with the lot of them!" Gnum's grimace dissolved when he saw the outcome of the attacks. The ship (we, the players inside of it still couldn't be attacked directly) remained unharmed. The forcefield worked as intended.

"My turn," Gnum rubbed his hands and pressed something on the virtual control panel. Portholes opened up all around the ship's perimeter, unveiling a thicket of ballistae. I frowned — instead of ordinary ammunition like arrows or pikes, the ballistae were loaded with ordinary nets. How would that defeat this mass of enemies?

"We can't hurt the players, right?" the gnome smiled and waiting for my puzzled nod, went on: "There! So we will use the tried and true method. On the count of three! Two! One! Fire!"

The GAS shuddered noticeably. I ran up to the railing and watched entranced as the broadside of nets hurled untroubled through the lightning bolts which only scorched them a little. A few of the players thought of getting out of the trajectory of the cloud flying from our ship, darting aside, but the nets were flying too quickly. And there were way too many of the players around us anyway. Hovering in place and pouring lightning on a motionless target is one thing.

Dodging a bunch of flying nets is something else entirely.

We didn't damage the players. That was forbidden. But like the GAS, the griffins were game objects that could be interacted with. The nets tangled up the mounts' wings causing them to plummet to the ground. And since Barliona has a relatively realistic physics engine, an uncontrolled fall to the ground from a hundred meters up...Again, a few of the players thought of casting bubbles and save themselves from respawning, but the majority of those who had surrounded the GAS were sent to take a break out in reality owing to a fatal lack of wits. Well, who asked them to attack me anyway?

"Again?" Gnum yelled into a device that looked like a loudhailer. The dozen of griffins that had managed to avoid the nets and remained circling around our ship put some distance between us and them.

"Bring her down," I decided, reading the notifications. Several clans were complaining that I had destroyed their players and equipment. Did they really think that I was about to compensate them? "Gnum, I need a manual for how to fly this ship."

"Here," the gnome handed me a pair of odd goggles similar to the ones he was already wearing. "There's no manual, but you'll figure it out. Ah! Look — the tournament's getting started over there!"

"Oh goddamn!" I blurted out when I realized

the scale of the tragedy. Until this moment, I felt fairly ambivalently about the tournament, shelling out the dough and trying to stay out of the event's overall organization. Now that the tournament had begun, however, I was shocked at its scale. A sea of people had taken up residence outside of Altameda. The tent city alone with its sharp points receded far into the horizon. Several auxiliary buildings had been erected near the castle, among which I could only identify the arena and the multi-colored merchants' tents mixed with small squares — and all of it roiled with people.

"The obstacle course," Gnum indicated one of the facilities filled with players. "That's where the opening ceremony will be held today."

I looked in the indicated direction and started back from the railing — Gnum hadn't finished his sentence when a myriad of fireworks erupted in the sky. Large, small, variously colored and shaped — the beauty of the event managed to overwhelm even the sun peeking from the clouds.

"Wanna make bets on who'll win the tournament?" Gnum offered when the ship began to slowly descend. "I'd guess the Celestial. Our boys have arms growing out of all the wrong places. Plus without Plinto or Anastaria, their chances will be zero."

"Astrum," I blurted out the first thing that came to mind. "They might be able to compete. Do you have any idea what the reward is?"

"Eh? Everyone knows that — whoever wins gets the Tomb of the Creator."

"Erm..."

"Ugh. I meant the 'Original' status — not the Tomb. As in, all the loot they find in it will be really sweet or something. Mahan, are you all right? Mahan, you're..."

The cocoon lid slid aside releasing me. Without thinking long, I pushed the external exit button on Stacey's capsule and, while the system got her ready for exit, dialed the Corporation on the phone.

"Put me in touch with the innovations department!"

The next half hour was full of unpleasant discoveries. The top prize in the tournament had been kept in complete secret. No one knew about it up until the last moment. It had been Stacey's dad's idea to offer the 'Original' status as a prize. He personally lobbied the Corporation on this issue, arguing that this was even "necessary in order to limit the influence that one player has on inter-clan relations." As James explained, the Corporation immediately agreed with this perspective — everything that pertains to a single player can easily remain his: Altameda, the Chess Set, his unique race — these are all toys for a single player. But as soon as the interests of a clan comes up, there should be some mechanism for doubling certain features, otherwise the player with the bonus can begin to extort other clans. By way of example, Ehkiller brought up my sale of the Tears of Harrashess and the tickets to the Dark Forest as vivid examples of virtual extortion. As a result, one of the tournament rewards was set as the 'Original' status for the Tomb of the Creator. You can't leave such a lever over others in the hands of just one player. However, James tried to cheer us up too, explaining that I could still win the tournament and thereby retain the status. Or rather, I would retain it in any case, but this way I would prevent anyone else from getting it. That would be entirely within the spirit of the game...

We ended up having to catch Ehkiller in the game — the tournament's opening ceremony was at its peak and he played one of its main roles. Sponsor, organizer, participant — Killer reveled in the general attention to his person, and we were forced to wait for him for a very long time. At last, Ehkiller deigned to answer us.

"I don't understand what you're so upset about. In the game, everything has to follow the game rules. This decision has been completely approved by the Corporation's ethics committee, so we have no other choice but to accept it and move forward. Prove that you're the only one worthy of this status! Mahan, it's in your hands — Shadows are officially allowed to participate."

"That's my Tomb!" I yelled enraged.

"This isn't some toy that you can have all to

yourself," Ehkiller cut me off tersely. "Mahan, you're starting to repeat yourself, so I'm going to go. Again — the decision was made with the Corporation's approval and all we have to do is abide by it. Signing off!"

"Stacey, this is a set up!" I looked at the girl with shock. "They stole the Tomb!"

"It's not as simple as it seems. I'm sure," judging by her tone, Stacey was trying to persuade herself more than me. "Dad would've never done this if there was even one way to resist. It's not as simple as..."

"Stacey, I really couldn't give a fig for what your dad decided with the Corporation," I told her in a cold voice. Everything inside of me was in an uproar, but it would've been dumb to go off on the girl. It wasn't her fault that her father turned out to be a complete bastard. "I won't let them seal that Dungeon. The Tomb will be completed and it'll be completed by my clan. And that's that."

"Dan..." Stacey sighed deeply, shaking her head. "We don't have the resources to interfere with them. They'll lock us in a respawn point and won't let us out until the winner completes the Dungeon. By the time that the Guardians get involved, they will have already...It's hopeless. We could've given it a shot if you still had your Blink ability, but in the current situation, the probability that we can even get to the Tomb is incredibly small."

"Small doesn't mean non-existent." An epiphany suddenly engulfed me. A fairly rare occurrence lately, but just the thing I needed right now when all visible paths to a solution had been cut off. Not a question — we'll look for another way. Like real heroes.

Handing Stacey the GAS, which would now play a not insignificant role in my plan, I didn't bother revealing my hand to my wife. First, I'd need to weigh everything and consider it carefully. The stunned Siren ran off to Gnum's workshop to see this wonder of Barliona technology with her own eyes, while yet another mind-numbing idea formed in my head. I'm actually afraid to imagine what the third one will be!

"Hey Plinto!" I got an amulet and began to bring my genius to life. "I need a partner for the 2 vs. 2 arena. We're going to..."

"Mahan, where the hell are you?!" as soon as Plinto understood who was calling, a wild yell burst from the amulet. "We have a Labyrinth scheduled in ten minutes! Get your butt over to the tilt-yard this instant! Call yourself a raid leader...Move it! We'll get disqualified!"

"Viltrius, I need a map of the tournament!" I yelled, dashing headlong out of Altameda. In my rush, I forgot that the amulet was still activated in my hand, and so for a little while I was cheered on by Plinto's motivational words about me, Stacey, the game and the entire world as a whole. Some of the expressions were so amusing that I couldn't help but laugh. It's a good thing that the Rogue couldn't see me — as that would've only added fuel to the fire. I suppose it's time to get used to playing with a standard character — I had gotten so used to blinking everywhere lately that I hardly paid attention to the time it took to travel anymore.

What really amused me as I ran from the castle to the tiltyard were the Malabarian and Kartossian players trying to get in my way and hinder me in various ways. At first I tried to run around them, but when I couldn't shift my weight and passed right through a groups of orcs from some clan I'd never heard of, I stopped caring and ran straight. PvP was disabled and anyone who wanted to pick up the loot from my body could take a rest. Come back and try again tomorrow, kids!

"Where?" I yelled from afar, seeing Anscenica. The Shadow players were standing in a heap to the side of the tilt-yard entrance, protected by two chains of security. Considering that the guards had their backs to them, the security was for my warriors, protecting them from their hostile surroundings. At first I thought this surprising, since players couldn't be hurt, and yet the vegetables and stones littering the ground in the vicinity suggested that the local NPCs were still playing their traditional roles. The roles of those who loathed everything about Shadow. Anscenica waved her hand in the direction of an enormous, colorful tent positioned close to the entrance, so I adjusted my course and literally came flying into the tent, slamming against an enormous guard.

"The Shadow raid is present and accounted for," sounded Plinto's voice as I tried to untangle myself from the armor of an enormous orc guard. All I had to do was curse the developers for turning the Kartoss guards into metal monsters. How did the designers decide that warriors decked out in spikes would be comfortable fighting? Or even just stand next to others? Let's assume that the Barliona physics engine lets the spikes of two adjacent guards clip through each other — okay, but I'm no NPC! I am strictly bound by my physical interactions with the world around me, in which the guards' spikes are like thorns that catch everything that's not well placed, at standstill or running.

Plinto handed a piece of paper to an important-looking, gaunt NPC in a dressy waistcoat from the time of Michelangelo or Leonardo da Vinci. This official even had a large hat with a long voluminous feather that brushed up against the tent's ceiling, completing his image. The image of a creature that hated the entire world. With unconcealed revulsion, the official accepted the document with two fingertips and instantly dropped it onto a massive desk cluttered with similar papers.

"Shadow," he seethed through his teeth.

"Registration confirmed. The Labyrinth will begin in three minutes...May you perish in it!"

"We need to register for the arena too!" I managed to yell, untangling myself from the orc. Rushing over to the stand with the blank forms, I found the one for the arena, paid the entry fee, entered my name and Plinto's and handed it to the official, who grimaced even further.

"Arena registration is closed!" he began, but there was no stopping me. I didn't need the hate of this shrimp, whom the Corporation would erase from the game's memory after the tournament. I needed the hate of the players! And only serious, hardcore hate.

"Is that an official rejection?" I hiked an eyebrow expressively.

"The second participant hasn't yet confirmed his participation, so you can't file a registration..."

"All right, I confirm it," Plinto looked at me attentively. "Mahan, the hell do you need the arena for? We don't have any tactics worked out and we've never even fought together. A Shaman and a Rogue are by default mincemeat for, say, a Paladin and a Death Knight, so..."

"Registered! Duo number 1,032,669," the official even smiled when he heard Plinto's words. An entrance fee was withdrawn from my account, forcing me to whistle — a thousand gold! Considering the number of participants, the Corporation had just made a cool billion out of thin air. I want to make money like that too!

"Come on," Plinto literally pulled me toward the exit. "The Labyrinth starts in a minute. We need to get ready."

CHAPTER TWELVE

THE ARENA

"ALL RIGHT, SURPRISE ME. What the hell do you need the arena for?" Plinto tore himself away from a mug of a stat-restoring liquid and leaned back in his armchair. The tavern that had been erected near the tilt-yard was full of people despite the fact that it actually consisted of several hundred virtual instances of its main hall to accommodate the insane number of guests.

We went through the Labyrinth like hot knives through butter. The designers hadn't bothered to come up with anything fancy for the qualifying stage of this competition, limiting themselves to two bosses with three attacks that we knew ahead of time. It still remained a mystery to me why they called it a Labyrinth even though it was no more than a straight hallway. There were no turns, no dead ends, nor any cozy out-of-the-way corners to take a nap. Two rooms, two bosses and one hour — this was how long each competitor had to complete the qualifying stage. We managed in twenty-three minutes, losing only two players along the way. The bosses here were Level 200, so whenever they cast AoE attacks, the low-level players had to be extra careful. Effectively, Plinto and I did the fighting, helped along by Anscenica and Endiga. The rest of our Shadow party hadn't yet reached Level 150 and the bosses were off-limits to them. To Plinto's chagrin, Lori wasn't there. She was practicing a new song with her band, wishing to rip the other competitors to shreds as early as the qualifying phase of the Battle of the Bards.

It was an unspoken rule that once a competition ended, the participants headed to the nearest tavern to celebrate. It's barely worth mentioning that the prices here were astronomical, while the crowd of players looking for a free drink was impassible in all 100 virtual instances of this place. Individual characters and even tables would pop in and out of existence in the tavern, but the general number of players remained about the same. The tournament competitors had started at the same time, so within a few minutes a mob of winners (vanquishers of two angry bosses — a two-horned rhinoceros and a slug) rushed into the tavern. The Celestial players had been the first to complete the qualifying Labyrinth, leaving the tilt-yard a mere three minutes and forty seconds after they'd entered it. The best time had been set very high. The results of the qualifying round didn't affect later standings, but Bihan clearly wanted to signal that his fighters had no equals at the tournament. Astrum had come in second with just over five minutes, while Phoenix wasn't even among the top three.

"Why?" I placed my glass on the tray that the waiter was carrying among the players and turned to face the Rogue. "I want to win."

"Not much of an argument," Plinto smirked but then grew serious. "It took me way too long to earn my 'Bloodied' title to see it evaporate in the arena. Do you think that anyone will be in fear or awe of me if I lose against two pimple-faced students? I may as well delete myself after something like that. So, please, be so kind as to explain the true reason for your wish to become mincemeat."

"The arena, as I understand it, scales everyone to Level 100," I paused waiting for Plinto's nod before continuing, "which means that you can't use any heavy artillery in it."

"That's exactly why we'll be mincemeat," Plinto interrupted. "All of my heavy artillery kicks in at Level 150. The entire arsenal I've been playing with for the last few years consists of Level 200 powers. Now I won't have them, and I'll be no different from a newbie who's just clambered into the capsule. So what's the point?"

"You see," I made a dramatic pause, evoking a frown of displeasure from the Rogue, and then went on: "I want to piss off anyone I can. I'll throw the gauntlet into Bihan's face, at his fighters, at Ehkiller,

Kalatea, whoever! I want to make it so that every arena participant only wants a chance to fight us."

"Let's say I know how to make that happen," little mad devils flared up in Plinto's eyes — the same ones that all of Malabar had learned to fear — yet again he grew serious: "Only, that doesn't explain how you plan on turning two meat-popsicles into fighters. I'll remind you again — you're a Shaman and I'm a Rogue..."

"When did I say I'd fight in the arena as a Shaman," I raised an eyebrow inquisitively. "And I never said that I need you as a Level 100 Rogue. That really would be stupid — to fight as such an odd combination."

"In that case, how..." Plinto began but here his face lit up with the comprehension of my greater idea.

"I'm only a Level 16 Dragon," I went on in an innocent tone, resurrecting the mad devils in Plinto's eyes. Unnoticed by those around us and perhaps even by himself, Plinto transformed into his Vampire Form: The little demons dissolved in the general redness of his eyes. Though the tavern was still full of people, an empty space formed around. The Shadow players that had been sitting beside us remembered that they had urgent business to attend to, the new players for some reason didn't rush to take their vacant seats or, if they phased in from another instance of the tavern, they quickly understood that the beer was colder in another instance. The aura of fear emanating from the

High Vampire worked perfectly.

"I'm terrified to imagine what will happen to a Dragon when he enters the arena at Level 100," I began to shake my head expressively, playing dumb. "There aren't any rules saying we can't use our race powers, are there?"

"You know, Mahan, I feel like taking a walk all of a sudden." If I hadn't been accustomed to Plinto's voice in his Vampire Form, I would've been struck by such a chill that my goosebumps would've been the size of eggs! Despite the disabled PvP, Plinto's voice caused toothaches among the players standing beside us, expanding the 'no-man's-land' around us even further.

"Whom would you like to piss off?" Two serious, red eyes fixed on mine. The joy evaporated from my mind like liquid nitrogen in the open air, so I replied in a voice no less terrible than Plinto's: cold and devastating, saturated with the same nitrogen.

"*Everyone!* The more people want to kill us, the better. I need to replace the cold calculation in people's minds with pure rancor. If I do that, they won't notice the obvious and I'll be able to snatch the Tomb from under their noses. That's the main goal of the arena."

"Stacey?"

"She's with us."

"Where are you going to get the other seventeen?"

"The clan raid," I almost stuttered answering this question. Plinto had caught on too quickly. Was my plan for winning the Tomb really so obvious?

"Won't work. They might leak the plan," Plinto paused pensively. "I have the right friends. How would you feel about some disinterested third parties?"

"Doesn't matter. Only the result is important."

"Like I once said, if there are two ways forward, a correct one and a wrong one, Mahan will always choose the third," said Plinto and after a long pause, during which each one of us thought about our affairs, Plinto thawed and turned back into a human, dispelling the aura of terror around him. The tavern all but sighed a sigh of relief. Noise and babble came pouring back into the space around us. The players looked around puzzled as if failing to understand why a moment ago they wanted to howl from misery, while now everything was buzzing with joy and celebration.

A sphere of negation popped up around us.

"I don't like to warm others' ears," Plinto explained, placing the scroll back into his bag. "I have an idea about how to piss everyone off, you can trust my many years of experience. Here's what I suggest..."

It took us an hour to hammer out a strategy for driving our opponents crazy. Plinto was full of napalm. I hadn't imagined that this small and gaunt Rogue would be so full of anger towards the surrounding world. He took most of the work on himself, leaving me some trivial actions, the general gist of which came down to nodding my head and saying: "Such is my decision. If someone doesn't like it, let's take it to the arena and figure it out." We discussed the upcoming battles too. Plinto assumed reasonably that our Dragon and Vampire ranks — didn't count as levels and wouldn't scale up. However, he remembered Thunderclap perfectly well and how we'd used it to slaughter our enemies in Kartoss and Krispa. He also remembered Draco who had the same power. And he remembered his own powers of control and suppression. In general, the arsenal at our disposal for turning the other players to mincemeat was quite expansive. At the same time Plinto insisted that we fight our first bouts in the arena as Rogue and Shaman. The million participants suggested that we'd have to fight a maximum of twenty rounds to reach the final, so it wouldn't do to play our aces right away. Even as early as the round of 64 everyone would be studying their competitors, so we needed to conceal the powers we'd use in the home stretch as much as possible.

"Gnum, launch the GAS!" When I returned to Altameda, I headed straight for the workshop. Stacey was still there, asking Gnum about the airship's various tactical-technical characteristics, which led to my order going to naught. I was forced to explain.

"I need to clear any aviation enthusiasts from the airspace above the tournament. Anybody that decides to fly must be sent back to earth. We net the griffins as before and reap the XP."

"Erm..." Stacey raised her eyebrows, demanding an explanation.

"I'm tired of being the good guy," I smiled bloodthirstily. "Both empires are out to get me without even explaining why. No problem — in that case, I'll give them a good reason. They will have such a reason to be angry with me that acting on their emotions they will give me exactly what I want. And the Tomb will be ours!"

"They won't remove the defensive perimeter around it," Stacey began but when she encountered my smile, her eyes went wide with surprise.

"Is Plinto with us?"

"Of course. It's his idea to knock down the flyers. We just discussed it."

"We need another 17 people..."

"Plinto promised to come up with them. Damn, is it really that obvious?"

"Hey what are you guys talking about anyway?" Gnum spoke up, demonstrating that it wasn't that obvious. At least someone doesn't see my plan in all its glory.

"Just family talk," said Stacey. "It's not that obvious, Mahan. It's just that I wanted to propose this option myself and was considering how to broach the subject. After all, this thing means a lot to you and to just destroy it...Especially right now. Still, you won't be able to piss everyone off with a single GAS. What else?"

Another sphere of negation appeared around us. Gnum pursed his lips demonstratively, expressing his displeasure at being left out, turned on his heels and walked over to his creation. What a wonder he was! It took me another ten minutes to tell Stacey about our maniacal plot. To my surprise, Stacey approved of it entirely, even though the word Phoenix popped up several times in my explanation.

"I'm with you," she concluded, dispelling the sphere. "I'll take care of Bihan and his lapdog myself, and...Heh, you know Dan, knowing the rules of the game sometimes turns out to be such an advantage...Gnum! I need you to do something for me! We need you to craft some enormous fireworks and attach them to some satchels. Mahan's right — launch the GAS! We're going to clear out the skies over Altameda."

Several hours later, the mood of the players in the camp had reached a boiling point.

"What the hell is Mahan up to?!"

"What is this outrage?! Why aren't we allowed to fly?"

"I call upon a Herald, I request your assistance!"

"Guardian, appear and punish the violators!"

"Do something about these assholes already!"

I walked to the Arena smiling happily and paying no attention to the enraged players. I had to admit that I understood Plinto perfectly. He had been living in an aura of reverence for several years now — the rancor directed at him not only spurred him on, but drove him to exacerbate the situation, do something that would cause the players not just to get in your way to express their anger, but even flee from this same path in fear. For, here comes Death!

In two hours, the GAS had sent about a thousand players to respawn. When we described to Gnum what we wanted him to do, he merely smiled. "Nets are so last century. I'll show them that flying is bad for their health," the gnome said meaningfully and headed off to his ship. I worried about the GAS at first, figuring that its creator's whimsy might be its undoing, but my fears were unfounded. Gnum exceeded all my expectations. Wizened by their initial experience fighting the airship, the enemy players didn't approach it and tried to hit it from afar, yet the GAS didn't fire a single net. Instead, it began to shoot small streams of what looked like sap at the griffins and other flying fauna. The sap gummed up the griffins' wings, forcing them to spiral to the ground. And the streams came flying so quickly that the players didn't have time to dodge them and began to plummet in flocks.

"That's a useful invention," Geranika's voice sounded next to me. I had stopped outside the entrance to the arena to take in another mass of players majestically tumbling out of the sky. The fallen were immediately revived by their friends on the ground and stubbornly flew up into the air again and again. At some point, it occurred to the players that the GAS could fire broadsides of twenty streams at once, so they began to group together in one place and came flying in for another round of revivals. And yet, despite being so 'last century,' the GAS still had its nets. "I propose you name this weapon the *Hailmaker*. It's quite the spectacle to watch the Free Citizens fall so whimsically, flailing their arms as if they were wings and cursing you so colorfully. Why do you need all this by the way? What's your angle?"

"Strange to hear that question from the Lord of Shadow, who's done nothing but try to destroy Barliona his entire career," I smiled. "I've been declared an outlaw and this is my way of showing the Free Citizens what awaits them if they come after me. Revival, revival and more revival."

"Here's a thought," Geranika shook his head. "Can I help you?"

"Erm...Actually there is one thing. Will you help me set up a private arena? Plinto and I would be happy to answer for our crimes before the Free Citizens. Anyone who wishes, will get a chance to regain their honor by battling us two versus two. If a duo of fighters manages to defeat us, they will get this," I handed Geranika a list of twenty Unique and Legendary items that I currently had knocking about my storage vaults. "However, there has to be some basic ante. An item of similar quality. We'll use this as a pool that will increase the winnings — every item will end up on the list. As for the number of bouts...Any contestant can battle with us as many times as he likes. And the selection of opponents will be automatic: Whoever commits the most valuable item will get priority."

"All right, I will set up a private arena," Geranika's eyes fogged over, yet he kept on speaking. A Corporate official had taken control over the NPC. "Why are you doing this?"

"Because I believe there aren't any worthy fighters among the players," I shrugged my shoulders. "And I couldn't care less what type of battle will be chosen. With a scaled level or with our current ones...who cares...I formally declare this and request that the following text is added to the description of the private arena: 'Mahan and Plinto consider you jerks a bunch of hapless crabs and want to have some fun at your expense. Anyone wishing to prove otherwise is invited to our private arena, at the entrance cost of some unique item.' And, by the way, the current list of rewards should be made public as well. So that everyone can see it and know what the prize pool consists of. Plinto and I are prepared to fight up to five bouts a day."

"You're so confident in your abilities?"

"Just make the arena. We can discuss my confidence later!" I interrupted curtly, unwilling to continue the conversation. I didn't mind chatting with Geranika, but Corporate employees — the same ones who had stripped me of my reputation — didn't warrant my attention. "Also we need a betting pool! I'll wager this miracle item that no one will be able to defeat us for ten bouts straight. The calling bet should match the value of the item."

I pulled out Lait's Stinger and handed it to Geranika. I didn't have any Death Knights who could wield this thing anyway. And I wasn't going to sell it. So I could risk losing it if something went off. After all, this is just a game! Let them try and win the staff. The item shimmered and vanished. The bet had been accepted.

"Anything else?"

"No that's enough. Bring Geranika back. He's more fun to talk to."

Attention all tournament participants!
Mahan and Plinto consider you jerks a bunch of hapless crabs and want to...

I couldn't contain my grin when the notification appeared. For some unknown reason the Corporation didn't bother censoring my arena description and literally forwarded my words without changing them. Someone would definitely get pissed at this — and after that the number of competitors wishing to win the prize would grow like a snowball. Humans are humans...

There was an hour left before the first bout. I went through the registration, entered the arena and frowned seeing my HP drop tenfold. Neither the players nor the spectators were there yet. They would appear at seven on the dot, so I sat down on the sand and opened my settings. I needed to figure out the powers I had as a Shadow Shaman.

We would be facing two players, so I didn't even look at my AoE Shadow summons. They'd be too weak. At Level 100 there weren't that many powers available to me, mostly just Medium Shadows. Healing, Battle, and Slowing — an ordinary assortment, similar to what the other classes had. I was about to open design mode to strengthen the Shadows through Crafting, when a curious idea occurred to me. Shamans have access to the Astral Plane, an alternate dimension where the masters of this class like to hang out. A highly advanced Shaman can visit it whenever he likes, receiving various bonuses and quests. I wonder who will act as the Supreme Spirits of the Higher and Lower Worlds to a Shadow Shaman like I was at the moment. Will there be anyone at all?

It'd be nice to find out while there's still time.

The Shaman has three hands...

A loading bar flashed past my eyes, informing

me that I was about to enter a location I'd never visited before. All the better — with my current reputation, I didn't really want to go to the Astral Plane anyway. The space around me shimmered and turned to fog. When it dissipated, I found myself in a small brick room, with two beings that resembled concentrations of white and black flame in humanoid forms. I could make out the eyes of each humanoid, which now focused on me with obvious astonishment.

"A Free Citizen?" boomed the white flame. "Where did he come from?"

"Are the shackles falling?" the dark flame asked with no less shock and boom. "Or is this yet another illusion of our endless torment?"

"I don't think so, brother," drawled the white flame and right then the space around us exploded:

"*WHO DARES?*" The humanoids flew aside like they were bowling pins. "*HOW?! YOU ARE NOT ALLOWED HERE! BEGONE!*"

"Destroy the Throne!" the white flame managed to scream.

"Free us!" the dark flame echoed.

The Vicegerent has expelled you from the Leprosarium. Your access to the Leprosarium has been revoked.

Scenario updated: 'Burden of the Creator.' Object of scenario: Meet the Creator. Current objective: Destroy the Alabaster Throne.

As I stared at the notification with surprise, another one appeared before my eyes:

Heroes of Malabar! Shaman Mahan is the enemy of all life in Barliona. From now, you are allowed to attack him within the limits of the tournament grounds and send him to respawn. Whatever you do, do not allow him to reach the Tomb!

Heroes of Kartoss! Shaman Mahan is...

Heroes of the Free Lands! Shaman Mahan is...

I smiled maniacally opening design mode. The Creator's Sons, for this is who the humanoid flames were, were locked in the Leprosarium. I should probably find out what that is. And neither the Emperor nor the Dark Lord want them to be released. Why? That is the question.

My access to the Spirits turned out to be entirely blocked — my reputation with the Shamanic Council had plummeted to Hatred as well, which meant it was now trying to help the empires. The hell with them then. I'll use the Shadows, since they're no different from the Spirits anyway. The same summons mechanics and the same strengthening mechanics in design mode. The only difference was some fog around my hands from which the Shadows would emanate. Hah! If someone had told me back in the

Dark Forest that I'd be fighting with Geranika and the entire game would be against me, I'd laugh them in the face. How's that possible?! I! A Shaman Harbinger! With Geranika?! Silly nonsense...

It took me half an hour to assign eight Medium Battle Shadows and two Heavy Healing Shadows to the quick cast slots. The system was willing to grant me the Heavy Healing Shadow, but refused to budge on the Heavy Battle Shadow. Thus it took me twenty minutes to realize that either my Crafting was too low or the Corporation had placed some limit on this functionality. And I found the first option more likely — the Heavy Battle Shadow slipped away from me at the last moment, when I had almost caught it. I'd need to increase my Crafting by another 3–4 points and then see what the deal was.

"You're already here?" Plinto appeared beside me, sliding his shimmering green daggers from their scabbards and examining their properties. "Mmmyeah...These babies really took a hit...Hapless crabs, huh? I like that. I know at least ten idiots who'll definitely get salty over such words, so you can be sure we'll have a few bouts ahead of us. Did you talk to Stacey?"

"Yes, here's what she came up with," I showed Plinto the fireworks and explained how we'd use them, causing the Rogue to holler: "I've never even heard of something like that! If we survive to the semifinal, we'll cause a real kerfuffle."

Plinto thought a bit, glanced up at the sky, at me and then asked wryly:

"You're don't mind my boys creating a diversion in your name? I've wanted to raze several castles for a while, the opportunity never presented itself though. It's not like things can get any worse now..."

"I'm all for it," I returned the wry smile. "Who are we gonna raze?"

"There're a couple candidates from among the top clans, who..."

"Welcome to battle!" roared a voice, interrupting Plinto. A haze filled everything around us. When it dissolved, we found ourselves standing on the sand of an enormous oval arena. The amphitheater was brimming with spectators and booming with screams, clapping, whistles and booing. Some of the spectators were on our side, some against and some had shown up randomly to see a fight. But there were very many of them. "May the strongest among you triumph!"

"Mage and Warrior," Plinto immediately reported, checking the frames. "Shall we make bets? We've got ten seconds..."

Like a top-notch bookmaker, the system had assessed our chances against our first challengers, giving us 5/1 odds of winning. Our opponents meanwhile were at 2/1. Even the Barliona bookmakers didn't believe that we could win. A Shaman and a Rogue were dead meat. Everyone knew that. Even the Imitators.

Silly of them.

"Hell of a bet," Plinto whistled when I placed ten million on us. According to the rules, participants could bet on their duel, but only on them winning it. Any attempt to bet on the opponent was viewed as an attempt to profit from the government and therefore punished with disqualification as well as criminal prosecution.

"Go big or go home," I shrugged as a countdown appeared before us: 5...4...3...2...

1...

To battle!

Off we went!

The enemy adopted a primitive tactic — the Mage began to teleport around the arena, leaving hunks of ice in his wake. Meanwhile, the Warrior began to advance on us with an axe, using the ice hunks as cover.

It didn't take much to guess what they had in mind — as soon as we enter the ice's AoE, the hunk would explode, freezing us for a minute and giving the Warrior the opening he needed to put his axe to use. Silly...silly...

"They're mine," I smirked, targeting the Mage. His teleport had a cooldown of 3–5 seconds, so I had plenty of time.

The Shaman has three hands...

It took one Battle Shadow to blow the Mage to smithereens. And he was blown to smithereens literally — he Teleported near us, within the Shadow's range and the Shadow happily entered him. I managed to see a look of surprise and shock as the player blew apart in various directions like a balloon that had been punctured by a needle. It's a good thing there wasn't any blood. Ours is a game for teenagers, after all. It's okay to see a creature explode, but blood is off limits. What's the logic behind that? Damned if I know.

The Warrior stopped, glancing between the bits of his Mage buddy and us. Plinto demonstratively traced a dagger across his throat, letting our opponent know just what awaited him in the near future and a system notification appeared:

You have completed the Round of 524288 of the 2 vs. 2 arena

The Warrior had resigned.

"Why don't you break it down for those of us who are slower on the uptake?" Plinto asked, once a shimmering field concealed us from the spectators, the remnants of the Mage and the surrendered Warrior.

"Crafting," I explained, happily regarding the 50 million gold that had appeared in my personal account. "I figured out how to use it."

"At last!" smiled the Rogue, clapping me on the shoulder. "It hasn't even been two years! How much of it do you have?"

"Thirty-one points."

"Whoa!" whistled Plinto. "No wonder it tore him apart. We'll change tactics. Do you have some other tricks up your sleeve?"

We only had another twenty bouts ahead of us, so the organizers divided them into four per day, wishing to complete the arena within a business week. A countdown timer appeared, indicating how long we had to wait until our next opponents. Thirteen minutes. So the bouts would happen every 15 minutes. The obvious question was what would happen if there weren't any victors in the allotted time? Would both win? No one? Whoever had done the most damage? I'd have to make sure to find out.

On Plinto's advice I adjusted my quick slots, replacing two Battle Shadows with Shadow Shields that would absorb incoming damage. When Plinto saw the amount of damage they would block, he burst out laughing: The enemy would have to wipe out one-and-a-half times my current HP before I would take any damage at all. As with the other stats, Intellect had been scaled to our levels, but I had so much of it that this steep decrease didn't really affect the final outcome. My Battle Shadows would detonate any players without the proper equipment like that Mage in the first bout.

It almost felt like cheating.

"Rogue and Paladin," Plinto remarked as soon as the second battle began. "Tough combo. If the Pal starts healing, we'll have a hard time of it. Check it — they don't think we've got a chance again!"

Ten million were again withdrawn from my account, and directed to the Corporation bookmakers. Our chances stood at 4/1. Less than in the first battle, but still large enough to make a nice profit. I checked the enemies' frames and frowned. The names were familiar: Silkodor and Chikan. I'd heard of them somewhere, but for the life of me couldn't remember where. Well, good luck to them. As far as I'm concerned, they're just more mincemeat.

Paladin Chikan headed our way from the other edge of the arena. Silkodor was nowhere to be seen — he'd gone into stealth mode. Plinto had gone into stealth as well and at the very beginning dashed off in the Paladin's direction, ready to fall upon him at any moment. More than likely, Silkodor is standing behind my back. That would be the most logical thing to do.

"*Odd couple, these two. They're too calm,*" Plinto typed into the clan chat. "*I'm sensing a trap. Cast a shield on yourself.*"

Chikan didn't make a move. Slowly but surely he walked in my direction. I was in agreement with Plinto — there was some peculiar confidence in how these two were behaving. I'd better protect myself.

A protective sphere appeared around me and as soon as Chikan entered the range of my attacks, I sent two Battle Shadows at him. Just in case!

"Reflection!" roared Plinto, popping up behind the Paladin and casting Stun on him. I managed to smile at our success just as I butted up against a wall behind me. The blow was so intense that a heap of debuffs descended on me: Stun, Daze, Petrify...A minute each. But before I could disconnect, my smile vanished — Silkodor appeared behind Plinto! Blast it all to hell!

During the minute that I was out of the fight, I watched Plinto's frame gradually but steadily crawl to zero. Scrolls of healing, like all scrolls, were disallowed in the arena. Damn reflection! Here's the power of a well-rehearsed duo! Chikan had acted as bait, causing the enemy to concentrate all the initial damage on him. At the same time that bastard had a Sphere of Reflection that sent any spell or attack back at the assailant. If it weren't for my protective sphere, the double Shadow attack would've killed me. Just hang on another 20 seconds, Plinto. Too much depends on it.

Petrification was the first debuff to expire and I, still Stunned and Dazed, immediately cast a second strengthened sphere on myself. Now I could consider...

A sunburst erupted before my eyes saddling me with Blindness for 10 seconds. I started back and cursed — a gray haze concealed the arena from my sight, while a series of damage notifications streamed before it. Silkodor was dutifully stabbing me with his daggers, trying to send me to respawn. Plinto's HP was barely over 10%, while Chikan and Silkodor were entirely unharmed. And now I got angry. As soon as the Blindness dissipated and the arena's yellow sand reappeared in my sight, I turned into my Dragon Form. Time to end this fight!

"Argh!" I roared, stunning our enemies with Thunderclap. Silkodor froze with his dagger in the air, green drops still dripping form it. I looked at the frames and swore again — the poison that covered the Rogue's daggers increased the debuff duration by 100%, lasting until the end of the battle. Without wasting time, I sent two Healing Shadows at Plinto. Bloody hell! I had basically been forced to use my entire arsenal to win the second bout.

Then again, win isn't even the word...Silkodor and Chikan were still kicking!

"Don't just stand there!" yelled Plinto, noticing my indecisiveness. "Take them out!"

Silkodor was blown to pieces right away, but Chikan required a little more work. I still had one Medium Battle Shadow that took 50% of the Paladin's HP. How is that possible?! He should've burst too! Where did this duo come from?!

You have completed the Round of 262144 of

the 2 vs. 2 arena

"That's what a well-practiced duo means," Plinto collapsed wearily onto the sand. "If it weren't for the Patriarch's Tooth, we'd never come out of there alive. Sucks that we encountered them so early on. Now everyone knows what we're capable of."

"You were a Vampire?"

"How else was I supposed to survive that?" the Rogue smiled grimly. "Damn! They were so polished. Imagine what would've happened if your Thunderclap had met their Reflection? See you later and don't forget to write! We should talk to those two — they seem promising."

You have completed Round of 65536 of the 2 vs. 2 arena

We won the next two bouts without any issues. A pair of Mages had nothing against my Shadows and went flying to bits all over the arena. As for the Warrior and Death Knight who were our last opponents of the day, I had to stun them with Thunderclap and then methodically cut them down. Nothing complicated.

As soon as we left the arena, a new notification appeared before us:

New   private   challenge   received.

Mahan/Plinto vs. Chikan/Silkodor. The bout will take place in 60 minutes in the private arena. Fighters' level: 100.

"They're salty," laughed Plinto, reading the message. "They want revenge."

"What are you so happy about?" I began to fret. "They just almost knocked us out and..."

"Mahan, I know what they're capable of now!" Plinto patted me on the shoulder. "Let's go celebrate our victory!" We need to leave a lasting impression on our opponents."

By 'lasting impression' Plinto meant gloating and gloat he did. He welcomed any high-level player who popped into the tavern with whistling and clucking. His scathing messages about the cowardice of various specific players periodically appeared in the general chat, accompanied by observations about the limpness of their wrists and other bodily parts. Several times we were approached by players asking us to shut up, but Plinto told them all to get lost, offering to resolve any salt in the private arena.

There weren't any takers, however, so the Rogue went on mocking everyone he came across.

Our grudge match against Chikan and Silkodor went off without a hitch. Two defensive spheres, a Minor Shadow at Chikan to check for Reflection and one more right after the first, then another one and only on my fifth shot did I send a Medium Battle

Shadow at the Paladin. Judging by his surprised grunting, he hadn't expected it. Finishing off the Paladin was a matter of technique — Plinto dispelled Reflection while I sent another two Shadows at the Paladin and Silkodor was left without a partner.

Fifteen minutes elapsed quickly and then the system automatically gave us the victory. We didn't bother running around the arena looking for the hiding Rogue. What for? He's one and we're two — we'd win either way.

"Mahan, Master Bihan wishes to see you," said a Celestial player with a deep bow as soon as we left the arena. "The head of our clan wishes to hold a meeting in Altameda, so as to avoid prying ears. To this end, Master Bihan wishes you to grant guest access to Bihan and Azari. What shall I tell my master?"

"Tell Bihan," I consciously omitted 'master,' which the messenger was trying to impress on me, "that if he wishes to meet with me, especially in pairs, then I will be happy to grant him this honor. With Plinto. In the arena. Two on two. All other meetings, especially in Altameda, are out of the question. I don't meet with mincemeat. Relay this message to the one you call 'Master.'"

"My school of diplomacy," smirked Plinto, watching the departing messenger.

"The hell with him!" I blurted out angrily. "What can he tell us? 'Stop acting like clowns and angering my warriors?' 'Follow us to the Tomb like a good boy?' 'Here's a bunch of money, now get on your hind legs and dance?' Tell me, what's with the main tournament?"

"Are you talking about the Labyrinth?" Plinto inquired. "If you mean seriously, then we don't stand a chance. There's no cohesion, the classes are all over the place, and we only have one tank and not enough healers. At the latest, we'll be out tomorrow. We won't pass the third day on time alone. Bihan's setting the bar too high."

"And if Stacey comes with us?"

"So it's like that?" Plinto grinned, but then shook his head. "All right, in that case, we'll make it to the day after tomorrow. But no further."

We were silent for a short while, each one of us thinking of his own business, and suddenly Plinto turned to me and asked:

"Mahan, you don't have some miracle up your sleeve do you? If the Celestial, Astrum, Phoenix and other top clans aren't in the tournament, we'll be able to reach the Labyrinth's final boss. And, at the risk of being sentimental, I always wanted to see him in person instead of just watching someone's recording."

"A miracle?" I looked at Plinto sadly. "Where from? All the miracles..."

A stunning thought pierced my consciousness like a bolt of lightning and goosebumps popped up all over my body. I snatched up an amulet, heard a response on the other line and yelled:

"Stacey, I need to see you in Altameda this instant! We'll meet in the main hall in ten minutes!"

"This instant and in ten minutes are different things," Plinto remarked, but I wasn't listening. Yelling at him to follow me, I ran off in the direction of the castle. I urgently needed the counsel of intelligent players. Stacey and Plinto.

"The map, Stacey!" I asked, forgetting that I already had the same map. Once Stacey had unfolded her map on the floor, I began to ask questions.

"How much time will the GAS need to get over here?" I indicated a point in the open seas to the north of our continent. "If we leave right now, how long will it take?"

"A week," Anastaria guessed. "Five days at least."

"Daaamn! Can we teleport it somehow? With a portal or some other way?"

"Impossible."

"Okay...Next question. Assuming that the GAS is at this location," I pointed at the northernmost tip of the continent. "How much time will it need to reach this point?"

"About twelve hours," Anastaria said pensively. "What do you have in mind, Mahan?"

"Hold on. Here's the most important question — the one that everything hinges on. Does Altameda's change of location count as teleportation?"

A silence filled the hall.

"Viltrius!" I called my majordomo without waiting for a reply. "Tomorrow, as soon as I go to Pryke, send Altameda to these coordinates."

"Master, we still need three months before the next jump is ready," the goblin began, but I interrupted.

"Bill the cost of the jump to my account. You can go."

"Ten million..." grumbled the goblin, but he didn't dare argue with me, leaving the three of us on our own.

"Question number two. What will happen if I will be gone for a week?"

Silence reigned again.

"Let me be more specific. I have an idea of how I can teleport to any point in the continent without violating any of the restrictions that have been placed on me. But I won't be able to return quickly. I'll need those five days that Stacey's talking about. How will my absence affect our progress through the Labyrinth and the arena?"

"Why don't you just tell us what you have in mind?" Stacey gave me a look. "And then we can come up with a way to put off the arena for five days."

"What I have in mind?" I made a dramatic pause, then laughed and began to explain. "I assume everyone knows why the Mage towers are always the northernmost buildings in our continent's cities? The next fog is expected no sooner than three years from now. I wish to accelerate its arrival. And not only by setting it on Malabar and Kartoss."

"That would force the Emperors to recall their warriors! To defend!" Stacey even jumped up from her seat from the news. "The tournament would be paralyzed!"

"Why would it be?" I blinked innocently. "The tournament is under way. No one has canceled it. If the invited guests and participants decide to abandon it, who'd be at fault? Obviously not me. I'm more worried about the five days that it'll take me to fly back on the GAS. I wouldn't like to lose out on the arena."

"How do you plan on reaching the north?" Stacey began but cut herself short, recalling my words.

"I was promised two teleports," I confirmed her guess. "One to Pryke and one back to Altameda. Whose business is it that my castle can change its coordinates?"

"I'll think about what I can do about the arena," Stacey drawled pensively. "At first glance, I'd say nothing — failing to show up is an automatic forfeit. Whatever the reasons might be. I'll need to read the rules. As for your mini-tournament, that's a simpler issue. Let your opponents queue up. When you get back you'll show them what's what."

"Mahan, I asked you for a miracle — not a

defeat in the arena," Plinto frowned unhappily. "Let's do it this way — tomorrow the arena is at 1 pm. After that you can go to Pryke. We'll come up with our next move later."

"Not even a question. Stacey, when are you going to come to terms with Geranika?"

"Erm..." Stacey froze. "That's right. I forgot about it entirely."

"Geranika, we need you over here!" I shouted into the air, certain that the Imitator and his NPC would hear us. After a short hesitation, I added: "I grant you guest access to my castle!"

"Thoughtful of you," said the Lord of Shadow. "I was starting to feel bad for your little hob-boogers. All right, out with it Mahan: What do you need?"

"I'll give you another player in exchange for the option to teleport to my castle from any location of the continent," I said as three pairs of eyes stared at me in puzzlement.

"And whom, may I ask, are you offering?" Geranika caught on quickly and began to ply his line. "Who am I supposed to violate the will of Barliona over?"

"Me," replied Stacey, without looking away from me. Her eyes told me that I should have discussed this with her first. "He's talking about me. If you grant Mahan the option of returning to the castle from a location besides from Pryke, I'll represent Shadow at the tournament."

"Do you understand the consequences of your decision?" Geranika asked seriously and it was clear from the motion of Stacey's eyes that she was reading the system text.

"I understand them," the girl stated with certainty.

"I accept your decision, Holy Paladin Anastaria," said Geranika in the same formal tone he had used when accepting Plinto to his ranks. "You are bound to me by your obligations, so there will be no reward for you when the tournament ends. Mahan will be allowed to return to his castle one more time. But only once!"

"We've solved the issue with the arena," I smiled when Geranika vanished and Stacey punched me in the shoulder. Or rather, she wanted to punch me: They system interpreted her action as aggression and kept her from doing damage to me. How I love Barliona! "Now the million dollar question — what will happen to us if we open Pandora's Box?"

"Hatred with the entire world," Stacey said resignedly, deciding that in Barliona she couldn't do anything to me and putting off my execution until we returned to reality. "Isn't that what you wanted?"

"Among other things. What about our clan? Is Fleita ready to become our new head?"

"Is there something I don't know?" Plinto asked with curiosity. We had to bring him up to speed on our decision.

"Makes sense," the Rogue agreed with our reasoning. "It's a nice way of getting the clan out of harm's way. Is the girl game?"

"Yes. I was actually dealing with this today when Mahan called screaming about this meeting," Stacey couldn't avoid sending a barb in my direction. "The documents are ready, all she has to do is sign."

"So get her over here then," I didn't bother reading the contract Stacey had drawn up. What was the point of working against my better half?

New private challenge received. Mahan/Plinto vs. Kei-Ten/Methodious. The bout will take place in 60 minutes in the private arena. Fighters' level: Current.

"Oh really?" Plinto grunted with surprise. "Check it out. We're going to fight Kei-Ten and Methodious."

"What?!" Stacey froze as if the names meant something to her.

"What you heard," Plinto grinned. "I was trolling everyone all day without any success. But as soon as Mahan told off Bihan, we're sent a new pair. Cool, huh...A duel at our current levels."

"Plinto?" Stacey gave the Rogue a serious look.

"We'll make it. If anything, Mahan will figure something out."

"Guys, hang on. What is this couple? Are they

veterans?" I reminded the two of my presence.

"That's one way to put it," Plinto explained. "The last three years, these veterans have put the kibosh on every taker. They're from Caltua but they work as mercenaries. They're the most annoying idiots in all of Barliona. Remember me before the Legends? I was a child compared to them. A Naga Rogue, Master of Venom and a Human Hunter, Master of Beasts. The Hunter will have his damn pet with him so in effect we're going to be facing a combat trio, and I'd be at pains to say which of them is the weakest. As for levels...They're both over 400."

"Kei-Ten is Level 403 and Methodious is Level 406. His cat alone is Level 410," Stacey offered. "He prefers to work with them the last two years."

"That doesn't absolve us from the need to sign the documents," I summarized, utterly unfazed by the famous names. Perhaps if I had any experience with this couple, my reaction would've resembled that of Plinto's and Stacey's, but at the moment these two names were little more than a collection of sounds, so I saw no reason to get distracted. I'll make my decisions when I'm in battle. Not right now.

"So we have to decide the most important thing — when do we start?" As soon as I signed the contract, the 'Enter' icon vanished from my avatar. I had left the clan entirely, not wishing to interfere in its business. Leaving Fleita alone with Mr. Kristowski, I pulled Stacey and Plinto over to the neighboring hall.

"Start what?" quipped Plinto. "We've been starting so many things lately that I'm all confused."

"Mahan is talking about the Eye," Anastaria guessed. "A two-sided problem. On the one hand, the Dungeons are all shuttered at the moment. But only the Dungeons of this world. The Eye opens a portal to another world, so purely theoretically, that Dungeon should remain accessible. The catch is that it would require a one-off run. If we start to do it, there won't be a way back. Or a second attempt. I suggest we try to do it anyway..."

"No second chance..." Stacey started saying something, but I withdrew into my own thoughts. "There won't be a second chance...A second chance..."

"Answer me, Mahan! Earth to Shaman Mahan, this is Houston!" Plinto's mocking voice drew me out of my half-daze, which I had slipped into without really noticing.

"Stacey, we'll need your help."

"Someone kill him!" Plinto even threw up his hands. "Are you going to show us some new miracle?"

"We will have a second chance. I once gave Evolett two portals. Did they ever complete those?"

"Not yet. But how would you..."

"What would happen if we activate the Eye, enter its portal and activate the Leg — or whatever it was — inside the other world. Will the system open another portal? Will the system lock up? Will the system simply send us to the final boss? Or will it simply send us to the beginning? Which would still be in the same world. WHAT?"

"Hi uncle!" Instead of answering me, Stacey called Evolett. "I need that piece of the Dark Widow that Mahan gave you.

"Hi niece," came the voice from the amulet. "Are you trying to conquer the world again?"

"I'm not alone," Stacey checked him, giving us an embarrassed look.

"So you're not even alone?" Laughter sounded in the amulet. "Hi, Mahan!"

"Hi!" I said when Stacey spread her arms in helplessness. "What's up with the Dark Widow?"

"She shriveled up and died. What else could happen with her?" Evolett went on having his fun. "I'll bet dinner that Victor doesn't know about this call."

"Will you help, uncle?"

"Mahan has been declared Barliona's most wanted, and you know how I feel about outlaws."

"Where and when?" A happy smile appeared on Stacey's face and she held up a thumb.

"Tomorrow at the tournament. It's too late today. I was going to exit. As for dinner, that wasn't a joke. Allie has been driving me crazy. She wants me to introduce her to the prettiest woman of Barliona."

"Are you there on the islands?" Anastaria clarified.

"Where else would a poor retiree spend his dying years, once everyone's given up on him?" The voice in the amulet sounded upset with the entire world.

"I love you, uncle!" Stacey sent an audible kiss and hung up the amulet, then looked at us with satisfaction. "It's quite rare that two pieces of the Dark Widow are in Barliona at once. Ok...Plinto, can we meet your fighters before the mission?"

"They'll be here tomorrow," Stacey's excitement infected the Rogue. He jumped to his feet and began to pace back and forth across the hall. "I have twenty, but it's better to find ten more. Stacey, do you have any candidates?"

The two began discussing names that I'd never heard before, so I quickly grew bored. This wasn't my line — vetting people, discussing their strengths and weaknesses. That's what I have my wife for. She'd already proved her competence in this issue by choosing me to begin with...

"Listen up." Fifty minutes later we were again on the arena's yellow sand and Plinto was again briefing me on the tactics. Which I had already memorized! If you ask me, the Rogue was nervous. A typical duel with typical fighters, what's the big deal? "Our job is as easy as a cork — we kill anything that moves. And if it doesn't move, we kick it and then kill it. Are there any questions?"

"Welcome to battle!" shouted the announcer's voice. Our surroundings came into focus and I couldn't help but whistle in astonishment: The arena had changed. As I had managed to learn, any spectator wishing to see the battle on the visualizer at home with a beer and a blanket simply needed to send his virtual body to the arena's seats. This was done in order to give the combatants a sense that they were being watched. If there weren't enough spectators, the gaps were filled in with NPCs whose purpose it was to simulate a crowded audience. But if there were too many spectators...We were inside a brimming, colossal edifice whose top rows disappeared in the sky above us. I looked over at the announcer's box and saw a constantly growing number that was currently a little over ten million. Wow! Do people have nothing better to do than to watch a battle inside a game? Found themselves some gladiators...

"May the strongest among you triumph!"

"Bets?" Plinto asked with a nervous giggle when the system reached the last few seconds of the countdown. As I had also managed to learn, neither team could cross the special line several meters from the fighters until the countdown expired. Otherwise the system would assign the violators a forfeit.

"Why not?" I opened the betting interface and bet ten million on our victory. I didn't even look at our enemies' chances, since the odds of 1/26 for our victory didn't really motivate me.

"Fight!"

On the other side of the arena, an ordinary Hunter with a spotted white/black tiger began to walk in our direction. Methodious. Like any decent Rogue, Kei-Ten went into stealth and was currently rushing to take up his position based on whatever the duo's plan was. That's okay, we've got plans too. I will try to do as Plinto asked me.

The battle's conditions allowed me to take full advantage of my character's specialization in Intellect. The Shadow Shields that appeared around me and Plinto at the very beginning of the fight wanted nothing more than to absorb two million points of damage, while I still had 241,000 Hit Points at Level 333. This duo is really much too strong for me, so I'll have to play the role I hate — a Shaman Healer. On the other hand, this was Level 395 Plinto's moment to shine. The important thing is that his nerves calm down and he comes to himself. Otherwise, we'll have a tough time of it...

"Mahan!" Methodious yelled, stopping beyond of my Shadows' range. "I was asked to relay a message to you: 'The insolent dog yaps at the tiger so long as the latter is in a cage. But when the tiger is released, the dog makes a puddle and runs to its master.'"

"How positively philosophical," I muttered. Methodious's self-assurance undermined my confidence in our plan. This duo had encountered Plinto many times and should be familiar with all his tricks.

"When you come flying out of the arena," I didn't feel like remaining indebted, "and stumble upon your kitty trembling in the bushes somewhere, simply pet him. Don't do anything else to him. Don't even take his money. Let this defeat be yours personally and not his. Let him continue to imagine he is a great and terrible tiger. If his courage consists of finding two griefers to deal with an insolent dog...then I truly sympathize with him who hired you. He sits there, frets and worries that the kids are about to get it. Pfff..."

"I like you," Methodious smiled. "It'll be a fun knocking you out and then hunting you. I heard there's a nice bounty on your head..."

"Uh-huh. Well. Shall we get to it, then? You see, I'd like to warn you, just so you don't waste anymore breath needlessly. I'll attack in 5...4...3...2..."

"Come here, Draco!"

"Coming."

"Maximum acceleration! Kill the enemies!"

"I'm on it!"

"One!"

Shield on Draco! To battle!

You have been stunned for 60 seconds!

Damage taken...

You have been blinded for 60 seconds!

You cannot summon Shadows for another 30 seconds.

Your Totem has leveled up! Current level: 301.

Battle completed.

"They died?" I heard Draco's voice through the fading white film of Blindness.

"This is an arena, it's just sport," I rushed to assuage the pacifist. Tactics, strategy...Like hell! You summon a Level 300 Dragon, have him accelerate to his maximum level of acceleration and then pour fire on everything and everyone. There's not a single tank that'll withstand that. Unless he has a healer, of course. And neither the Rogue nor the Hunter were that.

New private challenge received. Mahan/Plinto vs. Kei-Ten/Methodious. The bout will take place in 60 minutes in the private arena. Fighters' level: Current.

"Never imagined they would get so pissy," Plinto muttered pensively, patting Draco on the neck. "Hello, you scaly badass you! I'd forgotten about you somehow. You look good, kid!"

"Thank you!" Despite being five meters long,

Draco was a very flexible and mobile creature. He coiled around Plinto and took him in his...embrace? Coils? Vices? It's hard to find the word for the nightmare that I was currently witnessing. "It's nice to see you too!"

New private challenge received. Mahan/Plinto vs. Kei-Ten/Methodious.
New private challenge received...
New private cha...

It's a good thing that it had occurred to me to limit our bouts to five a day. Otherwise our enemies would simply wear us out! The tactics for this duo turned out to be simple as all hell — Draco would fly up, 'accelerate' to his sixth level of acceleration and in a few seconds wipe out the Hunter and his pet tiger. Then we'd wait around until the Naga appeared. He couldn't Stun Plinto due to the Patriarch's Tooth and it made no sense to Stun me since then Kei-Tan would be wide open to Plinto who was at his level and had a Shadow Shield to boot. Meanwhile, I'd set Draco free as soon as the Hunter had been wiped out — out of harm's way. The last thing I needed was to have my Totem sent to respawn!

"Mahan!" When it became clear that the duels had ended for the day, Plinto began to express his complaints: "Naturally, I understand that five unique items is quite a haul. And that we've just griefed those who are more accustomed to griefing others. That's cool and all! But your damn arena caused us to miss the most important event of the first day of the tournament!"

"W-what?" I even stuttered, not expecting such a dressing-down from Plinto.

"And he even has to ask! Lori was performing today! Come on, I still have a recording of it! We need to celebrate!"

"I kindly request a few minutes of your time." A goblin in a tuxedo appeared beside us. His voice instantly told us who we were talking to — the arena's announcer had blessed us with his presence.

"Under the rules of the tournament, you wagered Lait's Stinger as part of the betting pool." Plinto gave me a surprised look, unsettling me a little bit. I'd forgotten to tell him. "A raise was received, and under the rules you yourself set, it must be called. How do you prefer to call the raise, with gold or with items at their market value?"

"How much is it?" It occurred to me to ask before making my decision. It seems much easier to call using gold than to go around looking for...

"Six hundred, thirty-two million gold," the goblin deadpanned, staring at us with his hazel-blue eyes.

"HOW MUCH?!" Two throats hollered in unison. Plinto was no less shocked than I was.

"Bihan wagered his Castle of the Solar Wind

that you cannot win ten battles in a row at the status arena. The counting of the bouts begins tomorrow. Will you call his bet?"

"Understanding that this may cause a bit of inconvenience for you," squeaked the announcer after a short while, as we stood there in shock, "Bihan is prepared to accept your personal castle as a calling bet. "Altameda. In that case, the bets will be considered even and..."

"If Bihan wishes to wager his castle," I interrupted the goblin, trying to calm down. "That's his personal erotic problem. My wager has been made — Lait's Stinger. There's no mention of evening the bets in the betting pool I set up. If he reckons that the Staff is worth an entire castle — that's his business and his wager. If he reckons that I have to add to my initial wager, he is free to go to..."

"Sucker town," Plinto helped me come up with a good destination for Bihan.

"Precisely," I agreed and added: "I'd also like to point out that we've already fought five battles since the wager was made. It's not my problem that Bihan was navel-gazing and counting crows and decided to make his bet only now. He needs to be quicker on his toes! Or do you want to say that that would infringe on some law or rule?"

"Not at all, this will all be taken into account! Thank you for your explanation," the goblin backtracked shockingly quickly. He began to backpedal in a fit of bows: "All the best to you and may you have success in the arena!"

"What was that?" I asked myself aloud, but Plinto decided that the question was not a rhetorical one and required discussion.

"The Era of Dragons is trying to take Altameda from you!" The Rogue's outrage knew no bounds. "It's not enough that they've gobbled up all the other empires on their continent; they're trying to get their dirty paws on ours! This is just insolence!"

"The hell do they need with Altameda?" I asked puzzled.

"The hell?" Plinto thought for several moments and then fixed me with a serious look and asked: "Do you know your castle inside and out?"

"What?"

Plinto didn't bother listening to me, but waved his hand dismissively as if saying 'what's a Shaman gonna tell me, anyway?' He called Anastaria and demanded another emergency meeting. Some mega epic plot had occurred to the Rogue.

"...And that's why I believe that Bihan's main objective is Altameda. Now we have to answer the question: 'Why?'" Sitting in an armchair with a satisfied look, Plinto reached the end of his theory of what had happened. I shook my head. In my view, the Rogue had spent too much time in the game and was seeing spies, plots and conspiracies everywhere.

"Viltrius!" I called the goblin and asked him to

tell us about the castle's 'dark areas.' It's better to establish that 'white' is 'white,' than constantly fret about the opposite.

"The entire territory of the castle is under my control and that of the hobgoblins," the majordomo confirmed my belief that Altameda was no more than a castle. One that could teleport, but still a castle. "There are no closed areas, secret rooms, corridors or similar features in Altameda."

"There, you see? As old man Freud used to say: 'Sometimes a banana is just a banana,'" I held up a finger demonstratively, calling the people to a reasonable perception of reality, and yet Stacey's next question to Viltrius and his subsequent response, forced me to freeze with my mouth agape.

"Are there any unregistered portals in the castle? Ones that don't lead to anywhere?"

"Yes, three of them. At present, they are inactive and are therefore not included in the castle's reports. Judging by their properties, the first portal will be activated once the castle reaches Level 30, the second at Level 40 and the third at Level 50."

"Portals?" My initial shock passed and I fell onto my majordomo with questions. "Why am I finding out about this only now?"

"As I said, they're inactive and weren't included in the daily reports as a result," Viltrius replied nonplussed. "To be honest, the existence of the portals came as a surprise to me as well. They appeared right after the castle reached Level 26. Considering that in addition to the portals, the castle also acquired new rooms — allowing Spiteful Gnum to outfit his workshop — I deemed these new additions as specifics of Altameda."

"On the topic of global conspiracies," Plinto drawled sarcastically as soon as we let Viltrius go. "The Corporation had never before introduced a castle that could simply teleport. It's too simple and irrational. My heart senses that our mutual acquaintance has his own people among the game's scenario designers. Of course no one can prove anything, but the fact remains — he knows a lot more about Altameda than we do."

"It's a pretty move with the wager," Stacey agreed. "They got the announcer to just kind of mention that Altameda would be enough to call the raise and came up with this offer right after we'd trounced a duo that had been considered unbeatable until that moment...Had I a psychological profile of Mahan before the events of the Tomb, I wouldn't doubt for a second that — on a wave of success, emotions and internal sense of justice — he'd take a wager like this. Only Bihan isn't aware that Mahan's changed quite a bit over the last two months. I wouldn't say too much, but he's different. Do you understand why Kei-Ten and Methodious lost now, Plinto? You think a duo that's seen thousands of battles side by side doesn't know how to deal with an ordinary Totem? Even one that spits fire? This was all arranged ahead of time with the single goal of getting Mahan to wager Altameda. To put it simply, the Solar Wind is the second most important castle for the Era of Dragons. Would Bihan really risk it? Please..."

"In that case, the million dollar question: How can we level up the castle three times within reasonable time constraints?" Plinto looked at me inquisitively. "Mahan?"

I reclined wearily in my favorite rocking throne, which the Corporation had once gifted me. Yet another unique thing added to the game for the sake of pleasure. However, if I were to follow Plinto's and Stacey's logic, after some millionth rock in my throne, a portal would pop open under my butt and I would plummet off into some unknown dimension.

"'Mahan' *what*? I'm prepared to invest all my winnings in the castle. That's about 300 million. But what'll that give us? Let's imagine that we'll level up the castle and the portal will become active. Who'll go inside? We don't have the raid party for this. Shall we hire mercenaries? From Phoenix? Or bow down before Bihan? Insanity. Let's imagine a different situation — phantoms will start crawling out of the portal. The same ones that had once protected Altameda when we first appeared at its walls. Who'll defend the castle? Me? Plinto? Vimes and his pair of Tauren?"

"Stacey, did you already draft your will?" Plinto suddenly asked, turning to the girl. "The forecast has a high probability of a meteor shower today."

My wife stared at the Rogue in puzzlement for several moments and then grinned broadly.

"Mahan is worried about his estate? Is that what you're talking about?"

"What else? You're a bad influence on him. Before you know it, our Shaman will start using his head, thinking and asking inconvenient questions. The horror!"

"I'm of the mind that it doesn't make sense to rush the castle right now," Stacey brought the conversation back to the topic at hand. "I'd leave it alone entirely actually. If a new level grants something to the castle, we had better be prepared for it. Being at a state of war with the entire continent while pursuing these investigations at the same time is too much of a luxury. Now, who wants dinner?"

"I pass," Plinto shook his head negatively. "It's time to take a bath and go to sleep. We'll have to prove to everyone tomorrow that today's victories were earned, not granted. And I hope you two do the same. Get some rest. If Mahan pulls off his plan with the fog, we'll have a hell of a day ahead of us."

CHAPTER THIRTEEN
THE PRYKE COPPER MINE

"**W**ELCOME TO BATTLE!" Unlike in the private arena, there weren't many spectators in the 2 vs. 2 arena for the Round of 32,768. As far as I could tell there weren't any players at all — the noise here was being generated by an NPC audience which cheered as much for us as for our opponents (a duo of Rogues).

"May the strongest among you triumph!"

As per custom, I shielded us and we began awaiting our enemies' attacks, continuing our discussion of our upcoming bouts as we did so. It didn't matter whether yesterday's bouts had been rigged or not: Our opponents had bet Unique items, and the jackpot had grown a lot in the process. Even though Silkodor and Chikan had wagered a mysterious, yet not-very-useful Level 100 ritual dagger — Methodious and Kei-Ten's wager was so immense that I wanted to hop in the arena and defeat my own self to get my hands on it. When Stacey noticed the seemingly ordinary breastplate (or rather,

1/3 of a breastplate), she pressed me up against the wall and demanded I take it out of public circulation. In some sense I understood her — it's difficult to risk losing an item from the Luminous Set. I even tried to sneak this '**Luminous Breastplate Fragment (1 of 3)**' out of the pool, but the arena manager caught me, and warned me that the penalty would be a forced forfeit and a loss of something more valuable than mere Reputation. He was referring to status: I'd be marked as a player who didn't keep his word. After all, I had called the players a bunch of hapless crabs, and Plinto and I still had to answer for my words. Thus it wasn't mere reputation amid the NPCs that was at stake but status with the other players.

It was unclear whether Methodious and Kei-Ten had wagered this item on purpose or whether they merely wanted to show off what they had at their disposal. However, the end effect was that all the other players began to compete among each other for the chance to be the first to slaughter us. Initially, our challengers had been betting only simple and weak items. They were unique and all, but they were also low-level or largely useless. For example, a flower pot for a Florist that allowed the florist in question to forget about having to water the plants or repot them. The pot magically provided the perfect growing environment for any plant, allowing it to reach its greatest beauty. I wouldn't dispute the idea that this item was indeed a great wonder, yet who needed it?

You could count the number of florists in Barliona on one hand and given the item's restrictions, there were even fewer ordinary people who could even use this item if they wanted to. In a word, this bet was unique and absolutely useless — which the system instantly established on its own and sent the duo that had bet it to the very back of the 'kill Plinto & Mahan' queue. And yet, any betting party was always free to change its bet! And now it seemed like they had just been waiting for the opportunity! When I entered the game, the first place in the queue for the private arena was held by a duo that had bet a small jewelry box, large enough to hold a few rings. No more. The system had appraised this box so highly that over the next few hours only places two through five changed, while the first place remained the same.

Our old friends Methodious and Kei-Ten, were in fourth place. Stacey cursed when she saw this. Fourth place, according to her, was the best position to gain maximum profit from the betting pool. This duo was so confident in itself as well as us (it's worth pointing out) that they allowed three duos to step ahead of them in the queue. They wanted to maximize their final winnings. Why fourth and not fifth? So as not to risk some random rich kid beating their wager. These kids were playing smart...

"By the way, Mahan," Plinto smirked when the Rogue duo fell on him with their knives and daggers. "I think we've gotten distracted. We've got a fight on our hands here, seems like..."

"That's true. Let me help you with that!" I replied amicably and one of the Rogues went flying into bits and pieces — only a Paladin could survive two Heavy Battle Shadows at once.

You have completed the Round of 2048 of the 2 vs. 2 arena...

We encountered no problems in the ordinary arena. Druids, Death Knights, Warriors, Paladins with their Reflection and bubbles, Hunters, Mages, Rogues — the combinations were diverse, but the bouts ended the same way — our opponents played the roles of balloons and we the needles. They'd go flying in little pieces across the entire arena.

As soon as we left the arena, the system informed us of another challenge:

New challenge received. Mahan/Plinto vs. Kalatea/Antsinthepantsa. The bout will take place in 60 minutes in the arena. Scale: Level 30.

"Hum," drawled Plinto reading the notification. "Mahan, are you aware that we're missing the entire tournament because of this additional arena you set up? There're exciting events under way over there somewhere, and meanwhile we're over here toiling away in this arena you've created and all the headaches that come with it."

"What are you talking about?" I asked surprised.

"I'm talking about how until I hit Level 50, I have nothing. Not a single skill or power. I would have to rely entirely on my HP pool to survive, and uh, well...I'm a Rogue..."

"WHAT?! Oh no," I looked at my own stats and barely suppressed my outrage. "All of my Shadows require at least Level 50 too. What's the deal here..."

"The deal is that players who are just starting out and are really low-level can't play for Shadow. You know who caused this? Our lovely singer! Lori caused some kind of conflagration in her arboretum and the Corporation began changing the mechanics. To be honest, I figured that the changes would only affect starting players but...Damn! What about your Spirits?"

"Nope! Unavailable. They're locked. I'm at Hatred status with everyone, remember?"

"So we won't have any shields. Or healing. All right, we'll take that as a given. There's always your Totem and our racial abilities. It'd be nice to know who the hell Kalatea and Antsinthepantsa are."

"They're Shamans," I said sadly. "Two Harbingers. They know who my Totem is and have no doubt figured out how they'll neutralize him. Everyone must have seen yesterday's bouts by now. By the way, those two will be able to blink around. Like I used to.

And who the hell knows whether Blink is allowed in the arena or not! After all, they can only blink on their continent, but we're in..."

"Astrum brought its obelisk too. So they will be able to blink. That's the first thing. The second thing is that the arena is neutral territory as far as the continents are concerned, and any ability available at your home territory will be available here. Fun times, eh?"

"You could say that again."

"All right, let's go to the arena. We have an hour to figure out how we're supposed to win this one. I'm not about to forfeit without a fight..."

Design mode welcomed me with a terrifying emptiness. That is, not design mode itself — that was full of various items I had made — but rather the absolute darkness of design mode in which I had worked with the Spirits and later with the Shadows. As hard as I tried to summon a single Shadow or Spirit, nothing worked and all the embodiments I'd made earlier didn't work. They didn't have enough life!

The Shaman has three hands...

Your access to the Leprosarium is blocked.

Your access to the Astral Plane is blocked.

Tumbling out of yet another trance, I had nothing left to do but curse. Nothing worked! I couldn't wield either the Spirits or the Shadows at

Level 30! Despairing, I tried to do something with the Supreme Spirits or the Brethren directly, but encountered no success. The programmers had earned their keep — everything was blocked.

What to do? For the first time in a long time, I didn't have any idea for how to get myself out of this situation. Damn it! I wish I could blow them all up with Armageddon and...

Hold on!

I opened design mode and hesitated...I was so afraid that my idea might not work that I began to do everything with the patience and diligence of a sapper. It seemed as if any inaccurate movement, gesture or even breath might spoil the final result. When I opened my eyes, I saw Plinto blinking before me. Yes! I did it! I know how we can beat Antsinthepantsa and Kalatea! The important thing was to draw them in until they stood near me!

"Plinto! I have an idea! We can win, but I need to run over to Altameda really quickly!" I explained my plan to the Rogue and received another portion of wry laughter in response:

"You know, Mahan, even if they force us to fight Level 400 players while scaling us down to Level 1, I suppose I'll have to join you and fight alongside. Go on and run to the bank — we have very little time..."

"Welcome to battle! May the strongest among you triumph!"

Two women stood facing us at the other end of the arena. The founder and chief ideologue of the Shaman class — an enormous green orc — and her brightest student, the hope and light of the Shamanic movement, the apostate Antsinthepantsa — in the form of an ordinary girl. Why apostate? Because she had fled our continent in search of a better life and a better game for herself...

Well, good luck to them both!

I backed up slowly, watching our opponents approach. Plinto retreated alongside me. At Level 30 he didn't even have Stealth. The good thing was that the Harbingers weren't blinking. Either the arena's coordinate grid was unavailable to them or the penalty for using Blink was too great. Or perhaps they wanted us to savor our helplessness before landing the killing blow.

Suddenly, the Shamans' Totems appeared beside them. Bussy, a panther as black as tar and — I even shook my head from shock — a Tarantula! Kalatea's Totem was a Tarantula! A huge spider, one-and-a-half meters tall!

"I bet that monster can spit some kind of web thing," muttered Plinto. "They might paralyze your Draco and kill him."

"They might," I agreed, still backing up to the wall.

"Boys, where are you going?" Before I could blink, the Harbingers vanished from sight and their voices sounded behind us. I spun around to find Kalatea's green mug scowling in my face. Two steps in front of me. "It's pretty fun fighting without the powers we're all used to, isn't it? You know what's really odd is that my premonition is telling me to finish this fight as quickly as I can. It's as if you have even the slightest chance of winning! I like the mere idea of it, so I'll give you a chance. Just one. You get the first attack, Shaman! You have five seconds!"

"You know, Mahan, I like the way this orc broad thinks," smiled Plinto, unsheathing his knives. "If you have something up your sleeve, now's the time. As I understand it, we won't get a second chance, so uh, I'll leave you two be and go for a nice stroll I think."

Oh how I adore the overconfident! Were our places reversed, Plinto and I would have already been in the nearest tavern having a drink in mourning of all the items we'd missed out on. But as it stood we were facing your ordinary, overconfident, high-level player who had no actual experience with PvP. This couple thought they had our number.

Silly of them.

Plinto turned and broke into a sprint, putting distance between us as if he were on fire. Kalatea frowned with consternation, unable to understand exactly what was happening. She exchanged glances with Antsinthepantsa, began to raise her arm in order to point at the Rogue...and that was when design mode yanked me out of the surrounding world. Darkness enveloped me — darkness and two hundred Pendants just waiting for their moment to shine. And I do mean shine. My earlier trials with the Pendants had taken me to Erebus, but they had also taught me a very important lesson: If you want to blow something up, you have to create a masterpiece first! In my case, a hundred masterpieces. In Altameda I had picked up all the ingredients I needed to craft the items, and the only thing left now was to combine them with their projections.

There followed an immense explosion.

And yet there was no notification about our victory. As soon as all the motes of light had danced their scripted dance and their timer had expired, dispelling the Blindness debuff, I grabbed my staff and rushed in the direction of where Kalatea and Antsinthepantsa were supposed to be. I couldn't allow them to recover.

When my perception of the surrounding world had passed from two dimensions to three, and I began not only to see the objects around me but perceive my own position relative to them, a wave of surprise washed over me. The explosion had not killed Kalatea — the Shaman was still alive. In any case, that part of her that peeked out of the black crater in the wall was still alive. Screams, curses, groans and calls for help sounded all around me, but I didn't pay the collateral casualties any attention — instead, I was fixated on a strange quirk of the arena that my explosion had revealed: The explosion had destroyed a part of the wall, scattering stone blocks all over the arena, destroyed a part of the player spectators who had found themselves in its blast radius and — what surprised me most of all — hurled Kalatea into the opening that had been behind the wall. There wasn't anything there and now Kalatea's leg and arm were helplessly jerking side to side against an absolutely black background. It was these movements that made me conclude that the Shaman was alive and not dead. She'd merely gotten a little stuck in that place, which physically didn't exist in the game. She'd effectively clipped through the arena.

The system spent a long time thinking about the situation, about a minute. During this interval, the Stun that Plinto had managed to cast on the still-surviving Antsinthepantsa managed to expire as well. The explosion had thrown her not into the wall, but into the center of the arena, so if the Shaman had been killed it wasn't too violently. The good news was as follows: Bussy had been buried by rocks, completely freeing us from the threat of her claws and fangs. The panther was whimpering, trying to climb out of the pile, but it was beyond her.

Unwilling to allow himself the luxury of a revived opponent, Plinto turned into his Vampire Form and froze the girl just in case. Even if this was only for a minute, it would afford enough time to put the daggers to use and send the Shaman to respawn. When it became clear that we would be victorious, the system decided to have mercy on our opponents:

One of the combatants has left the arena and her team has been disqualified! Mahan and Plinto are victorious!
New challenge received...

Antsinthepantsa managed to give me a shocked-stunned look before my surroundings began to shimmer. Plinto and I found ourselves at a renewed, empty arena which bore no trace of the cataclysm that had just occurred. The system had generously granted us fifteen minutes to recover our powers and come to our senses.

"How many more of those do you have?" Plinto collapsed to the sand wearily. As brief as the first battle had been, its pressure was evident not in Plinto alone. I was shaking and shivering inside, as if I'd just overdosed on adrenaline. I wanted to jump and skip, even though there wasn't any buff on me.

"If we're talking about explosions of similar magnitude then enough for another 5–6 bouts. There're lots of Pendant orders."

"Beg your pardon," the arena announcer appeared beside us. "I must adjust the arena rules. You can't use..."

"You can't prohibit powers in the arena!" I

interrupted the goblin. "Facing professional killers without a single means of defending ourselves — is that within the rules too?"

"You didn't let me finish," the announcer whimpered. "From now on, there shall be no bouts below Level 50 and your powers will be available to you. But we must limit your use of your creative ecstasy in battle. There is no defense against it, so it would be unfair to permit it. It's enough if you sign an agreement about non-use and..."

"Is this the Corporation's official position?" Something odd struck me about the announcer's speech. "I am officially forbidden from using anything permitted under the rules?"

"No, not at all!" The goblin even started back. "This is merely a recommendation, not a position. The arena is place where the Free Citizens can demonstrate their mastery of their weapons. Who would agree to a battle knowing ahead of time that he would lose? It's unprofessional. For that reason..."

"*Rivarda ageloris!*" Plinto suddenly barked some incomprehensible gibberish and glared inquisitively at the goblin. The goblin faded from dark-green to a very light green bordering on white — paling from fear. The announcer's arms and legs began to tremble in fear and he whispered in a weak, terrified voice:

"*Rivarda riko!*"

"What were the odds?" Plinto continued to

surprise me.

"T-twenty-seven to one," the goblin replied with a stutter.

"Who hired you?"

"...?"

"I repeat — who hired you?" Plinto produced some kind of round object and demonstrated it to the goblin. Now the announcer became entirely white, like an albino. A very scary sight — an albino goblin — let me assure you. This terrifying creature collapsed on his knees and howled:

"Please, I beg you, don't kill me! They forced me! Too many terrifying individuals have bet on you losing in the fourth round! Please do not kill me!"

"Your life is in my hands!" Plinto growled bloodthirstily, the way only he could. "I. Need. A. Name!"

"Sig Crook Nose," the announcer collapsed entirely and froze, as if Plinto was the great god of Death. Although...I suppose there's much I still don't know about Plinto, so he could well be.

"Get out of here!" the Rogue barked and the goblin vanished like the wind.

"So...?" I hiked my eyebrow so high that Plinto was caught off guard:

"Have you considered a career on the stage? What mimicry, what emotion! Damn it all! The shadowy clans are playing against us. I noticed last time that there was something off about that goblin —

so that's what it was. Once upon a time, during my youth, I tried to set myself up in the Barliona underworld. That's where this code phrase came from: '*Rivarda ageloris.*' The Corporation ripped it off from an ancient bestseller. When a player earns the right to speak this phrase, an NPC that he addresses must answer him. That's how you can identify the thieves' guilds. Now it turns out that someone really wants us to lose the fourth bout. I can even guess who has enough money to pique Sig's curiosity."

"Who's that?"

"Well...If you want the short version — one of the wealthiest people of our continent. His clan is among the top ten, several castles, a well-developed infrastructure, lots of fighters. In general — he's an ordinary citizen. If it weren't for one 'but.' His entire business is focused on thievery, fraud, killing NPCs and keeping players locked in respawn areas. They say that in the real world he does pretty much the same thing. No one knows anything for certain, however."

"I don't really understand — what kind of threat does he pose to us?"

"The threat that the fourth bout, if you checked our schedule, is scheduled for 3 p.m., two hours after the third bout. We won't be able to spend that entire time in the arena and we'll have to step out to the city — where someone will be waiting for us. Some kind of kerfuffle will occur, enraging the local Guardian, the guards, whoever. And if we're in jail and can't show up to the fourth bout, we'll be disqualified and that will be that. Be sure to write, and sweet dreams."

"So why should we go out?" I asked baffled.

"Well, now it's clear that we shouldn't. But this very moment, that goblin is rushing to his boss to notify him of what happened. They'll cook up some other ruse. You think this is their first time? So don't relax and go set up your Shadows. We have a date with a new set of victims in five minutes. These guys'll be at Level 200. I mean, kids these days! Like that'll help them..."

We dealt with our second and third duo of opponents without any problems. The battle would start, I'd cast shields on Plinto and myself and turn into a Dragon, while my partner cast 'Blindness' on one of the enemies. Then I'd flit over to the other and Thunderclap him into paralysis, and then use four Battle Shadows to blow everyone out of the arena. I'm still not sure what the duos of Druids and Death Knights were trying to prove...or what they had hoped would happen. Did they think we wouldn't use our entire arsenal? Silly rabbits...

Everyone was waiting for the fourth bout. That would decide the fate of Bihan's castle and Lait's Stinger. In fact, it'd decide the fate of the entire arena! My premonition told me that if we won this one, no one else would even bother. We were about to fight the best of the best.

"Welcome to battle! May the strongest among you triumph!"

Plinto and Kei-Ten vanished into Stealth at the same time, darting off to take up their positions as per the plans. The audience hollered — the Rogues hadn't vanished for the spectators, merely become semi-transparent. Due to the restrictions, any contact with the outside world in the arena was limited, and exiting the game even for a moment was deemed a defeat, so the Corporation didn't risk anything, allowing the spectators to enjoy the beauty and horror of the tactics used in battle. As Plinto pointed out, the players would study the combat footage exhaustively and there were even specialized simulators which allowed them to face any opponent in the database. The players approached the task of killing each other extremely diligently, and the Corporation did its utmost to help them by offering any service it could. For money, naturally.

Our opponents had once again chosen to fight us without limitations. On the one hand this was bad due to the 70 level gap between me and the duo. On the other hand, thanks to the momentary pause between the third and fourth bouts, I had finally found the time to study the Shadows available at Level 333. And I had used this time to my utmost.

The Shadow Shaman class turned out to be a lot of fun. Figuring that only experienced players would play this class, the devs didn't bother assigning level caps to the Shadows. As soon as a Shaman reaches Level 50, every possible Shadow becomes available to him, with the strength of the summon determined entirely by the character's Intellect. If memory serves, Stacey mentioned that most players limited themselves to eight abilities, assigning them to the quick spell slots. I wouldn't argue — I did the same thing back in my Hunter days. And yet, reality was utterly different at the moment and using Shadows would lead to immediate defeat as there was nothing scaling down the level difference between us. So before the bout I sat down right in the center of the arena and began to craft.

And not Jewelry which would have been logical.

I began to craft Shadows!

Once upon a time the system had generously granted me the opportunity to craft hybrid Spirits. They turned out weaker than the originals, and yet they were also more versatile. For example, when healing an ally I could also cast a shield on him which could protect him from a subsequent attack...which formally speaking meant that I could choose between one large dose of healing and a smaller one with a shield.

This seemed all the same at best, but there were nuances involved to...or, as I like to say, undocumented features.

And these were what I wanted to find...

The Shaman has three hands...

A wave of Shadows emanated from my hands and sank into the arena's sand. The first thing I needed to do was to protect myself from Kei-Ten and his tiger. Traps wouldn't help here — given the level difference, they wouldn't even notice them. I had to find a more elaborate solution, even if it happened to be dangerous to me as well.

Quicksand!

The principles behind this terrifying phenomenon were well known to me, all I had to do was to make sure that the developers had translated the same physical laws wholly and entirely into the game. It didn't turn out too difficult to create a loose area of sand saturated with air. All I needed was the sand and several free Shadows of water and air. The water one would create a surface barrier that would keep the air in. My opponent wouldn't actually drown in this trap, but that's not what I needed anyway. I had to delay him. Plinto would do the rest followed by a Minor Battle Shadow. The Heavy one didn't work for some reason.

"Meth, we can leave the Shaman," Kei-Ten appeared out of Stealth, touched the quicksand I'd created with the tip of his tail and, even though his HP dropped by several points, began to chortle happily. "The idiot has cornered himself with his dumb sand trap. Let's go get Plinto!"

"Let's! This one's not going anywhere!" The Hunter replied with evident blood thirst; he stepped back several paces and suddenly fired into the air. Damn it all! I don't expect much of myself, but how did Plinto forget about this ability that Hunters had! Flare Shot was an ability that revealed all hidden creatures in a radius of forty meters.

"Plinto! Come on out!" Kei-Ten didn't bother going into stealth again, strolling demonstratively at the edge of the quicksand. It didn't cost that much Mana to maintain it, so I didn't pass up on the opportunity to send a Battle Shadow into the Rogue, keeping him on his toes...OH COME ON NOW!

As soon as the first Shadow reached Kei-Ten, his chortle broke into full on laughter, while Methodious's tiger licked its lips satiated — in some utterly baffling manner for an ordinary player (that is, me), the magical damage was channeled through the Rogue to the Hunter's pet, which in in turn, consumed this damage happily. He even licked his fangs and looked in my direction as if wondering whether there'd be more! The tiger was entirely immune to magic!

How am I supposed to play this game?!

"What, my darling, is this battle not working out for you?" Kei-Ten managed to contain his laughter and, without waiting for Plinto to appear, began to make fun of me. "You should try using that staff of yours! Go ahead! I won't even defend myself. Come on over and kill me! Oh, I'm begging you, oh great Shaman! Have your way with us!"

"It looks like they've wagered that they'll kill us during the last minute," Plinto whispered in my ear. I had to force myself to keep from starting back in shock — the Rogue's appearance was entirely unexpected.

"We can use that to our advantage," he went on. "How quickly can you dispel that quicksand?"

"Instantly," I replied without turning. Methodious went on shooting into the air, trying to illuminate Plinto, so I couldn't let on that the Rogue was beside me.

"There's ten minutes left in the bout. Act like you're shocked and don't know what to do. You can feed the tiger — it seems to like your Shadows! But meanwhile fill all your slots with shields. They'll come in handy."

It was incredibly easy to do as Plinto had told me. I really was shocked and had no idea what to do, so I didn't even have to pretend really. I'd periodically cast Shadows at Kei-Ten who went on pacing at the edge of my quicksand, but every time the result was the same — Methodious's cat ate them up with pleasure. At some point, I realized that they were playing with us like a cat with a ball of yarn. Our opponents were waiting for the last moments of the fifteen-minute-long bout to prove their might to the entire world. A kill in the last seconds of the bout wasn't just highly-esteemed, but pretty lucrative too if you made a bet on it ahead of time.

"When we reach the last minute," Plinto whispered, "you'll cancel the quicksand and cast the shields. But only on my command! I'll be in Stealth so you will take all the dps those two can dish out. We need to survive one minute. Don't let them do any damage! Here, take this. It'll come in handy."

Plinto took the Tooth of the Patriarch from his neck and handed it to me majestically. It was obvious how little he wanted to do this, but the Rogue didn't see another way out. I have to admit that our opponents did not behave in the spirit of arena fighters. Kei-Ten had set up training dummies and was practicing his attacks on them, leveling up one of his stats. Considering that the dummies dodged, twisted and even tried to parry his blows, it wasn't one of the basic stats either. Methodious, who hadn't managed to find Plinto, sat down near us and began to level up his Culinary stat. He made a bonfire, pulled a pot and ingredients out of his bag and a fairly pleasant scent of cooking began to spread across the arena. Every once in a while, the Hunter would cast a mocking glance in our direction, without forgetting to stir the food in the process. The outcome of the bout had been decided in our opponents' minds, so why waste time? Good players never have enough of that resource. Once a minute remained, Kei-Ten and Methodious took up their positions. Even the tiger hunched preparing for a leap and my premonition told me that the ten meters between us wouldn't pose much of a gap for this monster. Or for the Rogue. He'd come flying through in Sprint without even noticing the sand.

"They're getting ready," Plinto was following our opponent's movements. "At the count of three, get rid of the sand and pour everything you got into defense. One. Two. Now!"

You have been stunned for 60 seconds! Stun decreased to 2 seconds (Patriarch's Tooth).

You have been paralyzed for 60 seconds! Paralysis decreased to 2 seconds (Patriarch's Tooth).

You have been...

I stood surrounded by utter chaos watching with astonishment as the Hunter's pet was fruitlessly trying to break through the green sphere that had appeared around me. Methodious had become Legolas, sending arrows flying with such speed that they formed an unbroken line between him and the same green sphere. Kei-Ten was cursing somewhere behind me, but I didn't feel like turning to look at him. I was much more interested in the following entry in the list of buffs:

Disruption Field: All damage negated for 15

seconds.

In some mysterious way, the Rogue had managed to stick a bubble on me, granting me fifteen minutes of life. I'd figure out how he got this thing later and why he'd never mentioned it before. At the moment I had a much more entertaining affair to attend to. I clenched and unclenched my fists several time, trying to calm my trembling. Let's see how good of a Shaman I am! The shields blocked more than two million points of damage, I had eight shields, forty-five seconds and a panel which displayed how much durability each shield had.

I had to hold on...

You have been stunned for 60 seconds! Stun decreased to 2 seconds (Patriarch's Tooth).

You have been...

In the last seconds of the Plinto's sphere, I ducked, dodging one of the tiger's attacks. He went flying right over my head, growling unhappily in the process, his prey escaping his paws. And yet at the same moment, Kei-Ten's daggers began to strike my shield, while a stream of arrows formed a ribbon between Methodious's bow and my head. The shield's Durability went plummeting at a terrifying rate — in a few seconds it had fallen to half. Renewing the protection by 20% durability, I smashed the Rogue with my staff. Zero! No, not zero — I had managed to do several points of damage, but that didn't stop Kei-Ten. He didn't notice anything at all, continuing his terrible dance with his daggers. He had even shut his eyes, submerging into some kind of trance. The Rogue was relishing battle, with his strength, emotions and energy. He lived in the battle, he was the battle, he had turned into a true warrior, hypnotizing and demoralizing his opponent.

That's okay, we've got plans too.

A new shield appeared around me and here I forced the Rogue to take several steps back, interrupting his deadly dance. I turned into a Dragon and simply threw him away from my immense four-meter tall torso.

Thunderclap! Signed, sealed, delivered! Other people know how to stun their enemies too.

I won exactly five seconds, no more. Not even that — I won five seconds and took out one-and-a-half opponents — the tiger didn't have any protection from stun and turned into a pretty statue. For an entire minute. Kei-Ten and Methodious simply tossed their heads, regaining their concentration and coming to, after which our dance of death continued. It looked like the Patriarch's Tooth, that Plinto was so proud of, wasn't such a Unique item after all. But I couldn't help but be pleased with one thing — I had interrupted the Hunter's ability and now only ordinary arrows were flying in my direction. There were many, and they came in quickly and with lots of force, but they no longer resembled machine gun fire.

A shield! Another one! And another one!

"I'll help!" sounded Plinto's shout and I was suddenly left on my own with the Hunter. Kei-Ten stood quietly beside me, with his dagger in the air ready to land another blow — stunned. Plinto, who had left Stealth, was sprinting to the other end of the arena while dodging Methodious's arrows. Several blue flashes indicated that the Hunter had managed to strike the Rogue several times, yet my shield worked perfectly. I looked at the Patriarch's Tooth with renewed respect — it turns out that our opponents had a one-time way of avoiding stun while the Tooth worked constantly. I was happy to admit I was wrong. But the surprising thing was that Plinto didn't bother killing Methodious. He dashed out of the arrows' range and began to watch as the Level 400+ player turned on poor little me...

A shield!

A sudden silence descended on everything. I opened my eyes wearily, interrupting the casting of another shield and almost started — right in front of me hovered an arrow, a green venom oozing from its barbed point. The shaft was fluttering like a fish pulled out to land, thirsting to continue its flight and impale itself into the detested shield and shatter it, but this was no longer destined to be.

"Time's up!" The announcer's voice ended the

silence. "Team Kei-Ten/Methodious has done 0 points of damage. Team Mahan/Plinto has done 32 points of damage. The victor has been determined!"

Mahan and Plinto are victorious!
New challenge received...

I collapsed exhausted to the arena floor and began to giggle hysterically. We did it! We were the best! We won by doing a mere 32 points of damage, while my total HP amounted to several hundred thousand! We...

"Give me the Tooth back," Plinto deadpanned, as if we hadn't just bested the deadliest duo in the game. He stepped over to me calmly and held out his hand. "You've played with it long enough."

Neither a gesture nor a word from the Rogue suggested any joy at winning the bout — and yet the speed with which he put on the Tooth and his sigh of relief, small but notable, suggested that this person had nerves too. I had only one explanation for what was going on — in fifteen minutes we were due to fight our last bout and Plinto didn't want to lose his concentration. Agreed, if we let our victory go to our heads, we might accidentally lose through sheer carelessness. We could celebrate later...

"May the strongest among you triumph!"

The fifth duo seeking the incredible jackpot turned out to be a duo of Warriors. Choosing a restriction of Level 200, they decided to throw us off guard with dodges and feints that would make it difficult for us to target and focus them.

Silly rabbits...

Quicksand.

Thunderclap.

Cancel quicksand.

"Hold on, Plinto!" I managed to yell before the Rogue fell upon the Warriors. "Not like that!"

"Not like what?" Utter bafflement sounded in Plinto's voice. "What, do you want to duke it out with them one on one?"

"You misunderstood me," I hurried to calm my partner. What if he decides that I lost my mind a bit during the last bout and haven't recovered from it yet? I quickly produced the ten fireworks I had in my bag and showed them to Plinto. "We have this lovely little trick at our disposal! Let's see how it works, what do you say?"

"Monsieur knows how to get his kicks!" a cruel smirk appeared on Plinto's face. "You take the one on the right. Want to bet whose flies up higher?"

A combatant has left the arena and his team is disqualified. Team Mahan/Plinto are victorious!

New property acquired: The Citadel of the Solar Wind (Level 34).

"Good day, Master Mahan!" As soon as the

bout ended, a semitransparent creature that resembled at once a monkey, a person and god-knows-what else appeared before us. It took several more words for me to understand that I was looking at the Celestial equivalent of the Herald, or, as they like to say in those climes, a Rehadji.

"Allow me congratulate you on your new, marvelous castle. I have been sent by the Emperor to collect taxes on your new property. Taking into account the geopolitical position of the castle, the owner's relationship to your clan as well as the level of the castle, the amount adds up to sixty-eight million gold. Two million for each level. There are two methods of payment — a one-time sum, subject to a 5% discount, or a monthly payment. Which of these methods do you prefer?"

"If you are unable to make payment," the Rehadji went on, accurately apprising my confusion as an unwillingness to part with such an immense sum. Thanks to our arena wagers I had the money, but I saw no point in maintaining a castle in enemy territory. I couldn't ensure an adequate defense for the castle which would allow just about anyone to raze my property from Level 34 to Level 1, making me lose sixty million in the process...Stacey would not look kindly on such expenditures of the family savings. "Or you do not wish to do so, you will be granted a stay of two months during which you can sell the castle at auction. No one wishes to compel you to do anything. The castle will be sold and you will receive half of the proceeds. Everything is quite simple, transparent and lawful. Please make your decision!"

"Can the castle be transported to our continent?" Plinto came to my aid.

"The answer is a negative, Master Plinto the Bloodied," the Rehadji answered with a bow, unfazed by the Rogue's lack of tact. "This castle does not have a means of teleportation."

"Does that mean that other castles do?"

"I am not authorized to discuss this question. My goal is to determine whether Master Mahan will take ownership of his property or whether he prefers to put the castle up for auction."

"Can I make this decision a little later?" I inquired, wishing to discuss this with Stacey. Maybe the Solar Wind would come in handy...

"I'm sorry," the Rehadji shook his head negatively. "If I do not receive an answer in five minutes, the castle will be sent to auction. Such are the rules, Master Mahan. See clause..."

"If I take ownership of the castle, can I have a moving service move everything in it to Altameda?" A cute idea suddenly occurred to me. Any further growth for Altameda had to be effected through its decorations, which I didn't want to waste my time and resources on. However! If I had a Level 34 castle at my disposal, then no one could keep me from plundering it as much as I liked! If I set up an auction, the castle will go straight back to Bihan, who'll buy it for a few gold! Like hell! I would take the castle apart piece by piece, and stuff my vaults full of Imperial Stone and Oak. Loot's loot after all!

"Of course such a service is available," the Rehadji replied. "The price is equivalent to 2% of the cost of the transported materials, but no more than ten million. Have you made your decision?"

"I have. I will take the castle. Please withdraw the money from my personal account."

"The hell do you need that castle for?" Plinto frowned as soon as we were left on our own.

Indicating that I'd answer him when I got the chance, I got out an amulet and dialed Stacey.

"Stacey, listen..."

"You won! Danny, you won!" The torrent of joy emanating from the amulet forced me to smile. Pleasing a wonderful woman is always nice, and when that woman is your wife, it's twice as nice.

"Hang on, Stacey! We can talk about it at home. I have Plinto here. I have a favor to ask — I need to demolish the Solar Wind. Will you arrange it?"

"I'm all attention," the joy and happiness vanished in an instant. I was speaking to a veteran of all sorts of intrigues, ready to set out against her foe yet again.

"YEEEAAAH!!! WHOOO!!! THAT'S HIM!!!" roared a huge crowd of players as soon as we stepped out of the arena. I raised my eyebrows in surprise. The sea of players reached to the walls of Altameda. It was as though the players of the entire continent had assembled here and were trying to out-yell each other. Above the players' heads, I could see a projection of myself peering with shock into the distance: The Mages had provided a view of the action to the distant parts of the crowd. The guards were instilling some sense of order, forming passages in this sea of people and allowing the players to move among the buildings, yet beyond the passages an utter hell reigned. This was a terrifying mob.

"You managed to surprise me," Geranika appeared beside me. Looking at the monstrous crowd, he smirked and pointed at the players: "Do you still insist that they aren't a herd of sheep? Roaring, screaming, seeking revelation from their herd leader...A revolting mass of flesh! Who would call this creature a sentient?" Geranika made a motion and the projection of a mad, raving, hollering orc appeared several feet before us. The name above his head suggested that I was looking at a player, but his behavior made me have my doubts. The orc was shaking his head like there were voices in it, he was screaming, waving his arms in the air, sputtering with spit, and yet the scariest part of him were his eyes — they were insane.

"Only a sheep in a herd would consider being near its herd leader the highest blessing. Only so it could later tell its children about this 'epic' moment. You can be proud. This will be remembered for years to come. Beasts..."

I had nothing to say to Geranika's pronouncements. On the one hand, I couldn't permit an NPC to insult living players, and yet on the other...The projection Geranika had shown me was worth more than a thousand words. It really was quite a stretch to call these creatures humans. It was as if they had won in the arena instead of Plinto and I. Of course, it was possible that the rioting players had won a lot of money in the betting, but even that didn't justify the way they were behaving. Rational people don't behave this way.

"It's time for us to go," Geranika offered his hand without waiting for my reply. "The Pryke Copper Mine awaits."

"Plinto, launch Altameda and give this amulet to Stacey," I handed the communications device to the Rogue beside me.

"Launch?" I heard Geranika's surprised question, before the world around me turned into roiling fog. This jump didn't resemble teleportation. There had been no portal, shimmering or otherwise. Instead, a loading bar appeared, which in Barliona indicates that the location you're headed to, has never been visited before and is being loaded for the first time. Does this mean that the mines aren't on the main game servers? That can't be — my creation of the Orc Warriors from the Karmadont Chess Set had been announced to the entire game world. What's going on here?

"I will wait for you here," boomed Geranika, when the world around me came back into existence. The Lord of Shadow folded his arms across his chest, proudly raised his head and turned into a statue of the captain of some ancient ship, headed straight into the storm. No one and nothing could distract this captain, least of all the squad of orc guards pointing their pikes at us. The NPCs' faces betrayed such deep revulsion that I too adopted my most implacable face. I wasn't about to get emotional in front of some Imitators of the penitentiary system. The system had had three months to see plenty of my emotions as it stood. Enough.

"The boss is expecting you, minion of Shadow," one of the guards seethed with difficulty. Tension filled the air around us. I was hated. Purely, openly and whole-heartedly. You know, I was even enjoying this — I was tired of being a goody two-shoes.

"Just give me a reason," the guard frothed, prodding me with his pike in the back. In my view, this is going too far. Whatever feelings the devs had coded into the NPC, there should always be a clear line between the game world and how the player feels in it. When the game starts causing discomfort, it ceases being a game. People don't submerge themselves in Barliona for this — they have enough troubles in the real world.

"I didn't come here to play some two-bit part!" I yelled up into the sky, knowing full well that the game's moderators were watching my every word and movement. A player couldn't just wander into the mines just like that. "I request that you disable this physical coercion! My presence here has been approved by the administrators!"

To be honest, I didn't really expect someone to be listening to me, much less a response. My three months in the mines had dispelled any rosy conceptions I had about this camp among the cliffs, but the desire for justice triumphed over logic and reason. I'm not here to feel this NPC's hatred on my own body.

We reached the administration facilities without further incident. All of the convicts were in the mine, the guards were there too and I only tarried a bit at the smithy. However, instead of Rine — that whimsical gnome — I found a world-weary dwarf at the forge. A practically square torso, arms the girth of my legs, a terrible scar cleft half his face in half and passed through where the dwarf's right eye had been, watery gray hair, sooty chain mail — this creature bore no resemblance to Rine. Our eyes met. The dwarf frowned like he'd seen a heap of manure, spat and went on hammering the ingot on his anvil, having expelled me from his thoughts.

"Where's Rine?" I asked the guard escorting

me. It took a few moments to understand that no answer would be forthcoming. The guard merely smirked and indicated the administration building with his pike. We headed in that direction. When I get to the bottom of all my other problems, I'll need to figure out what had happened to this NPC. If he hadn't been erased, which was unlikely since he had a granddaughter and therefore a concrete history in the game's lore, I'll need to recruit the gnome to work for me. Smiths of his abilities don't grow on trees.

The mine governor's office hadn't changed much. The same elegant statues, paintings on the walls, a large crystal chandelier, carpets, carved wood and a light breeze...The only difference was that instead of two-meter-tall Prontho, the seat behind the desk was occupied by a dwarf. A new anonymous governor of Pryke Copper Mine.

"Your request was examined and approved," the dwarf said in a calm, business-like tone, offering me a seat in one of the armchairs. Had my yelling really had an effect? "Prisoner Izu shall be brought here in a minute. Would you like some water?"

"I won't say no," a copper mug with water appeared on the desk. The handiwork of one of the local craftsmen, dressed in a striped shirt. "Permit me a question — earlier, a gnome named Rine worked in the smithy. Where is he now?"

"How do you know him?" The governor tensed up notably, as if my question had been taboo. I had to respond honestly without hiding anything.

"I too was a prisoner here just over a year ago. Rine helped me set out on the Way of the Creator. I wanted to speak to him and say thank you but was surprised to see that he wasn't at his customary place. Has something happened to him?"

"He has retired," the dwarf replied, sighing with ease. "He returned to his family."

"How could I..."

"We do not issue the contact information of our former employees to former prisoners," the governor interrupted. "Please make your inquiries with the Heralds. This issue falls under their jurisdiction. The person you wished to speak to. You have half an hour!"

The door opened. An old man shuffled slowly into the office. I gulped. I had seen Donotpunnik — or Donald Izu as he was called in real life — in court, but over the last few months he had aged a great deal. A very great deal. Given that a convict's avatar reflects what he looks like exactly in real life, Don had aged by about forty years if not more. The only thing that remained of the old Donotpunnik were his eyes. Sharp, piercing, intelligent and filled with astonishment. I suppose I was the last person that Donotpunnik expected to see in the governor's office.

"Mahan," he nodded, sitting down across from me. Judging by your lack of a robe, you're here to ask me questions. Get on with it."

"What about 'I hate you,' and 'you damn bastard' and 'I hope you die?'" I couldn't keep from asking. The man before me had ordered that I be drowned in my capsule, so I didn't feel much sympathy for him.

"Did you not come for that?" Donotpunnik smiled grimly.

"No. I need information."

"What kind?" Donotpunnik even looked surprised. "They pumped me for everything I knew and even what I didn't know. A full memory scan — that's nothing to smirk at."

"They only recovered what you remember. I'm looking for your thoughts at the moment," I barely kept myself from swearing. Alex hadn't said anything about scanning Donotpunnik through and through. If I recall the law correctly, and I recall it very well, memory scans had to be approved by the President personally. No one else had the power to order the extraction of a person's memories from their mind. Human rights activists kept a particularly close eye on this kind of thing. All of Barliona was built on the principle that memory could not be extracted. An example could be Kart who refused to give up his corrupt boss. It was easier for the legal system to imprison someone for ten years than pull evidence out of their head.

"So it's like that? What kind of thoughts would you like then, buddy?"

"Marina. Tell me about her."

"Marina? What do you need her for?" The old man asked surprised, but went on: "An ordinary operator. She had several objectives. The first was to assemble a database of potential candidates. The second was to draw them into the game. The third was to arrange their exit into the wider game world. The fourth was to communicate with our people in the Corporation. She made no decisions. Are you here because of her?"

"Yes. Did you meet with her out in reality?"

"Of course. Every week."

"Is this her?" I brought up a photo of Roxanne and showed it to the old man. Alex refused to allow me to do this for a long time, but my ironclad reasoning proved convincing: 'I feel like this is the right thing to do.' He didn't find any counter-arguments to this, so he greed, waving his hand and muttering, 'Do whatever you feel like.'

"Yes," Donotpunnik looked me in the eyes piercingly. "I personally ordered her termination. The results were demonstrated to me. Is there something I don't know?"

"That is precisely why I'm here. Marina, the freelancer whom you hired actually looks like this," I brought up another photo and showed it to Donotpunnik.

"Go on."

"The girl you call Marina actually has a much

less typical name. Roxanne Vecchi. The first photograph is her. Here is what I've managed to learn so far." I related the story of my search for the truth and my meeting with Corporation officials.

"Well oh well," Donotpunnik muttered, staring into the window pensively. "So you've come to ask how I met her to begin with, correct?"

"Yes. Memories only record the fact of what happened — without thoughts, feelings or emotions. And those are exactly what I need at the moment. Where did Marina come from?"

Slowly as though unwillingly, Donotpunnik began to tell his tale. I'll admit that it's difficult to recollect your own defeat, but I wasn't too worried about the old man's suffering. I needed to get at the truth.

As I had guessed, Marina hadn't been found by posting an announcement in the classifieds. She had been recommended by one of her partners, to whom the old man had turned for help. An Eastern partner. Bihan. The girl was vetted, but the check didn't turn up any flags. Marina existed in all the databases, behaved entirely properly without raising any doubts and she really did look like the woman in the first photograph. Through her enthusiasm and emotions, Marina became 'one of the crew' within a few months, taking on especially sensitive assignments and completing them with astounding accuracy and cruelty. You need to send ten innocent people to prison? No problem. Marina ingratiated herself with the victims, seduced them and forced them to perform some act of folly. Hack the water management system, steal a painting, fight some juveniles and break one of their arms. The variations were diverse but the outcome was the same — everyone ended up in Barliona. Donotpunnik's brain trust agreed on eight candidates supplied by Marina and set in motion a grand game that resulted in my terrible defeat.

"So you weren't the one who selected us?" I asked surprised.

"No. I approved the selection, but she was the one making the recommendation. Although...You know, you've forced me to reexamine those events from a different point of view. Here's what else I have to tell you..."

The conspirators held daily meetings to discuss their plot and make decisions about its progress. At some point in time this group was pared down to three people — Donotpunnik, Hellfire, and Marina. And yet the main ideologue, the one who set the main goals, wasn't the old man. It was Marina. Donotpunnik even grabbed his head when he reviewed a typical meeting in his mind: Marina would propose the options, these were discussed and the decision that was made was generally the one the girl had preferred to begin with. Not the one Donotpunnik would have chosen. Marina had manipulated the entire process! The only decision that the old man had made on his own was to terminate the operator when the game had reached its conclusion.

"That's even among the scanned information," the Don glared at me with wide-open eyes full of surprise. "The decision to terminate you was hers. We never wanted to kill anyone! It was only later when I understood that you're in virtual space, I panicked and ordered your termination. Mahan, we were manipulated!"

The old man jumped up from his chair and started pacing back and forth.

"I know that our conversation is being monitored, otherwise Mahan wouldn't have been allowed to visit me. Check Roxanne! If Mahan is correct, the true mastermind is still free! Bihan recommended Marina, but only after I asked him myself. He gave me several choices to choose from, so I don't think that he's the one behind all this! He was trying to destroy Phoenix! The only person who ended up winning after everything was over and done with was..."

"Time's up!" The governor's office dissolved around me and I found myself beside Geranika. He was still playing his role of a statue — even his clothes didn't move in the breeze that blew through the Mine ceaselessly. Only his eyes — carefully studying me even now — let me know that this statue was a living one.

"Are you satisfied?" Geranika boomed.

"Entirely," I still couldn't calm myself after Donotpunnik's outburst. He hadn't had time to tell me the name, but I didn't need that either. I knew the name very well — the man who had won everything after the entire plot. The name was on the tip of my tongue and wanted to be uttered, but I refused to do so, despite all the logic to the opposite. This is just emotions and assumptions! This person wouldn't risk everything over the chance of a profit...

Or would he...?

.

CHAPTER FOURTEEN
THE TOMB OF THE CREATOR

"I HOPE YOU KNOW WHAT YOU'RE DOING," Geranika remarked, examining Altameda's new environs. On the one side, a dark-blue sea spread itself beside the castle. It was almost purple. The waves came running onto the shore and burst into a wall of spray as they crashed against an unexpected obstacle — the walls of my castle. The moat, which was ordinarily half-empty, filled with seawater and as I looked on, a pair of crocodiles swimming in the moat turned into terrible monsters — some kind of octopus and crab hybrid. I shuddered — despite my sensory filter, I felt a chill as if the bone-chilling sea breeze had found a way from this virtual world into the real world my body was in. On the other side of the castle, an endless plain stretched far into the horizon. There was neither a tree nor a bush nor even a stone to be seen in its expanse. Nothing but withered, yellow grass found the strength to stand up to the harsh climate of our continent's far North, filling the steppe with itself. But even that wasn't enough to fill the desolate gray landscape. There were neither seagulls, nor animals, nor people. There was no one.

"Everything's dead here," I whispered with astonishment, suddenly sensing the utter emptiness of the space around me.

"When at last I get my way, the entire world will be like this," Geranika replied salaciously, breathing in deeply and with evident pleasure. "All life shall be destroyed!"

I glanced at the Lord of Shadow from beneath my brow. Lately I've started to forget that he is the doom of all life in Barliona. The goal of this NPC, despite his seeming normalcy, is the annihilation of all life and one of my goals, as a player, is to keep him from reaching that goal.

"Is this why you want to help me reach the Tomb?" I guessed.

"Mahan, soon enough you will have no choice but to become my trustworthy ally. I can juxtapose facts and make inferences as well as you: You were in Erebus. You have a flying ship. I know what is located not far from this location. I imagine that you know that too. If you do what you're thinking of, there won't be a single Empire that will have you. Ever again. You will be enemy number one from now until the end of time. Every sentient creature in this world will hunt you. And that is precisely why I said: 'I hope you know what you're doing.' I will always welcome a warrior like you."

"Two warriors, Geranika. Two!" Anastaria joined us. "I go where my husband goes. Until the end of time."

"In that case, best of luck to you!" For an instant, an expression of sadness flashed across Geranika's face — immediately giving way to his customary smirk. Then the Lord of Shadow vanished. Without any sound or portal or other bells and whistles. I'll need to learn that trick.

"How's Don?" Stacey dropped what seemed like a neutral question, but I could tell she could barely contain her agitation. "Did you find out anything?"

"Bihan." So long as I lacked ironclad proof, I decided not to lay all my cards on the table before my spouse. "He recommended Marina and I'm sure that Alex is following up as we speak. We need to figure out why the Celestial Empire needs this."

"To eliminate an opponent!" Stacey exclaimed unable to contain her emotions. "Phoenix has been at their throat for a long time and using a third party to destroy them is exactly how the East prefers to achieve its goals!"

"Let's see what Alex comes up with. I'm sure he'll share whatever it is. He can't not. We'll make our conclusions then," I hugged Anastaria. "We don't have a lot of time. We need to go..."

"*I always imagined that there wasn't anything north of our continent,*" muttered Stacey, frowning from the frigid wind. The GAS struggled against the snowstorm, stubbornly moving forward. The airship had somehow gained a level during its extermination of the players, so our ETA turned out to be five hours instead of the original six. We were standing at the bow of the ship, staring ahead and trying to see anything at all in the blizzard raging around us: the odd patch of ice, gaps of dark blue water with a violet hue, but other than that, a white wall of snow before us. Nothing more. In order to dispel the 'Frostbite' debuff, I kept having to cast a Healing Shadow on myself again and again, as well as at Stacey and Gnum who flat-out refused to abandon his creation. Judging by the constantly falling temperature, soon enough all I'll be doing is healing, since we hadn't brought any warm clothes with us, while mailboxes didn't work outside of the continent's limits. The hastiness with which we had arranged this operation was making itself felt.

"*There shouldn't be anything here,*" I replied, congratulating myself for the foresight of arranging a Lovers' Pendant for us. We could communicate telepathically again. As slight as it was, it was some victory over the system that lately seemed stacked against us.

"*I know, but even then it's still a little too empty here. Why create a giant location without a single sign of life in it. It's a bit too wasteful even for the Corporation and...*"

"LIVING! WARM! DELICIOUS!" A sinister

whisper drowned out both Stacey's thought and the howling wind. The GAS shook noticeably as three enormous, fog-shrouded Shadows crashed onto the deck. At the same time, the ship's protective forcefield popped as if it had been made from glass instead of magical energy. The foggy monsters reared up on three legs, spread their flaming wings and turned into three-meter-tall, red-eyed demons, seething with Shadows.

"FOOD!" they yelled in unison, raised their hands or paws or whatever it is that demons have and thick Shadow snakes began to wind in our direction from their claws. Stacey immediately cast a bubble on herself, while Gnum put on some defense of his own, preparing for battle. I should have thrown up a shield too and prepared to fight this new incarnation of evil, but I shrugged off all logic and surrendered to my premonition. The arena was behind us. The continent was behind us. Everything was behind us. All limitations. All borders. I had had it!

The Shaman has three hands...

"HALT!" I took several steps forward and made the summons, pouring all of my anger, all of my hate, all of my hurt into it — all of the negative feelings I had amassed recently. The Corporation, the players, Donotpunnik and his suspicions, Marina/Roxanne, Bihan and his gang, the arena — I had amassed so many emotions that I was going to lose control one way or another. In this sense, the demons' appearance was actually quite propitious. For about the first time in my career as a Shaman, I summoned the elementals. Three Shadow Elementals, one for each demon. Judging by Gnum's stunned gasp, the effect was spectacular. The GAS shuddered again when three boulders shrouded in green fog plummeted onto the deck and instantly turned into stone defenders.

"WE ARE ALLIES!" I barked quite convincingly. I didn't know that I could yell like a demon. The demons froze in astonishment, as if they'd seen a ghost. Although, I suppose you couldn't scare these creatures with any old ghost. The roiling snakes evaporated, melting away into the snow storm, and one of the demons took a step forward:

"YOU ARE NOT THE KEYMASTER! WHO ARE YOU?"

"I am his messenger." It sounded like these NPCs were expecting someone, so I had better play along. "We..."

"We were sent to check your preparedness!" Stacey interrupted, stepping up beside me. I looked at the girl and almost lost it — the Paladin's entire body was shrouded with fog. The typically-glinting golden armor was covered with patches of fog which roiled along the armor against all laws of physics. It was as if the armor wasn't made from Imperial Steel, but from liquid that had in some miraculous way acquired solidity. And yet, what was especially stunning, were her eyes. The girl's normally hazel eyes were glowing with a red flame, as if she were an aggroing mob. I hadn't the strength to look onto these two embers and so I looked away, glanced at my hands and gulped — there wasn't much difference between me and Stacey. The same seeping fog, the strange armor and — I was certain of it — the red eyes. We had turned into true warriors of Shadow!

"The Keymaster is worried about the state of the world," Stacey went on. "He sent us to launch the Annihilator in order to distract the Free Citizens!"

"THE ANNIHALATOR STILL HAS TWO YEARS TO CHARGE!" boomed the demon.

"We need it now! Otherwise our plan will be imperiled!" I replied implacably, deciding to bluff. Something was telling me that this would work. "Are you really prepared to anger the Vicegerent?!"

"THE ANNIHALATOR SHALL BE READY IN AN HOUR!" As soon as I spoke the magic word, the demons did an about-face. Had I really guessed accurately? The redness vanished from their eyes as well as the fog and they even seemed to shrink several times, turning into mere two-meter-tall entities of Level 300. Quite slayable by me as well as Stacey. If it weren't for the horns and wings, they'd look like ordinary Barliona demons.

"*Who's the Vicegerent?*" Anastaria immediately

inquired, so I had to waste several moments to tell her about my accidental venture into the Leprosarium, the Astral Plane for Shadow Shamans.

"Is the work progressing as planned?" Stacey continued interrogating the demons.

"The Breach is ready," the demon with the colorful band across his torso answered in an ordinary voice. He seemed to be the leader of this trio. "Everyone awaits the Keymaster. When will he appear?"

"Soon," Stacey knew how to bluff much better than I did. "At the moment we need to distract the sentient forces to defend their cities. And not only of this continent," Stacey nodded over her shoulder in the direction of Kalragon. "All of them."

"The Annihilator won't handle such a load," the demon frowned.

"Why, we don't care one bit whether it'll handle the load or not," Stacey shrugged. "I have been issued an order and I intend on performing it. You'll be the ones who'll have to explain to the Vicegerent why the plan fell through. We're just doing our jobs."

"I don't sense any sacrifices on this ship," the demon sniffed the air with his nose and pointed at Gnum: "He alone won't suffice to charge the Annihilator."

"The Keymaster sent us in a hurry, so the sacrifices will have to be found on location," I interrupted. "How many of you are there here anyway?"

"WHAT?!" The demon started back from us like from holy water. By the way, does that even have an effect on them? "YOU WISH TO SACRIFICE US?!"

"Who else? What do you propose?" I hiked an eyebrow expressively. "Where else are we going to find the energy to charge the Annihilator? You were sent to this world with a single goal — to prepare the invasion. The goal has been completed, now everything depends on the Keymaster. You need to serve the Vicegerent one more time. Surrender your essence to him!"

"We shall do the Vicegerent's bidding," The demons bowed their heads obediently as if they were...

Oh hell!

Scenario updated: 'Burden of the Creator.' You may join the side of Char. The scenario objective will be changed as follows: 'Prepare the invasion.' The current objective will be changed as follows: 'Deliver the Alabaster Throne to the Breach.' Do you wish to join Char? (Time remaining to make your decision: 7 days.)

"*Stacey, do you understand what the hell is going on here?*" I asked in shock, swiping away the system notification.

"*There's nothing to understand — the*

Corporation has decided to roll out a new expansion. An invasion by creatures from a different world! Danny, I knew that I couldn't let you go on your own! How else could I find myself in this kind of thing? Are you going to switch sides?"

"NO!"

"That's what I figured. Let's wait to make our choice. Right now we need to pretend like we're basically ready but that we still have doubts. The more information we get right now, the better it'll be later."

"So the Tomb is the Breach point then?" I guessed. "That's why the other continents' players showed up! The prophecies! As soon as I created the full Chess Set, the system issued a quest to keep me from the Tomb!"

"I'm afraid it's not that simple," Stacey shook her head.

"We're here. We need to descend!" The demon interrupted our telepathic exchange. "The Annihilator is under water."

"I'll breathe for the two of us," Stacey assured me, interpreting my agitation accurately. I wasn't much of a swimmer. "I'm a Siren after all."

Gnum brought the airship down to the surface. Despite the blizzard, the sea was as placid as a mirror. There wasn't a single wave, to say nothing of a storm. Another infraction of the laws of physics? Or was this the effect of an anomaly? As in, check it out — there's something amiss here. Make sure to study it!

The dive took us a long time. The demons did not seem uncomfortable, swimming alongside us like they were dolphins or something. Stacey also felt completely in her element. Turning into her Siren Form, she moved through the water with the same agility as the demons. I, on the other hand, did not feel so comfortable. If the first ten meters had posed no difficulty to me, then further on, Barliona's physics kicked in. Stacey would swim over to me and kiss me to supply the oxygen I needed, resetting the 'Submerged' timer, but I would immediately start to rise. At one point, everyone got fed up with my struggling. The demons latched onto my feet and began to pull me down. Hello pressure and the 'Stun' debuff. It was only thanks to Stacey that I didn't drown: Even in her Siren Form she managed to send a Healing Shadow into me at the critical moment. Ultimately, though, the downside of the rapid descent became that I came to my senses in an underwater grotto without the slightest idea of how I'd gotten there. It was a good thing that Stacey was beside me, since I definitely had to remember this place.

"Armageddon would come in useful here," Stacey's thought sounded in my head and I had to agree with it entirely.

First of all — this cave was enormous. Even though there was plenty of light, the farther side of it was barely discernible. At first glance, the width added up to no less than seven hundred or eight hundred paces. There was a light source approximately in the center of the cave — a bright white sun that rippled with bolts of lightning. A portal from the looks of it. A host of strange demons were sustaining it from the ground — their paws raised beneath it. Demon Mages. First time I've heard of demons having a Mage class. Considering that any old demon is a Mage by default, it's hard to imagine what demons specializing in magic were capable of. Although, maybe it's not that hard. Evidently they can open and sustain a portal between worlds.

The rest of the cave was filled with demons of various shapes and sizes. Winged and horned, like our escorts, small and toothy, fat and clumsy, quick and agile — the various demon types vaguely resembled the specific divisions between the classes. Mages, Warriors, Hunters, Rogues...Char offered the same assortment of classes as any other race.

"The Annihilator!" The demon pointed at the white sun. "Before we can begin filling it with energy, you have to prove that you've been truly sent by the Keymaster. You shall speak with our leader!"

Stacey and I barely had time to exchange glances, unsure of how we would pass this test, when a small demon popped up right before our noses. This fellow barely reached my waist in height and had neither horns, nor fangs, nor claws. In fact, outwardly, the demon leader looked more like a reddish goblin who'd undergone some minor plastic surgery than a demon.

"Let's see now..." drawled the demon and the world around us dissolved into darkness. I lost complete control over my avatar, finding myself in some sort of suspended state. On the one hand, I could still do whatever I liked, yet on the other, my actions had no effect. Various debuffs flashed past my eyes so quickly that I could barely keep track of them. The demon had uttered merely three words, yet the effect was intense! Fighting him would be difficult indeed.

"It's odd that the Keymaster failed to protect you from the voice of the leader. He is well aware of its effects on uninitiated minds," the demon who had brought us to the cave remarked with surprise.

"He merely wishes to test us," I wheezed, getting to my feet. Once again I was forced to thank my lucky stars that I hadn't turned off my sensory filter — judging by Stacey's eyes, that had hurt a great deal. "To see whether we shall remain loyal to him, knowing what we've committed to. We have no choice but to bear the pain. Such is his will."

"May his will be done then." The small demon smirked, flourished his paw and two amulets appeared in his palm. They bore such a striking resemblance to an item I had seen before that I shook my head trying to clear my sight. This wasn't possible!

"It is entirely within the spirit of the Keymaster

to test his minions again and again," the small demon continued once we had donned the amulets. "I sense your kinship to him! You are blood kin! The blood of the Keymaster flows in your veins. There is no better proof that you've been sent by him. I have been informed of your quest. We are ready! The sacrifice shall be performed immediately!"

"Something tells me that Plinto owes us an explanation," Stacey muttered aloud when the demons began to hop into the Annihilator one after the other.

"Not Plinto," I shook my head, adjusting the Tooth of the Patriarch. "His father!"

The cave was rapidly growing empty. The demons were filing into the white sun one after the other without even uttering a sound as they did so. Excellent warriors — they'd been ordered to die, and so they did. Management knows best! Any attempt to speak to the small demon and pump him for more info turned out unsuccessful. The only help we could get from him was a tutorial on how to activate the Annihilator. All other questions such as 'And where shall the Breach take place?' 'How many demons will enter Barliona?' 'What are the demons' technical specifications?' as well as others, elicited nothing but a smirk. He seemed to have decided that my attempts to gain information from him was just another trial of the Keymaster. And if he talked, then he would be deemed weak and all of his subsequent incarnations would be as a footsoldier.

"Subsequent incarnations?" I asked baffled. "Death isn't the end of being for you lot?"

"We are the spawn of Erebus!" the small demon replied proudly. "Death is but a step towards unity! And my time has come to take this step! Tell the Keymaster that I have completed my task. It is his turn now. We shall open the door!"

"Okay, now I'm completely lost — what the hell is going on? How the devil did the Vampire Patriarch become the demon Keymaster?" I asked a rhetorical question once only two sentients remained in the cavern — Stacey and I. The space around us had filled with the roar and buzz of the charged Annihilator. The hovering orb had turned a deep red, illuminating the cave with a sinister hue.

"Damned if I know. Ugh. The people you'll meet...Let's get on with it," Stacey waved at the Annihilator. "It's time we wrap this up."

"Without searching the cave?" My astonishment knew no bounds. "Are you well, my dear? An army of demons just committed ritual mass suicide, leaving all its gear. What if we get thrown out of here once we launch the device? No! You can do whatever you like, but I'm gonna take a stroll. Maybe I'll find something useful."

The Altarian Falcon. Scepter of Power. Properties: Complete subjugation of an enemy's

mind (up to 1000 sentient creatures at once). The subjugation of a player is limited to 60 seconds, no more than 10 times an hour. Mind control resistance does not work against the Falcon. Limitation: Level 300+; Shadow Alignment. Warning: The owner of the scepter receives Hatred status with the entire world apart from Shadow.

Achievement unlocked: 'Orly?' You have reached Hatred status with more than 10,000 factions.

"Oh yeah, yup, that's useful all right," Stacey said sarcastically after reading the properties. My hopes did not pan out — the demons had hopped into the Annihilator with all their gear. The only thing they left behind was the scepter of power. "A few minutes ago, only our continent hated you. Now the entire game's out to get us. Fun."

"By the way!" I recalled Linea's tale. "Did you know that the Annihilator is also Karmadont's handiwork? It turns out that our ancient emperor didn't just want to enslave the world, he also wanted to destroy it!"

"Or enslave it by destroying it," Stacey added. "He was the servant of the demons, the Tarantulas, the Patriarch and who knows who else all at the same time. Anyone who was powerful enough. What are you going to do with the scepter?"

"Well it can't get any worse," I tossed the

Altarian Falcon into my bag. "Send me the coordinates. Let's get this party started."

Heroes of Malabar! A terrible evil is headed for Anhurs! The Emperor has declared martial law and bids you to assist him! Everyone to the defense of the Empire!

Heroes of Kartoss! A terrible evil is headed for the Nameless City! ...

Residents of Barliona. The inter-clan tournament has been suspended! All PvP limitations have been lifted.

Stop Mahan and Anastaria at all costs!

"Welp, they definitely hate us now," Stacey smiled sadly, sitting down on the sand. "Twelve years of playing all to..."

"Sucker town," I offered. "Plinto's suggestion."

"Speaking of that Rogue!" Stacey dialed an amulet. "Hey you bloodsucker, are you ready to do the Eye?"

"Always ready, my little serpent," replied the voice on the other side of the amulet. "When you vanished, everyone decided something odd was afoot. Not many were aware that castles can teleport. Now however...Kek. The Emperor is demanding that the people return to defend the realm, but no one has the gold for portals! They're stranded here! The castle's gone after all! You should see this! The PKers have woken up and they're hungry. And there's a herd of players running around in a panic. Hundreds of thousands! Are you sure you want to do the Eye right this instant?"

"That's right!" Stacey said firmly. "Gather your warriors."

"Already done."

"Wait!" I managed to jump in before Stacey hung up. The girl looked at me inquisitively, but didn't say anything. "Plinto, head over to Altameda right now, please, and pick up scroll number one from the storage vault. It needs to be urgently cast right in the center of that crowd."

"Where did you get it?" Stacey asked with astonishment.

"They returned all five scrolls to me. They revived Geranika, after all, so it was only fair that I get the scrolls back too. I threw them in storage and forgot about them. Wasn't any reason for it. Until now."

"On it!" the Rogue said happily. "Using numbered items, whether they be number one or number two is my favorite pastime! In this case, we'll have to wait six hours to do the Eye."

"We're going to head over to Altameda during that time. Geranika can't hear us here," I tried to summon the Lord of Shadow to no effect and realized that this wasn't possible outside of the continent. We'd have to return to Altameda on the GAS. That would take us about 5–6 hours. Plinto would manage to respawn by that time.

"What do you need a massive slaughter for?" Stacey asked, once Plinto had set off to perform my orders. "There's a lot of minnows there."

"I couldn't care less. I'll even reimburse them for their lost items," I explained. "But right now, well, just put yourself in their shoes...They've just been pulled out of yet another competition...They're all standing around buffed up, in their best gear, thinking their happiest thoughts...When wham! Armageddon, baby! Strictly for educational purposes...'Cause the hell with them!"

"Shadow is affecting you," Stacey shook her head. "You're becoming..."

"Cruel? Cynical? Calculating?"

"Prudent. Everyone who's not with us is against us. And the more we weaken everyone who's against us, the stronger we'll be."

Stacey got out an amulet and called Plinto again.

"What'd you want?" the Rogue answered, suggesting that he was a bit busy.

"Are you still in Altameda?"

"Yeah."

"Bring a helper with you. Cast two scrolls. We need maximum damage."

"Mahan?"

"Do it. The more of them we kill now, the fewer

will get under our feet later."

"A'ight. I'll bring...By the way! I ran into Lori here. She asked me to tell Mahan that she couldn't find Karmadont in the Gray Lands. Either he's well hidden or he's already departed to Erebus or...Well, figure it out for yourself. I'm off to the slaughter."

As soon as we entered the boundaries of the continent, my mailbox exploded. Hundreds, thousands, tens of thousands of letters came pouring in from all ends of the game world, trying to tell me a single, simple thing — I would die. I was a dead man. I was a very sick person and Barliona was no place for someone like me. I was forced to set up the mail Imitator to respond automatically: "Hi! If this is regarding the big ba-da-boom, please address your complaints straight up your..." I'll admit this wasn't very tactful of me. But I was pretty fed up.

In order to protect Altameda as much as possible from the players' ire, I was forced to make a deal with Geranika to locate the castle on his territory. The castle's coordinates would be listed in the castles register, so any clan that felt like vandalizing Altameda by way of revenge could find it in a few minutes. I wanted to avoid this, so the Empire of Shadow was the best hideout. Teleportation scrolls could send players to practically any point in the continent, with the exception of several locations, including the Empire of Shadow. So when a quite content Geranika gracefully permitted me to locate

Altameda not far from Armard, the capital of his Empire, my joy knew no bounds. At least one problem had been solved.

Three tanks, seven healers (including Anastaria and me), nine melee fighters and eleven ranged fighters — our raid consisted of thirty players of Level 250+. As we were on our way back from the Annihilator, Stacey demanded an industrial supply of healing and defensive scrolls for the entire raid. I didn't feel like arguing, so I turned my attention to crafting, sending my Shadows into the paper instead of my quick spell slots. In just over two hours I managed to create 50 scrolls for each member of my raid and, it seemed to me, completed my task of preparing the raid party. Like hell! As soon as Geranika teleported me to Altameda, which was already near the Armard walls by that point, Stacey dragged me off to the Cartographers. To study! While I was creating the scrolls, my Cartography specialization had grown up to 150, which allowed me to level up my 'Scribe' specialization to Level 3. It didn't seem like much — one level — what's the big deal? But Stacey held a different opinion entirely! Three levels of this specialization allowed me to create scrolls with a 1000 point stat limit. When it came to healing scrolls — from now on they would be five times as powerful as before and everything I'd made to that point was quickly sent to the storage vaults. Stacey simply smiled to my angry rant and told me to get back to work.

We decided to speak to the Patriarch after we'd completed the Dungeon. Stacey and I figured that the Corporation wouldn't have time to set the update in motion at the moment. A new threat in the form of the deadly fog, demanded that they stay on their toes, keeping the players supplied with arms, which all meant that we had at least another day. As soon as we complete the Tarantula quest, we'll go see the Patriarch. Everything in good time.

Message for the player! You have reached Char. +50% chance of finding a valuable item. +20 to Experience earned.

"That's right!" Stacey exclaimed happily. "I just remembered why Char sounded familiar to me! This is the Tarantula's world!"

"Okay, we've reached spiders' world," I muttered. Once activated, the Fleet Hound Paw opened a standard entrance to a Dungeon, though really we simply passed into another world. "What do we have to do now?"

"That's a question no one's been able to answer for about seven years now," Plinto approached us, examining the red mountain looming over our heads. "It's just a barren planet. Sooner or later, a player will get bored of wandering around here and he'll head back to Barliona. Or the local mobs will send him back."

The world of the Tarantulas, or the demons, or simply Char (the devil knows what the right term is), bore a close resemblance to Mars. Red sand, red stones, red mountains — I got the impression that it was simply painted red. Even the sun, in the middle of the sky, was reddish. It illuminated the lifeless barren nothingness with a bloody light. I've seen this before somewhere...

"Once upon a time, we spent a week out here," Anastaria said. "We killed everything that moved, but we didn't accomplish much. In the end we found ourselves outnumbered. There's a contact point with our world somewhere around here. We can use it as a shortcut into the Tomb. Only it's unclear how we can reach it. Maybe we need to activate the Eye and...Mahan? What happened?"

Step by step, I was moving away from the main group of players. I had the distinct impression that what we had to do next was right here somewhere nearby at arm's length and I need only to see it and grab it. In pursuit of this premonition, I began to stray from the raid party, which Anastaria noticed.

"Mahan! Where are you going? Are you being mind-controlled?"

I continued to walk, while a strange association occurred in my mind.

Control. A player could be mind-controlled for 60 seconds, ten times an hour. There would be a cooldown too. A minute or two. I no longer remembered exactly what it was. In any case, this mind control would be negated by the mighty Patriarch's Tooth and I had one of these now...

The Patriarch's Tooth. How would the High Vampire have five fangs? I saw two of them in his mouth and Plinto had another. Stacey and I now had one apiece too. How many more fangs did the demons have? One, two, ten, a hundred? Does the Patriarch give a demon his tooth every time he loses one? Come on, after all, they're...demons. Weird demons. They're not like the demons I have known. They're sort of a bit too...intelligent? Take the same old portal demon who runs the portal in Altameda. All he does is spend his time figuring out a way to make an extra piece of gold! Meanwhile these red-faced Char critters sacrificed themselves at the first order. Without even asking us for proof. All we had to do was prove that we had the Keymaster's blood flowing in our veins.

The Keymaster. The Keymaster's blood flows within me. He is my blood brother. But I only have one blood brother and that's Plinto. Even Draco is just a step-brother. Not blood. So this means that through the Rogue I became kin with the Patriarch and...

NO!

Blood relation only extends to two sentients!

The ones who exchanged blood! There can be no other bonds, especially mixed blood! Not in Barliona! But that could mean only one thing...

Blast it all to hell! What to do? Should I try it? You only live once!

This is just a game finally!

I returned back to the game. Stacey was standing beside me, anxiously peering into my face and no doubt screaming as loud as she could through our telepathic link...which, as I understood it, didn't work on Char. The other players were clumped up several dozen feet away. They were casting worried glances at the pillar of dust rising on the horizon. Our presence in this world had been noticed, and the first wave of locals was already on its way to meet its triumphant demise. I mean, this was a location designed for Level 100s, not Level 250s. And there were thirty of us.

"Stacey, what do players get at Level 100?"

"What's going on, Daniel?" Stacey tried shaking me back into a normal state. It's a good thing that this action is hard to perform in this game.

"What...Do...Players...Get...At...Level...100?" I repeated slowly and deliberately in the hopes that Stacey would realize the gravity of the situation.

"When a player climbs up through the levels sequentially — instead of skipping them like you did — then at Level 100 a forced initiation takes place. Not everyone manages to pick up their profession at

Level 10, Mahan. Some people get to Level 100 without a class profession and only then get their bonuses."

"Then that means that the player is modified at the hundredth level?" I guessed.

"No one modifies anyone! An ordinary ritual takes place, in which the head of the class confers the title on the player. And that's it!"

"Are the players gathered in one place? Or is this done remotely?" I went on inquiring. For some reason this felt important to me. So important that I could safely ignore the pillar of dust growing taller on the horizon.

"What the hell do you need to know this for right this instant? Yes. They're brought together in one place. Every class separately. The players take a knee, consume a class symbol, as if they're absorbing it, and that's it! There's no modification! That's how they get the first class title!"

It was like I'd been struck by a lightning bolt. A marker! Players who reach Level 100 receive a marker! And moreover, they're all players who've played passively and shown little interest to developing their characters until that point!

"Who among you received your first class title through initiation?" I yelled to the raid party. "Raise your hand! This is critical."

Hesitantly, even cautiously, the players began to raise their arms one after the other. A few moments passed and I was staring at twenty-two raised hands. Twenty-two...Three more than I needed! For, among the twenty players who'd come to Char, at least one had to be the head sheep. The rest were the herd. May the players forgive my thoughts...

"Okay. You've conducted a survey and determined that a part of the crew played unexceptionally. What now?" Stacey quipped and immediately started back when I yelled into the air:

"I have brought the Keymaster and the tribute! I seek a pass to see the Vicegerent!"

"What the..." Stacey began to say as a terrifying whisper filled the air around us:

"YOUR TRIBUTE HAS BEEN ACCEPTED, SHAMAN!"

Twenty-two players vanished with their arms still raised. The victims' frames went gray, signifying that the system was now preparing the cursing players to exit the game. The remaining five players exchanged glances and whipped out their weapons. So I had no other option but to yell to Plinto and Stacey:

"Take them out!"

Setting the example, I sent a Heavy Battle Shadow flying into the Warrior beside me. He grunted with surprise and collapsed on the ground with 0 HP — Plinto acted reflexively. Even though these were his friends, the order was more important. The remaining four tried to resist but in vain. It took Plinto several swipes of his daggers to leave only three living players in the Tarantulas' world.

"Keymaster," I took a knees before Plinto. "You are home!"

"Mahan, what the hell?" the Rogue cried almost upset, when Stacey, mumbling something under her nose, stepped over beside me and also took a knee. "What is going on?"

"He's not ready yet, Shaman." A painfully-familiar voice sounded beside me. Once upon a time, we had run the obstacle course to the sound of this voice — back then my sensory filter was off and I can't say that the recollection was pleasant.

"You are hurrying too much," the Patriarch went on, approaching his son. "He has too much light within him yet! He is not ready to lead the invasion."

"Only the Vicegerent knows whether he is ready or not." For whatever reason I had decided that the Patriarch and the Vicegerent were different creatures after all. What did we know about the High Vampire? Only that he was an extremely ancient creature. The son of the First Vampire, who defeated the mad Harrashess. Although I quite liked the latter actually.

"You have changed, Shaman!" the Patriarch said with surprise. "The Mahan I knew would stand up for kindness and justice. The current you...Can you imagine the vast quantity of rage and sadness was unleashed into the world when the two

Armageddons exploded among the unprepared Free Citizens? Another two or three such explosions and the Breach of Barliona will open on its own."

"The Mahan you knew died in the Cataclysm," I interrupted tersely, donning the mask of a villain. It's a good thing telepathy doesn't work in this world. Stacey's eyes told me that there was a lot she had to tell me. And it was obvious that none of it was positive.

"How did you understand that my son is the Keymaster? I did everything I could to have you suspect me."

At this point, another naughty idea popped into my head.

"The Prophecy. You know very well what it is about. With all due respect, confusing Plinto with you..."

"What prophecy are you talking about?" Stacey whispered, unable to control herself.

"Geranika..." the Patriarch seethed with a scowl. "Only he could have told you. I always knew that trusting that Shaman with a piece of the Alabaster Throne was a mistake! But why Plinto? I too am the son of the First Vampire! The prophecy applies to me as well as to Plinto!"

"Want to bet whose version is right?" I hiked an eyebrow. "Very well. Be so kind as to recite the entire prophecy. And I will show you the obvious reference to Plinto."

The Patriarch froze. His eyes were drilling into me — looking to see whether I was bluffing or whether I really knew the meaning of the ancient prophecy that the Emperor had mentioned back in the Dark Forest. It was back then that I heard: 'So, you finally found yourself a son? Do you not fear the Prophecy?' All of my current behavior was predicated on this single phrase. I was really hoping that Naahti hadn't made some mistake. At last, the Patriarch recited loudly:

"WHOEVER TEARS OUT HIS HEART AND REMAINS ALIVE SHALL DECIDE THE FATE OF BARLIONA. ONLY THE SPAWN OF A HIGH LORD MAY DO SO, BUT ONLY AFTER THE STRONGEST OF THE SPIRITS DECLARE HIM WORTHY."

"Ah-ha! And there it is!" I flourished a finger and grinned, frantically searching the text for the clue I needed. To convince the Patriarch, I had to find at least one reference to Plinto and...

"Even though Plinto is a High Vampire, he is a living creature," Stacey came to my aid. If there's any reason I love my wife, it's because she always helps me — even when she doesn't know what the hell is going on. I hope everyone can find a woman like that. "You, Patriarch are undead. You are not alive by definition. This seems quite evident."

"Evident..." the Patriarch echoed bitterly. "You are right, Siren. We're talking about my living son here. Not about me. Everything really is very evident."

"This whole tear your heart out stuff...it's not really my fetish," Plinto reminded us that he was there. "I like to keep my heart around, as a reminder of who I am and where I come from."

"I get the impression that no one cares," Stacey replied, still looking at me. Making my best stony face — as if everything was following my script — I stared steadily at the Patriarch, who in turn, remained staring at Plinto. Only the Rogue kept looking from me to the Patriarch, unsure of what was going on. What a clown circus. Clown cars, clown noses, clown pies, elephants and all!

"I shall lead you to the Vicegerent. He shall decide what to do," the Patriarch nodded and the red world around us vanished. And returned as a...

Stony cavern.

Unlike NPC Harbingers, I kept having to enter my Blink coordinates, so the habit of recording where I was spatially was automatic. It was no different now — the world was still blurry and coming into focus and I had already popped open the 3D map that showed my current location on Char. Comparing the coordinates with where we had arrived on this planet, I whistled to myself: We were practically on the other side of the world. If I hadn't committed the sacrifice, it would've taken us several years to get over here.

I should mention that the cave we were in was quite interesting. A portal burned bright red in the center. A portal to our world, by the looks of it. Or more precisely, to the Tomb. One-meter-tall Tarantulas stood one alongside the other around the perimeter of the place. A green beam emanated from the head of each Tarantula, intersecting and joining with all the other green beams a meter above the portal. In this manner, the beams formed a cocoon of sorts, within which hung an iron cage. An old man sat within the cage in a lotus pose. It was the same old man who had granted immortality to Lait. It was the Creator of Barliona!

But even that wasn't the most astounding part. The most shocking thing was the two-meter-tall Tarantula sitting on a terrifying imitation of a throne made of skulls. The properties of this monster were horrible: **The Progenitor (Level N/A)**. The Tarantula boss watched us with all eight of his black, lidless eyes.

"WHY ARE THEY HERE, SLAVE?!" A terrible voice roared in my head, causing a number of debuffs to fall on me at once. I regained consciousness on the floor and — thanks to the Tooth — a mere two seconds after hearing the question. The Progenitor's voice was the stuff of nightmares.

"They have brought the Keymaster, Vicegerent!" The Patriarch knelt and I felt the hair on my nape tremble. I'd never seen the Higher Vampire genuflect before anyone. Even if this was...A GOD?!

"THE KEYMASTER MUST BE IN BARLIONA! NOT HERE!"

I fainted again from the debuffs. For crying out loud! Deciding that I may as well stay sitting, I got comfortable on the floor. The upcoming conversation promised to be a lengthy one and I didn't feel like falling down every other sentence.

"I brought them here to deliver them to him! It is impossible to do so from Barliona!"

"*THIS SHAMAN WAS EXPELLED FROM THE LEPROSARIUM. HE SERVES THE BROTHERS!*"

"If I felt like doing their quest, I would've headed to Geranika a long time ago," I wasn't about to sit out the exchange, and as soon as the debuffs disappeared, I began to defend myself. "At the moment he possesses the Alabaster Throne and..."

"The Alabaster Throne is not subject to mortals!" To my immense relief, the reply came from the Patriarch instead of the Progenitor. "Geranika possesses a mere replica! A copy! One that enjoys a part of the original's power, but still one that is only a replica!"

"All the more," I replied, getting up. "I wasn't trying to destroy it. I never even considered it. You kicked me out of the Leprosarium over nothing. I don't work for the brothers."

"*THEN WHY DID YOU GO THERE?*"

Blast it all to hell! Why had I gotten up? Had I felt all-powerful?

"I needed the aid of the Shadows! I went to the Leprosarium for help, not to meet the brothers! I didn't even know they were there!"

"He speaks the truth, Vicegerent," the Patriarch intervened. "There is no deception in his words!"

The Progenitor didn't say anything, so I risked it and stood up again. To my surprise, Stacey and Plinto were out cold as if...POISON! Only now did I notice that the cave's floor was covered with a short grass, barely visible in the murk. A tiny green drop glistened at the tip of each blade, seething with a stupefying narcotic. Stacey and Plinto weren't paralyzed — they were high.

"Is this the Creator?" I asked the Patriarch, while the Tarantula was contemplating being and nothingness. "Or another replica?"

"His soul," replied the Vampire. "His body remained in Barliona, but we managed to transport his consciousness here."

"*YOU HAVE NOT JOINED CHAR!*" The Tarantula reminded us of his presence, accusing me once more of some crime against his reign. Like hell!

"I have my doubts!"

"*ABOUT WHAT?*"

"I'm not sure that you lot are dark enough for me. I need true allies! The entire world opposes me! Together with Geranika I plan on destroying Barliona and I don't feel like allying with any old passerby!"

"He speaks the truth, Vicegerent," the Patriarch muttered again. "He has become the enemy of all of Barliona."

"YOU SHALL LEARN THE TRUTH AND BEHOLD OUR MIGHT! WAKE THE KEYMASTER!"

I didn't fall! I managed to stay standing! I did it! I had had to lean on the Patriarch, yet I didn't simply collapse as I had earlier. Whoever this Progenitor was, he hadn't managed to drop me!

The Patriarch didn't waste time and simply pushed me into the portal. The world around me wavered for a few moments, and resolved into another small cave, no less strange than the earlier one.

This cave's perimeter was full of dead demons who formed another force cocoon around an iron cage holding the body of the Creator. In this sense, the two caves resembled one another. The difference was elsewhere — instead of a portal, the center of this cave was occupied by the Alabaster Throne — and the Throne in turn was occupied by an old acquaintance of mine.

Anastaria's stunned exclamation sounded beside me as she read the properties of the man. And indeed if Plinto hadn't told me that Lori had been unable to find the first Human Emperor amid the Gray Lands, I too would have been shocked. Karmadont sat in the throne and stared with a mad gaze at the Ergreis cuddled in his arms. Here he was, the first Emperor of the Humans.

"Stop, Mahan!" yelled a familiar voice. Geranika had decided to drop in! "You cannot destroy Barliona!"

"Don't you interfere!" the Patriarch stepped between me and Geranika, and yet he hadn't been the one who had spoken. Naahti and the Dark Lord stood shoulder to shoulder with the Patriarch, blocking Geranika's path towards Stacey, Plinto and me. "The time of reckoning has arrived!"

"Come to your senses, oh my children!" Eluna and Tartarus appeared behind Geranika's shoulder.

"*JUST GIVE ME A REASON!*" The walls of the cave shook around us. Back on Char, the Tarantula God was carefully following the current confrontation.

Karmadont laughed maniacally and began to clap his hands like a child: "Just like that the pieces are all in place but who will make the first move I ask?"

"*Mahan, do you have any idea what's going on?*" Stacey asked, simultaneously letting me know that our telepathy was back on line.

"There's nothing to understand Siren!" Karmadont went on giggling. "The Patriarch, the Emperor and the Dark Lord are trying to pop Barliona pop its very fabric and open a passage for the one true god to pop in the First God, the Tarantula God, the God of Char. And Geranika here is trying to stop them but poor fellow he's all alone and he'll be crushed because Eluna and Tartarus cannot interfere for if they do the Tarantula God, the First God will be able to get involved. So all in all when you add it all up and take a step back to appreciate it, you're about to witness a slaughter of the innocents! Awa-awa-hahaha!"

"Not so fast, you mad traitor!" Two old men appeared next to Geranika. A man and an orc.

"I thought you killed them!" The Emperor of Malabar exclaimed with astonishment. "It can't be!"

"But it is, Naahti. Anything's possible in this world," the ancient orc replied hoarsely. "The throne's power is not limitless!"

"Three versus three!" Karmadont started clapping again. "What'll it be, Freemies? Come on and join the party already...By the way! I still haven't chosen a side either! Now who should I fight with? Ho-hum...let me cogitate...but eureka and but of course! Minions! Defend your ruler!"

The space around us began to vibrate, changing the cave. The walls and the ceiling vanished. We found ourselves in an enormous open area, with Geranika and the old men on the one side facing the Patriarch, the Emperor, the Dark Lord and several dozen enormous Tarantulas on the other.

In the center stood the Alabaster Throne with Karmadont.

Eluna and Tartarus stood to the side, looking disconsolate and near them stood three players, looking astonished.

"I don't have enough pieces!" Karmadont went on babbling. "I need more! Slave! Heed my summons and appear you winged nightmare!"

"Sovereign!" the world shuddered as Renox, my Dragon Father, appeared to Karmadont's call. "I am ready to serve, your lordship!"

Renox had taken the side of the Patriarch.

I was tired of being surprised by all these twists and turns, so when Geranika summoned the Siren Nashlazar and Kronos the Titan, I hardly even reacted. I was drained.

"New pieces!" Karmadont applauded. "It's too bad there's so few of you! The game would've been so much more interesting otherwise! Have you made up your minds yet, Freemies? You have but one minute!"

"They will choose the right side, traitor!" The Hermit stepped out from Geranika's back.

"Oh no! Who will save me?!" Karmadont went on chortling. "Barliona herself has dropped in for tea for two...but...but without your husband, you're nothing! A useless hag! You have neither power, nor energy, nor...Scram, you wench! The adults are busy! What do you say, Keymaster? Look what you'll get!"

"Well I'll be damned," Plinto whispered, reading a system notification only he could see.

"You too shall be blessed, Siren! Look what you'll get!"

"Hmm..." Anastaria frowned, reading the text.

"Dragon!" Karmadont addressed me. "You are really cracking me up lately. As a result, I will be happy to accept you to my banner! Look what you'll get!"

You have the option of joining Char. In the event that you accept, you shall receive the following bonuses: +200 to Crafting; +200 to Dragon Rank; +200 to Level; Title of Vicegerent of Char; +200 to Blessed/Cursed Artificer. Do you wish to join Char?

"Aren't you a craftsman?" Karmadont continued to seduce me. "I shall teach you everything I know. I shall teach to create items like the Imperial Throne! It was thanks to the throne that I managed to enslave the Emperor and the Dark Lord, since the seat of power requires sacrifices, sweet delicious sacrifices, don't you think?" Karmadont giggled. "There are hiccups, sure, and every once in a while someone escapes the throne's fetters but this has happened only twice and those are the two standing right there. But look at them, they're practically decomposing from their advanced age! The throne drained their strengths long ago!"

"Make your decision, my son," Renox decided to back up Karmadont. "This world is rotten. It must be destroyed to pave the way for a new one built from its ruins! I shall teach you everything I know! You will become the first among my Dragons!"

"Basically, we can become the top players in Barliona," drawled Plinto, without addressing anyone in particular.

"It's not like we can prevent the expansion from

launching at this point. All that's left to decide is which side we'll be playing on," Anastaria agreed. Both of my friends looked at me. Like I was the one who had to choose.

"The time has come! What did you decide?"

"Stacey, didn't you solve all of the Chess Set's riddles?"

"Erm...Yes. Are you sure that this is a good time to be thinking about that?"

"Send me all the solutions, will you please?"

"Here you go...but why?"

"What is your choice, Mahan?" Karmadont cried again. "If you do not make a decision, I will consider you an enemy and..."

I produced the Chess Pieces from my bag. It's curious — they had been created by Karmadont, who'd infused the essences from the greatest sentients of his era into them. But was that the truth? Had the essences merely been infused? What if these weren't simply replicas? Something tells me that I'd better check!

The orcs came first. Finding the Chess Piece — I entered '13.8175802' into the text box. The die had been cast!

"I don't like to play like this!" said Karmadont when eight two-meter-tall orcs came trudging out of the whirlwind that had appeared. Grichin, Grover, Vankhor...Eight great orc Warriors stood before us, their scimitars bared.

"Defend us, oh brothers!" I asked the orcs and reached for the dwarves. If I remember correctly, I'd need to enter...

"Stop him! Kill him! Kill them all!" Karmadont began to scream hysterically and the space around us went dark. The battle began, but I paid it no attention. I had much better things to deal with than watch a fight between some NPCs. I noted the bubble around me, indicating that Stacey was somewhere nearby, but it was useless here. The orcs were protecting me.

The dwarves. The masters. Eight stumpy subjects of the kingdom-under-the-mountain had appeared to my summons.

"The Throne!" I pointed at the hunk of white stone beside us. "It must be destroyed! Only you can accomplish this!"

"Onwards, brothers!" shouted Borhg Goldhand, shifting his hammer from one hand into the other.

"We shall reinforce you!" growled two of the smaller orcs.

"And we shall cover you!" boomed the two Giants.

"We shall escort you!" hissed the Lizards.

"We shall bear you!" whinnied the War Horses.

"We shall suppress the foe for you!" announced the Elves.

"We shall ambush their flankers!" muttered the Trolls.

"I shall summon Spirits to aid you!" said the orc Shaman.

"I shall cast wards to protect you!" proclaimed the Archmage.

"I shall lead you!" growled the Leader of the White Wolf Clans.

"I live!" cried Lait.

"Your staff!" I handed Lait the staff that had been charged by the phantoms and only now did I get the chance to look around. Blast it all to hell! I wish I hadn't.

The army of Tarantulas had summoned a host of terrifying creatures to its banners and was now pushing back Nashlazar and Kronos. Geranika was playing tag with the Patriarch, blinking all over the field of battle, without it being clear who was 'it.' The Emperor and the Dark Lord fell upon the old men who, as I had already guessed, were the former Emperor and Dark Lord. The young bloods were fighting the old bloods. Experience or strength? The answer was evident. Renox poured fire and flames onto Plinto and Anastaria, who were aided by the Hermit, and the King and Queen from the Chess Set. The Dragon was toying with his enemies, still at Acceleration I. Hardly had he engaged Acceleration II, when Anastaria and the Archmage collapsed to their knees and blood sprayed from the mouths. The Dragon was too strong for them. Eluna and Tartarus had vanished, but I was sure that they were nearby, watching the battle. Surrounded and protected by the other Chess Pieces, the dwarves were hammering at the Alabaster Throne with their sledges. Cracks had appeared in it. Karmadont had cast aside the Ergreis and set on Lait. And I stood apart, alone without an opponent. Everyone was fighting without holding anything back. But I stood frozen with no idea of whom to help — in my view, we were losing all over the place and everyone could use my help.

DING!

With a deafening ring, the Alabaster Throne shattered into little pieces and two sentients appeared in its place. The Sons of the Creator.

"FREEDOM! AT LAST!" cried Harrashess joyfully and the world winked into darkness. The Progenitor, the god of the Tarantulas, had entered Barliona.

"*BARLIONA SHALL FALL!*" came his telepathic roar.

"TO BATTLE, GODS OF BARLIONA! DEFEND YOUR HOME!" Eluna and Tartarus finally entered the battle, accompanied by a myriad of lesser gods. Now the battle was taking place across all levels of being — physical, mental and spiritual. The world began to shudder around us!

"*Dan, if you have a plan B, now's the time!*" Anastaria's hoarse voice sounded in my mind. "*We won't hold much longer!*"

"Thank you for giving me another chance to

fight for this world, Mahan! You are a true and worthy Shaman!" A ghost orc suddenly appeared before me. I believe it was Grichin. But before I could say anything, he dissolved like a patch of fog scattered by a gust of wind. Over by the where the throne had been, one of the Chess Pieces collapsed to dust. We were one fighter less.

"Thank you for giving me another chance to fight for this world, Mahan! You are a true and worthy Shaman!"

"Thank you for..."

The Chess Pieces turned to dust one after the other, forcing me to clench my fists. The hell do I care if you think I'm a true Shaman when we're losing and...

A cold sweat covered me from head to toe.

The strongest of spirits had declared me worthy! Renox was the high lord and I was his son! Plinto wasn't the Keymaster! I was the Keymaster! All I had to do was tear out my heart and...

THE ERGREIS!

"Stacey, I need a bubble!" I yelled, rushing in the direction where Karmadont and Lait were locked in a death embrace. Shadows whirled around me, lightning, fire, ice, but I was certain that nothing could stop me. For I had protection from all types of damage.

"Stacey's gone, kid," Plinto creaked hoarsely. "It ain't a bubble, but it'll protect you. Do what you must!"

The same mysterious Disruption Field that had saved me in the arena appeared around me. Plinto gasped and collapsed to the ground with 0 HP. Renox accelerated once again and began to smash through the Hermit's defenses. Another set of notifications from Chess Pieces declaring me a true and worthy Shaman flashed past my eyes, and then I reached Karmadont...

"It is too bad you came to our world," Karmadont was standing with his back to me, reveling in Lait's agony. The Death Knight was being immolated from within, yet the gift, the curse of the Creator still refused to let him die. "You shall beg me for...EH!"

I snatched the Ergreis from the evil Hunter and almost suffocated. Even with my sensory filter set to full, the pain pierced me through and through. My breathing became ragged, circles of light swam in my vision, my consciousness screamed for release, but the Hermit's hoarse voice pulled me back.

"*I shall take your pain, Shaman! You must think. You must feel. You must understand what you are to do!*"

Scenario updated: 'Burden of the Creator...'

Swiping away the system notification and understanding perfectly well that now was not the time, I yelled to Lait:

"Delay him! Five seconds!"

"Do it, Shaman!" Charred, Lait rose to his feet and locked Karmadont in his embrace. "Five seconds!"

The Eye of the Dark Widow. The item that I had received back in my first months as a Shaman. The item that I had argued so much with Stacey over, the same one that drew the attention of the shadowy factions of Barliona and caused me so many headaches because I didn't want to sell it. The item that I had wanted to use on Char, to reach the center of power.

How nice it was that I hadn't done this earlier. For, now, I needed a passage to that red world as much as I needed a breath of air. The world where the Creator's soul was held.

"*NOOOO!*" I managed to hear the squeal of the Tarantula as I dove into the portal. I whipped out the Altarian Falcon, opened the 'Blink' input box and entered the cave's coordinates. How nice it is to know your work so well that you do it reflexively! Let the Mages think about their deeds and misdeeds. I am a Shaman! I only had to feel!

"Submit!" I had no idea how to use the scepter, so I simply pointed it at the nearest Tarantula. "Remove the barrier!"

"Remove the barrier!" the Tarantula echoed obediently and the beam emanating from his head blinked and vanished.

"Submit! Remove the barrier!" I immediately trained the scepter at the next Tarantula. "Submit! Remove the barrier!"

As soon as the last beam vanished, the cage plummeted straight into the red portal beneath it. Eh! Wait a second! I have the crystal! Without thinking much longer, I dived after the cage and — stars began dancing before my eyes — someone had Stunned me for two seconds.

"That belongs to me worm!" Karmadont growled with hatred. "I will open the gateway not you I will open it myself! I am the Keymaster always have been!"

The battle had all but ended. Renox was pouring fire onto Nashlazar and Kronos, the Hermit was dead, Eluna was crawling away from the fire tornado like a broken doll, dragging a dead Tartarus behind her. The old rulers of the Empires were still holding on, but it was clear that they were being toyed with — the Emperor and Dark Lord could finish off the old men whenever they wished. Lait had been cut up to pieces and even the gift of the Creator could not sustain him any longer. As for Geranika...I could see neither him nor the Patriarch, but the general trend suggested that he wasn't doing so hot either. Plinto and Anastaria had been sent to respawn without leaving their bodies — they were watching to see what would happen. Karmadont raised Lait's Stinger above me, wishing to send me to respawn, when suddenly everything went still. A snow white portal opened in the air — and two lifeless bodies came falling out of it to the ground. The immortal sons of the Creator had been slain. The Progenitor peeked his head out behind them and Barliona shuddered:

"*THIS WORLD SHALL BE MINE! TREMBLE, BARLIONA! YOUR NEW RULER HAS ARRI...WHAT?! N...NOOO!!!*"

The portal began to collapse like something incredibly powerful and unimaginable was sucking it from the other side. The Tarantula twisted and contorted into himself and was pulled back in. There was a pop and a grim notification appeared to everyone:

Mourn, Barliona. The Creator of this world has left his creation forevermore!

The shock wave from the collapsed portal swept across the field of battle, scattering the combatants like some bowling pins. Karmadont flew off somewhere to the side, granting me several moments of life. Trying to use these to the utmost, I crawled over to Eluna. I hadn't even the strength to stand. Even though I was still in a game, I felt completely shattered.

"We've lost, Mahan," Eluna noticed me and sadness tinged her incredibly beautiful face. "I have no more strength. The Creator has died. His children have died. Our power has been exhausted."

Eluna collapsed helplessly beside Tartarus. It's strange but even on the verge of death, the goddess had done everything she could to drag the god of Kartoss away from battle. The Dark God breathed, hoarsely, but he breathed. How can I help two powerless gods? I have no such power, unless that is...

"Eluna! Do you take Tartarus as your lawfully wedded husband?"

"WHAT?!" Eluna found the strength not only to exclaim but even to sit up.

"Do you promise to love and cherish him until the end of time? Till death do you part?"

"Mahan, what is wrong with you?"

"ANSWER ME!" I don't even know where I found the strength to scream so loudly. The devs couldn't simply let this couple end up like this. Having killed off all the leading NPCs of this world, they had to come up with something.

"Yes! I do!" Eluna's shock was so great that she simply agreed to my demand.

"Tartarus! Do you take Eluna as your lawfully wedded wife? Do you promise to love and cherish her until the end of time? Till death do you part?"

"Yes...I do..." It was difficult to tell what the god was saying through his wheezing, yet I made it out.

"By the powers vested in me by, um, myself — I declare you husband and wife! From now on, you are the supreme deities of Barliona! From now on, you are the Creators!"

I placed the Ergreis into Eluna's hand and placed Tartarus' hand on top of it. That was it! Where's my respawn?

"When are you going to die finally?!" Karmadont cried, appearing beside me. He raised his staff and brought it down directly onto my chest. Sparks erupted from the place where the blow landed and the world went dark. The Gray Lands welcomed me in their gray embrace. Here it is — respawn.

Eluna wishes to revive you. Do you Accept?

By my estimate, an eternity had gone by — but it had only been about forty seconds. That was how long it took for the system to process that our continent had a new god. Two in fact!

Stacey was already there, as was Plinto. The lifeless bodies of the Hermit, Geranika, the Emperor, the Dark Lord, Renox, and Kronos lay on the ground with pieces of Lait among them. Nashlazar and the two old men were covering the bodies with shrouds, demonstrating that even gods weren't all powerful.

"It's over, Shaman," said Critchet, wearily taking a seat on the ground. "We failed to stop the Breach. But we have defanged the serpent and we shall have the chance to expel it once and for all from Barliona."

"Critchet, will you tell me what the hell

happened?" I basically began to shake the ancient orc, demanding the truth. "Why was good on the side of evil and vice versa?"

"Good...evil...These concepts are much too relative to rely on them. Consider this hypothetical: A lumberjack decides to fell a tree in order to heat his home and keep his family warm — when suddenly he is attacked by an angry orc. Where is evil here, where is good?"

"But it's clear — the orc is evil and the man is good."

"That's from the perspective of the human. Look at it through the eyes of the orc. The soul of his family is implanted in that tree and in several years a cute baby orc will be born from its wood. Suddenly this man appears and seeks to cut down the orc's child. What is evil here, what is good?"

"Erm..." I was at a loss.

"It's the same story here. That which took place cannot be called good or evil. It simply took place."

"Will you tell us how you managed to survive?" Anastaria sat down next to me.

"Honor your wife, Shaman! She is quite the rare one." Critchet grinned before beginning his tale:

Once upon a time there was a Hunter named Karmadont, who wanted nothing but power. He sought it in various ways and came upon a servant of the Progenitor — the god of the Tarantulas. The children of this god had already populated Barliona, preparing the arrival of their god. A loyal servant of the Tarantulas, the father of the Vampire Patriarch persuaded Harrashess to conduct an experiment — to create a powerful weapon against the Progenitor. The Alabaster Throne. The brothers agreed, not suspecting the trap and as a result found themselves imprisoned in the Alabaster Throne. The Father of the Patriarch was killed by the Creator for his betrayal, but the Creator lacked the strength to fight the Progenitor. He decided to leave the throne alone. And at this point something happened that no one expected — Lait appeared in our world and with him the heart of the fallen god. As soon as the Ergreis appeared, it destroyed, or drove mad all the Tarantulas. The power locked in the Heart of the fallen god was so unbearable to the Tarantulas that they shriveled up as soon as they encountered it. The Creator sighed with relief and went off to gather his strength in order to free his children, leaving Lait to guard his throne.

But then Karmadont found the opportunity to lock the Creator inside the Tomb. Through his crafting he created a key, investing it with the essences of the greatest individuals of all the races. Barliona was left without a god. Here the Tarantula appeared and became the Vicegerent. The temporary god of Barliona.

Karmadont made a mistake while creating the prison for the Creator and found himself trapped in the Tomb. Along with the Ergreis — the item that continued to stave off the Tarantulas. The Ergreis did not have an effect on the demons, so it was decided to have them lead the invasion. As the rulers of their realms, the Emperor and the Dark Lord were aware of the coming invasion, but couldn't do anything about it. They had become slaves of their respective thrones, which the ingenious Karmadont had created. Through these thrones, Karmadont controlled the Emperors, forcing them to do his bidding. The Emperor and the Dark Lord began to fight Karmadont's influence, issuing orders to stop me, but in the end fought for the Tarantulas.

So began preparations for the second invasion. First, the Patriarch created the replica of the Alabaster Throne. Then, in order to allow the Tarantula's main force to enter Barliona — the Shadows were harnessed. The Ergreis blocked the effects of the original throne, but it did not have enough power to curb the power of the replica. Darius and Critchet, the former Emperor and Dark Lord, decided to fight until the bitter end. A sentient was found who was holy enough to resist the power of the throne. This was an ordinary Shaman named Geranika. A sham assassination was arranged, a spectacle, after which Renox proclaimed the new rulers of Kartoss and Malabar outside of Beatwick. Darius and Critchet began to seek a means of blocking the power of the Alabaster Throne and a way to free the Creator, while Geranika did everything he could to mitigate the damage to Barliona. Geranika aimed his entire blow against the Free Citizens, who could return from the Gray Lands anyway — and it seemed like everything would work out. Until Mahan and his friends showed up.

"It looks like I'll have to ascend to the throne of Kartoss yet again," the orc concluded his tale. "It's time to return your powers to you. It's not your fault that Karmadont turned out to be stronger."

Attention all players!

Have you had enough of stamping on one patch of ground you call a continent? An ancient enemy has breached Barliona seeking to enslave it. Let us stop this threat together! Everyone to the defense of Barliona!

Speak to the heads of your class to sign up. A new continent and new adventures await you!

Welcome to a brand new Barliona!

"He became the Keymaster after all," Darius shook his head. "The Entrance is open. Mahan, permit me to take the scepter. It doesn't do to have such items lying around Barliona..."

No sooner had I handed the scepter to the old man, than a strange notification appeared before me:

You shall be disconnected from the game in

30 seconds.

Excuse me?

"Despite our losses and our grief, we have managed to vanquish the Progenitor!" Eluna appeared beside us. "That alone is honor enough for our heroes! I know what Karmadont offered you, but you refused his offer and..."

"*Stacey, I'm about to be disconnected. Something is broken. Accept the reward for me, please. I'll try to re-enter as soon as I can.*"

"*Okay. Is it serious?*"

"*I don't think so. Some kind of glitch maybe. The system seems to...*"

The cocoon lid slid aside returning me to reality. I'll need to check the uplink and...

My head exploded in a million pieces sending me to unconsciousness.

CHAPTER FIFTEEN
THE GREATER EVIL

"**Y**OU HAVEN'T OVERDONE IT, HAVE YOU?" A familiar voice said through the darkness.

"Not at all! He's alive!" another voice replied in a chipper tone and I was struck by the disgusting and sharp smell of smelling salts. My brain cleared in a moment, snapping me back to reality.

I looked around. I had been here before. I had been rudely transported to the office of Victor Zavala, otherwise known as Ehkiller. The owner of the office sat in front of me in his favorite chair. And he did not seem pleased to see me.

"Victor," I tried to reach my hand out to shake his and suddenly realized that I couldn't do anything. My hands were tied behind my back!

"What is going on?!"

"Try asking yourself the same question," Victor cut me off tersely. "What have you done?"

"I don't understand..."

"What the hell did you launch the expansion for?!" Ehkiller exploded. It was about the first time I'd seen this person raise his voice. It took a lot to push him to this point. And I had done it — even though I had no idea how.

"Maybe you'll explain what the hell you're doing?!" I knew how to blow my lid too. Being tied to the chair didn't mean that my mouth had to stay shut. That was their oversight.

"Mahan, you had a simple job to do: Follow my orders calmly and quietly instead of sticking your nose where you were explicitly ordered not to stick it," Victor said in a cold voice full of anger. "You were not the one who was supposed to launch the expansion!"

"Your daughter launched it!"

"Why I couldn't give a damn which one of you it was! You and she are two sides of the same coin!"

"Okay, maybe you'll explain what's happening now?" I yelled again. "The hell did you tie me to this stupid chair for?"

"Because it's time to answer for everything you've caused, you idiot." Even a viper would envy the amount of venom in Victor's voice.

"All we did was launch the expansion," I growled back angrily. "Who else was supposed to do it? Phoenix? Or maybe...not the Celestial?" Ehkiller twitched as if he'd been shocked and at the same moment all the puzzle pieces fell into place in my mind.

I'LL BE DAMNED! This simply couldn't be! It wasn't possible!

"So you're behind all of it?" I said, shocked. If I'm right (and I'd give myself a 90% chance of being right), Victor is a terrifying person. Unprincipled, unconscionable and completely ruthless. I mean, is he even a human after all this?

"I am behind all of it," Victor said calmly. "From the moment you entered our life to your imminent departure from it. You are no one! You are nothing! I created you and I will destroy you!"

Victor seemed so convincing in his wrath that the emerging picture grew sharper by the moment. I couldn't contain a smirk — Ehkiller struck me as some spider spinning his web. Carefully, confidently, year after year — yet when a fly got trapped in it and, struggling to free itself, disrupted its delicate ornament, the spider had lost his temper.

"You think this is funny? Do tell, what's making your soon-to-be-dead corpse grin so?"

"We'll all be corpses sooner or later," I remarked philosophically. "I'm simply amused be the scale of your plot. Let me guess — everything started when you realized that Anastaria can't have children with ordinary people?"

"What would you know about that?" Victor interrupted in a rage, but since he didn't go on, it was clear that I could continue.

"Maybe not a thing. The doctors suggested in vitro fertilization, but Stacey was opposed. She wanted a family, love and other things that woman want. This is when you came up with your plot. Correct?"

"Yes!" Victor hissed. "I will do everything I can for my family! Stacey wanted to be happy and she will be!"

"But at what price! You've killed so many people!"

"I couldn't give a damn about them! Family is all anyone needs. You had a chance to become part of the family, but you blew it!"

I smirked again.

"A chance? I never had a chance. You never gave me one. Correct me if I get something wrong..."

The daughter of one of the wealthiest and most powerful men of the continent was ill. Hundreds of tests in all the labs of the world only reinforced one and the same sad fact: It would take a miracle for Anastaria to get pregnant. That, or in vitro fertilization, which the girl refused to do. The father refused to give up. In violation of all privacy laws, he had his men examine the medical records of all males who had ever entered Barliona — and a miracle happened. Several hundred men were discovered who could indeed make his daughter happy. Anastaria could have children with them. Victor rushed to his daughter with the good news, but right then she fell into a depression due to her breakup with Hellfire. The boy had wanted more, while Anastaria could not give it to him. Ehkiller was faced with a dilemma —

either he could make his daughter happy here and now or give her the chance to earn her own happiness and live a fairy tale. The loving father won out. He decided to grant her the fairy tale. He had psychologists select ten candidates who were best fit to be husbands. Victor then revised their selections, carefully checking all ten and eliminating all but one. I was the last one remaining. Then a global plot was set in motion with the single goal of making Ehkiller's daughter happy.

I was forced into the game and equipped with everything I needed to get out of the mines. Roxanne, a trusted accomplice of Ehkiller, with whom he'd already worked for several years, arranged everything perfectly — and an in-game competitor, Donotpunnik, was brought in as a patsy. The idea of making a ton of profit from this scheme caught Ehkiller's attention, so much so that at times the main goal was put on the backburner.

All the game's actors played their roles perfectly. Donotpunnik ended up in prison. Anastaria fell in love with me. I fell in love with her. And Victor made an immense amount of money from the Corporation. Happiness for all seemed right around the corner if it wasn't for one 'but' — Roxanne.

"I went to her house," I went on. "I met her husband. He's crazy about the East. Alexander Vecchi loves his dragons. The question occurs — where did he get this obsession from? Where had he seen it all?

The answer is simple — he as well as Roxanne lived in the East for a long time."

Roxanne turned out to be a woman with a secret. She worked for Bihan.

The old fox did not want his partner to die, but he could not refuse being the first in everything, including the launching of a new expansion. He was simply incapable of it.

Victor received an ultimatum — either he reigns in his daughter and her uppity husband, or all the info that Roxanne had carefully amassed about Ehkiller will find its way to the police. Nothing personal, you see, it was only business.

Victor agreed to allow Bihan onto the continent. The two made a deal and Victor lobbied the Corporation to put up the Original status as a reward for the tournament winner. Then he told us off and stepped back into the shadows.

When it came to the conflict of interests between the two in-game clans, Phoenix was the weaker one. So Victor had to back off and accept Bihan's will.

There were some details, however. Among them, Mahan and Anastaria. Ignoring all orders, requests and threats, they managed to launch the scenario.

Bihan was enraged — it turned out that the gods of the continent where the final battle of the scenario would take place, would become the gods of all of Barliona and the head of the Celestial Empire really wanted to launch the expansion on his territory. It didn't happen.

Victor received another ultimatum — either I would be punished, or the information about Ehkiller's plot would be handed to the Corporation. People were sent after me, in an attempt to interrupt the final battle, but they only reached our place after everything was decided. The only way to pull me out of the game was through the disconnect button, since the cables were all tucked away in the wall now, and these extra 30 seconds had been enough for me to receive the scenario's rewards. I was knocked unconscious, tied up and brought to Victor.

"And here I am," I concluded my monologue. "Sitting across from the man who raised me from my lowly state — awaiting his decision."

"It's too bad..." Victor said after a minute of dead silence. "It's too bad, Daniel, that you did not heed my advice. I cannot permit you the luxury of prison. You have given me no other choice. Security!"

An enormous guard the size of a wardrobe emerged from the shadows.

"Daniel is very tired. He wishes to rest. Ensure he does so. Quickly and painlessly. Kill him!"

I looked on as the guard reached for his handgun and leveled it at me.

This is it!

The Shaman fairy tale has come to an end.

When suddenly...

"Victor Zavala! You are under arrest for suspicion of organizing a criminal enterprise and the attempted murder of Daniel Mahan. You have the right to remain silent. Anything you say can and will be used against you in a court of law..."

EPILOGUE

"AND WHAT ARE WE SUPPOSED TO DO NOW?" Alex sat down next to me and watched the EMTs cover Victor's body and load it into the ambulance. The spider's heart had given out.

"Nothing," I answered calmly. "Nothing at all."

"I spent three years getting one of my men into Victor's organization! Three years on this operation which you almost ruined two months ago and which you completely ruined just now!"

"Alex, what's the point of this? Evil has been punished. There he is, dead as a doornail. What else do you want?"

"Justice."

"What justice? He's dead. Do you understand? Dead! Isn't that some degree of justice?"

"What are you getting at?" Alex frowned.

"That if we unwind this whole thing to its logical end and bring it to light, Anastaria will discover the truth. I'm getting at the fact that I'm merely a carefully selected partner for her. You don't need to see the future to know how she'll react to this news. She'll follow in her father's footsteps! Everything she believed turned out to be a lie! I'm sure your brainiacs have already considered all the outcomes. Are you going to lock her in a nuthouse with her hands tied so she can't hurt herself? Is that the justice you're looking for?"

"No..."

A silence followed. I had nothing to suggest to Alex. Everything depended on him now, but he remained stubbornly silent.

"And you're ready to come to terms with the role you've been given?" Alex asked suddenly.

"I love her. More than my own life. I'm ready to forget what I know, to process it and go on living, if it'll make her happy. The Phoenix must arise from the ashes, whatever happens to her. That's my decision."

"It's yours all right. No one can argue with you...Okay. I will help you..."

FROM THE BARLIONA NEWS NETWORK:

"Victor Zavala, one of the best players of Barliona died suddenly yesterday. He was 56. Mr. Zavala founded and led an enormous Barliona clan known as 'Phoenix.' The Barliona Corporation wishes to express its sincere condolences to his family, to which Mr. Zavala was a true support and a caring father. Mr. Zavala's eternal memory shall forever be cherished by the Barliona community!"

Somewhere in the vast reaches of the Celestial Empire:

"Master, the Ergreis has been destroyed!" Azari bowed deeply before Bihan. "I have confirmed that Mahan has transferred the power of this crystal to his gods."

"Our gods, Azari. Now they are our gods. But it is no matter. The main objective remains the same. Altameda will be ours!"

THE END

Want to be the first to know about our latest
LitRPG, sci fi and fantasy titles from your favorite
authors?

Subscribe to our NEW RELEASES newsletter:
http://eepurl.com/b7niIL

Thank you for reading *Clans War!*
If you like what you've read, check out other LitRPG books
and series published by Magic Dome Books:

Dark Paladin LitRPG series by Vasily Mahanenko:
The Beginning
The Quest

**The Dark Herbalist LitRPG series
by Michael Atamanov:**
Video Game Plotline Tester
Stay on the Wing
A Trap for the Potentate

The Neuro LitRPG series by Andrei Livadny:
The Crystal Sphere
The Curse of Rion Castle
The Reapers

**The Way of the Shaman LitRPG series
by Vasily Mahanenko:**
Survival Quest
The Kartoss Gambit
The Secret of the Dark Forest
The Phantom Castle
The Karmadont Chess Set
Shaman's Revenge
The Hour of Pain (a bonus short story)

Galactogon LitRPG series by Vasily Mahanenko:
Start the Game!

Phantom Server LitRPG series by Andrei Livadny:
Edge of Reality
The Outlaw
Black Sun

Perimeter Defense LitRPG series by Michael Atamanov:
Sector Eight
Beyond Death
New Contract
A Game with No Rules

***Mirror World* LitRPG series by Alexey Osadchuk:**
Project Daily Grind
The Citadel
The Way of the Outcast
The Twilight Obelisk

***AlterGame* LitRPG series by Andrew Novak:**
The First Player
On the Lost Continent

***The Expansion (The History of the Galaxy)* series by A. Livadny:**
Blind Punch
The Shadow of Earth

***Citadel World* series by Kir Lukovkin:**
The URANUS Code
The Secret of Atlantis

***The Game Master* series by A. Bobl and A. Levitsky:**
The Lag

***The Sublime Electricity* series by Pavel Kornev**
The Illustrious
The Heartless
The Fallen
The Dormant
Leopold Orso and the Case of the Bloody Tree

Moskau *(a dystopian thriller)* by **G. Zotov**

Point Apocalypse
(a near-future action thriller)
by Alex Bobl

You're in Game!
(LitRPG Stories from Bestselling Authors)

The Naked Demon (a paranormal romance)
by Sherrie L.

In order to have new books of the series translated faster, we need your help and support! Please consider leaving a review or spread the word by recommending *Clans War* to your friends and posting the link on social media. The more people buy the book, the sooner we'll be able to make new translations available. Thank you!

Till next time!

Made in the USA
San Bernardino, CA
07 December 2018